INNATE HOSTILITY

INNATE HOSTILITY

Remastered

Brian David Simmons

LUMINARE PRESS
WWW.LUMINAREPRESS.COM

Innate Hostility Remastered by Brian David Simmons

Published by Bright Crescent Sky. Bright Crescent Sky can be emailed at brightcrescentsky@pmt.org . Follow us on Facebook for events, information, reviews, and new releases. To contact Brian Simmons, email us at brightcrescentsky@pmt.org with Brian Simmons in subject line.

Library of Congress Control Number (LCCN): 2022904532

Library of Congress Cataloging-in-Publication Data is available upon request.

International Standard Book Number (ISBN):
979-8-9859323-0-0 (print)
979-8-9859323-1-7 (ebook)

Cover by Melissa Thomas, Luminare Press

Printed in United States of America

*The best things in life happen when
the love of my life is by my side.*

Chapter One

INCOMPETENCE, INSANITY, AND INJUSTICE

Hamilton Cole Davis sat on his front steps listening to the city sounds. The noises of never-ending traffic up and down Ogden's Twenty-Third Street drowned out most other sounds to all but the careful listener. A block over, maybe two, an argument was escalating. It was too far to hear what was actually being said but the dispute definitely included a man and woman. Farther off in the distance he could hear a siren. Cole speculated that the sounds might be related as he popped the top on another can of beer.

It was doubtful that the siren was heading for the domestic dispute. Cops in this part of Ogden had more serious things to deal with than a simple argument unless it escalated to a shooting or stabbing. Even then it would probably just get documented, filed, and eventually forgotten. Government statistics reported crime as being down, but from Cole's point of view, it could only be down in elite suburbs. Shootings and stabbings seemed to be a regular occurrence in the downtown area. One day it was a random drive-by shooting. The next day it was a Jack-the-Ripper murder, and then there was the newest form of intercity warfare—bombings. The violence came from all sides: gangs, Proud Boys, BLM, Antifa, and even the cops.

Ogden cops couldn't seem to grasp the insanity that gripped the inner city and exploded beyond their power to control. It was a small town police force, overworked and underpaid, fighting twenty-first century big-city problems with 1970s tactics.

Down the street Cole could hear shuffling footsteps and muffled voices coming his way. He couldn't make out how many, but it was a pretty good bet that they were gang-bangers. Nobody else would be out at this time of night, especially in this neighborhood. They had probably just come from his drug-dealing neighbor halfway down the block. The thought that they might try to harass him or in some other way accost him concerned Cole but it also excited his senses. His hearing became keener to capture and segregate each sound. His vision cut through the blackness of the night to extract fragmented glimmers of information for his mind to augment and create the vision. His mind cleared all inconsequential thoughts to record each and every detail and to consider the events of the moment. His body accelerated internally and tensed externally with the rush of adrenaline. He feared, yet feared none. Mind, body, and soul were alive with exhilaration.

There were six thirteen or fourteen-year-olds; all were male. Each wore gang-banger attire with only a few subtle personalizations: drab-colored baggy

   Brian David Simmons

pants, white T-shirts under long-sleeved flannel shirts, expensive new tennis shoes, and to top off the look, each had slicked-back hair. One wore a dainty gold chain around the neck; another twirled a stick or club. Two of them sported cigarettes.

As they approached Cole's front step, their pace slowed. One of the bangers whispered something to the one next to him and momentarily studied Cole. Cole returned the glance with the cold icy stare of challenge. One of gang-bangers shoved the boy in front of him and asked, "Thirsty?" All eyes turned in Cole's direction. He took a last swig of beer, tossed the can behind him on the porch and tensed himself for the attack. His heart pounded faster and his eyes swelled with increasing blood pressure. Cole glared intensely at each one of them.

As they reached the walkway leading to his doorstep, their pace slowed further—almost stopping. There was a flurry of whispered contemplation and quick glances at Cole. Cole's lungs filled and his biceps hardened as he prepared to stand. Then, without another word, their pace resumed and they passed by, looking for an easier target.

Cole stood and quickly took the two steps to sidewalk level, but their pace quickened and the little wanna-be gang-bangers never looked back. He knew that real gang-bangers would have at least challenged him up for "spare change" or the rest of his six-pack. Cole's intense stare followed them all the way to the corner and then they were gone.

The city seemed too quiet. Cole's senses relaxed with the passing of the potential confrontation. He finished another beer. The encounter had thrust suppressed memories from his past to the forefront of his mind. He thought of his mother and father and life in the mountainous Northern Idaho compound where he spent his early years. The Patriot Rebirth Society compound of his youth resembled an 1800s wilderness fortress complete with inner and outer defensive structures, which could be manned at a moments notice. The compound was home to more than a hundred people living in the compound itself or in cabins in the surrounding forest. For the children of the many families, school was central to their upbringing. Math, reading, writing, history, science, were all taught with the interweaving of white supremacist hate and brutality.

He had been born in a cabin located within the confines of the compound in the dead of winter with two feet of snow preventing a way out to the hospital in Coeur d'Alene. His father had been an officer and leader within the Patriot Rebirth Society and his mother an avid organizer and teacher within the community. He could vaguely remember his early educational beginnings at age three with the colors, alphabet, numbers and hand-to-hand combat. At his early age, it was just boxing with a five-year old counterpart, but the root of the lesson was to inflict as much pain as possible in any manner possible.

 Brian David Simmons

As he grew older, the boxing evolved into a mixture of Karate, Brazilian Jujitso, Judo, Sambo, and twelve other marshal arts skill-sets taken from the Marine Corps Martial Arts Program (MCMAP). All tactics were allowed in sparing matches, except for those intended to maim or kill. The forbidden skills were taught with vigilance but only allowed to be exercised on black dummies dressed in gang attire. He remembered how it pleased his mother when he was five-years-old and beat his eight-year-old opponent in hand-to-hand combat training. When he was eleven, he won the Society's annual Summerfest Combination Award for marksmanship, hand-to-hand combat and pursuit tactics for sixteen and under. By age twelve, he was sparring with multiple combatants of all ages.

Even at age twelve, he knew he could have easily put all six of the little gang-bankers in the hospital. Cole went inside his little two-bedroom rental house. It wasn't much but it was a bargain in this day and age at nine hundred per month. It was over a hundred years old; it had been built before you had to worry about hearing your neighbor's toilet flush. Houses on this block were only separated by the distance of a single-car driveway. It was close living, but at least he didn't have to share his walls, floor, or ceiling with neighbors like comparably priced apartments.

Cole turned on the TV to catch the midnight rerun of the 6:00 news as he stripped down to his skivvies for bed:

"George Connor's legal battle continued today with testimony from two of his sons' former acquaintances. They testified that Malcolm James was not responsible, in any way, for Connor's son's death. Both testified that James was, in fact, not a drug dealer and that he had never sold drugs to Connor's son. Television series star Connor is being sued for allegedly making slanderous public statements about James in relation to his son's drug-related death.

In local news, Salt Lake Mayor Jimmy Callaway announced his resignation today stating that allegations about his Dominican Republic financial affairs were taking a toll on his personal life and he was no longer willing to make the sacrifice of public office. City Council members predicted his resignation after special investigators uncovered suspected, unreported Colombian investments linked to bank transactions from Callaway's foreign accounts.

Melissa Vandyke has been following another police investigation of the execution-style murder of a West Valley aerospace engineer. Melissa?"

"Yes, Bob. Police authorities believe they are close to identifying suspects in last week's shooting death of William Roskeller along the shores of the Salt Lake. Chief Sansberry stated that tire tracks and soil samples led to a car rented at the airport. Through further thorough police work following up on a footprint, shell casings and other clues. An arrest can be expected within the week."

"Enough," mumbled Cole as he switched off the television. It made no sense. Has insanity run rampant? Judges, drug dealers, and politicians all out of control. Roskeller's death an execution—who would execute an aerospace engineer? For what? Cole climbed into the unmade bed and lay awake confused and frustrated trying to make sense of it all. Eventually, the frustration passed and Cole dozed off, only to find deep sleep just before the alarm went off.

When Cole woke, he knew the day would be as confounding as the evening news. As a master's degree graduate in mechanical engineering, he had landed a summer job in the aerospace industry to gain experience as an aerospace engineer. He had plans to return to MIT in the fall to begin work on his Ph.D., but the exciting vision of rocket science that had motivated him through five years of painstaking study was quickly eroding. Maybe it was because he was just a co-op, a temporary employee, that got all the dullest of dull assignments.

Like every day, Cole was running late. He dug through the dirty clothes and came up with a white shirt that didn't look too bad. With a tie wrapped around his neck, he bolted from the house and jumped in his Buick Sun Fire. It had served him well through five years of school and was now approaching two hundred thousand miles, but it still had enough spunk to get on the freeway with the fastest of them. Cole kept the accelerator deep in its travel, passing cars to the left and right as he headed for the Space and Defense Manufacturing Company. As the car neared the remote facility and the traffic waned, he pushed even harder on the accelerator pedal until the front end started to shimmy. He arrived at five before eight, just in time for his meeting.

Today was Issue Review Board, IRB, for engine discrepancy issues. It meant a meeting that started at eight o'clock and ended at who knows when. Cole waited his turn to make his presentation to the IRB about a small spot of residual adhesive on the flame surface of the engine nozzle. It was ludicrous that such an innocuous issue had to be presented to the IRB. What was essentially bathtub caulking wouldn't survive more than a fraction of a second when exposed to the extreme thermal environment of a LOX/Hydrogen rocket engine. But this discrepancy was a first time occurrence and therefore had to be presented.

Cole's turn finally came and he made his presentation to the IRB and a conference room full of bored onlookers. His purely technical presentation was met with a barrage of questions on historical precedence for the discrepancy. He had a convincing argument that the caulking would have no technical effect on the engine, but failed to provide any historical precedence. His presentation was over in less than fifteen minutes and the decision was predictable. Based solely on political considerations and lack of history, the multimillion-dollar piece of hardware would be set aside until a repair procedure could be developed. To Cole, it was ludicrous.

This wasn't why he had gone to years of school at MIT, one of the finest technical institutions in the country. Nothing had prepared him for this insane level of conservatism throwing his whole life's purpose into a state of confusion. Whatever happened to the greatness that once existed in America's space programs? Where are the brilliant scientists and engineers who had developed the hundreds of new technologies that made space exploration a reality? Are there no more Wernher Von Brauns whose visionary boldness defined most of the rocketry vehicles in use today? Are the brilliance, vision, and calculated risk taking of yesteryear gone? Are politics and historical precedence what the future holds for me?

Thank God it was Friday and thank God it was over. The meeting lasted until almost four o'clock. Cole desperately needed to escape. As he left the gates of the SDRMC, he pointed his Sun Fire west and headed for the solitude of the desert.

Chapter Two

Cyber Assassination

Kevin McKuel was glued to his monitor at Omage Corporation. Jumper wires criss-crossed his cubical and modular tabletops to connect open computer towers, loose circuit boards, drive units, and diagnostic equipment. The smell of warm electronics drifted upward and floated over the cubical walls before being picked up by the ventilation system. A high-pitched squeal from the prototype laser read-write drive unit on his right sporadically drowned out the constant hum of the computer tower on his left.

His hand brushed back wires as he moved the mouse into position and clicked. Then, with lightning speed, his fingers attacked the keyboard and it clamored in a rhythmic tune. A passing voice behind him said, "You can go home now. Have a good one, dude." But the vociferation of the keyboard continued without interruption. Half an hour passed before Kevin paused and hit the enter key. The squeal of the read-write drive transitioned to a deep-throated howl as the speed of gigabytes attaching themselves to the cloud interfaced digital disc accelerated. Kevin's focus switched to the diagnostic equipment and he smiled.

Another voice came from behind. "Kevin, are you going to stay here all night?" asked the VP of Product Development. Kevin's eyes switched back to the monitor;

again he brushed back the wires and swirled the mouse.

"Kevin!" shouted the VP. He received no answer. He stepped into Kevin's cubical, stumbled over a wire and put his hand on Kevin's shoulder. "Are you all right, son?"

"Huh?"

"I said it's time to go home now."

"Oh, what time is it?"

"After five."

"Oh yeah," came Kevin's excited reply.

"I'll see you on Monday. Go do something different this weekend, will you? Go hiking, rent a boat, take a drive. Just don't log onto a computer. Will you do that for me?"

"Sure, see you Monday." Kevin always did the same thing on evenings and weekends, and this weekend would be no different.

There were only two other cars in the parking lot when he exited the Omage main entrance. His red Porsche was there waiting for him; waiting to whisk him home where he could play his "game."

The Porsche was his symbol of accomplishment. His innovative genius could be directly linked to Omage's boost to the Fortune 500 list. He had conceived and developed numerous pieces of innovative, secure software and state-of-the-art computer drives that directly integrated with cloud based media. It was relatively simple stuff for Kevin and he was well paid for his technical contributions. But that was all work and his game was all play.

Kevin loved the sound of the turbo when it engaged. He turned right onto the highway and squealed through the stop sign with exactness that only his Porsche could provide. The tires chirped as he paddle shifted into third and then again when he shifted into fourth. The computer-controlled precision of the engine optimized the balance of its strokes and gave Kevin all that he demanded as he flew toward Ogden. Home was an hour away but it felt like minutes.

He pulled into the garage of his upscale condo, turned off his faithful companion, and patted it good night. It was now game time; he was about to wreak havoc on the lives of politicians, businessmen, sports figures, and any other member of society operating outside his vision of right and wrong.

The Internet and telephone were Kevin's boxing gloves and his victims had no clue that they were in for a fight. For Kevin's game of information and misinformation, a simple piece of data, true or false, carefully deposited within the tentacles of the Internet would grow, multiply, and accelerate to eventually return to his victim like a right hook. His targets were those who cheated society. Some were politicians who stunk of graft and self-serving manipulation of their position. Others were white-collar crooks who were guilty beyond all reasonable doubt but beat their sentence with a slick attorney or legal technicality. Kevin picked one fight at a time and gave it his undivided attention.

 Brian David Simmons

Since the Internet was scanned by thousands daily, an individual's life could be made miserable overnight with a little carefully placed misinformation. The amazing thing about misinformation is that once it's out there, it's almost impossible to change. After a while, it essentially becomes true. Attempts to refute it simply make it more believable. If it's good juicy stuff, and a member of the media believes the tidbit of misinformation has been uncovered as a result of his or her detective work, then it's even more believable. This was the most intriguing element of the game. Who would pick up what piece of information and what interpretation would they make?

One of Kevin's favorites was to get a digital photograph of his victim, modify it in any number of suitable ways, and then distribute it on the net. With the right photograph, anyone could easily become a park flasher, porno star, child molester, or wife beater.

Other elements of the game were equally as brutal: erroneous credit card purchases, bills for goods never received, driver's license suspensions, redirection of incoming telephone calls, and requests for hundreds of magazines and bundles of junk mail. Each one was not very serious by itself, but taken as whole, it was quite overwhelming.

With a couple of clicks of the mouse, he was in. First, he checked on the local news at www.xkl/news. Kevin scanned down through the news stories: two stabbings, more on the execution of the engineer, another rape, one car bombing, methamphetamine lab bust, and Salt Lake Mayor Jimmy Callaway's resignation—interesting and almost the story he was looking for.

With a few more clicks of the mouse, he backed out and brought up his electronic passport. Kevin had a very special passport for playing the game. It was a multi-layered tailored disguise that allowed him to be free of his electronic profile and emulate others'. Tonight's custom-built passport was a disguised link that emulated Salt Lake City Councilman Harold Hubbard's website, Facebook page, and Twitter account. Hubbard was Kevin's choice because it was apparent from television reports that he wanted the mayor's job. Hubbard was probably as crooked as Callaway. Maybe he would even be Kevin's next victim if he misbehaved. But for now, Callaway was the subject of the game at hand and Hubbard would get all the credit.

Kevin thought about the Callaway resignation story as he clicked through several screens to check on his special passport. It was interesting that Callaway had not refuted any stories of reported money dealings with Colombia. Especially since this had been discovered by a web-snooping reporter for Channel Two. In fact, it was nothing more than Kevin's fabrication. All he really knew was that Callaway deposited huge sums of money, millions, in the Dominican Republic Bank. Also, this sometimes corresponded to transfers of almost equal amounts to Colombian banks several days later. Since the amounts were sometimes inconsistent, a correlation was purely speculative. However, if Callaway didn't deny the news story, then maybe there really was some dirty money moving between Callaway, the Dominican Republic Bank, and Colombia.

Kevin swirled and clicked the mouse to check the last piece of misinformation placed through the Internet. Unknowingly, Jimmy Callaway had rented two storage bays from Airport Storage using his VISA card two weeks earlier. Yesterday the Environmental Protection Agency received a report through email for a hazardous waste spill in Callaway's storage bays. As is required by any business selling, receiving, or transporting potentially hazardous waste materials, the Emergency Planning and Right to Know Act mandates self-reporting of any spill. And of course, with Kevin's help, Callaway had complied and reported on himself.

Kevin's first thoughts were that Callaway should have a radioactive hazardous waste incident. That might lack credibility so he considered other possibilities. PCB was overused in the media and might not attract the interest of a web-snooping media hound. He needed something hazardous, believable, and yet slightly unusual. He needed something that would get attention. Eventually Kevin decided that Callaway had had an acetone, naphtha, red phosphorus, and hexamethylenetetramine spill. It sounded impressive, took half a line to write, and might even be used in a meth lab. With his Colombian money connections already exposed, it was probably in the back of every reporter's mind that Callaway had something to do with drugs. At least a clever reporter might think so.

When Kevin filed the electronic report, he implanted a special cookie of his own creation that allowed him to track anyone who accessed the report. The EPARTKA database had been visited by the Salt Lake Journal and, by the looks of the keystrokes recorded in the cookie, the only thing that had been accessed was Callaway's report. But there was no report of it in the news. Maybe they were waiting for Sunday. Kevin wondered if he shouldn't call the Haz-Mat guys and let them know that there really wasn't a spill. After all, it might cost these guys their day off and Kevin really didn't want to do a disservice to anybody except Callaway. Then again, maybe they wouldn't mind if it got them out of church with double pay to boot.

Enough misinformation for now, thought Kevin. It was time to move on and see what real information could be misused. Kevin had set himself up to monitor and record all incoming and outgoing calls from Callaway's cell phone. It was really rather simple to capture a conversation broadcast across the airways, regardless of the cellular service used. The hardest part was obtaining the phone number. With a little

          Brian David Simmons

Internet surfing, even that could be readily found. It was amazing to Kevin that so many cell phone users were oblivious to the ease of cell phone transgression and were confident that their phones were personal and private.

Kevin had modified a police scanner purchased from Electric Shack and hot-wired it with an old 286 PC. It was programmed to scan only for pre-selected phone numbers. The 286 was a whole lot more than he really needed but it was what he had. Actually, a simple logic board would have done equally as well. The PC also did an adequate job of running trial and error routines to capture the access code. The third element of the system was a telephone answering machine, also purchased from Electric Shack. The only reason for the answering machine was that he could get instant playback along with the day and time of the call. He could have had DOS record the time and day and then Kevin could have matched phone call to conversations captured on a simple tape recorder. But the answering machine did all that for him—kind of like a secretary for his game.

Kevin could also eavesdrop on Callaway's landline phone, but he just hadn't spent the time to set it up. People seemed to believe their cell phones were more private than their landline. After all, they could make calls from the privacy of their own car, a bathroom stall, or the middle of a football field. As Kevin knew, cell phone security was essentially nonexistent.

Hopefully, Callaway would feel the sense of cell phone security and reveal something of interest. However, Callaway was a careful sort. Often his phone conversations seemed to be innocuous, yet they had a cryptic air about them. They included references to commonplace items that seemed out of context. He spoke in terms that led Kevin to believe Callaway was more concerned about being overheard, rather than suspecting his cell phone was being monitored.

Kevin listened to the recorded phone conversations for almost two hours. There was nothing of any significance; the calls were legitimate business and personal chitchat. The only thing of particular interest was how sexy his wife sounded over the phone. Kevin wondered if she looked as good as she sounded. He didn't remember ever seeing her in the paper or on TV.

 Brian David Simmons

Chapter Three

ACCIDENTAL ENCOUNTER

THE SUN FIRE RACED FROM THE BONDAGE OF THE Space and Defense Rocket Manufacturing Company and headed toward the empty plains. Cole was strangely attracted to the west desert. He found great simplicity in the solitude of the barren countryside. He often explored the region looking for artifacts of the past and always carried a sleeping bag and camping equipment in the back of his car. He also had a .22-caliber rifle hidden from inspection by the rocket-cops at work. It was against the rules to bring any firearm or ammunition onto company property. Of course, at the Space and Defense Rocket Manufacturing Company, most things were against the rules. Nothing was against the rules in the desert.

He pressed on, never dropping below 60 mph as he hit the end of the paved section of road. The car shook violently, drowning out the radio, and skittered back and forth across the washboard road. More speed smoothed out the washboards and Cole accelerated, leaving a huge dust cloud in his trail. In some places where the road bordered stagnant poisonous water pools it would have meant disaster if the car wandered from the washboard path. Or at the least a long walk back to civilization. After thirty minutes of white-knuckle driving, Cole slowed and turned north on a jeep trail.

With low rolling hills to his right, he maneuvered the Sun Fire around on what was probably once a well-traveled road. The Sun Fire wasn't much of a four-wheel-drive vehicle, but as long as it was dry he didn't worry about getting stuck. At least if he did, it wouldn't be too difficult to get unstuck. The road was sandy in some places and hardpan in others. There were a few rocks to dodge here and there, but it was for the most part quite passable with a two-wheel drive vehicle. He turned off the jeep trail onto an even lesser traveled path. Sagebrush scratched at the Sun Fire's paint and the front tires spun in the sandy soil as he maneuvered the vehicle down the path. When he reached a small wash, he stopped. This was as far as he could go in the Sun Fire; the rest of the trip would be on foot.

Cole had discovered a low-lying area out in the flats that was undetectable from a distance. This was where he was headed, but it was still several miles away. He traded his dress shirt and slacks for a T-shirt and jeans, readied his gear, and closed up the Sun Fire. Cole estimated that he had less than four hours before dark and headed down the trail with canteen, hunting knife and the .22 rifle. The canteen was essential to survival in the desert and he never ventured far without it.

Cole moved slowly and deliberately, watching everything in his advance. His senses intensified with

     Brian David Simmons

the anticipation of game: a glimpse of a live target and the momentary opportunity to raise the rifle, aim, and fire at fleeting prey. With the single shot .22, he had learned that it had to be one shot, one kill. It was the same with his big game rifles when hunting white tails in Massachusetts or mule deer in the mountains of Utah: one shot, one kill. This was his credo for success.

He intensely studied every mound of dirt, every dried-up sage bush, every desert weed, and every rock. Leaves clung to delicate branches on little flowering weeds hoping for a hint of water to sustain life, but the ground was too parsimonious to give up its precious moisture. Any moisture was stored deep out of reach of the roots, nature's pipeline to the dying leaves. The leaves were the rabbits' food of preference and if there were any rabbits to be found, it would be next to one of those little plants.

His stomach growled. He hoped for a bunny, but a jack would do. He moved on further west—not even a jack had showed itself, much less a bunny. It was probably going to be a hungry evening and an even hungrier morning.

Cole picked up the pace and hurried on to the trail's end. It was a half-acre in size, recessed in the flat countryside. From even a short distance away, the low-lying area was undetectable. If a person didn't know it was there, they would never find it. Cole had originally walked into the area while hunting rabbits, but rabbits weren't the attraction. The place had a strange familiarity—almost as if he had always known it existed. He returned many times to search out little pieces of wood, nails, iron scrap, and other miscellaneous tidbits. There was probably some historical value in the findings, but even if there wasn't, it was still very intriguing. What could have once stood here? A house? No, nobody builds a house in a low-lying desert region like this because of flash floods. Why no central location to the artifacts? What secrets did this place hold? Why this remote location? The questions bounced around in Cole's mind aching for an answer. Someday he would put the pieces of the puzzle together. Often, he fantasized about finding something of real value or something that might reveal answers to at least some of the questions.

There were still unanswered questions, but there was also something else. That "something else" that rational people don't acknowledge. That "something else" that brings goose bumps and shortens breath. It was something that's sensed rather than seen, heard, or felt. Like believing someone is behind you, but when you look, no one is there. That "something else" that is mystical, yet almost within grasp. Cole was engrossed with the sensation, and his body shivered as if attempting to drive off the embodiment. His hands and feet grew cold and an abysmal chill struck deep into his chest and momentarily stopped his heart. Intense ethereal sense blocked rational thought and reason gave way to feeling. Rational thought resisted

     Brian David Simmons

and discounted the feeling but in the end, lost to the sensation that he had been here generations before. Humbled by things beyond his understanding, Cole blocked his senses from probing for the answer. Some things are best left to rest.

He began the trek back to the Sun Fire. Following the trail wasn't a priority, and he moved in the general direction of the car. Just walking east was good enough. Nothing seemed to matter except the ethereal feeling that had touched his existence.

Distance and the imminent onset of darkness alerted Cole's sense of reality. His camping gear was at the car and the desert was no place to just snuggle up to a bush for the night. He had missed the trail by quite a way and found himself making a gradual climb up a small, rolling hill. The sun was setting behind him as he advanced up the hill. Cole's sense of direction placed the north-south road just over the hill. It would be an easy walk, even in the dark, down the road, and then only a short jog to the right would put him back at the Sun Fire.

When Cole reached the crest of the hill, he instinctively hit the ground, falling flat on his belly. He concentrated on events unfolding on the road below. Two cars and four men having an intense discussion were not more than four hundred yards away. One man with his hands behind his back was bent over the hood of the car in the rear. Another man, also with his hands tied, faced the other two and was enjoined in a desperate conversation.

Cole's adrenaline gushed and his senses awoke. His sight and hearing reached out to gather details of the altercation, but he was too far away to satisfy his desire to know more. He was also potentially detectable on the ridgeline at dusk. He needed to drop down off the ridge where his outline would blend into the hillside and an onlooker would be blinded by the sun in the background.

He carefully began his descent down the hill, inching his way closer, keeping his body in full contact with the ground, sometimes loosing sight of the drama below, but always moving closer in search of a vantage point. His body, mind, and soul were electrified with the fear of potential detection and the challenge of going unseen. Vegetation crackled beneath his slithering body as he reached the safety of a clump of tall grass to observe for a few minutes before trying to move closer.

The two men didn't have their hands tied; they were handcuffed. All four men were in suits. They were all large, well-built men. One handcuffed man backed away from the two in control and turned as if to flee, but he was quickly hurled to the ground. He struggled to his knees and said something to his partner, still bent over the hood of the car. Cole thought he heard one of the men say "shut up," but the distance was still too great even for his keen hearing to capture the sounds. The two men in control moved to the rear of the car and leaned against the trunk. They each lit a cigarette and seemed to joke about the whole thing. Or maybe they were talking about next year's basketball season and recent draft picks.

Cole lay motionless, peering between blades of dried grass. The man who was bent over the hood of the car had his head turned in Cole's direction—maybe he even saw Cole. The sun had now settled behind the hill, which meant that Cole was more visible than before. The men below, not having the sun in their eyes, could probably have picked him out on the hillside if they had just looked. But they were too secure in their pre-selected, isolated location to be on guard for somebody slithering down the hillside. Cole inched closer.

Every move was carefully planned. He targeted cover below and then made every motion slow and continuous, with no abrupt movement, even to avert the pain of cacti and stickers and varmint holes in his path. As he got closer, more detail was visible. The man on his knees had a beard and the other three were clean-shaven. The two cars were dark brown, almost black, full-size outfits, maybe Lincolns or Mercurys. A metallic case lay on the trunk behind the two men, now on their second cigarette. Cole could now hear their muffled voices. His mind focused to segregate and ascertain the meaning of the words, but they escaped him. He crept closer.

With another fifty or sixty yards behind him, Cole took a sitting position behind a sage bush to capture fragment sounds from the two still leaning against the trunk. From garbled sounds, he extracted the words "disappear," "more money," "Mexico," and finally "okay, do it." At which time, the conversation came to an end; one of the men nodded in some kind of agreement with the other and then stepped away from the trunk. He walked to the handcuffed man on his knees and pushed him face down into the dirt with his foot. Then, without even a pause, he pulled a pistol from beneath his jacket and shot the handcuffed man in the back of the head. It was a large caliber gun. A serious weapon. There was no doubt that the man had just died. The shot boomed, echoed, and vibrated throughout the desert silence, shocking its inhabitants, sending birds flying and varmints seeking refuge in their holes.

Cole was no different; he rolled from his sitting position and with a burst of adrenaline, his legs launched him up the hill. His ears now captured a distinct cry from below, "Get him!" Another shot boomed, only this time Cole heard the bullet whistle over his head. Loose soil on the hillside gave way under his scrambling feet, and he fell forward as the third and fourth shots rang out.

The man bent over the hood bolted from his position and Cole heard the fifth shot ring out, but the sound was different and not in his direction. The second handcuffed man had obviously just died as well.

     Brian David Simmons

Fighting upward on hands and knees, he was going nowhere. A flurry of gunfire reverberated through the desert sky with each bullet making a dull thud in the hillside, first to his left and then to his right. He managed to get to his feet in his upward charge only to step in a varmint hole and be driven back down. He looked upward toward the top of the hill as a bullet buried itself in the sand only inches from his face. He wasn't going to make it; it was more than a hundred-yard dash back to the crest of the hill, with no cover. Cole's mind cried in terror and then exploded with adrenaline overload in a scream at death.

The release freed Cole's mind and he began to gain control of his fear, but something was different: the sense of deja vu, the sense of his past, the sense of his Patriot Rebirth Society origins, and the sense of knowing had returned. His hand felt the stock of the .22, still clinched tight. A bullet jolted Cole's left foot as it nicked the edge of his Nike. He rolled over and assumed a sitting position with the .22 firmly pressed deep into his shoulder. He was one with the rifle, as if it was just an extension of his body. In the seconds that followed, rational thought contradicted chival-rous feelings and an inner battle waged reason against resurrected instinct from compound training of his childhood. Who do I think I am? White supremacists extraordinaire? .30-06 no problem. .22 no way. Who am I kidding? A 250-yard shot with open sights and a dainty little bullet wouldn't hit the target, much less penetrate it. Bullet ballistics aren't that good. Why do I even point the rifle? Safety off. Who am I kidding? Come on. The Patriot Rebirth Society was wrong. Killing is wrong. The Lord is my Shepherd and thou shalt not kill. Easy, put an "X" on their forehead and squeeze the trigger. Why would I even pull the trigger?

One of the men below ejected the clip from his gun and reached for another. The other man steadied his aim by positioning his feet and grasping the pistol with both hands. Cole's focus crystallized. A bullet thundered from the man's gun and raced up the hill toward Cole. It passed through his shirt under his right arm leaving a slight burning sensation; Cole didn't move. Instead, his heart rate slowed. His mind came into tune with his body, including the .22-caliber extension of his hands. He sensed the pulsing of his heart through his eyes and between beats the rifle was dead steady. He instinctively calculated: 250 yards, plus a little. Elevation seven, maybe eight, inches. Shooting down hill. Back off an inch or so. Slight breeze from the north. 100 yards no compensation. 200-plus yards—better make an allowance. Two inches to the left. One shot. One kill. Then, as if by accident, the rifle fired.

A clap of the hands, a door slamming, or maybe even the pop-top on a cola can would have made more noise. But a moment after the shot, the gunman's arms fell to his sides, and he dropped to his knees. He was motionless for what seemed like minutes to Cole. He

     Brian David Simmons

seemed to be looking directly at Cole. Cole imagined he could see the man's eyes glaring at him as if piercing his very soul and seeking revenge. Breathing was difficult as the man's thoughts reached out and touched him. Then, slowly, the man fell forward, face down into the dirt.

The other man withdrew with a frantic flurry of gunfire. No target—he just fired, as if using his gun as a shield in a guarded retreat to the rear of the car behind him. Cole pulled back the bolt on the .22 and ejected the shell. He pulled another little rim fire round from his pocket and inserted it into the chamber. He closed the bolt and resumed shooting position.

Occasionally the man bobbed up and then back down behind the trunk, as he fired in Cole's direction, but he had lost his target in the rapidly disappearing daylight. The man had succumbed to fear, and the fear of the unknown is always worse than the fear of the known.

Again, Cole did the mental calculation of the shot and took steady aim. Movements of the man below were barely discernable. But Cole's focus cut through the dim light to study the rhythm of man's movements. His head peered up over the trunk periodically and every third or fourth time up was to the left as he searched for a target. Then his head was back to the right with an occasional peek around the back of the car.

It would take a half of a second for the bullet to reach its target and Cole included this in his new calculation. Cole was one with the rifle and, with his newfound courage, this all felt natural. Elevation, windage, rhythm, anticipation and again, as if by accident, the rifle fired. The bobbing stopped and tranquility returned to the desert.

Cole laid back against the hillside in relief and closed his eyes. For a few seconds, his mind went blank and he sighed in a slight slumber of relief. Then the questions crept in. What the hell just happened? Who would believe this happened to me? What next? I will tell the whole story to the police. What were those guys doing out here to begin with? Have I really just killed two men? The killing really isn't a result of my past; it really was just self defense. Wasn't it? The action brought back buried memories as it wasn't the first time he had killed. He suppressed the memories and his mind rejoined the present.

He needed a closer look. To be safe, Cole reloaded the .22 and put the spent casings in his pocket. Only an inkling of the day remained to light the sky. The sky above was a dull dark blue and provided only enough light to see those things that were directly in his path as he made his way slowly down the hill. He stopped and knelt when he neared the cars. He could see three men lying motionless in the road between the cars. He studied the man nearest him for any signs of movement. Did I really kill this man? questioned Cole's rational sense. The man was face down in the dirt, legs straight, hands by his sides with palms up, and no signs of movement. Cole had his answer.

Curiosity lured him on. Silently, careful with every step, he moved parallel to the road to the front of the first car. With increasing trepidation, Cole moved around the front of the car, rifle ready, to see the fourth man. He was lying on his back with his legs half folded underneath him. The position was too uncomfortable for anybody to maintain, even if they were playing dead. The man had to be dead, guessed Cole as he moved closer.

"Damn," stuttered Cole. There was no entry wound and he saw chest movement. He jumped back, took aim with the .22, fired, and then leaped back behind the front of the car. Leaning against the bumper clutching the .22 in ready position, he quickly reloaded and peeked around the front of the car. The man was in the same position.

Cole stood and stepped out from the car with the rifle pulled deep into his shoulder and pointed at the man. His eyes searched for signs of movement; chest, hands, and legs were all interrogated. The body twitched several times and Cole almost fired again, but eventually, it became motionless. Cole took a step and then another, gradually approaching all the while maintaining his aim at the man's head. He stopped with the barrel of his .22 resting gently on the man's cheek. Only then did Cole realize that his first shot had been deadly.

Several tiny streaks of red, almost iridescent in the starlight, hinted at a trail of opaque liquid coming from the man's right eye. His first shot at the man had entered the eye, been funneled by its socket into the skull, and then rattled around inside the man's head doing who knows what damage. Cole's only remorseful thought was, not enough windage. The second bullet had entered the man's head a little low and to the left, just behind his ear.

In the movies, the good guy always runs off and throws up after killing, not so for Cole. He continued his systematic visual interrogation of the man he had just killed. The man still gripped his semiautomatic pistol and its holster was exposed by the open lapel of the man's jacket. A glimmer of reflected light from the man's breast pocket caught Cole's attention and he knelt down to get a closer look. Pulling back the pocket, the object became visible: it was a badge! With two fingers, Cole warily extracted the badge and its leather pocket carrier. The I.D. that came with it was visible, even in the almost non-existent light, "Special Agent—Federal Bureau of Investigation."

Cole let out concerned sigh. "Now what? I just killed an FBI agent," he mumbled in the desert silence. He marched over to the second gunman, rolled him over, threw back the suit jacket, and pulled out another badge. Cole studied the photo on the FBI I.D. comparing it to the dead man's face, but it was covered with a mixture of dirt and blood. With continued scrutiny of the man's muddy face, Cole learned the accuracy of his shot; it was just to the right of the bridge of the nose at eye level.

Cole put his hand over his mouth and breathed through his fingers as he contemplated his next course of action. He had done and seen enough; it was now time for the cops. He dropped the badge on the man's chest, stood, and glanced at the other two men. The police can figure out who they were, he concluded and began his hike back to the Sun Fire. He took one final glance back as he passed the second car and then walked down the road, but his pace soon slowed as his mind reconstructed the scene, including an image of a metallic case.

He stopped and again breathed through his fingers. The night was quiet and it was extremely unlikely anybody would just happen by. Time really wasn't that important and nobody would care. Just one peek, Cole convinced himself.

The case was sitting on the trunk of the car where the two men had been smoking and strategizing. Cole glanced at the special agent's face and then popped the latches. He took a deep breath and his heart skipped a beat as he opened the case. It contained neatly stacked bundles of hundred-dollar bills. Cole didn't have to count it, the mathematics were simple enough: maybe a hundred bundles, a hundred bills per bundle, a hundred bucks per bill. That's six zeros.

"Sweet Jesus!" echoed through the night sky.

Cole slammed the case shut, paced away, kicked the dirt and the agony began. A million bucks. I could just grab it and run. But then what? The cops would track my butt down, and I'd go to jail for something, if not murder. Nope, I gotta just walk. Besides, what would I do with it anyway? Cole turned and looked back at the case. He paced first one way and then another with repeated glares at the case. It would be so easy. Who would ever know? Nobody ever walks away from a million bucks. If I leave it to the cops, who knows what they'd do with it? That money probably isn't FBI money. If I turn it over to the cops, would the owners of the money be mad that I fouled things up? Would they come after me? Finally, the torment climaxed and was replaced with a nauseous acceptance of his childhood that accompanied his decision.

He needed a plan. Cole sat on a rock and stared at the hateful metallic box while thinking it through. He'd stomped around enough to leave his foot prints everywhere and it would be simple matter to find his trail back up the hill and then eventually to the Sun Fire's tire tracks. They would identify tire brand, age, local retail outlets, condition of the car's front end, and then come up with a list of customers. Even if he was only one of a thousand possibilities, that was too many. In parallel, they'd go after his Nike prints to establish height, weight and stride characteristics. Urine on the trail might shortcut the whole investigation with DNA and other tests establishing blood type and age. These were just the things he knew about, not to mention a whole list of other unimagined possibilities. It was clear that he could never have been here—or never

     Brian David Simmons

have been at wherever the crime scene ended up. Cole searched his pants pockets for a foil gum wrapper – none. Something else would have to do. Cigarettes, they were smoking. It would work. He had his plan.

The police were only half the problem. If he was going to do this successfully, he would also have to elude anybody affiliated with the dead men, whoever they were. They could actually be the worse of the two threats. If drug dealers, foreign spies, assassins, or whoever were going to be after him, he ought to at least know who they were.

Cole began a survey of the other men and cars. Both of the handcuffed gentlemen were a mess. Entrance holes in the back of their heads were small, but there wasn't much left of the other side. Even the world's greatest forensic scientist would have a hard time restructuring the shattered facial features. Identification would have to come from some other clue.

He searched glove boxes and trunks of both cars. The front car belonged to the FBI agents and was registered to Avis. That meant that these other two men had followed the agents out into the middle of nowhere for their own execution. It made no sense.

By moonlight and interior lights of the cars, Cole collected and examined wallets, IDs, the contents of the dead men's pockets, cell phones, and miscellaneous paperwork from the glove boxes. The executed men were Amal ibn-Gabirol and Strabo al-Hamdani; at least that's what their international driver's licenses said. The second car was also a rental. No wonder the cars were look-alikes. They had been rented that afternoon from the Salt Lake Airport. Amal and Strabo had reservations that night at the Holiday Hilton in Ogden. The agents didn't have a hotel reservation even though both of them had home addresses in Washington, D.C.

Cole placed the case and collected articles off the road, out of sight. Then came the distasteful task; Cole took a deep breath and hefted the first of the Arabic men into the backseat of the Buick and came away with his whole front side covered in dirt mixed with blood. The smell reminded Cole of mule deer entrails. Loading the second Arabic man was just as distasteful a task.

Next it was time to move the FBI agents. Cole depersonalized the work at hand by renaming them Mr. Muddy-Face and One-Eyed-Jack. Again, he thought he should feel some remorse, but not now. Cole loaded One-Eyed-Jack into the front passenger seat of Amal's car and Mr. Muddy-Face into the passenger side of the front car.

With a little re-enactment of the day's events and the help of an emerging half moon, Cole was able to recover the majority of the shell casings. For sure, he got Mr. Muddy-Face's shell casings. He dropped them on the front seat next to him along with his gun. But he wasn't exactly sure how may rounds One-Eyed-Jack had fired and with him being on the move they were scattered over a wide area. Cole was careful not

     Brian David Simmons

to leave any fingerprints on the shell casings and cut the front pocket from his jeans to serve as a little bag.

He looked around one more time and then climbed in alongside Mr. Muddy-Face. Cole started the car, pulled it into drive and drove off. The headlights came on automatically and this was unsettling to Cole; the whole desert seemed to light up, reflecting off sandy hillsides. If anyone was out there, even miles away, they could see the headlights.

The road was rough in places, frequently changing from rocky to hardpan to sand and then back again. Cole watched the odometer and when it reached two-tenths, the countryside opened up. There were no visible hills or obstacles off in the distance, at least with as much visibility as the half moon provided. Cole stopped when the road turned back to hardpan.

Cole pulled One-Eyed-Jack over into the driver's seat, buckled his seat belt and pulled the arm down through the bottom half of the steering wheel. Even in death he clung to his gun and Cole wondered how many people it had killed. Cole positioned the stiffen-ing leg to apply pressure to the gas pedal and closed the door.

Cole carefully began his hike back to Amal's car. As soon as the hard pan turned to sand, Cole moved off the road and searched out a path that most obscured his footsteps. The half moon seemed especially bright, illuminating the beauty of the desert. It was a warm, still night, full of sights and sounds. An owl hunting for nocturnal rockchucks could be heard searching through the night sky. The outline of each bush, rock and ridgeline became clearer as Cole's night vision improved and so did his pace. When he could, he ran. When there was chance of leaving a print, he planned and executed each footstep with caution.

He was relieved to be back at Amal's car, until he opened the door. He instantly felt his stomach coming to his throat when he caught the scent of drying blood and secreted bodily fluids. Cole backed off and took a deep breath to quell the shock. He questioned his choice of actions, but it was too late; he had already started down this path and now he had to finish it. He got in the car.

Two-tenths on the odometer didn't come soon enough; Cole mashed the accelerator to shorten his stay in this car of death. When he pulled up behind the FBI car, Cole had had all he could stand and burst from the car to fill his lungs with the desert air.

Cole held his breath and forced himself to make repeated trips to position Mr. Muddy-Face behind the steering wheel, similar to One-Eyed-Jack. He then took the shell casings out of his pocket, wiped them one by one and carefully laid half of them lengthwise in the gap between the trunk lid and the quarter panel. Similarly, he placed the other half in the hood gap. He assumed that they would withstand mild forward acceleration, but would bounce off with any kind of significant bump. Next he punctured the gas tank with a thrust of his hunting knife and filled his canteen with the leaking gas. He dumped the gas in the interior of One-Eyed-Jack's car and then with several repeated refills, soaked the interior of both cars.

With One-Eyed-Jack stiffening around the steering wheel, Cole removed the cigarette pack from the man's pocket, dumped the cigarettes on the seat and removed the foil wrapper from inside the package. He opened the passenger door and started the car; its little V-6 revved to at least a couple of thousand RPM. Cole soaked the cigarette wrapper with gasoline, poured a small quantity into the cell phone charger, shoved the wrapper into the hole and forced the cell phone charger in on top of it. Simultaneously, Cole pulled the shift lever down. The car took off as Cole fell backward out the passenger door. The door slammed shut as the car accelerated away; it stayed right with the road until the cigarette foil began to glow and the interior burst into flames.

Cole quickly repeated the same trick with the second car, only its engine hovered at little more than an idle as it drove away. Fearful that gas leaking from the tank would explode, Cole took off in a dead run before the interior ignited. But the gas tank didn't rupture and car continued slowly down the road.

He could see the first car speeding away off in the distance and watched as the two blazing vehicles continued on their journey out into the desert. The first car drifted off the roadway and was bouncing through the desert at a good pace. The second car crept along nearly following the road for at least five hundred yards before it stopped. The other car, further off in the distance, also stopped at about the same time and then, as the flames violated their gas tanks, the cars exploded to further illuminate the desert with the burst of flames.

Cole turned and hurried his pace back to the metallic case. As he mindfully made his way back, stepping only on rocks and hardpan, his thoughts were of how the investigation would stack up the facts, clues, and unknowns. Some facts should be simple to establish while others would just create a quandary. Hopefully, tire tracks of the cars would be overrun by sheriff, FBI, coroner, and maybe even media vehicles. The initial assumption would be that the murders occurred at the location of the cars and that somebody had then torched the cars to destroy any evidence. But the position of the ignition switches and shift levers, along with only one set of tracks would confuse that assumption. Some smart detective would probably find the spent shell casings, maybe even backtrack their positions to some point where it all must have happened. Then there would be no physical signs of anything at any single location; they would look harder and still find nothing and eventually they would discredit the entire scenario and start over. Maybe they would imagine some kind of moving gun battle, but that

     Brian David Simmons

would be contradicted by other evidence, which was still further confused by the fires. Whatever scenario they hypothesized, it would probably be contradicted by a coroner's report and again they would start over. Or maybe, with hierarchical pressures from above to provide answers, they would fill in the details and just make it so.

Would the reasoning powers of the police ever imagine that someone would load up corpses and send them driving off into the desert in flaming cars? Doubtfully, at least that was what Cole hoped.

Maybe they wouldn't even find the cars for a week or two, in which case any identifiable footprints, vehicle tire marks, or anything else Cole may have forgotten would be obscured by desert winds and time. In which case, it really didn't matter. What mattered was to finish his camouflage job at the real shooting location get away as quickly as possible.

The half moon that had illuminated the desert faded as the sky began to brighten. Cole sat down next to the metal case for a few minutes to catch his breath and study his stratagem. He found two more shell casings and then began obliterating all footprints and tire tracks with a sagebrush.

Continuing with the sagebrush in one hand and the case in the other, he worked his way toward the Sun Fire. The sun rose before Cole got back to the car and the unsettling feeling that he had made the wrong choice crept in.

He reeked of a smell he was becoming accustomed to and peeled off his clothes to the reveal the dried blood that had penetrated the pores of his skin. He scratched and dug at it, but it wouldn't come off. Finally, Cole just wadded up his bloodstained clothes and put his dress shirt and slacks back on to cover his defiled body.

Chapter Four

ADDICTION

As the Sun Fire hit the pavement, Cole agonized over a single question, Who's going to want to find the perpetrator of the desert crime? The cops and FBI, yeah. Mafia? Drug dealers? Arabs? Counterfeiters? Maybe. Maybe the money is counterfeit. Why Arabs? They don't deal in drugs—do they? Cole glanced at the cell phones lying on the front seat and realized they might hold some answers. At least if he was going to be looking over his shoulder, he should know whom to look for.

He reached over and picked up an I-Phone. It was locked with facial recognition and no chance of guessing a passcode. He tossed it back on the seat. The second phone was a Samsung. Face recognition hadn't been activated and it wasn't even password protected. The more he studied the phone, the more it bothered him. With today's high-tech tracing ability, he wasn't sure what was possible. Could somebody pinpoint his whereabouts by tracing a signal or was there some GPS link that identified his longitude and latitude? The cell phones had to go, but not until he had the phone numbers out of the Samsung. As he pressed on toward Ogden, he punched through and wrote down preprogrammed numbers. He also viewed the cell phone's own number.

As he concentrated on the phone, the road made a slight curve to the right and Cole found himself drifting into the left lane. With the cell phone still in one hand, he grasped the wheel with both hands to gently maneuver back into the right lane. In the process, his thumb touched the screen and the display on the phone now flashed. Cole wasn't sure what he'd done and put the phone to his ear. It delayed, clicked and then rang.

"Beech."

Startled by the voice on the other end, Cole said nothing.

"Beech!" came the second and louder demand for a reply.

Cole quickly judged his options: hang up or reply. Radio background music, wind whistling through the open window, maybe the guy wouldn't recognize the voice.

"Crossac here."

"Did you get the transfer?"

"Arabs dead. Money lost."

"What the hell are you talking about? If that money's lost, it's gonna come out of your pocket! You find that money and don't tell me different! I have obligations and that money has places to go. You find it, pay off the SDRMC guys and get me the rest. Do you understand?" shouted Beech.

"Right."

Beech didn't respond; the phone just went dead.

Cole's imagination raced wildly. "Delay, roaming, then ring," Cole replayed the phone call over and over again in his mind. It wasn't a local cell phone; the call transferred somewhere else. The phone only rang once; the guy sure wasn't sleeping in, and it's a Saturday to boot. Seven-fifteen here, eight-fifteen in Denver, nine-fifteen in New York. Probably back East somewhere. The acronym SDRMC was too close to home. And which guys? Beech, what kind of name is Beech? Was it John Beech or was it son-of-a-Beech? Silliness from lack of sleep was sneaking in, but the thoughts continued. Money coming out of your pocket—probably not his money, but he's still gotta pay somebody? Who? And he didn't care that the Arabs were dead; they were obviously not his drinking buddies.

This was a dangerous game, but Cole just couldn't let it rest. He knew he would have to come back for more, especially since he was feeling cocky about the phone call. First he needed to get rid of the soiled clothes and figure out what to do with the suitcase. The money was now becoming a secondary factor; it was the chase, the conquest and the curiosity that was the allure. And, as of yet, it wasn't doing harm to those who didn't deserve it. If it ever got to that, he would back out.

Cole wiped the phones clean of fingerprints and chucked them out the window. The first one went over the roof and into the ditch on the right. The second one he chucked as hard as he could off the road to the left. If they survived the impact and were traced, it could have been anyone discarding the phones since this was the only paved road returning to the freeway.

Once on the freeway, Cole realized he needed to make one more stop. Like the cell phones, what if the metallic case had some kind of tracking feature or bug? Cole pulled into the first rest stop. It was early enough that the rest stop was for the most part vacant. A couple of motor homes and cars were scattered throughout the parking lot, but the occupants were sound asleep. In the back of the car, Cole emptied the contents of the metallic case into his partially unrolled sleeping bag, inspecting each bundle as he went. The count was 240 bundles—2.4 million!

Cole deposited his bloodstained clothes in a trashcan beneath a stinky disposable diaper and other nauseating waste. He left the metallic case free of prints, sitting curbside, inviting itself to be stolen and transported to places unknown.

He pulled off the freeway shortly after eight, turned right onto Ogden's Jackson Avenue and drove toward his house. He passed his drug-dealing neighbor's house only to admire all the toys in the yard. A twenty-foot, Sea Rage ski boat was hooked to a brand new F-350 crew cab with a turbo diesel. It was parked on the grass extending fully across the front yard. In the side yard, there was a dual axle flatbed trailer with four wheelers and two motorcycles strapped down. Behind the four-wheeler trailer there was another flatbed with four mothballed snowmobiles. If the doper gets any more toys, he'll have to get a bigger yard, thought Cole as he looked down the street to his empty front yard. He was too tired to moan about such things. All he really wanted was sleep.

Turning off the ignition of the Sun Fire was a welcomed end to the adrenaline high that had raged within him for most the night. Cole hugged the partially rolled-up, bulky sleeping bag with both arms to keep its contents secure as he entered the house. With the door locked behind him, Cole went horizontal on the worn-out couch in the front room and was asleep in seconds.

KEVIN WAS UP BRIGHT AND EARLY TO RESUME THE game. He checked the previous night's cell phone activity. The answering machine spoke to him when he hit the play button: "You have three new messages. Message one at 8:22 P.M." Then the phone conversation began, "Hey Bud, this is Jimmy Callaway. I need some help with tax strategies. Are you going to be around this weekend?"

"Well, I hadn't planned on it. I was going to run over to Flaming Gorge and do some fishing this weekend with my neighbor..." The conversation continued with nothing but chit-chat. Just another bunch of nothing to go with yesterday's eavesdrop recordings. Then the second recording started: "Message two at 7:21 a.m."

"What's going on out there, Callaway? What are you doing with my money?"

"What are you talking about?"

"You know what I'm talking about!"

"Look, Beech, your money is on its way from Bank Islam with two of the best transporters we've got. It'll be in your hands when the hand-off is made, just like we agreed. Don't forget that when you get yours, we also get our twenty percent. There's nothing to worry about."

"That's what you think. You aren't going to get your twenty percent and your 'transporters' are dead."

"Bull."

"Hey, you aren't listening, Callaway! I just got a call from Crossac, and he says the Arabs are dead and that my—no, your—money is gone. Now, I figure the hand-off was never made which means the money had been entrusted to you and you owe me two million."

"Don't get excited, Beech. I'll check it out. I'll get back to you when I know something."

"You better make it fast. I've got payoffs to make en route and a big bill to pay for Shir Ali Kahn parts."

"I'll get back to you." Click.

"Message three at 7:32 A.M.," announced the answering machine.

"Melvin, this is Jimmy. I know you like to sleep late and I'm sorry to wake you, but I need you to check on something for me real fast. There is a potential disruption in the delivery from Iran. We may have lost 2.4

mil, some of which belongs to the man on Wall Street. I need you to check it out and get back to me as soon as possible."

"Consider it done." The caller hung up.

Kevin could hardly believe his ears. He had had his doubts about how dirty Callaway was, but there was no question now. This was even better than Kevin expected. Dead Arabs, two million in cash, and Callaway's take of a cool twenty percent. Kevin not only knew Callaway's profession but now he also knew how much Callaway made. Callaway's sideline was moving dirty money, which also meant that his speculation on money going to Colombia was exactly right. Callaway had probably been skimming that for twenty percent as well.

Callaway was like a blackjack dealer who had just flashed his down card. Now Kevin just had to figure out how to play. Double down or take a hit, but he wasn't about to fold. Now he had something real to go on instead of just speculation. In order to win this hand, he had to link Callaway to dead Arabs, 2.4 million in cash, and this guy named Beech. Who were the Arabs and this guy named Beech and where was the 2.4 million now? If it had been two Colombians, a simple scenario could have been formulated based on Callaway's confirmed Colombian connections and his real occupation. Beech could be a drug king using Callaway to launder his money and a hand-off went bad; maybe he was even ripped off by some rival drug gang.

"Wow!" spoke Kevin, feeling so much excitement that he couldn't contain himself.

But why was the money coming from Iran instead of going out? The Arabs just didn't fit, unless it was part of some complex laundering scheme. For now, that was it; at least until he could figure out who Beech was.

There were probably a hundred thousand Beeches in the United States. Kevin could modify his search engine to try and figure out who this Beech guy was. He could run the name against personal property tax records, state-by-state, to identify the most affluent and maybe cut the list in half. He could then cull out those who were registered voters and again maybe cut the list in half. Drug dealers don't usually register to vote, unless of course the state had a "motor-voter" registration program. Since an affluent drug dealer probably traveled outside the country for business, a check for U.S. passport holders might cut the list again by half, or maybe even a fourth. Some other runs might cut the list further, but Kevin knew he was probably still looking at a list of at least five thousand candidates.

There was another approach to tracking down Beech. Kevin could clue the media in and let them do the detective work. If they knew about two dead Arabs, two million dollars, and Beech, they could put lots more resources on it than Kevin could. Then all Kevin would have to do is wait for the news reports

     Brian David Simmons

to develop and eventually the authorities would catch up and go after Callaway.

If Kevin just told them, they probably wouldn't believe him. Media people are funny that way. They need to find out for themselves through their own detective work and develop the "exclusive story." Otherwise, it doesn't carry the same weight and probably ends up on page C-17 instead of the front page.

Kevin decided to file a report with the Salt Lake City police and hope they reacted. The report read:

> "Callaway suspected of ordering the death of two Arab couriers and theft of two million dollars from yet unidentified gangland operator. Identity of Arab couriers is unknown. Arab couriers killed at, or in vicinity of, Callaway's Park City residence and then transported to unknown location. Gangland operator from whom two million dollars, plus twenty percent commission, was stolen is probably named Beech. Recommend inquiry into Callaway's business dealings with individuals of Arabic decent and develop a list of probables for Beech. Please respond to www.slc.ciuu.com."

The server site was real enough. It was one that Salt Lake City was paying for every month but only Kevin had access to it. He had set it up as part of his disguised passport system and had used it in the past to receive messages when he wanted to ensure anonymity. It was password protected, and he was sure nobody knew it existed, other than the accounts-payable people who just paid for it along with thousands of other unquestioned bills. He was a little concerned, however, that he would now have to give it up. If anybody really investigated, they would try to find the owner of the website and it would get enough attention that it would become useless to Kevin.

Kevin modified his passport to emulate www.slc.ciuu.com, accessed one of several clandestine host servers, and sent the message. He hoped it would be received with confusion by some rookie who wouldn't have a clue what to do with it, other than to just electronically file it and then forward it to somebody for evaluation on Monday. Police reports are favorite sources of new stories for the media hounds and they monitored them on weekends as well as during the week. If some Channel Two or Salt Lake Journal media hound found the report, he would be asking questions before day's end.

Kevin had expected too much of the police. He checked back every couple of hours throughout the morning to see if anybody accessed the message, but no action. Maybe they didn't know how to access the file, or maybe the right people just aren't there on weekends. He'd let it ride, unanswered, until Monday evening. Then if it didn't get some action, he'd try another approach.

     Brian David Simmons

The other piece of data he had was the name "Shir Ali Kahn." Country, person, pet, or what? pondered Kevin. He initiated several Internet searches, all of which came up empty. Then, unexpectedly, he found two references to Shir Ali Kahn when he simply looked in the electronic encyclopedia. The first was the Amir of Afghanistan in 1825, obviously of no relevance to today's search. The second reference was in a discussion about the Middle East maritime shipping industry. The Shir Ali Kahn was a small cargo ship, less than 100,000 tons, of Turkish registry transporting goods primarily in the Mediterranean. It was a strange finding and Kevin didn't know whether to dismiss it or try and fit it in as a piece of the puzzle. It just added to the confusion and the intrigue. He needed to know more.

The phone rang and broke Cole from a deep sleep. Reconstructing the previous night's events in his head, he cautiously picked up the phone, paused, came to a full upright position and peeked out the front window. When he finally spoke, it was slow and deliberate, "Yes."

"Hey, Cole, I thought we were going to do something today," said a sexy, deep-south voice on the other end of the line.

It was Carol Meeks. Carol, a southern belle in every sense, had been relocated to Utah by her husband and then dumped when hard times hit. He had abandoned Carol and her daughter, Tamra, to pursue an easier life without the responsibilities of a family. Carol had to survive in a strange place with no one to help her through the tough times. But she was a remarkable woman and had made a place for her daughter and herself without complaint. She had charm, capability, and determination. Cole couldn't help admiring both her spirit and beauty. If he had been looking for marriage, she would have been his first choice. But he hadn't been mentally or financially prepared for what he thought marriage should be and therefore the relationship hadn't developed beyond deep friendship.

"We were, Carol, but I'm going to have to cancel. I've got some problems to take care of that can't wait."

"What kinda problems? Can I help?"

"I wish you could. But this is stuff I gotta do. What I want to do is get things taken care of today and then take care of you tonight. How about running down to Salt Lake for dinner at the Playhouse?"

"Okay. I'll get a sitter for Tamra. How'd your presentation go yesterday?"

"Oh, fine. But they didn't buy."

"That's too bad. Maybe next time. Maybe next time you'll be caught up on your laundry so you won't have to wear wrinkled shirts. That would make you look more professional, ya know. If you'd let me come over, we all could get you caught up."

"You know I appreciate the offer, Carol, but we've already had this discussion. You don't need to spend your Saturday washing my dirty underwear. I'm a big boy; I can take care of myself. Got to go. I'll call you later this afternoon. Okay?"

"Well, ya know, I'd take it out in trade. I still need the oil changed in my car."

"We'll see. Gotta go now, Carol."

"Alrighty. Luv ya. Bye now."

Cole knew he would change the oil in her car just as an excuse to spend time with her. She always made him feel good. The conversation with the wonderfully adorable woman made Cole forget the previous night's events. The conversation with her would have left him elated for hours except that the sight of dried blood on his arm and hand brought back vivid mental images of Mr. Muddy-Face and One-Eyed-Jack. It should have been a dream, but it wasn't; it was all too real and it wasn't over yet. The smell of the dried blood suddenly bothered Cole and he raced to strip off his white shirt and slacks and get relief in the shower.

It was a relief to stand under the cool, clean shower water. Cole watched red water run off his stomach, arms, and hands. Although he knew better, his imagination pondered whether the water would wash off the repugnance of the previous night and cleanse him of his actions. It was clear that there was no going back and Cole mentally debated the day's activities to distance himself from the killings. He had to ensure that he was beyond identification with, or even associated with, the murder of four men in the desert.

He had done all he could in the desert. He had obliterated all physical signs of his presence, relocated the apparent location of the shootings, and left confusing evidence to mislead any investigation. It would have to be enough; if it wasn't, it was too late now and not worth fretting over. The evidence that remained was the money, a handful of IDs and paperwork, and his scribbled notations of preprogrammed cell phone numbers.

The shower felt wonderful and his thoughts turned to the money. What am I going to with 2.4 million dollars? I could use a little of it; maybe buy something nice for Carol, replace the Sun Fire, or glide through my Ph.D. at MIT. Probably not. I could give the majority of it to a charity, but which one? If I did decide to spend it, the last thing I need is for somebody to notice a change in spending habits. Whatever I do, it has to be circumspect. Maybe I should keep a little and hide the rest for a rainy day. With shower water running off his head, he devised his plan.

After his shower, he donned work clothes somewhat reminiscent of a construction worker, including a baseball cap and work boots. Temporarily, and for lack of a better place, Cole put $399,000 along with the IDs and paperwork under his mattress. He put a thousand dollars in his wallet as mad money, just to see if he could really spend it. He packaged two million in his sleeping bag and left it by the front door.

Cole had to do something about the building mountain of laundry in the closet. He gathered up his dirty clothes and stuffed them into a duffel bag. But this time he wasn't going to take them to the coin-op. This was one thing he could now afford to have done for him. He put his dress shirt and slacks from yesterday in a separate bag of their own. They were destined for deep hole in the mountains. With sleeping bag and laundry loaded into the Sun Fire, he headed for the full service laundry and the lumberyard.

He dropped off his laundry and then at the lumber store he bought a small plastic storage box for a pickup side well, rubber gloves, shovel, big metal wash pan, other miscellaneous supplies and eight ready-mix concrete sacks. He paid at the cash register with a hundred-dollar bill. It worked; it was actual money and his fears about somebody not accepting it disappeared. Cole drove around to the lumberyard to pick up his bags of ready mix. When there was nobody around to show him where to go or help him load, he tracked down the bags of cement himself and did his own loading. Cement bags come with their own fine dust that finds its way out of every folded seam in the bag and by the time Cole got through loading, he was covered with cement dust and looked like a real contractor.

The load was all the Sun Fire could carry and the rear suspension buckled to its capability. With close to a thousand pounds of supplies in the back, the load rating on the rear tires was exceeded and they bulged as if under-inflated. Under ordinary circumstances, Cole wouldn't do this to the Sun Fire, but this was all very extraordinary and called for calculated risks.

As he was about to depart, Cole recognized an approaching man. Idle home improvement chitchat might bring up questions about the cement and Cole would have to develop a cover story. Then there would probably have to be some follow-up questions and phony discussion at work about the weekend project. Cole wanted to just avoid it altogether.

Cole was about to say something when the man spoke. The man looked right at Cole, handed him a sales receipt and said, "Can you load me up? I'm parked over there."

It was a Systems Safety guy that Cole had talked to numerous times and just yesterday Cole had been at the front of a conference room, in the limelight, and this jerk was in attendance. How could this fool not recognize him? Every time this guy had seen Cole in the past he was wearing a white shirt, tie, and jacket. Now, Cole in his contractor's garb was a complete stranger. Were people really so unobservant that simply being out of context made him a stranger?

Cole responded jokingly, assuming he would figure it out. "No sir. I'm going on my break now. You'll just have to get somebody else." To Cole's surprise, the man still didn't recognize him.

"Okay, but I don't see anybody else. Where are they?"

 Brian David Simmons

Cole couldn't help but provide a concocted and somewhat punishing response, "Don't you know we don't load during break? Didn't you read the sign? It's right up front on the fence. I can't believe you didn't see it. If you want me to load during my break, it'll cost you extra."

With that, the Systems Safety guy got red in the face and walked off mumbling something about how this "stupid place will never get another dime of mine."

"Amazing," returned Cole, as he watched the man march toward the main building, no doubt to register a complaint about the yard help.

Cole slammed the deck lid on the Sun Fire, climbed in, and left. He set off north where he would venture into another desolate region of Utah. Utah has extreme contrasts. To the west, it's nothing but desert. Some areas have soil so enriched with salt and beaten by the sun that the land is uninhabitable and useless for all practical purposes. To the east, it's mountainous terrain covered by feet of snow in winter and accessible in the summer only by four-wheel drive or horseback. Cole wasn't sure how far the overloaded Sun Fire would make it. The destination he had chosen would provide safekeeping for the money. It was isolated, hard to get to, and almost completely inaccessible for part of the year, all of which would minimize the chance of somebody stumbling across it. Of course, if he needed it in the winter, it would be extremely difficult to find.

Cole turned east toward the mountains and exited the highway onto a dirt road that led deep into the interior of the mountains. The Sun Fire's underbelly bumped and banged rocks in the road as Cole navigated to keep the tires out of deep ruts. Even in a four-wheel drive vehicle, the road would have been challenging. Some of the ruts had evolved into wash areas deep enough to fully capture even the tallest tires on a big four-wheel drive pickup. Cole had made the trip before in the Sun Fire, but never with a load like it carried today. He feared more than the ruts; every time the car's suspension bottomed out, he thought of the fragile rear axle and how easy it would be to break something. Or if he rolled over a sharp rock, he might lose a tire and the miniature spare was no match for the load or the difficult journey.

The Sun Fire took the beating and eventually made it to the chosen hiding place. A creek ran down the little ravine with the road carved into the steep mountainside above. Across the creek, it wasn't nearly as steep and that was where Cole was going to hide the money. Cole unloaded his supplies and carried his cargo across the creek to the chosen spot, including the eight ninety-pound bags of concrete, which was no easy feat considering the terrain: steep on one side, through the creek and then up the hill on the other side. Cole dug a hole just slightly deeper and larger than the small pickup cargo box. The cargo box, having been designed to fit in front of the wheel well without interfering with cargo

 Brian David Simmons

space, was just large enough to hold the two million. Using water from the creek below and the metal wash pan as a cement mixer, bag by bag Cole built a below-ground, sealed, concrete tomb for the cargo box and its contents. He put the finishing touches on the tomb by covering it with dirt and pine needles to obscure it from detection. When Cole finished, the location of the cache was indistinguishable from its surroundings and would certainly never be found except for the geometric references locked in Cole's mind. Cole envisioned the location defined by two intersecting vectors: one extending through points at a distant mountain peak and the saddle of a ravine and the other running through two large and irregular rocky outcroppings on the hillside above. The vectors defined the location like two lines intersecting in three-dimensional space.

Cole felt relieved as he cleaned up and loaded his supplies. The burden of having the money was gone and he had further distanced himself from the previous night's events. Cole turned the Sun Fire around and made the journey back down the trail. Before reaching the highway, he stopped, dug another small hole, and disposed of his dress shirt and slacks. The pounding and jarring of Sun Fire ceased when he pulled to a stop at the edge of the pavement. The Sun Fire had ventured deep into the mountains and gone places no ordinary car could travel. Cole was extremely pleased with its performance and haughty that hiding the money had gone so well.

Cole proceeded back onto the roadway and then on to Ogden where he picked up his laundry. He proved for the second time that the hundred dollar bills were real, at least real enough to spend. After another shower and a thorough cleaning of the Sun Fire, inside and out, Cole was ready for an evening with Carol. He was looking forward to her company and what followed. This southern woman knew how to please a man and sometimes he secretly thought of her as his "little southern snapper."

As evening approached, Cole's yearning for Carol's sweet company grew stronger. He also realized that it had been more than thirty-six hours since he last ate and he was hungry. Tonight he would satisfy primal needs for food and companionship. Cole showed up at Carol's apartment promptly at six o'clock. It was a two-story, deteriorating multi-unit complex built in the mid-fifties. The brick building was covered with unintelligible graffiti that only had meaning to those that understood the gang culture. The only thing Cole could make out from the cursive scrawling was the Roman numeral "XIII." Carol's apartment was on the second floor with an entrance overlooking the parking lot. When he arrived, she was leaning over the rail smiling down on him. She was a gorgeous dark-haired, blue-eyed woman wearing skin-tight black jeans and a black reverse zebra striped top. She had on a black vest trimmed with silver to add a touch of country girl class. With her boots, she was slightly taller than Cole, which further complimented her thin shape.

     Brian David Simmons

"How ya all doing?" were the first words she spoke. That southern drawl spoken with a sweet, sexy tune just made Cole fold.

"You all is doing just fine. But I am starving. How about you?"

"If y'all give me just minute, I'll say bye to Tamra and be right down. We'll take care of your starvin', darling."

Cole missed her presence even though she was gone only a few moments. When she stepped out of the apartment and headed for the stairs, Cole just admired her. She had a prim and proper walk with just a little swing; no doubt a lady's walk she learned growing up in the South. As far he was concerned, with her tall thin shape and simple-girl hairdo, she was the most desirable woman in the world.

Cole's reward for patience was a gentle kiss on the lips and a full hug. Like the gentleman she expected, Cole opened the car door for her and she seated herself. She squirmed in her seat seeking the most comfortable position as he closed the door. Cole couldn't help his wandering eyes from catching a downward glimpse at the perfect features of her special place.

Cole felt inebriated by the mere presence of the woman as they drove off. She began talking about Tamra and their day at the Dinosaur Park. She talked about the fossils, the garden hike, and the dinosaur playground. Cole loved to hear her talk. She spoke fifty words to his one and so the conversation was mutually enjoyable. She began to recount the story of a co-worker who had been beaten and robbed for just twenty-seven dollars in his wallet. As Carol spoke, Cole's imagination led his mind down paths of ugliness. He didn't want to think about it, but his night actions could lead a path to Carol's front door.

Cole turned down Jefferson Street and headed north past what was once one of Ogden's finer residential areas, but had now deteriorated into city slums and gangland territory. Jefferson ran along the fringe of the slum and connected middle class homes to the north with shopping areas to the south. It was well traveled by people that streamed past the mix of innocent homeless and nefarious shadow dwellers.

Cole, taking every opportunity to glance over at Carol as she talked, noticed the car in the lane beside. It got his attention when the brown, full-size car moved ahead and then fell behind again. It was very similar to the cars he had "set free" in the desert. The driver wore a suit, not too different from One-Eyed-Jack's or Mr. Muddy-Face's, and he kept looking over at them. Maybe he just couldn't help himself from staring at a beautiful woman or maybe it was something else. It didn't matter; he couldn't take any chances. Without notice, Cole slammed on the brakes and jerked the steering wheel left.

Carol screamed, "Cole! Watch out!" as they made an immediate left turn across traffic causing two oncoming cars to brake and divert around the Sun

Fire before it darted down a side street. Cole made a second left and then a U-turn to come to stop alongside the curb.

Carol wasn't the least bit impressed, "What are you doing? You almost ran into that car back there!"

Headlights killed and engine running, Cole didn't respond. He concentrated on the street ahead and his mirrors for any sign of a would-be follower.

"Cole, talk to me," demanded Carol and she slapped his shoulder with an open hand. "What's going on? Come on, Cole!"

Cole was occupied with the intensity of a potential conflict and didn't respond until he felt they were safe. There was only an occasional car on the side street, which made it easy for Cole to keep a watchful eye for full-size cars driven by men in suits. He had made more than one decision this morning; he didn't realize it at the time but now he knew it.

Carol demanded again, "Speak to me, Cole. What's the matter with you? Do you hear me, Cole?"

Finally, Cole spoke, "Carol, we all live our lives in our own ways and we only hope that the things we do don't bring harm to others. I can't let the things I've done bring harm to you or Tam. I need some time."

"What are you talking about? Do harm? Whatcha going to do? Bite me?" she asked.

"Seriously, Carol, just listen. I care too much to let anything happen to you. Just being with me puts you and Tam in jeopardy. That guy back there in the brown car, or any other stranger, could be somebody out to collect from me. They won't settle for just my wallet. They will want me dead and if they ever catch me, you need to be as far away as possible. We need to break off our relationship for a while."

"You listen here. I'm a big girl and I make my own decisions. There's nothing you could have done that could be so terrible. I can handle the consequences. What have you done? Tell me, Cole."

"How about Tamra? Make it easy, Carol. Let me take you home."

"And who's going to hurt Tam?"

"Men who perform cold-blooded, execution-style murder, that's who."

"No way."

"Yes. I know what I'm talking about. Right now things are just all screwed up and I don't want you involved."

"Who's after you? What did you do? You know, you could talk to the cops. They could help."

"I don't think so. Besides, it's nothing I will ever talk about to anyone! It's simple. We have to end it for your sake and for Tamra's sake. Please make this as easy as possible."

"Good God, Cole, I thought we had something." she pleaded tearfully. "Something that doesn't come along very often."

"We do, Carol."

Carol didn't know what to say. She felt the emptiness of loss but she also felt betrayed. Why couldn't he at

 Brian David Simmons

least confide in her? Hurt and disappointed, she folded her arms and pouted as Cole drove toward home.

It was a long, tense drive for both Cole and Carol. Neither had any words to ease the pain. For Cole, there was more to his decision than caring about Carol and her daughter's safety. He had alternatives to his decision that went unspoken. He could have recovered his cash and taken Carol and Tamra to some obscure place back east or maybe even left the country. But that would have left them always wondering, always looking over their shoulder. It wouldn't be fair to Carol.

There was another reason Cole had to end the relationship. He needed more. The excitement in the desert had triggered a desire that wasn't yet satisfied. He made more than a decision; he made a commitment to sacrifice companionship, love, family, and all those things that are normal to satisfy his need.

Finally, they arrived at Carol's apartment. Cole started to get out of the car to go around and open the car door, but Carol didn't wait and opened the door herself. Briskly, she said, "Bye, Cole," and closed the door.

It was over. Cole sat there struggling with his decision, emotionally suffering his loss and contemplating his future.

The drive home was miserable. Carol's sweet scent still lingered in car and the absence of her chitchat drove the emotional loss deeper. Cole's emotions hit rock bottom when he arrived at his empty little house.

Chapter Five

LIMITATIONS AND CAPABILITIES

AS THE DAY WORE ON, KEVIN BECAME MORE AND more impatient. No more phone calls. No bites on his phony police report. It just wasn't happening. He needed access to more information to continue his game. The Internet was just too limited and didn't provide him with avenues to the data he wanted.

If he could have tapped into the phone company for access to phone records, his eavesdropping could become unlimited. He would know who called whom and when. But that would require a considerable amount of effort to create the necessary software to sneak in. He would have to crawl inside an unknown system without detection, circumvent the main arteries of data flow, hide in upper memory, create a device, find the storage medium, gain access to it, convince it to talk to his device, compress the data and then smuggle it out.

All doable, but very time consuming. Given an assignment like this at work, it might take as long as a couple of weeks. Kevin decided to start this new project, but it wasn't going to help him with his current game.

For the short term, it would be simpler to upgrade his system to respond faster and pick up the number of the dialed call. That was easy to do. He just needed a system that would perform a rapid scan of a select list of cell phone numbers and tie his 286 in to record the digital transmission, but at this time of day Electric Shack was closed and it would have to wait until Monday. The thought of having to wait until Monday left him frustrated. If there was anything he could do between now and Monday, he would do it. But what?

The silence of his eavesdropping setup was exasperating. He couldn't believe Callaway wasn't making any calls today. Maybe the system dropped the access code. He could take the system offline and give it a thorough checkout but then he might miss a phone call. Maybe Callaway just hadn't charged his cell phone battery. In any event, Kevin couldn't risk taking the system offline. He would just have to sit it out, no matter how frustrated or impatient he got.

Hamilton Cole Davis had jilted the most incredible woman he had ever met. Even though he hadn't eaten in a day and a half, he felt sick to his stomach over his loss. He sat staring at the interior walls of his little house, which now seemed more devoid of life than ever before. The walls were barren and cold and quiet.

Cole had no desire to eat but recognized the necessity of bodily nourishment. His choice was cold cereal, "the breakfast of champions," even though he didn't feel much like a champion. Cole grabbed a banana from the counter to make the cereal more tolerable.

He broke the stem on the banana, began to peel back its protective covering, and his mind formulated an analogy. His situation was not so different from that of the banana. Its contents shielded and protected by a vulnerable, yet removable, covering. The shielded and protected banana survives intense heat, voracious insects, brutal bruising, and deprivation of nourishment. Once the banana has been peeled, its survival is short-lived. Once exposed, the banana discolors quickly, is readily damaged by mild impact and is a prime attraction for a variety of insects. What if he simply peeled back the protective covering from around Beech and his associates for police, media, and the world to see? Would their loss of two million be that important to them if they were struggling for their very survival?

Cole retrieved the phone numbers he had jotted down earlier in the day and selected a couple to try. He would try the last number dialed on Special Agent Crossac's cell phone first and then start down the list. He had a total of six numbers to try. Cole set off on foot down the street and around the corner to the convenience store. Pay phones were mostly a thing of the past, but he knew there was one available in this neighborhood at the convenience store. He hoped the pay phone was operational; in his neighborhood, one never knew.

The convenience store had been modified to defend itself against would-be smash and grab perpetra-

     Brian David Simmons

tors with multiple surveillance cameras, bulletproof cashier enclosure, and a robbery hot button. Customers were expected to scan their purchases past the electronic eye under the supervision of the cashier protected behind the bulletproof glass. The cashier had a small tray built into the counter top to allow for exchange of money beneath the bulletproof glass. The measures were extreme, but it was the only way the convenience store could survive this neighborhood.

Cole entered the store and, being sensitive to the surveillance cameras, avoided glancing up. He felt like a criminal. Maybe he was. Cole approached the bulletproof enclosure always keeping his head tilted forward to only give the camera a view of the top of his head. At least this way there could be no conclusive identification. Cole glanced at the "out of order" sign on the phone card machine and then spoke to cashier through the shielded vent slot, "I need quarters for the pay phone." Cole thought the less said the better, which was a contrast to his normally friendly and outreaching approach, even with strangers. It felt awkward to him. He was, in a sense, acting, and that was new experience for him.

"How many?" said the clerk.

"How many you got?"

"A couple of rolls."

"Give me both rolls."

Cole slid a twenty under the glass through the vent slot and the exchange was made. Nothing more was said. Cole kept his head down and exited the store. The phone was in working order and Cole broke open the first roll of quarters. He made even stacks with the quarters and readied pen and paper to take notes.

He deposited a stack of quarters into the phone and dialed the first number on his list. It wasn't a cell phone number; it was a 202 area code. Cole hadn't bothered to look it up, but it wasn't anything local. The phone rang and rang and was finally answered. Cole tipped the phone away from his face and committed to limit his end of the conversation.

"Debbie."

"Crossac."

"Who?"

"Crossac."

"This ain't Tim. Who is this?"

Cole quickly came up with a different tact, "Tim asked me to call. He's in trouble."

"Yeah, he always in trouble. You tell that boy if he want lovin' from Debbie, hurry his white ass on home. Who are you anyway? Tim never tell anybody bout me and him."

"Special Agent Simon."

"Ha, special my fanny. You just as mental as Tim. You come too. We do a party. I take care a both a ya. You going to bring me a special present? Timmy say he bring Debbie a special present when he come back from Utah."

"Tim probably ain't coming back. He took a little trip."

"That boy better not be going without me. He promised me. He said we be rich together. I love him and do anything for him, specially what he likes. Why can't he call?"

"Tim is gone and he's never coming back. I'm pretty sure of it. Maybe we should tell Beech?"

"You silly. That don't matter. If Tim gone, Beech already have army looking for the money. Why didn't Timmy take Debbie? Did he say?"

"I'm sure he wanted to, but sometimes things just don't work out. It was because of a couple of Arabs that Tim didn't have a chance to say. Do you know about the Arabs?"

"That's why Timmy gotta hide good. It Arab money, but it be Halladay, Callaway, or something like that, that be responsible for delivering the money to Timmy. Tim really afraid of him."

"Why's he so afraid?"

"Don't you know? If you be Tim's friend, you should know. Who are you, anyway?"

"Special Agent Simon. Look, Tim never told me much of anything, so I really don't know."

"You don't know about Halladay? Tim said everybody knew."

"Well, not me. I must be a little slow or something."

"You better not be slow, boy. Halladay got people that hunt you down. Then they cut you up and put ya pieces in garbage bags. Timmy told me all about it."

A lump formed in Cole's throat and he couldn't

swallow. He struggled to continue, "Did he tell you anything else?"

"The guy that does the cuttin' is from Atlanta."

"Is that it?"

"That ain't enough. If you Timmy's friend, you better hide 'cause they come looking for you, too. That's why Timmy is taking me with him." Debbie paused and then added, "Curse that boy!"

"Thanks, Debbie. Good luck," concluded Cole and he hung up.

The call was unsettling to Cole; it was as bad as he feared, but he was committed. He couldn't back out now. The second number on his list was the last number dialed on Crossac's phone. Cole dialed the number and it was answered immediately. Unknown to Cole and the man on the other end of the phone, the answered phone call began the wheels spinning on a rigged answering machine in a North Ogden condo.

"Callaway."

Cole tilted the phone away from his face to gather as much background noise as possible and obscure his response, "Crossac."

"Your boss is looking for you. You better call him ASAP."

"Money's gone. Arabs are dead."

"Yeah, so I heard. But it's not my problem anymore. There's a gentleman you need to meet. He's flying in tonight. Go to happy-hour tonight at the Salt Lake Grand."

"Who is he?"

"I wouldn't worry too much about that. I'll tell him you'll be there. He'll find you. You sound funny. Are you all right?"

"Fine. I'll be there. Why do I need to meet this guy?"

"He's going to recover the money and make an example of somebody. You know it's as important to send the right message as it is to recover the money. I'm sure you heard of how we made an example of things in Atlanta: castration, broken bones, wife, kids, you know."

"I'm not sure I want to meet this guy."

"You better or he'll come looking for you."

"What time?"

"Let's say eight."

"How will I know him?"

"Like I said, he'll find you. One other thing: don't call me on this phone anymore. I've been instructed to use the secure line. In fact, you don't ever need to talk to me again. From now on, Melvin will take care of it. Just be there at eight."

Cole hung up and the wheels on the North Ogden answering machine quit spinning. His actions in the desert were about to anger some horrible people, but would it have been different if he had just gone to the police? Probably not, concluded Cole; somebody would have still wanted retribution and they would have come after him just the same.

Cole had made two successful calls in row and

felt haughty that he had managed to fool and act his way through. It was surprising that they believed him just because he had called them. It was so simple. Cole deposited another handful of coins and dialed the third number. After half a dozen rings, the phone was answered.

The mechanical male voice said, "The cellular phone you have dialed does not answer. Please check the number you have dialed or try your call again at a later time."

Cole deposited another stack of coins and dialed the 405 area code number. The phone rang and rang and was eventually answered.

A recorded feminine voice said, "Space Sciences Corporation is here to serve your propulsion needs. We are sorry that we are unable to take your call at this time. If you will leave your name, phone number and a brief message, we will return your call as soon as possible."

Cole scribbled to take down the message as quickly as possible and then hung up before the beep on the other end. He wiped the phone free of fingerprints, gathered his remaining quarters and departed. Cole had a date with some guy named Melvin, and not much time to get there. On the short walk back to his house, Cole thought through what might happen that evening. Just surveillance: ID this guy, see where he goes, see if he talks to anybody—be the hunter and then come home, nothing more. Cole reached

     Brian David Simmons

the back of the Sun Fire and opened the deck lid. He uncovered the .22 and loaded it without removing it from the back of the car. That was just in case. Next, since this was a stealth operation, the dome light in the Sun Fire had to go. He opened the fuse box under the dash and removed the courtesy light fuse. Cole went inside, grabbed a denim jacket, locked up, returned to the Sun Fire, and then was on his way. He headed south on I-15 toward Salt Lake.

The trip gave him time to recount what he knew and what he didn't. It started with Beech. It was the Arabs' 2.4 million. It was supposed to be delivered to Beech. If the money was lost, Beech was on the hook for some or all of it. He had mentioned SDRMC guys. What would anybody at the plant be doing mixed up with people like these? None of it made sense. If it were gone, would Beech really have to replace it? Could he follow the next 2.4 million and find out who the recipients were to be? And what was it for? Drugs, maybe? But Arabs aren't known for their drug dealing. Crossac and Simon weren't real FBI agents; they worked for Beech and after his discussion with Debbie, it was clear they were double-crossing Beech and running with the money. The money was Arabic, but the Arabs worked for Callaway. Beech and Callaway both knew the Arabs were supposed to hand off the money; but neither seemed to care that they were dead. Then there was this other character, Melvin. How did he fit? Callaway was involved somehow, but not directly.

All he did was make the appointment for this evening and tell Crossac to call his boss.

Cole exited the freeway on Sixth North in Salt Lake. He realized only too late that he could have saved time if he had gone further south on the freeway before exiting. He made his way on the surface streets toward the Salt Lake Grand. It seemed like he got hung up at every streetlight but eventually arrived.

Cole parked among the other cars some distance from the entrance. The Sun Fire blended in but was outclassed by the abundance of sports and luxury cars. As he walked toward the entrance, a security guard in a golf cart passed in front of him and then continued on his way, criss-crossing the rows of high-dollar cars. A security camera was mounted above the well-lit front entrance and Cole ducked his head as he entered. Inside the door, a man greeted him and let Cole pass but only after establishing the purpose for his visit.

"Can I help you, sir?"

"You sure can. I'm looking for the bar."

"Just through the doors and around to the side of the courtyard. You can't miss it," said the doorman as he pointed the way.

Cole entered the courtyard and studied the setting like a keen hunter looking for a game trail with an ambush spot. The Grand was a large, multi-story, rectangular hotel. In the center, the hotel opened into an atrium, complete with a running creek and large Japanese goldfish. The atrium was enclosed with a

     Brian David Simmons

glass roof that allowed illumination by sunlight during the day and starlight at night. The hotel rooms all opened up to the center of the building, each level with its own walkway overlooking the courtyard below. Two glass-cased elevators serviced the walkways and provided riders with a panoramic view as they ascended or descended. Cole felt hunted. If Cole was the game, he was now in plain sight of any hunter and there was no avoiding it.

He kept his pace brisk and crossed the courtyard to the bar. Once inside, he quickly surveyed the layout of the bar and its patrons. He chose his spot and strolled over to the bar counter next to the main pickup, sat down, and halfway turned to watch the entrance and patrons in the bar. He glanced up at the ornate clock above the liquor display; it was only 7:30; he was a half an hour early. Just right, thought Cole. Now he was the hunter with the best vantage point in the bar. The bar maid returned from one of the tables with a tray of empty glasses and gave Cole a hinting little smile and half wink. She was attractive and about Cole's age wearing a skimpy, low-cut shoulderless dress that left little for the imagination.

"Can I get you something?"

"A beer would do for starters."

She raised her voice at the bartender and said, "Get this man a drink. Can't you see he's thirsty?" Then she turned her attention back to Cole.

"I haven't seen you in here before. Are you traveling or something?"

"No, I'm just kind of lonely tonight and I thought I'd check this place out."

"Well, there's not much action around here, but you're welcome to stay, and I'll keep your glass full."

"I knew I came the right place. What's your name?"

"Hilda. What's yours?"

"Ah...Cody."

"Kind of a cowboy name, huh. I like it."

So started the conversation that continued between bar orders as Cole waited for eight o'clock. Cole was good company for her since most of the bar clientele were affluent traveler types, more interested at looking at her cleavage than what she had to say. She didn't realize it but she was doing Cole a big favor. Outward appearances of the two could have suggested boyfriend and girlfriend. Further speculation could have been that he was just waiting for her shift to end and then the two would run off together. As she leaned on the counter and talked, Cole peered past her to study the occupants of the bar.

There was a couple in the corner. They looked like business acquaintances; he well dressed in a suit and she in a very conservative dress. It could have been a business meeting except that they were playing a little game of "accidental" touch. Her legs were crossed and her foot was gently swinging beneath the table. She "accidentally" rubbed against his leg and then he responded by positioning his leg closer to her foot so he could feel her every movement. It didn't take long before the two had shifted positions in their chairs to allow their legs to fully embrace. They thought their innocent embracing went unnoticed, but Cole saw it as if it were lime-lighted.

In front of the TV, there were two men, probably mid-forties, in leisure attire. They became more vocal as time passed, obviously having had too much to drink. Their attention occasionally diverted from TV and conversation to ogle Hilda when she delivered a drink. No doubt they would give her a big tip. There was an elderly foursome: two men and two women at a table in the middle of the bar. They were probably old friends out for an evening together. The only likely candidate for Melvin was the guy sitting at the table by himself near the entrance. He was a candidate, but he didn't look like the bad guy Cole had envisioned. This guy was probably in his early twenties, reasonable in size with light hair and pale white skin. He fit into the bar setting all too well with preppy white shorts and an argyle sweater. He was probably the spoiled kid of some well-to-do venture capitalist or something.

It was pretty clear to Cole that Melvin hadn't arrived yet. Cole continued his conversations with Hilda and kept a watchful eye on the occupants of the bar. The romance in the corner had progressed from leg rubbing to hand holding under the table: his hand on her knee and her hand on top of his. The business types watching TV just kept ordering. The preppy kid slowly sipped a strawberry margarita and watched

Hilda as she made an occasional round of the bar to be sure everyone had a full glass.

The love affair in the corner finally developed to the point where a hotel room was needed. Cole watched them as they got up and headed for the exit. As they passed the exit, Melvin entered. At least, Cole was pretty sure it was him. He was a tall man, about fifty, wearing a gray suit. Cole was more than sure it was Melvin when he passed by and momentarily glared into his eyes. The man was frighteningly cold. He took the corner table once occupied by the lovers and slid the chair around so he had a full view of the bar. The only better vantage point in the bar was that of Cole's. Hilda left Cole's side with her tray in hand and collected the two glasses and the tip on Melvin's table. He ordered a screwdriver and shooed her away to clear his view of the bar. Hilda returned to the counter and relayed the order to the barkeep. She commented to Cole that "it takes all types." Cole didn't look over at the man. He didn't want to give himself away and this guy was no amateur. Cole needed all his hunting skills to avoid becoming the hunted. Hilda delivered his drink and quickly returned.

Out of the corner of Cole's eye, he caught a glimpse of something that surprised him. The preppy kid took a picture of the guy in the corner. No flash, he just slid a cell phone out from under his sweater, pointed it at Melvin, touched the screen and then tried to conceal the phone back underneath his sweater. Cole wasn't

     Brian David Simmons

the only one doing surveillance! He tried to continue the conversation with Hilda, but had difficulty maintaining his concentration when it happened again. What was he doing? He wasn't doing a very good job of it, either. The kid tried to conceal his actions, but if Cole had seen it, then so had Melvin. The kid was in trouble. This Melvin character was not somebody to take pictures of. Cole knew Melvin was going to retrieve the phone and have a private discussion with that fool kid.

Cole speculated on Melvin's reaction to being photographed: assume the preppy kid was going to follow him, move off but not too far, verify the kid was following and then lead him to some private place. That's what Cole would do if he were in Melvin's shoes.

Cole chose his course of action, but first he needed to take care of Hilda. He reached into his pocket, pulled out a hundred dollar bill and held it concealed in his hand.

"Hilda, do they make you report tips here?"

"Yeah, all of them and then I split them with whoever is working the bar."

"Don't look at this and don't include this in your tips tonight," said Cole as he slipped his hand in hers and left the bill. He was pretty sure Melvin didn't see him and certainly nobody else in the bar did. If anybody came looking for him, he didn't want Hilda implicated. Cole got up from his seat without saying goodbye to Hilda and affecting a slightly inebriated gait, made his way to the exit. He could feel Melvin's eyes glaring at him, studying him, and hopefully drawing the wrong conclusions about him.

Cole exited the bar and continued his gait along the edge of the courtyard to the elevator. He pressed two, promptly arrived at the second floor, and then proceeded around the walkway to a vending area in the corner of the building. He found his vantage point in the shadows of the corner. Now, remaining motionless, Cole could observe anybody exiting the bar and he could do it without fear of detection. He was the hunter.

Cole didn't have to wait long. Melvin exited the bar with a meandering stroll. He pretended to study the vegetation, trickling stream and giant gold fish, as if he was a tourist. The preppy kid followed shortly but didn't see Melvin on the other side of the courtyard. Looking lost, the kid hurried down the path that cut directly across the courtyard and then, when he finally saw Melvin, stopped.

He tried to look inconspicuous but it was now more obvious than ever that this kid was nothing more than a fool. Maybe Cole was as well. After all, the only real difference between Cole and this kid was hunting skill. Melvin resumed his pace now that he had his tail and strolled toward the entrance.

Cole skirted along the wall, staying out of sight of the men below, to the stairway. He hit the push bar on the heavy steel door and flew down the stairs. He needed to get in front of them to again gain another vantage point. He exited the hotel side door and studied the parking lot. The Sun Fire was as good a place to observe from as any, especially since he didn't know which cars he needed to watch. As Cole briskly walked toward the Sun Fire, he looked for the security guard, but the man wasn't in sight. Cole slipped into his car and slid down in the seat to peer unnoticeably through the back window. It was several minutes before anybody exited the hotel. A valet made a beeline for the cars nearest the entrance. He brought around a full-size white Buick and parked the car, with the engine running and driver's door open, directly in front of the entrance. Melvin met the valet near the rear of the car and handed him a tip as he passed. Melvin got in the car, pulled up to the street, and waited.

The preppy kid came out of the entrance as soon as Melvin pulled away. He looked over to see that Melvin hadn't departed the parking lot yet and then, in a dead run, made his way down the lane toward Cole. He stopped short of Cole and got into a red Porsche. Melvin was still waiting, probably just watching the kid through his rear view mirror. As the kid backed out, Cole started the Sun Fire. The kid engaged the turbo to zoom past the hotel entrance and catch Melvin just as he pulled out into traffic. Cole didn't move until both cars had left the parking lot. After all, it would be pretty difficult to lose a big white Buick with a bright red zooming tail.

Cole caught sight of the pair in a few moments. The kid was following the Buick two cars back and Cole was following them about half a dozen cars back. They turned on Third West and traveled south for several miles. At one point, through cars making lane changes, the kid ended up directly behind Melvin at a stoplight. The kid dropped back as soon as he could after the light changed, but it probably scared the life out of him for a few moments. Cole thought about moving up through traffic past the two cars and then falling back again. It would give him the opportunity to get license plate numbers and he was sure he could do it without detection. There would probably be time for that later and it was quite comfortable and amusing to just sit back and watch. They passed the downtown area and proceeded into the commercial area.

The Buick slowed, signaled, and made a right turn into the parking lot of an industrial business. He drove up to the front of the parking lot and stopped in front of the office. The Porsche did it right, probably the only thing the kid did right that night; it passed the parking lot and pulled to the curb out of sight from the Buick. Cole passed them both and made a right turn at the next street. He stopped the car just past the entrance to an alley and then quickly proceeded on foot down the alley.

It was unlit, and it took Cole a few minutes for his eyes to adjust to the dark. As he quietly moved closer to the back of the industrial building, his adrenaline

   Brian David Simmons

began to intensify his senses. His eyes cut through the darkness to search for movement ahead and his ears filtered out the city background noise to capture the sounds of the alley. A cricket halted its chirping as Cole sneaked silently past a dumpster. When he reached the back of the building, he slowed his advance further and crept carefully, placing each foot delicately on the ground with slow, even movements. In his blue jeans and denim jacket, with his soundless pace, he was imperceptible in the dark alley. He stopped in a doorway near the corner of the building to concentrate his senses on any signs of movement. A slight change in the dim light emanating from the street out front or subtle thumping of footsteps would warn him not to approach the corner. He strained intensely to visualize around the corner and then, just as he was ready to step out of the doorway, he caught a hint of a familiar smell.

Cole froze in the doorway analyzing what his senses were telling him. It wasn't the smell of a cigarette but rather the smell a recently smoked cigarette on one's clothes. Without the slightest movement, Cole's eyes searched the alley way ahead—nothing. He strained to pierce through the darkness and aid his eyes with imagination to fill in what they couldn't see. Then it came together; Cole saw someone. He was almost directly across the alley from Cole, standing against the fence. Cole was too close! He chastised himself for being stupid. He should have seen that guy before but the figure was motionless with his shape obscured by the discoloration and irregularity of the deteriorating fence. Cole wasn't sure what was next. Did the figure know Cole was there? Could he back off as quietly as he had arrived? If he stayed, how long would it be before he was detected?

He didn't need to decide. His attention was attracted to footsteps coming from around the corner. As they came closer, the figure across the alley shifted his weight from one foot to the other in anticipation of the approaching visitor. Cole knew that his presence had gone undetected. The figure pulled something from his pocket and then again resumed a motionless stance in anticipation of the approaching visitor.

The argyle sweater glowed like a neon light when the kid rounded the corner. He stepped out into the middle of the alley and looked first one way and then the other. As the kid looked in the opposite direction, the figure across the alley quietly stepped toward the kid. Cole instinctively followed. The object in the man's hand was a knife and Cole was now close enough to hear its blade click into lock position. Cole reached into his pocket and retrieved the unbroken roll of quarters. The figure was now clearly Melvin. Cole reached out and touched him on the shoulder just as he reached for the kid. The kid turned around just in time to see Cole deliver a solid right hook to Melvin's jaw. Melvin went down and hit hard. The knife bounced off the pavement and scooted down

 Brian David Simmons

the alley to come to rest in the light emanating from around the corner.

The kid started to run away but stopped when he stepped over the knife. He looked back at Cole standing over Melvin and then in a submissive voice asked, "Who are you?"

"Your salvation. Who the hell do you think I am? You were about to become the subject of great pain and fifty questions."

Standing at a distance from Cole and postured to charge away, the kid blasted back, "Oh, how do you know? Who are you? FBI, ATF, who?"

"I'm just anybody. Let's say you just call me Cody. Now what's your name?"

"Uh, Casper Johnson."

"Okay, now your real name. If you don't give it to me, I'll just have to track you down from your license plate number and then come to your house for tea and chitchat. What's your name!" demanded Cole.

"Kevin McKuel."

"Okay, come on over here. Let's do a little a research on this guy."

Cole knelt down next to Melvin and began emptying the contents of his pockets. Kevin cautiously approached. Cole started with the front pants pockets, removing keys, pocket change, and a money clip. With an outstretched arm offering the keys and change, he beckoned Kevin to take the final few steps and become a party to the search. Kevin watched as Cole removed a wallet and cell phone from the man's suit jacket pockets. Cole put the wallet in his jean jacket pocket without showing it to Kevin. He knew what was inside. Cole inspected the cell phone in the near non-existent light and then handed it Kevin. He pulled a .45 automatic out of the man's shoulder holster and a silencer out of the inside pocket in the jacket. He screwed the silencer onto the .45 as he stood to face Kevin. The two men stood in the dark alley studying each other and wondering what the future was going to bring.

"Can I have this?" said Kevin in reference to the cell phone.

"No! You sure got yourself into a mess. This guy is going to wake up and come looking for you."

"Why me?"

"You still haven't figured it out, have you? This guy knows your fancy car, knows your license number, can get your picture from the hotel, and by noon tomorrow he'll be knocking at your front door. You're screwed. What did you think you were doing?"

"I just wanted to see who he was and who he met."

"You just wanted! What kind of a stupid answer is that?"

Kevin got indignant and pointed at Cole, "Hey, I've had enough of your high-and-mightiness. I'm not going to take anymore of that from you."

"What are you going to do? Bonk me with your cell phone?"

"You, you—!" Kevin raised his fist.

Cole almost laughed at his stance and then tried to calm him down, "All right, all right, settle down. What are you going to do?"

"What do you think I should do?"

"Disappear."

"Hey."

"Settle down. I mean you need to erase the last hour of your life. You need to get off the surveillance tapes at the hotel and make sure this guy never remembers this evening. Melvin isn't the only one who expected a meeting tonight and anyone wanting to see if it occurred has a perfect record of everybody in and out of the hotel."

"How did you know I was at the Grand and how did you know there was supposed to be a meeting?"

"For now, let's just say I knew."

"No, you were there. You were flirting with the top-heavy waitress."

"Let's just say I knew."

"You're on the surveillance feed, too."

"Maybe, but I'm not identifiable."

"So the surveillance feed has to disappear, huh?"

"That's only one of your problems. Melvin here is a bigger problem. How do you get him to forget that you ever existed? Do you want to use this?" said Cole as he pushed the .45 automatic at Kevin.

"You're nuts. Kill him? No way."

"If you don't, he's liable to find you someday and then put one of those little bullets in the back of your head."

"In cold blood?"

"Yep."

"I just wanted to see Crossac and anybody else that showed up."

"What do you know about Crossac?"

"He was who Melvin was going to meet."

"How do you know that?"

"Uh, well," stuttered Kevin. "I've been watching."

Cole read the lie but didn't let on. He kind of liked the man. Like Cole himself, he was an amateur playing outside his league. Though Cole didn't feel like an amateur. His Patriot Rebirth Society training and childhood experiences reignited by the desert encounter had stirred something inside him that made this feel all too natural. Cole knew these were bad men and this kid would surely be dead tomorrow, if he didn't help.

"I want you to do exactly as I say. First, very quickly and very discreetly, take this stuff and go to Melvin's car. Use the keys to open it up and go through the glove box, under the seat, over the visor, everywhere and collect everything you find. Don't touch anything, and I mean anything, with the full print of any of your fingers. Don't forget the trunk. Leave the keys on the roof and take everything you find with you. Get in your car and drive home. Get anything from your home that you might need for a week. Load it in your car and drive to Ogden. Take the Twenty-First Street exit and go to the bar called Raedeux on Twenty-Fifth and Wall. Park your car out on Twenty-Fifth at least a half a block from Raedeux. Wait in the bar."

"I've seen that bar. It's a biker bar."

"Yeah, you'll be safe there. They're a friendly bunch once you get to know them. But take off that ugly sweater."

"What are you going to do?"

"Leave me the gun."

"Are you going to kill him?"

"Don't ask. I'll meet you at Raedeux sometime after closing. Just stay there."

Kevin did exactly as Cole had instructed. He cleaned out Melvin's car, including the trunk, and was soon en route to Ogden. In the dark alley, Cole undressed Melvin, leaving him lying on the cold asphalt in his underwear. Cole dragged him over to the fence and used Melvin's belt to cinch up his hands behind his back. He left him hanging from the fence in an unpleasant, head-down position. Cole undressed and put on the suit, complete with holstered .45 and tie. The pants were too long, but with his boots they fit well enough. He didn't need the belt; he could hardly get the pants buttoned. Cole carefully folded his clothes across the top of the fence and then carefully approached the corner of the building. Traffic out on the main street was starting to diminish. He proceeded around the corner and then to Melvin's car.

The keys were on the roof, just as he had instructed Kevin. Cole had a plan that might work but only time would tell. He got into Melvin's car, started it and exited the parking lot. Melvin had selected the alley for a reason. He must have known it was a good place to have a private conversation. Cole returned to the alley and pulled in past the Sun Fire, stopping momentarily to retrieve a six-pack of beer. In his headlights, he could see his still unconscious victim hanging from the fence. He pulled Melvin's car alongside, stopped the car and turned off the engine. It was time to see what Melvin had to offer.

Cole untied Melvin from the fence and then cinched his hands even tighter. Cole pulled Melvin over to the back door of the car, opened it and then positioned Melvin's right hand in the door jam. Cole slammed the door shut. The unconscious man's body reacted to the pain with a straightening of the legs that pushed him forward but didn't rouse him. Blood was already seeping through constrained vessels to swell the fingers and soothe the broken metacarpals. Melvin wasn't going anywhere.

Cole reached inside and hit the lock button on the door. He popped the top on a can of beer and then squatted down next to the fence to take a swig. Cole studied the man; he wondered just how hard he had hit him. He took another swig and then dumped the rest of the beer on Melvin's head. Then he opened another and poured it over the man's head and down the middle of the man's bare back. He got a little reaction and then slowly a shaking of the head and a few unintelligible mumbled sounds.

"You look kind of uncomfortable."

"Oh God," cried Melvin as the signal of pain from his hand reached his brain.

"Nope, just me. Come on now, wake up."

Melvin brought his knee up under him and then screamed with pain when he tried to jerk from the car.

"Now, be civil about this."

"Civil? You're a dead man," said Melvin as he struggled to find a position that reduced the pain.

"We'll see. I think it's you that should worry." In a monotone voice, Cole explained his purpose, "I don't want much from you. I just want a few little facts. If I get what I want, everything will be fine. If I don't, I'll drive this car back and forth in the alley until you beg to tell me. So everything will work out much better if we just talk freely. What do you say?"

"Who are you?" cried Melvin.

"Well, I'm not here for your salvation. That you can be sure of. And, depending on your level of cooperation, I may be your executioner."

"You're insane. You're dead."

"Let's worry about you instead of me. What's your name?"

Without thinking, Melvin said, "William," and Cole swiftly knocked him off his knee sending a shriek of pain to Melvin's brain as punishment for lying.

"Not true, try again."

"Okay, okay. Melvin Roberson."

"Good. Now who were we going to meet tonight? And don't lie."

"Nobody."

Again, Cole kicked Melvin's knee out from under him and his brain registered the shriek of pain as the consequence of lying. "We'll just keep trying until you get it right. Now who were you going to meet?"

"Tim Crossac."

"Good. It's much easier when you tell the truth. Now, how much money are we talking about?"

"What money?"

Cole swiftly kicked Melvin off balance and he screamed in pain. Cole screamed at him, "I'm losing patience with you. Just answer the fucking question!"

Melvin caught his breath and replied, "Okay, don't do that again, please. You're right. We lost some money."

"How much?"

Melvin hesitated but when Cole started to move, responded, "We lost a transfer worth just over two million."

"Two-point-four is more accurate. Who's we?"

"Do you know who you're messing with? You can drag me up and down this alley a hundred times and then kill me. But it ain't going to help you. They run everything and they'll find you. You're dead."

"I'll ask again. Who's they?"

"Callaway."

"That's real good for starters. Now who else?"

 Brian David Simmons

"Sugar Ike. I work for Sugar Ike."

"Where's this little ant in your company?"

"I don't know, I uh, think he works for Laughlin. You know, the Wall Street Laughlin."

"Did you enjoy the service you provided last April in Atlanta?"

"It's a job. How do you know about that?"

"It's my business to know and I ask the questions," said Cole as he kicked Melvin's knee out from underneath him for the third time. "Just a reminder. Nothing but the truth. How much did you recover?"

Melvin, unsure what his tormentor knew, began to respond without hesitation and Cole got more than he expected with each successive question. "Cater skimmed twenty million, but I only recovered half. It was all he had. I'm sure of it. If he had had more, he would have talked when I made his kids scream."

The questioning continued. Cole got more than he wanted about the Cater incident. Melvin also revealed the primary business of his company: money laundering. But something still didn't fit and Cole continued his questioning to get a picture of the organization. Cole also began to pick up some of the jargon and used it in his questioning.

"How much cleaning is Sugar Ike doing?"

"I don't know, but we make a profit of at least forty million a year."

"And what about the 2.4 million you lost? Do the Arabs know you lost their money?"

"Our boys lost it. You better believe they know it."

"Tell me about it."

"Sometimes our clients take payments through Bank Islam. We just pick it up and deliver it. It's not laundered. It's not our money. I don't know what it's for. It's just a customer service and we get paid just the same."

"You mean the money isn't Arabic?"

"Could be. I don't know."

Cole had slipped in his questioning and sensed that Melvin had caught it. But there was no way to be sure. Melvin could still be holding back and Cole floundered in further questioning, "What do you mean you don't know?"

"Exactly that. I don't know. We just pick it up and deliver it."

Cole anted another piece of data to try and regain the position knowledge superiority, "With Beech as the recipient, who's the client?"

"Just Beech. We're just moving money for Beech."

Again, Cole suspected Melvin was stonewalling. Melvin had now learned the limits of Cole's knowledge and Cole felt that he had extracted everything he was going to get going down this line of questioning. He shifted his tact to probe an off-handed comment from earlier and explore a plausible excuse for Kevin's actions, "Tell me about customer service."

"You know. We're better than the bank. We can't lose money. Customer service and all that."

"It's good you brought it up," stated Cole as he planted the seed of a deception he was formulating. "Customer service is why I'm here. Now, what do you know about the kid in the Porsche?"

"Newspaper reporter or something. I don't know."

"Come on, let's have it."

"I swear, I don't know."

"Tell me what you do know."

"He was taking pictures of me in the bar at the Grand. He followed me here. That's all."

"Did you get the license number or anything?"

"Yeah, I wrote it down, it's on the pad in the glove box."

"Is that it?"

"I'll get the shrimp tomorrow."

"No, you won't!" stated Cole and then continued with his deception. "Do you know who your customers are? How do you think Sugar Ike would feel if you messed with one of his customer's kids?"

"How was I supposed to know?"

"You know now. You also know I'm looking out for the kid and I won't tolerate anybody—I mean anybody—pulling a knife or anything else on him. Do you understand?"

"I got it."

"Couple other things you should consider about tonight's events. I know who you are, who you work for, and where you live. You, on the other hand, know only that I'm wearing your clothes. I can track you down anytime and finish this conversation and you'll never see me coming. Now, this is how it's going to be. You're going to forget ever seeing the kid. You can report being mugged tonight, and tomorrow, when you call Sugar Ike, tell him you're still looking for the 2.4 million. Don't ever look for the kid. Don't ever talk about the kid. Forget this little conversation. Let your hand be a reminder of what happens if you don't obey."

"Yeah, got it."

Cole's voice lowered to a whisper, "You better. Let me paint a picture for you. You're in bed, sound asleep, in some obscure hiding place. You're safe from all harm. You're in hiding in a place where nobody can find you. You're all relaxed, comfortable and warm. Then from out of the darkness, I wrap my hand around your throat and squeeze. You grab my arm with both hands and push with all your might, only to feel my cold blade penetrate skin just above your crotch and then slowly slice all the way up to your sternum. I relax my hand around your throat to get clear of your intestines oozing their way out of your stomach cavity. You reach down in the dark and feel the warm, wet expulsion from your body. You get a whiff of the stench. You hug your bodily organs and try to pull them back into place, but they continue to ooze from around your arms, and then you die. And if you doubt my resolve, Google Kootenai County Sheriff for details. Clear enough?"

"Don't worry. I've been doing this a long time. I know better. You can count on me."

     Brian David Simmons

"Now, you've been really cooperative about this incident. You just hang around here for a while and the police will come to help you." With force Cole added, "Remember, you were mugged!"

Cole thought about killing Melvin, but the thought that he might visit him again for more information gave Melvin's life purpose. Cole left Melvin, naked and struggling to keep the weight off his hand, hanging from the door of the car. By now his swollen hand had taken the shape of the door jam and would take weeks to heal. That was enough for now. Cole checked the glove box of the car to see if Kevin had done a thorough job cleaning it out. The note pad mentioned by Melvin wasn't there. Kevin had at least done that much of what Cole had instructed him to do. Cole collected his clothes from the fence and used his shirt to give the inside of the car a quick wipe down. He paid particular attention to the steering wheel and glove box. He made a quick trip around the car, wiping door handles and the trunk lid. Melvin tried to see Cole's face as he wiped the door handles above him but Cole didn't give him the opportunity. Without saying a word, Cole picked up his beer and empty cans and then walked back down the alley and around the corner to the Sun Fire. He had one more illusion to pull off.

It wasn't his problem but he was about to risk revealing his identity, maybe even his life, to erase Kevin's blundering. He didn't even know if his plan would work. It would be much easier if he had had time to set it up and think it through, but it was now or never. He had been successful so far. He had fooled Beech, Callaway and Debbie on the telephone and he had impressed Melvin with the importance of customer service. With a little luck, he thought he could do it again.

Cole drove back to the Grand Hotel. Only this time, he drove past the parking lot. Surveillance cameras now seemed to be everywhere and videotape of the Sun Fire could provide a link to his identity. He would be especially careful this time. Cole parked the Sun Fire within a half a block of the hotel and walked toward the entrance. He took Melvin's folding leather wallet out of his pocket and removed the identification from the slip pocket. He slid his own driver's license into the slot, closed it and put it back into the breast pocket of Melvin's suit jacket. As he walked, he played the deception through in his mind and anticipated the variations he might encounter.

The hotel entrance was quiet. He could see a security guard inside dozing on a guest couch just inside the front door. Cole looked down as he entered the surveillance camera's field of vision and stepped inside. He walked silently over to stand directly in front of the security guard. The sleeping guard let out a little snort when Cole nudged the man's shin with the toe of his boot. The guard awoke to see a well-dressed young man towering over him. He rose, struggling to recover from his

    Brian David Simmons

nap, and started to greet Cole. Cole didn't give him a chance. He pulled the wallet from his breast pocket, being sure to give the guard a glimpse of the holstered .45. He flashed the ID and badge to the guard. The guard's eyes were drawn to the words Federal Bureau of Investigation, and Cole flipped the wallet closed.

"Agent Jackson. I'm looking for my partner. Have you seen him?" said Cole as he handed the guard Melvin's ID.

The guard studied Cole and shook his head.

"Are you sure? I was supposed to meet him here at eight."

"I'm pretty sure I haven't seen him."

"How long have you been here?"

"For the last hour or so."

"And how long have you been sleeping? I could report you to hotel management, you know. I need to know if my partner has been here," asserted Cole.

"I'm sorry. I can't help you."

"There must be some way for me to find out."

"I'm sorry," said the security guard as he timidly shook his head.

"This is not good," scowled Cole and then continued. "How about your surveillance cameras?"

"The surveillance room is upstairs. But it's locked and nobody goes in there."

"You have a key. Don't you?"

"Yes, but nobody goes in there."

"Well, it wouldn't be necessary if somebody hadn't been sleeping. And we won't bother anything. We'll just look."

Under duress, the security guard conceded with the condition that Cole didn't touch anything. The guard led the way as the two proceeded to the second floor via the elevator. In the elevator, the security guard looked uncomfortable with his decision, but Cole reassured him that this was all right. Cole also explained that his partner was to complete a precarious surveillance mission tonight. If he hadn't returned to the hotel, his life was in danger. The knowledge of whether his partner had been at the hotel around eight was critical and the guard could help. The security guard gained some sense of being a part of the machination and became a voluntary participant.

The surveillance room was just above the front lobby. The door had an eye-level brass plate that read: NO ADMITTANCE. Inside, there were six monitors, a computer keyboard, a tower computer, and a disc drive tower of a type that was unfamiliar to Cole.

"Where are the tapes?"

"Oh, we're computerized now. We don't have any tapes. Everything goes into the computer and onto those fancy computer drives. See that one with the light on? Every camera in the hotel is being recorded on that drive. Then when it's full, the computer will automatically start recording on the next one. It just keeps going. Cycling through, I think, every four days."

"How do I find eight to nine tonight?"

"Uh, I was hoping you would know."

"What if I change out the drive with the light on with one from the shelf."

"Shoot, I don't know."

"Let's try it. Shall we?" Cole pulled on the drive with the LED. The whole unit slid out. It was about the size of a paperback book. One of the monitors beeped and displayed an interrupt notice and then the LED came on the drive unit just below the one Cole had removed. With confidence, as if he knew what he was doing, Cole replaced the unit with one off the shelf. Then, just in case, he also removed and replaced the one directly above it in the tower.

"I'm going to take these over to the Federal Building. They can read them over there for me," said Cole with dominance. Cole read the concerned look on the security guard's face and provided further reassurances. "Just don't tell anybody I was ever here. They'll never know. The system is still running and in a couple of days it'll cycle back through. The only thing they'll know is that the drives off the shelf are missing, or just unaccounted for. It'll be fine. I really appreciate your assistance. I wish I could tell you more. Then I'm sure you would understand the importance of your help. Believe me when I tell you that this may just may save a man's life."

The guard locked up after the two left the surveillance room and followed Cole to the elevator. Cole continued to assure and divert the concerns of the security guard as the elevator descended. "Have you seen the sweetheart in the bar? They don't give her enough clothes to hold her in. She's a fine looking woman."

The security guard picked up the conversation with some drivel about wanting to see her bend over. The two parted with a common admiration in mind, which helped the security guard feel comfortable with his actions. He resumed his position on the couch. Cole again looked down as he exited the hotel. As the guard watched Cole walk away, he tried to remember the special agent's name, but he couldn't. It really didn't matter anyway. He was never here.

How easy, thought Cole as he walked back to Sun Fire. Just tell somebody something and once they accept it, it becomes true to them and goes unchallenged. Cole concluded that he was actually pretty good at deception. It also dawned on him why Mr. Muddy-Face, One-Eyed-Jack, and Melvin all carried phony FBI IDs. It allowed them to assume the role of authority and therefore, whatever they did, couldn't be wrong to the unchallenging naive. It was all too simple.

Cole quickly undressed in the stillness of night alongside the Sun Fire. He put his own clothes back on and left Melvin's at curbside. The clothes wouldn't be there long. It was still warm and there were enough street people out at night that they would get picked up before too long. Cole accelerated the Sun Fire away from the curb and headed to meet Kevin. He had almost forgotten Melvin. By now he was probably getting cold, maybe suffering some degree of hypothermia. His hand was, by now, irreparably damaged and he was longing for relief. It might drive home the motivation for forgetting Kevin. Cole pulled into a convenience store and gas station next to freeway and parked next to the pay phone. It was quiet, with little activity in the convenience store, and probably nobody would observe his call. Cole used one of his quarters and dialed 911. He made it short. All he gave the 911 operator was the address, the report of a robbery, and a description of the man's dangling position.

As he talked, he thought of Carol. She worked days as a 911 operator and the act of making the call brought back his longing for her. She was probably at home in bed, thought Cole. Would he ever be able to reunite with her? Would she take him back? Could Carol, Tamra and he someday make a life together?

Cole left the convenience store and entered the freeway. It was shortly after midnight. It hadn't taken as long as Cole had figured to complete his plan. He had done all he could to erase Kevin's evening and now he had to figure out what to do with the man. He was a danger to Cole's own anonymity and he couldn't just take him in, so to speak. Rather, he needed to just hide him out in a motel for a couple of weeks until he was sure Melvin had forgotten. Once he was sure, Kevin could resume his life and things could be normal for him.

It was Saturday night and Cole made sure not to give the appearance of a drunk or a speeder. He maintained a careful and precise 67.5-mph, just slightly over the speed limit. The last thing he needed was to get pulled over. Traffic was light and he reached Ogden in good time. Cole was familiar with Raedeux and parked out back. It was part of Ogden's underbelly and very unlikely that anyone would recognize him. It was a little bit rough and different from most of the places he took Carol.

Cole locked the Sun Fire and left it sitting in the dark. One advantage of the Sun Fire was that it wasn't very enticing to car thieves or burglars and he walked away without concern for its safety. He stepped around a large fellow sitting, passed out, next to back door of the bar and entered. He glanced around and didn't see Kevin at first. Then Cole spotted him sitting in the shadows in a booth with clear view of both rear and front entrances. The crowd was pretty lively and nobody even acknowledged Cole's entrance.

"Glad to see you made it, Kevin."

"Did you kill him?"

"No, but I don't think he'll bother you. I convinced him otherwise."

"What do you mean?"

"Let's just say the thought of paying you a visit will bring pain and terror to his mind."

"You beat him?"

"No. Not really. I just left an impression in the form of an unpleasant memory. I also got the video recordings from the hotel so you don't have worry about being identified, even if he does want to find you."

"Oh, you did," said Kevin sarcastically. "I've been busy, too. I also got the video recordings."

"I don't think so. I went right there after I got through with Melvin."

"Yeah, well, I got them electronically. Security on the hotel computer system is non-existent to those with the know-how. I just went in through the reservation system instead of the front door. And, Mr. Hamilton Cole Davis, I also got some other things."

This wasn't part of Cole's plan. He struggled to decide what was next. Kevin had identified him and that was the last thing he wanted. If he walked, what would this guy do? If his name got out, he could be the one lying awake at night waiting for an unwelcome visitor.

He had just saved this guy's life and now contemplated giving him the same treatment as Melvin, or even worse. These thoughts weighed in his mind with the fact that this was obviously a "good guy," innocent of the baneful crimes committed by his desert acquaintances or Melvin. One thing Cole did recognize was that whatever "other things" Kevin had gotten, their relationship had just reversed and Kevin now had the upper hand.

Timidly, Cole asked, "What other things?"

"How about the fact that you're a MIT grad, or that you make $6,127 per month as an apprentice engineer, or that your mother's maiden name is Trent. Want to know where you live and who your grandfather was?"

"You little four-eyed twit! Where'd you get all that?"

"From the license number on the Sun Fire parked at the entrance to the alley. You gave me the idea, remember?"

"Oh, right. Quick study, huh? I still don't understand. Where did you get all that information?"

"It's all out there on the information highway. You can find almost anything you want to know with just a few bits of information to get started. I started with your license number and confirmed it when I saw the variation of your name. Do you go by Cole or Cody?"

Cole didn't answer.

"I went to the bar to check out Melvin and Crossac. What were you doing there, Mr. Engineer-in-training?"

"Same as you, only I have a real reason for it."

"What reason?"

"I, ah, inadvertently interfered with their money transferring activities. Just a little mistake on my part."

Kevin insisted on knowing more, "What do you mean money transferring? Who was it supposed to go to? Come on, give me a name. How much money?"

"None of your business! What makes you think I should tell you anything? You're the spoiled rich kid that just waltzes in, struts around and then takes pictures like some kind of la-di-da tourist. You couldn't have done a better job of saying here I am, bend me over, take me now. Who do you think you are, anyway?"

"Are you a jerk or do you just always act like one?"

"I'm a jerk, all right. I'm going to jerk you out of that chair and bounce you off the wall!"

"You know that fits. You can't deal with people so you resort to violence. I'll bet you did a real number on Melvin. Did you bounce him off the wall a few times? Maybe punch him the face a few times?" added Kevin with a little boxing motion and sarcastic smile. "When you got him down, you probably kicked him in the nuts just for the fun of it."

"No, you scrawny little punk," whispered Cole as he leaned forward. "I stripped him down to his underwear, tied his hands behind his back, and then twisted his arms up behind him so I could slam his gun hand in the door of his car. Then I kept kicking his legs out from beneath him so he had to hang from his hand. I kept it up until he answered my questions and was persuaded to leave you alone. I did it for you."

The sarcastic smile left Kevin's face and he replied in a penitent voice, "The game went too far this time. I should have just let it be."

"What game?"

"Nothing," mumbled Kevin.

"No really, what game?"

"Just the whole thing. Me going to Grand and everything else. So what's next?" said Kevin meekly, avoiding eye contact.

"You camp out in a hotel for a week or two and I keep my eye on your house. When we feel comfortable that Melvin got the message, you go home."

"It sounds so simple."

"It is."

"Hey, how much do you really know?" asked Kevin in an amicable voice. "I don't really expect an answer. I have my secrets and you have yours, but I'll bet if we told all there would be some real synergy."

"I doubt it. There is no synergy in what I know. Trust me. "

The bar was getting ready to close, which really meant that it was time for the regulars to hurry up and make their last order and stockpile enough beer to finish out the night. With the evening coming to an end, Kevin was compelled to make a confession, "You know, Cole. I don't deal with physical situations very well. Usually, I try and talk my way out of things or run like hell. I'm sure I would have died tonight if it hadn't been for you. I just wanted to let you know that I appreciate it. Thanks."

"It's no big deal. I would have followed Melvin wherever he went. It just turned out he followed you. Besides, I learned a few things that I would have been guessing at, otherwise. That Melvin is one bad mother."

"I'll give you a piece of data, if you don't already know it. Melvin and his boss are in the money laundering business."

"Yes, they are."

"I'll give you one more," said Kevin as his eyes darted side to side. "My private goal is to make their life so miserable that they will turn themselves into the police and beg for punishment. What do you think of that?"

"I'm not sure. What did they do to you?"

"You have to understand. They prey on society. They rape it, steal from it, spit on it, and then they have a party. That's why I went to the Grand tonight. With a good picture of Melvin, I can plaster him all over the web."

"You mean last night. It's morning and I'm kind of hungry. How about some breakfast?"

"Sure."

"Is the truck stop okay?"

"I don't know of many things that could be more dangerous, but let's do it."

Cole and Kevin made their way to the back door and stepped into the dark. Cole nimbly stepped past the obstacles on his way to the Sun Fire. Kevin followed and tripped over the drunk outside the back door, stumbled into a trashcan, and sent a beer bottle skittering across the gravel.

Chapter Six

Membership Holds No Secrets

Ogden's Twenty-Fifth Street was once the heart of all decadence in Ogden but had taken on a transformation in recent years. Five-dollar hotels and deteriorating bars were part of Ogden's historical heritage and had been designated as historical sites. Owners of cheap hotels, strip joints, and biker bars had been forced out and the buildings renovated. Raedeux was one of the last holdouts of the renovation and had eventually become an accepted novelty of the street's historic past.

Cole and Kevin circled the block to check on the Porsche. They crept past a police car that had pulled over a biker. The biker was in the familiar position with his hands on the hood of the cop car and feet back and spread. He was being patted down by one of the cops while the other admired his Harley.

"Why don't they go find some real crooks?" commented Cole.

"That guy looks pretty criminal to me," observed Kevin as he studied the biker's black leathers and unkempt appearance.

"Looks are about as far as it goes. Those guys in Raedeux are just out enjoying themselves, doing no harm to anyone. It's just an easy bust for the cops. That's all. They oughta clean up my neighborhood or go after somebody like that Callaway crook."

The offhand comment caught Kevin by surprise and a lump formed in his throat. Did Cole know something about his cyber attack on Callaway? He didn't respond.

Kevin had parked the Porsche just as Cole had instructed, half a block from Raedeux. It was in front of a pricey hair salon with legal offices on the second floor. By morning, it would be surrounded by vehicles equally as nice. Even though Kevin had concealed its contents with blankets, its mountains of stuff might still draw the attention of the police if it sat there too long.

The truck stop on Twelfth Street was nearly empty when Cole and Kevin arrived and finding a table was no challenge. Kevin bent and twisted at the frame on his glasses while their waitress, Katie, took their order. Finally Kevin got just the fit he was looking for and then gave Katie a full smile. She didn't respond. Kevin and Cole both admired her shapely figure as she walked away.

Katie returned to their table with increasing frequency to check on the level of coffee and anything else they might need, but she focused most of her attention on Cole. To Kevin's ire, Cole responded with some mild flirtation. By her fourth visit, she had her hand on Cole's shoulder and the two of them were making goo-goo eye love.

He managed to maintain his composure and used the intervening moments to get some answers on what was next. Cole displayed a good-spirited moment of weakness and solved Kevin's problem of keeping out of sight for a couple of weeks. If somebody were looking for him, the owner of a Porsche, the last place they would look would be in Cole's neighborhood. Cole extended the offer and Kevin accepted, but the Porsche could never go anywhere near Cole's house.

Katie got cold when the two men finished breakfast and she realized Cole's flirtation wasn't going anywhere; Kevin smiled to himself. They left the truck stop and returned to the well-lit Twenty-Fifth Street. It was after 4:00 A.M. and the Porsche stood out like a red flag, alone in the empty angle parking slots. Even the Harleys that previously lined the street in front of Raedeux were gone.

Cole waited for a police car to round the corner before pulling alongside the Porsche. Kevin and Cole jumped out and quickly popped rear hatches on both cars. The contents of the Porsche were quickly moved to the Sun Fire in relay fashion. Most of what Kevin had taken from his house for a week away from home was his computer and electronic equipment. It filled the back of the Sun Fire with a computer tower just clearing the deck lid. They were backing out as the circling cop car re-emerged on Twenty-Fifth Street. Cole gently accelerated away, fearing they were going to draw the attention of the police car, but luckily the

     Brian David Simmons

cops were more interested in a street bum loitering at the entrance to Raedeux. With a quick left, they escaped Twenty-Fifth Street and then drove the short distance to Cole's house.

Kevin wasn't impressed with Cole's house; it wasn't what he expected for an aerospace engineer, even an apprentice. It was in a lousy neighborhood, but was well kept, as were several of the other adjacent houses. It made for a strange mix between slum and "homes." Cole opened the hatch as he passed by the rear of the car. Kevin grabbed a load and followed Cole inside. There was plenty of space for Kevin's things; the front room only had a couch and TV. Kevin set his stuff in the corner and then he and Cole finished carrying in the rest of his computer and electronic equipment. In the last load, Cole carried in a cell phone that got his attention.

Nervously, he asked Kevin, "This isn't Melvin's, is it?"

"Yeah, I thought it might it come in useful."

"No way. I've got to get rid of it," said Cole as he took it from the box and headed toward the front door.

"No, wait. I can use it."

"Sure, it'll be real useful to help Melvin find his way to my front door."

"No, he can't. Not with that phone."

"You sure?"

"Yeah. It's got some neat features on it, but there's no signal to track. I could add one for you if you want."

"Smart aleck. I just thought, well... Hey, what do you know about a secure line?"

"Why do you ask?" questioned Kevin nervously remembering that his eavesdropping on Callaway had been thwarted by a "secure line." Again Kevin wondered if Cole knew something about his clandestine relationship with Callaway.

Cole's ambiguous response didn't help. "I just heard that somewhere."

"Yeah, that's one of the features on this phone. It's got encryption features to code and decode outgoing and in-coming transmissions."

Cole popped the top on a warm beer that had come in with the load from the Sun Fire. The look of anxiety on his face exposed his ignorance of the electronic world and he asked his next question, "So nobody can listen in on an encrypted phone conversation?"

"How much do you really know about encrypted phone conversations?"

"Not much," conceded Cole.

Kevin popped the top on a beer and then explained, "Not even the NSA, with their eavesdropping Eschelund project, can listen in. And they have hundreds of receivers and a gazillion computers monitoring and searching for threatening conversations. But they can only listen in on unencrypted conversations."

"What about you? You listen in on Callaway, maybe?"

Kevin neurotically took a swig of beer. It tasted terrible but he didn't let it show. He squirmed on

Cole's spring bound couch and then broke with a coy, "Maybe."

Cole glared at Kevin in the silence. A realization came to Kevin and a childlike smile gradually grew on his face. The look of anxiety returned to Cole's face when Kevin didn't speak. And then, without saying a word, Kevin got up, went over to the corner and shuffled some of his things aside to find his answering machine. With a witty glance in Cole's direction, Kevin plugged in the answering machine, hit the play button, and then turned back to Cole to ask, "This is you, isn't it?"

The recording played:

Voice one: "... Money's gone. Arabs are dead."

Voice two: "Yeah, so I heard. But it's not my problem anymore. There's a gentleman you need to meet. He's flying in tonight. Go to happy-hour tonight at the Salt Lake Grand."

Voice One: "Who is he?"

Voice Two: "I wouldn't worry too much about that. I'll tell him you'll be there. He'll find you. You sound funny. Are you all right?"

Kevin stopped the recording and stared at Cole, "Are you Crossac? Or are you just a you-sound-funny Crossac?"

"So you got me. At least now I know how you got the invite to the party with Melvin."

"Yeah, but you've got some explaining to do. If you're tonight's Crossac, then where's the real Crossac?"

"Look, I only met you a few hours ago."

"But now I'm your roommate. Like it or not, that's the way it is. Whatever you did to these people is now my problem as well. So, tell me!"

"Fair enough," started Cole. "The truth is that I—ah—look, I just kind of ran into Crossac a couple of days ago, ripped off some money, and stole his ID."

"So where's Crossac, now?"

"He's probably on the run. I mean, if you killed somebody, wouldn't you?"

"The Arabs?" Kevin was suspicious.

"Yeah."

"Sounds a little like a fish story to me."

"Screw you! Maybe I killed Crossac, Simon, and the Arabs, too. Does that make you nervous?" replied Cole with a glare.

"Just being around you makes me nervous. Did you kill them?" asked Kevin timidly.

"Nah," said Cole as he waved his hand. "I didn't kill the Arabs. Crossac and Simon did. I'm just too close to it all because I snatched their cash."

"How much?"

"A bunch."

"How much?

"About four hundred thousand."

"Dang! I guess that would make them mad. What are you going to do with it?" Kevin silently wondered what happened to the rest of the money.

"I don't know."

"What about the police? You worried about getting caught with the money?"

"Not really. It's the Ike character that Melvin talked about that really bothers me. I don't think these guys play by any rules and I'm dead if they ever catch me. I'm a lot worse off than you, that's for sure."

"Not if they don't play by any rules. I suspect I have as much to worry about as you."

"Could be."

"What about the money? What are you going to do with it?"

"Heck if I know. At this point, I don't really even want it."

"I've got some ideas. How about a short-term loan? Maybe fifty thousand or so?"

"What, are you going to pay me back?"

"Sure, when this thing goes away, I've got stocks and stuff I can pay you back with."

"Then knock yourself out. You're welcome to it. It's in the bedroom under the mattress."

"Not a very original hiding place."

"It's the best I could do on short notice. What are you going to do with it anyway?"

"I need some computer equipment and this will go a long way toward setting up some things I've been thinking about."

"Each to his own."

"Hey, what about the case from Melvin's trunk? Think it has more money in it?" said Kevin as he pulled it out from underneath the stack of stuff in the corner. He slid the long rectangular-shaped, hard-sided black case out into the middle of the floor and depressed the two buttons to release its lid. As Kevin lifted the lid, its contents attracted Cole. Foam pockets cradled a rifle, scope, six rounds of ammunition and a pair of binoculars. Cole had never seen a rifle like it. To Cole, its dull black barrel and unpretentious stock were beautiful. Kevin removed the binoculars and inspected the military features. As Kevin admired the binoculars, Cole removed the rifle from the case and jerked the extendable stock into place; it slid to the rear on two steel rods that left eight inches of air space between the stock and the pistol-like grip. The stubby stock was custom shaped to provide a resting spot for the shooter's chin, which added to the unique appearance of the rifle. He stuck his little finger in the barrel to estimate the caliber; it was only a quarter inch wide. The butt plate had a mechanical recoil shock absorber that fit comfortably against Cole's shoulder. It felt good, but was heavier than any rifle Cole had held before. Cole removed the scope from its cradle and rotated it into position on the rifle. The eyepiece had a knurled, rotating ring with numbers showing magnification adjustments in fine increments of two. The scope was adjustable from six to forty-two magnification and its objective lens was almost five inches in diameter. With

     Brian David Simmons

the scope securely in place, Cole raised the rifle and pointed it toward the front window. The addition of the scope noticeably increased the weight of the rifle, but Cole focused it, dead steady, out the front window, across the street, through his neighbor's window to put the cross hairs on a cat.

"Holy crap! This is a rifle."

"What is it?"

"I'm not sure exactly what it is, but one thing's for sure: it's not for hunting rabbits. This is a sniper rifle. It's a small caliber Browning model 1500 Special Application," finished Cole as he read the markings on the barrel.

Cole reached down and removed a round from its cushioned position in the foam. Its case was over five inches long. The oversize diameter necked down to clamp around the smaller bullet. Cole pulled back the bolt on the rifle and slipped the round into the chamber. He slammed the bolt shut, startling Kevin.

"You scare me. Put that thing away."

"Don't get excited. Check this out. The barrel elevation is independent of the scope mount. You adjust the elevation of the barrel to account for bullet drop using this adjustment here," said Cole excitedly as he pointed to a knurled knob between the scope mount and barrel. "This says the adjustment is between one hundred and fifteen hundred meters. Incredible!" Cole made Kevin nervous as he continued to babble like a kid at Christmas, admiring the newfound toy.

The binoculars were equally as impressive, complete with range finder and switch to infrared capability.

With a long day coming to an end, Kevin slipped down on the couch and closed his eyes. In his mind, he summarized what he thought he knew. Callaway was part of some kind of local franchise that transferred and laundered money for their customers. The Arabs were working for Callaway and were making some kind of an incoming payment to Crossac. Special Agents Simon and Crossac were supposed to pick up 2.4 million, but Cole snatched it from them. Cole was also lying about it only being four hundred thousand. The money had a purpose, but what? Cole was holding back; he knew a lot more than he was letting on. Somebody had sent Melvin to recover the money. Cole's little stunt in the alley won't scare off the mob or whoever they are, concluded Kevin as his last thought before dozing off.

     Brian David Simmons

Chapter Seven

IMPETUOUS REACTION

COLE AROSE FIRST. IT WAS AFTERNOON AND MOST OF the day had passed, so there was not much reason for coffee. He stepped out onto the front porch and picked up the Sunday paper. It was too hot outside for a comfortable read of the paper so back inside he went. He stretched out on the floor where he had slept. Kevin was fully laid out on the couch and occasionally let out a subtle little snore. His glasses hung from one ear, but he seemed quite content to just be left alone.

The headlines were "Hansen to Seek Council Job," "New Witnesses Nail Olympic Scandal Coffin," and "Weather Bleeds Farmers Dry." Cole quickly concluded, same news, different day.

He flipped through to the local section. Surprise, surprise, Kevin strikes again, thought Cole. "Callaway has got his fingers in everything," mumbled Cole as he began to read:

"SALT LAKE CITY. Ex-Salt Lake Mayor Jimmy Callaway was questioned Saturday in regard to allegedly warehousing methamphetamine chemicals. Detectives commented that the substances in question are commonly used in the manufacture of street drugs. A search warrant is being sought for Jimmy Callaway's residence and select business locations…. No arrests have been made at this time but the investigation is continuing…. This suspected link to illegal drug manufacture follows investigations into Callaway's alleged illegal transactions between the Dominican Republic Bank and Colombian drug cartels."

Cole thought about waking Kevin but he looked far too serene to disturb. Cole just let him sleep and went on to satisfy his hunger. He pulled two trout, with their heads still on, from the refrigerator and started them frying. He added his own special mountain man seasoning of cayenne, garlic, cilantro, lemon pepper, butter, and peppers.

"Pew, what stinks," groaned Kevin as he rolled off the couch. Cole ignored him and continued to bathe his fish as they fried. Kevin grunted at Cole on his way to the bathroom and was again ignored. Cole noticed how surprisingly different he looked without his glasses and made a mental note to pick up a pair of glasses for himself before he went "undercover" again. The two ate fish, talked about women, and then turned back to the subject at hand.

Kevin had a solution to the problem of the Porsche. By now it was surrounded by early diners visiting Twenty-Fifth Street restaurants. Kevin said he had a specialty shopping list to fill and a Porsche to sell.

     Brian David Simmons

Californians love Porsches and have all the latest in high tech gadgetry, legal and illegal. A trip to California was in order. Cole thought it would be a good idea since it would keep Kevin out of sight for a few days.

After dinner, Kevin set up his computer and logged in to search catalog offerings on the net. Most of what was offcred was simple, commonplace stuff; after all, real eavesdropping equipment was illegal and not explicitly offered for sale. But he got enough leads from the search to go directly to obscure server addresses with exactly what he wanted. He'd surfed through them before, but never with the intention of buying. He placed his requests at several different clandestine websites and waited for responses. He hit in several different Los Angeles locations: San Fernando, Palmdale, and Anaheim. He made arrangements for door pickup and cash payment. He would leave in the morning.

While Kevin swirled his mouse, Cole grabbed a six pack of beer and went out to sit on the front steps. It was a beautiful evening; sun was still up but the temperature had cooled considerably. Some of his neighbors were out doing yard work making their homes stand out from the drug dealer, gang and condemned houses. Cole drank several beers and checked on Kevin several times. Kevin was consumed by whatever world the computer was providing access to. As the sun set, Cole went back inside. Kevin was still hammering keys and swirling the mouse.

"Hey, don't you gotta go pee?" yelled Cole. He got no reaction. Kevin was on some kind of mind merge with the cyber world and completely oblivious to his surroundings. Cole yelled again, "Your mother called for a cyber geek. I told her you were having cybersex with the electrons." Still nothing. "She said that was the only way you could get it." Cole still got no reaction.

ANOTHER MOUSE SWIRLED AND CLICKED IN Atlanta as David Laughlin scanned national news stories. His private phone next to the computer rang.

"Laughlin."

"Business in Salt Lake isn't what we expected."

"Where've you been? I expected to hear from you last night."

"I just got out of the hospital. Some punk screwed me up bad."

"What?"

"Some jerk worked me over. Slammed my hand in the car door and then beat the crap out of me trying to get information. I'm going find him and kill him."

"What'd you tell him?"

"Don't worry about it. I told him I worked for Sugar. I had to give him something; he knew an awful lot about our business. He knew about the missing cash, Beech's boys, and Callaway's couriers from the East. I had no choice but to give him Sugar."

"Melvin, this is not working. I can't afford to have this kind of thing happen. This was supposed to be a simple pay-out from Bank Islam, nothing more. And now I'm going to have to cover Callaway's mistakes by fronting another two million. Callaway is becoming a liability; not only is he costing me money, but he's in the news every day becoming a public spectacle and the focus of police investigations. I need him taken care of very quickly. Can you take care of it?"

"I'm not really up to it. I'm feeling sick and my right hand is pulsating in this soft cast like you can't believe. Can you send somebody else?"

"I need you, Melvin. This can't wait. It needs to be done today."

"Okay. I'll see what I can do."

"Good. Anything on the money or Beech's goons?"

"Nothing, other than that jerk I met last night was not Crossac. I suspect he has your money. Callaway said Crossac was going to meet me last night. Instead, I got lured to an isolated alley by what I thought was a camera-toting fool and then somebody got me from behind."

"That doesn't sound like you, Melvin."

"I got enough of a look at the camera fool and his car that I can track them both down. Then, I'll get your money back. I'm really going to enjoy it."

"Take care of Callaway first."

"I will," confirmed Melvin and then continued with an after thought, "the son-of-a-bitch that fucked up my hand said something strange. Can you run it down for me? It had something to do with a sheriff in someplace called Cootie, Cantenae, or something like that, Idaho."

"Sure," Laughlin swore as he slammed the phone down. "What kind of freakin' mess is this?"

Kevin was in a world all his own. He was building a file on Sugar Ike and "Wall Street Laughlin." Laughlin had a variety of business enterprises with the one of most interest being his Atlanta convenience stores. It was a limited partnership with the principal partner being David Laughlin. Everything Kevin found linked Laughlin to business enterprises, but the other partners were well hidden from Kevin's queries.

As the hours passed, he found more and more. IAB Convenience Enterprise was managed by Isaac Bartrum, who was most probably Sugar Ike. The company held two shell companies: Supply Management Corporation and Account Managers, Inc. Both of these companies also had subtler ties that led to warehousing, storage, inventory management, and supply companies. Outward appearances of the business structure were that Laughlin had vertically integrated his convenience store business with supply and service companies. It all looked completely legitimate but from what Kevin could tell, was only a marginal, break-even company. Yet it had a tremendous yearly cash flow of over eighty million dollars. The initial source of all the cash came from just six convenience stores. Some simple mathematics showed that each one of Laughlin's stores had to be taking in money at a rate of thirty seven thousand dollars per day. Possible, but it seemed like an awful lot for simple convenience stores.

He heard some of Cole's mumblings from behind but it didn't deter his investigation. The thought crossed his mind that Cole was an undesirable distraction and he wished he would just leave.

The hours passed as Kevin investigated further; Laughlin was indeed a Wall Street player. He had personal holdings of futures contracts as well as managing accounts for others. The more he investigated, the more he suspected that Laughlin's futures trading enterprise dwarfed the convenience store business.

Kevin felt Cole jab him from behind and mumble something about "Oh my God!" The TV came to life just in time to catch the late night re-broadcast of the ten o'clock evening news. The headline story broke Kevin's focus on cyberspace. A woman in her early thirties was reporting live from outside the security gate at Ex-Mayor Jimmy Callaway's estate.

"…Mayor Jimmy Callaway has apparently taken his own life. Police spokesmen say that at approximately 9:45 this evening Mayor Callaway went into his private library, locked the door behind him and then allegedly shot himself with a small caliber handgun. His condition is not known at this time. Paramedics are inside working on Mayor Callaway, preparing him for transport to the University of Utah

Medical Center. This horrible turn of events occurred only hours after Callaway's reported involvement in the death of two Islamic businessmen and the theft of a large sum of investment capital. Police authorities have declined to comment about the deaths, but they have scheduled a news conference for tomorrow morning to provide a detailed accounting of all of today's events. We will keep you informed as we learn more throughout the evening. This is Melissa Van Dyke reporting live from the Mayor's mansion. And now back to you, Tom."

"We'll be back with more on Mayor Callaway's apparent suicide as well as other top stories after this brief commercial break."

Kevin spoke deliberately, "He's dead?" Then came the realization that this wasn't a suicide and he knew who had done the real killing. Kevin's tear glands swelled and a lump formed in his throat. He hung his head and let out a faint sigh.

He had provided the information and misinformation reported in the press that had forced a decision to terminate Callaway. Callaway was too much of an embarrassment and under too much scrutiny for him to be of any further use to his money-manipulating partners. His partners would have perceptibly had no further need for him and terminated him, but the real blood was on Kevin's hands.

     Brian David Simmons

Chapter Eight

COMMAND CHOICES

THE NEWS OF CALLAWAY'S APPARENT SUICIDE CON-
fused Kevin and delayed his trip to Los Angeles. The
game wasn't supposed to be deadly. Kevin found himself engrossed in computer chess and Free Cell in an
attempt to escape from guilt. Kevin called work and
advised them that he was sick, which was not a lie.

In his suffering, Kevin renounced his web mastery; henceforth he would limit his search activities
to established search engines that touched only major
servers. Remote servers and global e-mail searches
would be off limits. He would bench his correlation
routines and customized passports. Access to the web
would only be done using his own identity and he
would let the cookies be deposited as they may, without interference. Avenues that allowed him access to
law enforcement, API, credit reporting, tax records,
vehicle registration, driver's license, and other limited access databases would be forgotten. He would
become just an ordinary web surfer. He told himself
the game was over.

COLE KNEW HE HAD TO KEEP UP APPEARANCES UNTIL
the bodies were found in the desert and things settled
down. Before going to work, Cole drove down Twenty-

Fifth Street to check on the Porsche. By now, somebody was probably starting to get suspicious. The car had been there for more than twenty-four hours and it wasn't an easy car to miss. The police had surely noted its presence and had maybe even called it in to verify that it wasn't stolen. It was imperative that they got the car out of there that evening if they were going to remain invisible to anyone interested in their whereabouts or actions. A simple license plate run by an inquisitive cop would provide a time and place record that needed to be avoided. In Cole's mind, it probably wouldn't lead anywhere; but it would still be better to leave no tracks for anybody to follow. The car would have to move tonight.

Cole drove on toward the freeway. He was late and he didn't want anything to be unusual about actions today. He entered the freeway and accelerated to cruising speed as he merged across lanes to the left. The Sun Fire was aging but it still had enough youth to jump when the accelerator was fully depressed. He had made the long trip out to the Space and Defense Rocket Company many times, but today was different. How could his job compare with the excitement of the weekend's events? But it had to be done. Any appearances that things were different might start a trail leading to the events in the desert. No matter how monotonous it was, he would just maintain normalcy and go through the motions of performing a job that no longer mattered to him.

     Brian David Simmons

Kevin sulked most of the day, consumed guilt. He played Solitaire and Free Cell until he could stand it no more. He checked news stories on Covid, BLM, potential Presidential candidates, and more. Gradually, as he scanned the various news articles, the lure of the game and the realization that maybe Callaway had gotten what he deserved, began to pull him from his depression. He evolved to an understanding that Callaway, Sugar Ike, Laughlin, and Melvin played a game on a whole different level. They had no inhibitions about murder, graft, theft or probably any other crime. Maybe they were even involved in drugs, child prostitution, or worse.

Cole's day was long and miserable. Everything at work seemed insignificant compared to the weekend events. Cole didn't go straight home from work. He had some soul-searching to do and the desert was the ideal place. He didn't dare venture near his favorite hunting ground but instead found a place equally as isolated. He went for a short walk and took a seat on an uncomfortable rock outcropping to watch the sunset.

Everything had happened so fast that this was Cole's first chance to reflect on what he was becoming. He had suppressed it for so long, but now it was growing full force; hostility of the Patriot Rebirth Society compound was now blossoming full-force within his very soul. He could no longer suppress the memories.

Chapter Nine

First Kill

At age twelve, life in the compound changed. It was summer and he vividly remembered the conversation at the breakfast table that started it all. His father recounted events from the night before; Leroy Manson, sheriff of Kootenai County, had been sneaking around the mountainous perimeter of the compound. Several times previously Cole's father had spotted the sheriff spying on the compound through high powered binoculars. The night before, Cole's father had crept through the wooded terrain to circle around behind the sheriff and catch him spying. Silently inching up behind the sheriff, with skinning knife in hand, Cole's father relieved the sheriff of his sidearm and made it absolutely clear that if he ever came up here again, he would be gutted like a hog and fed his own entrails. The words "gutted like a hog" echoed over and over in Cole's mind.

The sheriff did come back two months later in a night raid on the compound. FBI helicopters, armored personnel carriers, and a small army of FBI agents assaulted the compound killing seventeen and arresting or detaining surviving men, women and children. Cole's mother was among the dead. Cole's father had been shot in the arm and, after losing a slugfest with six FBI agents, taken into custody. Cole was processed through child welfare services and eventually released to his grandmother from Boston.

Cole's father received medical attention, such as it was, with the amputation of his left arm. It delayed his transfer to a federal facility like the other compound combatants and he was temporarily placed in the custody of the sheriff. Custody didn't last long.

News reports said Cole's father had become combative, which required Sheriff Leroy Manson to exercise defensive measures. With Cole's father's remaining arm handcuffed to his waist, he had repeatedly charged the sheriff and had to be repeatedly repelled into the cell bars. Cole's father had continued his attacks on the sheriff until Leroy Manson had no choice but to use deadly force and fired a single shot to the head. Video cameras within the jail had failed and explanation of events relied solely on the sheriff's account. Kootenai County and Idaho officials were just glad the bad press associated with the white supremacists would finally come to an end and consequently the sheriff's questionable accounting of events got little attention.

Cole was whisked off to Boston, given counseling, entered into public school and expected to put the past behind him. He didn't. He had a purpose and only one. Cole excelled in school attaining straight "A"s and being placed on the honor roll. Cole convinced his grandmother to enroll him in martial arts classes.

Cole was careful not to display too much of his skill but still attained some nonsensical black belt status. In tournaments, Cole made sure to loose some matches in order to avoid drawing attention to himself. It was all nonsense but it helped keep him practiced. Late into the nights, Cole surfed the internet studying everything from security systems to city bus schedules to DNA. As the end of his seventh grade neared at age thirteen, the middle school principal and faculty decided to jump him an entire grade and have him attend the high school in the Fall. His grandmother was so proud of his accomplishments that nothing was denied; all he had to do was ask.

The look on her face went from beaming parent to pure terror when Cole told her he was going to disappear for a week and she needed to be prepared to swear that he was at home the whole time. Cole sensed she knew what he was about to do. She cried the entire night. Cole kissed her on the cheek the following morning before heading out to catch the city bus.

He worked his way across the Country by catching rides in truck stops and taking short-run city buses. He picked up supplies along the way in anticipation of the end goal. In thirty-six hours, he reached the truck stop on the outskirts of Coeur d'Alene Idaho.

As evening approached, Cole studied the small house through binoculars from the safety of tall grass on the hill side. The sun was still at full blaze when a vehicle arrived at the house and backed into the

     Brian David Simmons

driveway at 6:05. Cole studied the vehicle occupant and wasn't sure; he'd only seen photographs which could be impalpable confirmation, but it was the correct address and the vehicle markings were correct. He breathed through his fingers and adjusted his plan accordingly. Cole watched the light traffic on the road in front of the house as the sun set. Traffic became almost non-existent as the hours crept onward.

Cole slipped on coveralls, gloves and a ball cap from his small duffle bag. He crept down the hill, crossed the street and inspected the mailbox, which had just numbers and no name. He put the duffle bag under the front of the Kootenai County Sheriff's pickup and then used his boots to go after the vehicle with a vengeance, making as much noise as possible. He worked his way around kicking in every body panel, until the sheriff stepped out of the front door. The sheriff yelled "what the fuck," but Cole payed him no attention and continued to inflict damage to the truck. Cole had insipidly noticed that the sheriff was still wearing his uniform shirt; that would simplify verification of identity. The sheriff darted back inside and then quickly returned pistol in hand to charge towards Cole. As the sheriff reached Cole, he pointed the pistol and screamed, "Knock it the fuck off or I'll shoot!"

Cole stood still, with his back to the sheriff, and slowly raised his hands over his head. The sheriff advanced and yelled, "You fucking little punk. What the fuck do you think you're doing?" The sheriff was at least a head taller than Cole, which was good, and he silently visualized his next move. He heard the jingle of the cuffs coming from the sheriff's belt. Pistol in his right hand, the sheriff was reaching up with his left to cuff Cole's left wrist. Before the cuffs reached Cole's wrist, the explosive speed of his MCMAP training went into action; Cole's body's began a leftward rotation and he started the trajectory of his left hand. As the speed of rotation increased, Cole's hand trajectory began it's upward path to forcefully plant his Karate formed hand directly into the sheriff's arm pit. The sheriff's pistol fired from reaction to the blow but Cole's rotation had cleared him from the bullet's path. Taking full advantage of the continued rotation, Cole's right elbow popped straight to maximize impact of his fist driving inches deep into the sheriff's solar plexus. Cole's mind captured the name from the uniform's tag; it was him. Identity confirmed: Sheriff Leroy Manson. With the sheriff's heart now reverberating in shock and his lungs paralyzed from the solar plexus blow, his concentration wasn't on the pistol in his right hand and Cole grabbed the wrist to lift it high and deliver a full force knuckle driving punch to the man's right armpit. Cole delivered a final blow with his foot to the inside of sheriff's left knee, snapping it and starting the sheriff in a downward path to the ground. In less than a second, the sheriff had gone from the over-confidence of arresting a scrawny, little, mischievous

     Brian David Simmons

punk to having only gasps for breathing, both arms incapacitated and only one good knee.

Cole pulled an eight inch skinning knife from his boot and crawled onto the sheriff's belly to look him directly in the eyes. The sheriff's mouth gasped for air and moved as if to say something, but Cole interrupted, "Did anybody ever tell you not to come back to the compound? Did anyone ever tell you that you would be gutted like a hog if you did?" Horror entered the sheriff's eyes and he squirmed and coughed for breath as Cole inserted the knife just above the sheriff's pelvic bone and began to slice upward. Cole felt the warmth of the man's entrails through his gloved hand as he sawed upward. The man managed a scream. Cole reached inside to grab a handful of intestines and then shoved them into the man's mouth; it brought silence.

Chapter Ten

ANSWERS

COLE SEARCHED HIS HEART FOR ANSWERS THAT would determine tomorrow's life. Was I destined to the insane morality of the Patriot Rebirth Society forever? Who would ever teach a three-year-old to inflict pain on another before he ever learned his colors? Could I ever again suppress the hostility and just be normal? Could I resume my relationship with Carol? Only this time, I would ask her to marry me. Would she accept? What would the cops do when they found the two cars? Would I elude their investigation and Laughlin's hunt? If he did, his life could return to normal. Then the choice was entirely his. But is normal what I really want? By any psychologist's assessment, I should probably be committed. His choices were simple. Normal life offered Carol and all the pleasures of the heart. The hunt offered excitement, pursuit, evasion, challenge, accomplishment and the adrenaline rush that came with it. He chose the hunt and the hostility that came with it; addiction was stronger than love.

The sun set and Cole made his way home. The mood was noticeably different when Cole got home. Kevin had also been doing some soul-searching and had come to grips with his responsibility for Callaway's death. Kevin confessed his private game. It had

     Brian David Simmons

begun because things weren't right in the world. He had the skill and knowledge to use a weapon more mighty than the sword or the pen to effect change and make corrections in the world. This was what he believed and this was what he was ready to continue with. As for Callaway, he deserved what he got.

When Kevin finished his confession, a solemn quietness filled the small living room and Cole was compelled to make a guarded confession of his own, "You aren't the only one with blood on your hands. I haven't exactly told you everything, you know."

"I do know. You think I'm stupid or something. You killed those men, and it isn't just four hundred thousand—it's more like two million four hundred thousand."

"How do you know?"

"The 2.4 million is on my answering machine, and as for the rest of it, it doesn't take a rocket scientist to figure out. You're the only variable in this whole thing that could have killed Crossac, Simon, and the Arabs."

Cole felt naked; he had covered his tracks so well and yet his actions were transparent to Kevin. Cole could only attempt to justify himself; "It was more like self-defense. And I didn't kill the Arabs. You see, Crossac and his partner killed the Arabs—I just witnessed it."

"But you did kill Crossac and Simon."

"Only in self-defense. If I hadn't killed them, they would have killed me for sure."

"If it was self-defense, why didn't you go to the police?"

"The money and fear of its owner. I couldn't just walk away from 2.4 million and even if I had gone to police, I figured somebody like Melvin would have still come after me. Do you think they would have just let me walk away after screwing up their transaction? It was better that I was just never there, so to speak."

With a few more questions, Cole confessed all, including the cover-up and torching of the cars driven off into desert by Mr. Muddy-Face and One-Eyed-Jack. It was actually a relief to share the details of his secret.

Both men had now willingly chosen and fully accepted the endeavor they were about to undertake and began to formulate a plan. They agreed that Kevin should go ahead and make his trip to California, and that Cole needed to go on a reconnaissance mission to Atlanta. Kevin would leave in the morning and Cole would leave as soon he could get away from work. Kevin briefed Cole on everything he had learned about Laughlin's convenience store enterprise and futures market manipulations. He didn't understand how Laughlin was laundering money through the futures market, but he made too many strange transactions for it not to be part of the overall laundering business.

Cole's reconnaissance mission in Atlanta was simple. He was to verify addresses; take pictures of

Laughlin, Sugar Ike, and any others that might be involved; survey the operation; establish people and money movements; and look for any opportunities to hurt them and relieve them of their laundered cash.

The following morning, Cole dropped Kevin off on Twenty-Fifth Street, half a block from the Porsche. Cole could hardly stand the thought of going to work, but he couldn't afford to let anybody suspect that things were anything other than normal. When he got to work, he scheduled Wednesday through Friday as vacation time and made reservations for a flight out of Salt Lake to Atlanta.

Chapter Eleven

CITY OF PAIN:
HUNTER'S NIGHTMARE

THE MONOTONY OF THE DAY FINALLY ENDED FOR COLE and he accelerated the Sun Fire past the guard at the SDRMC gate. He made the left onto the highway and the Sun Fire flew with the pedal deep in its travel. He had a six-forty-five flight out of Salt Lake International and no time to spare. The exhilaration of the hunt was already starting to affect him and he had to exert self-control to slow down. He made record time to airport and found a spot in long-term parking. The shuttle bus was there before he got his bags out of the Sun Fire and he had to make a hurried dash to catch it. He forgot his Covid mask and the bus driver had to provide him with one. He hated the damn things, but then they also helped with anonymity. Kevin had helped Cole pack and he wasn't taking just clothes. He had a large suitcase, a duffel bag, and his briefcase.

He made the terminal in plenty of time for the flight and paid cash for his cattle class ticket. He could have easily paid the first class price but that would have made him stand out even more than paying cash, and standing out was not part of the plan. Cash made him suspicious enough. He checked his duffel bag and suitcase, leaving him with only the briefcase to carry.

Sure enough, the cash ticket purchase flagged TSA, and he got the full treatment. When he finally boarded the plane, he settled into his window seat and shoved the briefcase under the seat in front of him.

It took a lot of effort and concentration to find a mid-level state of slumber. He knew that once he got to Atlanta, sleep wasn't going to be a priority, and the flight offered him the opportunity to get a little rest ahead of time. Sleeping in a window seat on a night flight in the cattle class section meant that even airline attendants wouldn't notice him, much less anybody else. It was a relatively short flight, lasting little more than three-and-a-half hours, which meant that with the two-hour time difference, he would be in Atlanta by one o'clock. He managed to sleep for most of the flight, which reduced the monotony.

The 737 touched down gently. That roused Cole, but he consciously maintained his appearance of sleep. There was no reason to wake and chance having the guy sitting next to him try to start a conversation. When the plane pulled up to the gate and people started struggling down the narrow aisle, Cole retrieved his briefcase and merged in. The attendant looked at him and Cole was pretty sure she smiled at him under the mask. He was sure when she briefly pulled her mask down. She was attractive in a different sort of way; her facial features and a slight gap between her front teeth gave her a Lauren Hutton kind of look. Cole made his way up the jet way, following the other passengers in line to the terminal, and then set off to the baggage claim area. En route, he passed the escalator to the underground tram. The E terminal was surprisingly still full of people. He just hoped that the rental car office would still be open since he had several things to do before he could get there. Instead of making his way directly to the baggage claim, he headed back down the E terminal wing toward the escalator. He ducked into the restroom closest to the escalator and jammed into a stall with his briefcase.

It was time for a new Cole. The suit, white shirt, and tie were traded for faded blue jeans, gray T-shirt, baseball cap, and wire-framed glasses from the brief-case. Cole emerged from the stall with a good ol' boy contractor look. His next stop was the underground tram where he ran into the Lauren Hutton look-alike. She stood right next to him waiting for the tram. Cole wondered how observant she was. Would she, after having briefly seen him only minutes earlier, recognize him?

Cole turned and spoke to her. "Must be a warm evening. It's sure warm down here."

Her eyes squinted a little and replied, "Yes it is."

Cole studied her eyes searching for any recollection, reaction, or questioning thought. There was none. She simply looked away without mentally recording his true facial features or linking him to the very recent past. His simple disguise was enough. He followed her onto the tram and then gave her a second chance to

     Brian David Simmons

recognize him as the tram accelerated toward terminal D. Again, the reaction was the same. He got off at terminal D and left her standing there grasping the padded post, unaware that she had been the subject of a test. He made his way to the baggage claim and then on to the rental car desk. He could see his folder in one of the reserved slots. It was easy to recognize by the bold name "Roberson" marked on the folder.

"Yes, sir. May I help you?" Cole loved the sweet southern words spoken by women of the South. He melted every time one of them talked to him.

He responded without hesitation. "Melvin Roberson. I believe you have a car for me."

"Yes, sir. Right here. I'll just need your driver's license and a credit card."

Cole handed her Melvin's driver's license and waited to see how close she would really look. As a distraction, Cole counted out six hundred-dollar bills on the counter. It worked. She concentrated more on the cash on the counter and the wad in his hand than she did on his facial features or the obvious difference in age between him and the delineation on the license. With the pertinent information entered into the computer, she handed the license back to him. It cost him an additional three hundred dollars for insurance and a damage deposit before she handed over the keys, but it wasn't his money anyway. As he departed the counter, she said, "Y'all come back now." Her voice was so alluring he almost did. The duffel bag and suitcase got heavier as he made the trek to the rental car. The shuttle ride was a welcome break. The car he had been given was a mid-size something; it was hard to distinguish one model of car from another, as they all seemed to take on similar appearance. It turned out to be a Buick and Cole put his luggage in the trunk, but kept his briefcase with him. He opened the briefcase before touching anything inside the car and retrieved a pair of surgical gloves. This was the way it was going to be every time he got inside in the car. Eventually somebody might want to fingerprint the car and Cole needed to make sure he was never there, so to speak.

With the briefcase at his side, he started the car and proceeded to the exit. He again opened the brief-case and pulled out the map Kevin had made for him. He followed the map to the first of six circled locations.

He pulled up across the street from Big IAB Food and Liquor. It was a small convenience store with no gas pumps, tucked away off the main thorough-fare. It was nearing two A.M. and the store was still open. It was an aging building with graffiti scrawled on its exterior. Glass windows on the front of the store allowed for full view of the entire inside. Inside, Cole could see a single cashier reading a magazine. There were no cars parked out front and no custom-ers inside. He opened the briefcase and withdrew the set of binoculars. He studied the interior of the store and observed the typical shelves filled with candy and

     Brian David Simmons

snack foods; the cashier station had the typical cigarette advertising overhead. There was nothing out of ordinary, nothing to generate suspicion, and nothing that could have done thirty-seven thousand dollars in sales today.

Cole moved on to the second location on the map and pulled into the parking lot in front of the second Big IAB Food and Liquor convenience store. It was now closed with all the lights off, except for the cigarette sign over the cashier station. In overall appearance, it was similar to the first store, including its probable inability to have much of a cash flow. Cole pulled out of the parking lot and drove on to the other stores marked on his map. In each case, the story was the same. All of the stores were in small, deteriorating buildings suffering from neglect in aging low-income neighborhoods. Kevin had been right.

The last store Cole visited was on Dresden Drive Northeast directly across from a three-story apartment building. Kevin had made arrangements for a street-side apartment there. It was still early and Cole had some time to kill before he dared approach the building manager. He would wait until eight o'clock. Cole drove down the street to a breakfast house. It was as good a place as any to kill a couple of hours.

Cole blended in with the early morning breakfast crowd. It was about half full of working men dressed in attire similar to his own. He ordered a big breakfast and settled in to read the national newspaper. Their feature story was on money laundering, a subject that Cole was learning about first hand.

Financial Crimes Enforcement Network (FINCEN) had developed databases and completed analyses that resulted in identification of six money-laundering schemes, all using different variations of the same three basic steps. The first step was to dispose of the cash itself. Cash was transported and then deposited in foreign bank accounts, used to purchase real estate, converted to art works or other collectibles that could then be converted via check to money in a bank account. This was a simple step, but provided FINCEN with multiple opportunities for detection. The second step was to lose the origins of the money through complex wire transfers and stock market transactions. The third step was to make the increases in gross income or assets of an individual look legitimate. This third step could be accomplished through phony loans, bogus invoices for goods and services, and other artificial financial obligations that offset increases in gross assets or income. Cole could easily relate what Kevin and he knew about Laughlin to the story and it really offered nothing new, except that he had no idea of the magnitude of money-laundering activities in the U.S. FINCEN estimated that somewhere between four and five hundred billion dollars were laundered each year. But not anymore, thought Cole; it's now going to be five hundred minus…Cole finished his coffee—he had had more than he could ordinarily stand—and left a

     Brian David Simmons

small tip. He avoided direct eye contact with anyone as he paid his bill and left the restaurant.

The sun was now breaking up the morning haze and the day was already uncomfortably warm. He drove back toward the apartment complex, circled the block, and then parked half a block away. He locked the car and headed down the street toward the apartment building. The little convenience store across the street had a single car parked in front and it was apparent that business was slow. He entered the apartment building and found the manager's apartment on the first floor. After a few repeated knocks at the door, a big black man answered the door. He was wearing a stained white T-shirt that was too small and stretched near its limits to accommodate the man's beer belly. He looked as if Cole had woken him and he wasn't the least bit cordial. Cole managed to complete the apartment rental with cash paid for first and last month's rent, and a two-hundred-dollar security deposit.

The apartment was on the second floor with a view of Dresden and the convenience store across the street. It was perfect. The apartment had furnishings that had probably been around since the sixties; bright orange seemed to be the predominate color. He needed some bedding and some other miscellaneous items to make it livable. Cole retrieved his luggage from the car and then started to set up.

He closed the drapes and then opened the suitcase and took out a tripod and high resolution, extended recording time video camera. He set up the video camera with the lens obscured in the shadow just behind the slightly opened drapes. After letting it record for a few moments, he checked its playback for clarity. It was a little obscured by the window but it was good enough. He reset the camera, plugged in its power source, and took one last peek through the drapes. The camera would record for twelve hours, which meant that if he were to capture everything that went on at the convenience store he would have to return to the apartment frequently. Of course, if he missed a few hours, it probably wouldn't make any difference. He really didn't know what he was looking for, except that anything unusual might help build on what Kevin and he already knew about Laughlin.

Cole made a trip to the local department store to purchase bedding, picnic plates and utensils, cookware, and miscellaneous toiletries. This was going to be home for the next several days and it needed to have all the normal conveniences. The time wasn't wasted but it wasn't spent on reconnaissance, which was why Cole was really there. His first recon into enemy territory, as he characterized it, was to investigate the Big IAB Food and Liquor across the street.

Cole left the apartment building and used the crosswalk on the corner to disguise his trail to the convenience store. When he entered the store, a stout, older black man greeted Cole. Cole replied in kind, but didn't let the man get a good look at his face. He went about gathering up groceries and supplies he thought he might need for a week's survival. As he shopped, he studied the interior of the store, looking for surveillance or other equipment. The little store had neither cameras nor a burglar alarm to protect itself. How strange, thought Cole, especially in this neighborhood.

Cole finished his shopping and set his hand basket on the counter in front of the cash register. It was a modern, computerized cash register that looked out of place in the aging store. The man behind the counter was extremely friendly and kept trying to start a conversation with Cole as he rang up the groceries. Cole resisted but eventually gave in, still managing to avoid eye contact.

"The baked beans in the generic can are 17 cents cheaper than these and they're twice as good. If you like, I'll trade 'em out for ya."

"No. These'll be fine."

"It's your money. I'll bet it's going to be another warm one today. I don't envy you fellas that work outside all day."

"It seems like it's kinda slow around here. You're not doing a lot of business."

"No slower than usual. We mostly just get people that buy a few items instead of doing all their shopping here like they used to."

"Is that so? What changed?"

"I used to own this store. Now I just manage it. When I sold out to the IAB, they started managing my inventory and setting all the prices. Now people don't like my inventory and they get their groceries cheaper down the street."

"That doesn't seem right. How do they make money?" said Cole as he handed the man two twenties.

"I don't have a clue. But I get paid just the same, and it's a living. So I can't complain. By the way, my name's Joe Atkinson." The man handed Cole his change. "You need anything, you just come on back now, you hear."

"I will." said Cole and then he picked up his grocery bags and departed.

Again, he took the long way back to the apartment building, back down to the corner to cross at the sidewalk, even though he knew that if Joe Atkinson was watching he could have easily seen him enter the apartment building. Cole made his way up the stairs to the second floor and through the heavy steel door. There were two kids playing in the hallway; it was probably safer than playing outside. He passed the kids and entered his apartment. It took only a few minutes to put his groceries away; forty dollars didn't buy much. Cole rewound the video camera and then replayed in fast-forward. He watched himself enter and leave the convenience store; it was clear enough that he could make out facial features for identification. It reminded him that he would always have to be on his guard. He reset the video camera and was off for

     Brian David Simmons

a tour of the residential areas of Atlanta. His first site was to be the residence of Sugar Ike.

Cole searched for an alternate exit from the building but there were none that were unlocked. It was unnerving to walk past all the peepholes in both the first and second floor hallways. He never knew who might be watching him. Cole exited out the front of the building, and as he headed for his car, he glanced across the street at the IAB Food and Liquor. The parking lot was empty. Joe was right about it being slow.

When Cole opened the door on the car, he was hit with a blast of hot, muggy air that reminded him instantly that this was Atlanta. Cole was really beginning to dislike the surgical gloves; they made his hands sweat and there was nowhere for the moisture to go. The car started instantly and Cole was off to Atlanta's Buckhead area. It wasn't too far, although traffic made it a long trip. Cole circled through the area, up and down residential streets, until he felt like he knew the streets in the immediate vicinity of Isaac Bartrum's house. All of the houses were of the upper-middle-income variety, each one sitting on a large lot with lots of open space between the houses. Probably a doctor-lawyer neighborhood, thought Cole as he cruised in and out, back and forth.

Cole knew he could afford only two or three passes in front of Ike's house if he was going to avoid drawing suspicion. He made the first pass very slowly while holding a second high resolution video camera at the base of the window opening. It was a modest home in comparison to the others, set well back off the road on a slight hilltop. Large locust and dogwood trees obscured the front of the house. It may have been equal to the others in the neighborhood, but from the road it didn't look like it. The only unique feature about the house was a four-foot chain link fence that encircled the entire lot. All of the other houses in the area were unfenced. Cole made his second pass with the video camera in one hand and then just as he passed in front, he raised the binoculars with his other hand, leaving the steering for his knee. He spotted a surveillance camera over the front door and maybe another pointing down the long driveway, he wasn't sure. Unnerved by the surveillance cameras, Cole decided not to take a chance on a third pass.

The next stop was Laughlin's house. From the map Kevin had provided, it was supposed to be near the intersection of I-85 and I-75 but Cole didn't find it immediately. It was almost in downtown Atlanta and with the freeway nightmare of overpasses, on-ramps and off-ramps, Cole was sure Kevin had made a mistake. Eventually, Cole passed Piedmont Hospital and then things transitioned from intermingled, busy roadways to quiet, narrow residential streets. Cole found Lorring Street and then made a left on Garden Road. He was close and began his surveillance of the surrounding neighborhood. There were fewer houses than in Sugar Ike's neighborhood and they were larger.

     Brian David Simmons

Some of the houses had acres of grass to mow and the distances between houses assured privacy. The area had its own private park with a fishpond. It had miniature forests of mature trees and paved walkways winding throughout. The spaciousness of the area was surprising considering how close it was to downtown. Cole counted only sixteen houses before deciding to drive past Laughlin's house.

He turned off Garden Road, down the narrow lane, and the house was immediately visible. The arc of the road crested at Laughlin's circular driveway and then turned back to rejoin Garden Road. Cole started the video camera and drove slowly past a mansion on the left, and then two more, one on the left and one on the right. He steered the car slightly to the right to round the arc as he passed Laughlin's mansion. It was truly a mansion, resembling a pre-Civil War plantation house. It had two stories with pillars spanning both floors to support the extended overhang of the roof. A first-level veranda with white picket railing surrounded the entire house. Sweeping rounded steps led up to the veranda and double-door front entry. A much shallower veranda, also with picket railing, spanned across the entire front of the second floor. It was a grand house and had to have cost Laughlin millions —and he didn't get it from the convenience store business.

Cole circled back to Garden Road and readied the binoculars for his second pass. As he turned back down the narrow lane, he studied the driveway. It led past the side of the mansion with a side-loop providing for a circular drive in front of the house. No vehicles were visible in the front, meaning that most of the daily traffic, in and out, used a rear entry. This, along with the fact that there were no good vantage points, would make it extremely difficult to see who came and went. Cole again used his knee to steer while videotaping and looking through the binoculars. He thought he could see several surveillance cameras along the eaves and over the front door. Something else caught his eye, too. The roof had an unusual set of dormers. Not that dormers themselves were unusual, it was just that they didn't seem to fit the style of the mansion.

Cole didn't dare make a third pass. He would wait for night, when he might have a better advantage. Cole's next stop was the IAB Food and Liquor main office. It was in downtown Atlanta, in a multi-story office building. Cole checked it out and concluded that it had to be just a front of some kind. It was a single room office tucked away amongst a hundred others, with only a mail slot in the locked door to conduct business.

In route back to the apartment, Cole stopped at a mail service. He sent the videotape and his notes related to convenience stores in an overnight envelope to his home address. Kevin and Cole had agreed not use telephones until Kevin could ensure private communications. The mail system was actually more private.

     Brian David Simmons

Back at the apartment building, Cole parked the car across the street and just passed the IAB Food and Liquor. Joe was pretty free with his words about IAB and maybe Cole could learn some more. Cole entered the little store and walked past an elderly, frail woman on his way to the beer cooler. Her clothes were neat and complimented her perfectly ladylike appearance. With a six-pack in hand, he returned to the counter.

"Howdy, ma'am. Where's Joe?" said Cole, unnaturally trying to emulate the southern drawl. After he said it, he realized how stupid he sounded.

"Oh, you know. He's getting a little sleep."

"No, I didn't, ma'am. Is he all right?"

"Sure. But he spends so many hours minding the store that he needs to get some sleep sometime. In here at seven to open and then keep the doors open till eleven, ya know. He'll be up and about in hour or so. You need something from him, I can call across the street and wake him if ya like."

"Oh, no, ma'am. I'll just stop by later."

Cole paid for his beer and went back to the apartment. A couple of beers would help him get an early evening nap. Cole expected it to be another late night. He returned to the apartment building, passed all the irritating little peepholes on the first floor and then up the stairs to the second. As he walked down the hall, a door opened and Joe stepped out.

"Looks like we're neighbors."

"Yes, sir."

Cole quit trying to be elusive by avoiding eye-to-eye contact and let his normal outgoing nature take its course. Joe, being at least sixty and a store clerk, was obviously of no threat to him.

"Haven't seen you around here before. We don't get many nice young men in this neighborhood, especially white ones. You must have just moved in."

"Yes, sir. Just looking for a job that pays well." And Cole wasn't lying.

"Well, we're glad to have you in the neighborhood. If you got that six-pack across the street, then you met my wife."

"Yes, sir. I did."

"Well, I gotta go relieve her. We'll talk later."

"That we will, sir."

As Joe walked off, Cole noticed his invigorating stride exhibiting the overall physical shape of the man. Inside the apartment, Cole reviewed the day's videotape in fast-forward mode while he drank his beer. The tape showed nothing unusual, just hour after hour of six or seven customers buying one or two items. Cole reset the video camera and dozed off.

Cole didn't wake until nearly midnight, which was still early for what he had in mind. He reviewed and reset the video camera, which was now becoming a non-productive routine. He put on black jeans and a black long-sleeve turtleneck to cover as much of his skin as possible. At this point, he also had a three-day beard on his face, which would help a little. He put on

     Brian David Simmons

his baseball cap and left his glasses at home. He didn't expect anybody to see him this evening.

Outside the building, the car was noticeable, sitting at curbside all by itself. Cole would have to find a better place to park it. With surgical gloves on, Cole drove off back toward the intersection of I-75 and I-85. Traffic had died down and the trip took half as long as before. This time, he also knew where he was going. Tonight's objective was to evaluate the parking arrangement at the rear of the mansion, determine accessibility of the rear entry and see what more he could learn about the security system. Eventually, he knew he would have to go inside. The more he learned now, the easier it would be later.

Cole slowly turned down Garden Road. He rolled down both front windows to take in all the evening sounds. The air was warm and still. Cole could hear the faint roar of the freeway off in the distance to the right. Railroad tracks had to be not too far off to his left; he thought he could hear the rumble of a locomotive under load. But the overwhelming sound was that of the locusts hiding in the trees. Listened to intensely, the sound became deafening. Headlights off, Cole made the turn down the narrow lane and idled the car toward the mansion. The front of the building was fully lit as if to show it off. The street was dark and Cole stopped momentarily in front of the mansion to study the surveillance cameras. The binoculars worked well in the partial light and Cole counted four cameras as he passed.

Cole prepared for his second pass with the high resolution video camera mounted on a short tripod leg. He edged the car down the narrow lane. While studying the mansion through the binoculars, he held the camera out the window by its tripod leg to slowly pan across the entire front of the mansion. As the car crawled past the second leg of the circular drive, he saw headlights heading up the lane in front of him. The approaching vehicle was a dark, full-size sedan and just before it got to Cole, it turned sharply to the left, blocking the roadway. It was then that Cole saw the second car just turning up the lane behind him.

Cole mashed the pedal and veered off the narrow lane to hug the side of the borrow ditch. It worked and he cleared the sedan. As he passed, he saw the passenger getting out of the sedan with a frightful weapon: a submachine gun with a silencer. Cole wrenched the steering wheel hard to the left to pull the car back up on the roadway. The car overreacted and returned to the roadway cross-wise. It was then that Cole heard the rapid, muffled, ti-ti-ti-ti-ti sound of bullets coming from the gun. The sound was almost masked by destructive, metal-ripping noise coming from the rear quarter panel of his car. Cole pulled the wheel back hard to the right to regain some element of control and keep the car from going off the other side of the road. But the momentum of the car, along with the now-destroyed left rear tire, was too much to overcome and the car dived off the road, plunging

     Brian David Simmons

into the drainage ditch and then flipping over onto its top. Stunned but unhurt, Cole heard more bullet impacts from the silenced machine gun and scrambled out the window.

He made a hundred-yard dash like he'd never run before, hearing only the ti-ti-ti-ti behind him. Cole triggered a sensor when he entered a neighbor's yard and huge overhead lights clicked on to illuminate the whole acre-sized front yard. Cole's adrenaline raced and he turned on even more speed. He heard the sedan behind him squeal its tires as it got turned around. Cole was now on the pavement, running with adrenaline-fueled speed like he'd never known before. The car behind him was accelerating, coming closer, coming faster, and coming for him. Cole dived off the road into the borrow ditch just as the car got to him. The car slammed on its brakes and passed Cole. He scrambled to his feet and took off across a yard, only to hear the ti-ti-ti-ti-ti of the silenced machine gun behind him. He didn't look back; he just dug from the depths of his strength and ran like hell. He passed between two mansions and turned to his left, never looking back to check on his pursuers. The machine gun fire stopped and he started to believe that he had eluded them. Cole breathed a little easier and slowed his pace as he approached Garden Road. He glanced back and didn't see anybody; but as he turned his head back he heard the sedan accelerating down Garden Road. He didn't see it but it was coming.

Cole poured on the speed again and, as he crossed the road, he saw the sedan coming at him with its headlights off. It pulled up short and Cole saw two men get out, each carrying a machine gun. But Cole was now in the park and, with trees for cover, confident that he could evade them. He entered a small stand of trees and found one just inside that he could momentarily hide behind. Like a scared deer in the forest, he froze with only his head peering out from behind the tree. His eyes struggled beyond all normal expectation to penetrate through the darkness and find his pursuers.

The tree exploded next to his left cheek and splinters pelted the side of his face with violent force. He screamed in pain and bolted from the tree; but where had the shot come from? Was he running in harm's direction? With an instant of indecision, Cole stopped at a tree providing a vantage point of the opening behind. Where had the bullet come from? Cole searched with his eyes but could see nothing. Cole's face hurt. He felt the blood running down his neck and the growing sensation of his shirt becoming wet.

A small branch on the tree in front of Cole broke with a crack and swung down, dangling, as Cole heard the bullet whistle past his head. Cole broke to his right, charging through the edge of the trees. Momentarily, he would emerge from the trees becoming fully exposed. It wasn't a machine gun he was now eluding; its sound was distinctly different. It was the

     Brian David Simmons

familiar sound of a high power rifle, not too different from one of his own.

The image of Melvin's rifle formed in his mind: thousand-yard capability, recoil mechanism, night scope, and bolt action—a sniper's weapon with no other purpose than to kill from great distances. But with a bolt action to eject the spent shell and load another round, he guessed that he had seconds before the rifle could fire again and emerged from the trees at a full gait, only to encounter a machine gun-carrying pursuer. Terror cried out in Cole's mind. How did they know? He made an instant left, losing his footing on the wet grass and going down as he heard the ti-ti-ti-ti of the machine gun. Like a sprinter coming off the starting block, Cole was up in an instant and off at a frantic pace. But he was headed in the direction of the high-powered rifle. Out of terrified instinct, Cole dodged right to avoid another shot from the rifle and then put on the speed. His normally composed and calculating mind gave way to stark, raving terror and he ran like only a madman can. He turned and blasted into another small stand of trees, taking a whipping by unseen tree branches as he crashed through. The branches stung as they ripped past his face, arms, and torso, tearing clothing and taking skin. He didn't stop this time to check behind him; he just ran.

Back out in the open, running at full speed, Cole began to regain control of his terror and evaluate his situation. The lessons nature had taught him about being invisible didn't work here. It was their hunting ground and he was the hunted. They knew his every move and spotted him when no one could. They had eyes; he was blind. They were many; he was one. The odds against survival were nil unless he gained an advantage, any advantage.

Cole could see the glimmering streetlight at Lorring and Garden. He veered to his right to flank the machine gun goon and charged on toward the light. A few sparsely spaced trees obscured full view of the street but a sedan was clearly visible under the streetlight. With the sniper now to his rear and gunmen in the darkness, he had no choice but to race on toward the light.

As Cole fled across the open expanse of the park, he sensed the touch of the rifle sighting in on him. The cross hairs first lining up on his torso and then, estimating movement, moving ahead for the shot. It was the high-power rifle that he feared most. He knew that it could reach out with one shot and kill. The rifleman now had to be across the park to his rear and slightly to his left. Cole couldn't see him, but knew he was there nonetheless. With calculating instinct, Cole erratically jogged left and then back to the right toward the street light. The intersection was now less than a hundred yards away and he pressed on, anticipating his escape. He again made an erratic pair of turns. If the rifle fired, Cole didn't hear it. He detected movement from his peripheral vision off to his left, but didn't see anything

     Brian David Simmons

when he glanced over his shoulder. Gut feel for the timing of the rifle and the sensation of its cross hairs told him it was time again; he repeated his sudden jog to the right. This time he heard the bullet whistle past as he jogged back to the left and ran faster toward the streetlight. The sedan was empty and there was no one in the intersection; he was close. The rifleman could get, maybe, one more shot off.

Cole was within twenty feet of the sedan when he realized the movement he had detected earlier was a pursuer running at edge of the trees. He heard the distant ti-ti-ti-ti-ti of the machine gun spraying a random blast into the air with only a hail-Mary hope of hitting him. Cole didn't slow as he passed the front of the sedan and ran through the lit intersection. He had escaped the terror of the park but he hadn't evaded his pursuers, yet. He was several hundred yards ahead of them and with a little luck, he could beat them to Piedmont Hospital. There had to people there at all hours of the night and if he could get there, he would no longer be the only possible target. His pursuers would have to question every face and wonder about hundreds of hiding places.

Cole saw the emergency room sign and cut across the corner to the well-lit entrance. The door opened automatically as Cole approached. Still wearing the surgical gloves, Cole grasped his shirt and wrung out enough blood to leave his hand dripping wet. He slung his hand at the pavement, leaving a distinct line of red speckles. Grasping the frame of the door, he ran his hand across the glass to leave a brilliant red streak. He squeezed his shirt to again milk more blood, then flung it inward to splatter the white floor.

Cole heard the squeal of tires rounding the corner and dove over the planter adjacent to the entrance. On his hands and knees in the shrubbery, he made his way along the edge of the building and out of sight of the emergency entrance. He didn't look back to see if his deception worked; if it didn't, he would know soon enough. He kept going.

Cole had learned all too well that his pursuers had eyes in the dark, and he knew he still wasn't safe. As he skirted the building, he watched the road for oncoming headlights, both from front and behind. Except for the rumble of the nearby freeway, it was quiet and the side street was empty.

He detected the glimmer of headlights and dropped to embed himself in the vine ground cover. With his toes, he inched himself forward to force his body under ground-clinging vines and obscure himself from view of the road. He peered out from his hiding place to see the sedan stop directly in front of him. Fear told him to bolt and run, but instinct told him to stay put. He was close enough to make out facial features on the passenger. He was a young Caucasian man, with a small mustache and crew-cut hair. He was wearing a suit that would have been the envy of most businessmen. He had on a strange headset with a

    Brian David Simmons

microphone positioned directly in front of his mouth. He was talking quietly. Cole couldn't hear what he was saying. The conversation had the man's attention and he stared straight ahead instead of in Cole's direction. He adjusted the position of the microphone and turned to the driver. Then, the sedan roared away with a sudden burst of acceleration. Cole watched it as it made a tire-screeching U-turn at the next intersection and then sped past him. It headed back to the emergency entrance. Now was Cole's chance.

He broke from his vine entanglement and ran along the hospital until he was sure it was safe to cross the street. With the few needed minutes of rest and a chance to catch his breath, Cole's stride was now refreshed and he darted across the street, cut the corner at the intersection, and was quickly clear of the hospital. He maintained a steady pace, pounding the pavement with every stride, toward the freeway. He had eluded his pursuers but now he had to preserve his anonymity.

Cole had lost the rental car and was now without transportation. A taxi ride would have given his feet a welcome rest but it would also provide a trail. The buses weren't running at this hour and that was not an option. The subway was an unknown. It wasn't that far back to the apartment, at least as the crow flies, and he was still in good enough shape to make the hike. He estimated it at three, maybe four miles, and decided that he could make it before sunup. Cole crossed under the freeway and turned back north along a side street through a residential area. He would follow the rumble of the freeway, using it as is his guide, and stay in the cover of small side streets. His problem now was to avoid detection—a cruising police car, barking dog, roadway traffic, or anything that would call attention to himself.

Cole alternated jogging and walking to increase his distance from the hospital. By now, his pursuers would have figured out that they had been deceived and would have resumed their search. Or maybe they would have returned to the rental car to look for clues. What would they find? A briefcase with only a pair of binoculars, video camera, and videotape. The briefcase came from a secondhand store and had no traceable markings. The video camera was unique and unusual but still not traceable. The only thing on the tape was Laughlin's mansion. He had put his tape of Sugar Ike's house in the mail for Kevin's analysis. The binoculars were Melvin's. Would he recognize them? Maybe, but then maybe not; they probably weren't uncommon for people in his line of work. Cole had left his glasses back at the apartment. He had lost his baseball cap in the scramble, but that too was generic. There were no notes or paperwork in the car, not even a rental contract; he had cleaned out the entire car. There were no fingerprints; he had been careful to wear his surgical gloves and never pulled on a door handle or touched anything else in any way that would have

     Brian David Simmons

left a fingerprint. If they found the little rental car sticker in the windshield or traced the license number it would lead to them to the airport and a two-week rental agreement for Melvin Roberson. Cole analyzed the loss of the car and concluded that he was probably safe, unless Melvin was involved and started putting ordinarily innocuous facts together. If he did, he might conclude it had something to do with his unpleasant experience back in Utah.

It started to rain. It wasn't a delicate, cool rain like Cole was used to in Utah; it was a downpour of warm water that soaked him instantly. Cole estimated he was halfway home and tried to keep up the pace. He jogged as much as he could, but he was tiring and walked more and more often. He replayed the events in the park as he pushed on. How did they know I was there to begin with? He had taken no aggressive action, he hadn't trespassed, fired a gun, or anything. He just drove by. Maybe the video camera on its tripod looked like a gun from a distance? Then, in the park, they knew and anticipated his every move. A rifle had made long-range shots in nearly complete darkness. Whoever was doing the shooting was good; thank God he wasn't good enough. Every time he advanced, they anticipated his move and intercepted. They must have had infrared night vision. That was the only way. They also had communications allowing them to hunt as a team, driving and trapping their game.

The little side street emptied out onto Dresden. He was only two blocks from the apartment. It had stopped raining and the sky was starting to glow through a thick haze. Cole walked at a rapid pace down Dresden. Traffic was light but seemed to increase with every step. Hopefully, nobody would give him a second look in the dim light or, if they did, just write him off as a street person. He had to look terrible; maybe that was a disguise in itself. Cole crossed Dresden at the corner and was soon inside the apartment building.

All those irritating little peepholes seemed to be watching him and he hurried his pace. He hit every other step on his way to the second floor only to meet Joe in the hallway.

"Sweet Jesus. You all right, boy?"

"Yes, sir," said Cole, not realizing how bad he really looked.

"You don't look it. You should be in the hospital."

"No. I'm fine, really. But I need to go now. I'll stop by and we'll talk later."

Cole hurried down the hall, afraid he would run into somebody else, to his apartment, and once inside, realized why Joe seemed so concerned. In the mirror, he saw his face. It was a bloody, swollen mess with scabs starting to form around protruding splinters on the left side and tree-whipped lacerations on the rest. His clothes were tattered, torn, and bloodstained. He had been through hell and he looked like it.

Cole took off his clothes, got in the shower and let the warm water soften and wash away the scabs from his splintered face. By feel, he began the process of pulling out the splinters one by one. Blood ran down his cheek and mixed with water, turning the shower floor red. He got the largest ones in the shower and finished up in front of the mirror. Naked, in front of the mirror, he heard a faint knock at the door. Quickly, he put on a pair of pants and with trepidation, approached the peephole in the apartment door. It was the old woman from the convenience store.

He hollered through the door, "I'm busy. I can't come to the door right now."

"Joe said you needed some help and I wasn't to take no for an answer," came the reply.

"Just a minute," said Cole as he scrambled to hide the video camera. He returned to the door and opened it. Cole towered over the small frail woman who stepped through the door and instantly took charge.

"Joe wasn't kidding. Now you just sit right down on the couch and let me have a look," said the woman as she put her hand on Cole's bare chest and gave him a push.

Cole did as she said and let the woman mother him. She delicately probed Cole's swollen cheek and removed the remaining splinters. Her touch was so delicate that Cole could hardly feel her work. She probed, cleaned and then applied soothing liniment to Cole's wounds with motherly love. She enjoyed the mothering as much as Cole needed it.

"I don't suppose you want to tell me what happened?"

"No, ma'am. I'm a little embarrassed about it."

"You were the young man in the store yesterday. Joe told me we had a new neighbor. He said no white boy, or other for that matter, had called him 'sir' in a long time. He thinks you'll be a good neighbor."

"Yes, ma'am. But I don't know how long I'm going to stay."

"Well as long as you're here, you just let Joe or me know if you need anything."

"Yes, ma'am."

Sylvia went on as she worked, "You know, I met Joe in a hospital. That's where I learned my nursing skills. I wasn't a real nurse, just an aid. But when things were bad, there wasn't much difference between nurses and aids; for that matter, sometimes there wasn't much difference between nurses and doctors. Joe broke his arm when a flatbed load fell on him. He was hauling for Denk's Trucking out of Memphis and when they brought him into the hospital, there were only two of us on duty in the emergency room. You know, when I set his arm, he didn't holler or even flinch. He's my iron man. Then, when he came in to get his cast off, he asked me on a date and that was it. We got married a month later. The only problem was the color thing. Back then things were different; Joe's friends all wanted to know how come he married a 'wetback' and my family didn't speak to me for two years cause I married a 'darky,' as they called him."

     Brian David Simmons

The one-sided conversation went on as Sylvia worked to bandage Cole's cheek and the larger of his lacerations. Joe had retired from truck driving and invested their life savings in the little convenience store. He had done his homework and anticipated owning a convenience store years before he finally bought. He evaluated locations and predicted the sprawling growth of Atlanta to select just the right store. The store was a converted gas station and wasn't much to look at. But it was nestled between two suburban areas along a side street with ever-increasing traffic and the potential for ever-increasing profit.

Social security and the pension of a truck driver were only enough to provide for mere survival. The convenience store offered them the opportunity to catch up with life, and maybe even get ahead. However, when Sylvia had a mastectomy, the burden of the store and medical bills was too much, and Joe was forced to sell.

Under duress, he had sold the store to Isaac Bartrum with the agreement that Joe and Sylvia would continue to operate the store for a flat five thousand dollars a month. It was hardly the dream they had hoped for, but it supplemented their income enough to hopefully someday make their dream a reality.

With insight and intuition, Cole interpreted what she didn't say. Isaac Bartrum had cheated them and now had them as captive employees. It was a sad conclusion to what should have been their retirement and it bothered Cole, but he kept his insights to himself and let the woman finish with her maternal work.

"There, all done. In a few days, you'll be as handsome as ever."

"Yes, ma'am."

"Now you need anything, you just let me know. I'm right down the hall in two-sixteen," said Sylvia as she re-packed her first aid kit. Cole could tell she was tiring from the exertion and it revealed her fragile physical condition. He didn't let on. Instead, he just carefully helped her to the door.

"Yes, ma'am," he said as they walked, arms locked, to the door. "Thank you very much. I don't know what I would have done without you."

Cole closed the door behind her and retreated to the bedroom. He was exhausted and it felt good to stretch out on the bed. Cole was thankful for the help but he didn't want friends that he would have to leave behind or that someday might have to identify him. He thought more about the old couple and marveled at the bonds that tie a man and woman together for a lifetime. He was her iron man and she was his jewel. How wonderful. Momentarily, he thought of Carol as he dozed off into a deep sleep.

 Brian David Simmons

Chapter Twelve

CITY OF SURVIVAL: MORE THAN SIMPLE SURVEILLANCE

COLE SLEPT MOST OF THE DAY. IT WAS MORE SLEEP than he had gotten in a long time. It rejuvenated him and he felt as good as ever. He had forgotten to reset the video camera before he went to sleep and was contemplating what to do next. First, he wasn't going back to Laughlin's. Second, whatever he decided to do, he needed transportation. Cole painfully slid the frame of his glasses past his bandage and then adjusted them for a tolerable fit. He had become accustomed to a baseball cap and glanced around the apartment before he realized that it was now probably the best clue Laughlin had about his identity.

His mood changed when he remembered what he already knew. After a Patriot Rebirth Society training exercise, essentially war games, they had always held a post event debrief. Cole compared his actions, or lack thereof, from the previous night to what his training had taught him. He had failed. His father and other commanders would have chewed his ass. Regardless of the situation, regardless of the strength of the opposing force, regardless of armaments, the tactic was always action – not reaction. Last night he had done nothing but react, being driven, pursued, and nearly killed. He had gotten lucky. Best odds for survival in any situation were always with action. Cole imagined the rebuke from his father: "You might die, but your survival odds are still better than reacting, being a puppet, waiting on the action of others. You need to control the situation by acting first and putting your enemy on the defensive. Only then will you gain the advantage." Next time it would be different, he assured himself.

Cole found the bus stop nearest the apartment and caught the first bus without regard for its destination. He watched out the window as the bus made its way through the city until he spotted a used car lot. It had just what he needed. "All Cars for Less Than $10,000.00, " read the sign. Cole got off the bus at the next stop and walked back to the car lot. He felt the stiffness in his legs from the previous night's activities and it reminded him of his high school football days. He found a jewel on the car lot; it was American-made minivan. It was silver gray and came complete with a dent in the rear and factory paint peeling off the hood—it was perfect. There were at least ten just like it in every supermarket parking lot in America. The salesman was there in an instant, and Cole was soon negotiating a price. With a short test drive, Cole and the salesman sat down in the office to complete the necessary paperwork.

"Eight thousand even, including tax and license. That's a bargain," congratulated the salesman.

     Brian David Simmons

It was no deal at all; in fact, it was nothing but robbery. But it was a car. Cole shook the salesman's hand and nodded.

"Now just give me your name again and we'll have you on your way with a new set of wheels."

"Isaac Bartrum," replied Cole.

The salesman looked at him strangely and asked, "Are you sure?"

"Yes."

"And the address?"

From memory Cole recited Sugar Ike's home address and the paperwork was finished, at least as far as Cole was concerned. Cole pulled a wad of cash out of his pocket and counted out eight thousand dollars. The salesman handed Cole the keys and the deal was done.

Cole wiped down the steering wheel before putting on another pair of surgical gloves. He pulled out of the car lot and went immediately in search of a gas station. The needle was on "E" and the low fuel light glowed. No doubt the used car lot wasn't about to give anything away, even a few meager gallons of gas. Cole found his gas station and also picked up a new baseball cap when he paid for his gas.

It was early evening and sun had just disappeared from the sky. Cole didn't have a specific plan. He just drove around the city, retracing his earlier travels and contemplating his next move. He drove past the rest of the IAB convenience stores to confirm his conclusions about Laughlin's lack of business. In each case, there was no more than one car out front and an equal lack of activity inside. The last stop was the IAB across from the apartment building. He parked the van in an unassuming place and went to the IAB to thank Joe. Joe was inside alone, reading the evening paper and was glad to see Cole, or anybody for that matter to break the monotony.

"You're looking a lot better, Cody. How you feelin'?"

"Just fine. Sylvia fixed me up just fine."

"Yeah, she's just that way. That's why I married her. How about you? You got your eyes on any little sweet thing?"

"No, sir. Not at the present. Sure seems slow around here." said Cole, changing the subject.

"Tomorrow things'll pick up. We do most of our business on Friday and Saturday."

"Is that right?"

"Yep, sell beer, mostly. Of course, Friday's pickup day, too."

"Pickup day?"

"Sure, IAB security picks up the week's take and changes out the register disk. Every Friday, the armored car shows up at five and backs up to the front door. Two armed guards march in like the Gestapo, clean out the safe, change the register disc, and march out. They don't even bother to say hi."

Now Cole had something to go on. With a few more friendly words, Cole determined that the pickup

     Brian David Simmons

occurred sometime in the late afternoon and he started anticipating tomorrow's adventure. For now, he would just have to wait. The conversation turned back to Sylvia as they watched her step out of the front of the apartment building. Joe had many fond memories of life with the woman. He glowed with the light of love when he shared them.

As Sylvia slowly moved toward the corner, four hands reached from the alley shadows and pulled her in. Joe screamed and started to move toward the end of the counter. Cole was already out the front door. He dodged an oncoming Toyota and brought a red pickup to a screeching halt as he flew across four lanes of traffic.

Cole passed a defunct Mexican restaurant and bounced off the wall as he entered the alley. Three men, startled by Cole's abrupt entrance, fled down the alley with the contents of Sylvia's handbag. Sylvia was okay, just tearfully upset by the incident and happy to have Cole's arm around her.

The three men jumped into a 70s vintage Chevy and it roared as it came to life. The tires chirped as it began its full-throttle charge toward Sylvia and Cole. Cole swept Sylvia into his arms and dashed toward the alley's entrance. The Chevy caught Cole just as he reached the sidewalk. Its fender thumped him in the butt, bouncing him, with Sylvia cradled in his arms, into a spin. Cole cushioned the full brunt of their fall as he skidded to a halt on his back, just outside the

Chevy's path. The Chevy never left Cole's sight as it turned right out of the alley and squealed away.

Joe was there moments later and the tearful but unharmed Sylvia hugged him with all her strength. The two were so engrossed in each other with the celebration of reunion that they didn't notice Cole slip away. Cole was back across Dresden in seconds and standing at the door of his ugly duckling minivan in only a few more. Cole put on his gloves as he climbed in. It started instantly and he turned left down Dresden, momentarily glancing at Joe and Sylvia, still in an emotional embrace.

How better to get to know Atlanta than to spend an evening learning about its underbelly, thought Cole. He had lost sight of the Chevy but frantically maneuvered the minivan in and out of traffic. The minivan was gutless, forcing Cole to keep the speed up and avoid traffic with erratic maneuvers. He caught the Chevy in two blocks and slowed to blend in with traffic. He used all the tricks he instinctively knew, staying well back but never losing sight completely. It only stayed on Dresden for another two blocks before turning right. Cole followed. The Chevy's final destination was a rundown section of northeast Atlanta. It stopped in front of a house that reminded Cole of his drug-dealing neighbor back in Utah. Two men got out and went to the door. They returned to the car a few moments later and then drove down the block. It turned right again and then pulled in the driveway of

     Brian David Simmons

a small, deteriorating house. The house was barren of all paint and had several boarded-up windows. Cole cruised past the house as the three were getting out. He parked the van down the street, out of sight. He was in the mood for a real direct conversation with this bunch.

Cole figured they had just made their buy and he didn't want to give them the opportunity to get fuzzy minded; they needed to feel some pain. He went straight to the house and tried to peer through windows with drawn curtains. He got a glimpse inside but didn't see anybody. As he moved to the back of the house, he formulated his plan. Just like high school football, he would barge in the rear and charge through the house, using his body to run over the opposition. If it looked too ugly, he wouldn't stop. He would just bust through the front door and be on his way back down the street. They would never know what hit them.

Cole picked up a warped two-by-four at the rear of the house and then crept up the back porch. He turned the door handle and the rear door creaked open. Three black men were sitting at the kitchen table cooking white powder in a spoon. They turned to look as Cole rushed in and whacked the one closest with the two-by-four. Another turned to reach for a gun on the kitchen counter, but with rhythmic motion, Cole popped the man still sitting at the table with the butt end of his club, then dropped him cold with a whirling blow to the head, just as his hand reached the gun. The other two men were on the floor, scrambling to get their feet.

Cole screamed, "Sit," as he turned, swinging his two-by-four, to break one man's kneecap and return him to the floor. The third man made a break for the door, but Cole made a standing tackle before he got through the doorway and whirled him around to thrust him into the lap of his sobbing partner with the broken knee.

Cole closed the door behind him and calmly said, "Conversation time."

The third man leaned forward, as if to get up off his friend's lap. Cole let go with a field-goal kick to his face. "Didn't you hear me say sit," screamed Cole, and without hesitation, picked up his two-by-four and let go with another full swing to catch the man's arm as he raised it to guard his head. Cole caught the arm right below the elbow. The two-by-four stung Cole's hands as it fractured and drove the man's radius and ulna bones out of the synovial cavity, ripping tendons and exposing broken bones. The man cried out with pain and folded over, face down on the floor. Cole let go with a sharp jab with the two-by-four to the man's back and again screamed at him, "Turn over, now!" The man rolled over and assumed a sitting position next to his friend. Both men were bawling and babbling. The third man lay unconscious. Cole had control.

     Brian David Simmons

"What do ya want? We ain't done nothing," balled one of the men.

"Shut up," replied Cole as he mildly jabbed the man in the face with his two-by-four. "Not one word out of either one of you unless I ask."

The pair quit babbling but couldn't completely contain their misery and continued to whimper. Cole momentarily stepped away and with the blunt end of his two-by-four, jabbed the man on the floor near the kitchen counter. He got no reaction. He was either dead or out cold. Cole turned back to the other two. The man with the broken kneecap started to move as if he might try an escape down the hallway, but quickly changed his mind when he realized Cole was looking at him.

Cole jabbed him in the chest with the two-by-four and said, "That's for thinking about it." Cole turned off the light in the kitchen and set up a chair to face the two terrified men.

"Now, we are going to have a little chat. I ask the questions. You provide the answers. If I don't like the answer, your reward is a face full of two-by-four. Understand?"

Cole got a nod from both whimpering men and continued with his demands, "Give me your car keys."

"They're on the counter."

"All right, where you boys been tonight?"

"We, ah, we out looking for a—a whore. Yeah, that it—a whore." Which got the man an immediate rap to face with the two-by-four. His head bounced off the refrigerator and even in the dark, Cole could see he had hit him too hard. Blood gushed from the man's nose and he fell forward, his head hitting the floor between his legs with a thud. Cole didn't let up.

"Now look what he made me do. If he would have just told the truth, he could have lived. Now, what about you?" Cole prompted the other man with his two-by-four.

"We out scrounging for money. Hit some old lady. That's all, man."

"Why the old lady?"

"Just thought she was Mex'is, man, that's all."

"Maybe Mexicans are my friends. Why not the Food and Liquor down the street?"

"No way, man. That's Sugar Ike's."

"So?"

"Hey, man. Everybody knows not to mess with Ike."

"Why not?"

He hesitated to speak, but looked at his hunched-over friend next to him and then released his answer. "Look, man. Sugar Ike is king. Nobody messes with him and lives to tell. He knows everything about everybody and if he wants you, he'll find you. Sugar moves everything in the city. He runs all the crack, smack, ludes, juice—you name it, he moves it. You cross him and you're out. He puts your name out and no more stuff."

Cole went on with the questioning and obtained names of local kids who idealized Ike and had gone on to become local legends in Ike's organization. It was surprising how much common street knowledge there was about this Sugar Ike. The man talked for an hour or so, until Cole figured he had enough. As a distraction, Cole left the man with confusing thoughts.

"Now, I have a sixteen-year old sister down here. She has blond hair and three rings in her nose. Have you seen her, huh?" asked Cole as he jabbed at the man's chest.

"No. No, man."

"If you do, you best not touch her. If you do, I'll be back with this two-by-four and you'll look like your friends. Now you spread the word. Anybody sees my sister, they better leave her alone. Got it?"

"Yeah, man. Yeah, I got it," blurted the man excitedly, realizing that his torment was almost over.

"Okay. Here's the way it works. You live if you sit here for five minutes and think about my sister. If you move, I'll come back in and kill you. If you tell anybody what I look like, I'll come back and kill you. Got it?"

"Yeah. Yeah, I got it," said the man with a ring of excitement to his voice.

"If you want to live, remember what I said about my sister," said Cole as he opened the back door and stepped outside.

Cole dropped the two-by-four as he started his full-out run for the van. God, I hope it starts, thought Cole, but realized he didn't have the right to ask God for anything. Cole reached the van and it started. Only seconds after leaving the house, Cole was around the corner and headed back toward Dresden. What did God think of his actions tonight, and why don't I have at least some small feeling of remorse? I killed two people tonight for no real reason at all and I might just as well have gone to a ball game. This is the path I've chosen and it doesn't bother me at all. I am fucked in the head. I am destined for hell.

Shortly, he neared the apartment, parked his minivan back in its nondescript parking place, and returned to his apartment. The day was over and tomorrow he would track this Sugar Ike character. He stared at the ceiling planning the day's events until nearly dawn when he managed to finally doze off.

It was near noon when Cole finally woke. It was another hot day and the refrigeration unit in the apartment couldn't keep up. Cole dawdled around the apartment, straightening up, resetting the video camera, and cooking bacon to go with his cold cereal. The bandage on his face was discoloring around the edges from sweat and oozing purulence; it was in need of replacement.

Cole finished with his morning activities and ventured out to get first aid supplies. He also needed to replace the handheld video camera and binoculars he had lost. He found everything he needed at nearby Bass Sporting Goods and Circuit City stores, and was soon back at the apartment. The binoculars and

     Brian David Simmons

camera were nothing compared to the ones he had lost, but they were the best available. He checked out the clarity and magnification of the binoculars by watching Joe across the street in the convenience store. They were ten by fifty and were adequate.

Cole stood in front of the mirror, slowly and painful peeling the bandage from his face to reveal his swollen, damaged cheek. The body's defense mechanisms were fighting the impending infection and expelling the depleted antibiotic fluid to encrust on the surface. His face looked terrible. When he got back to Utah, he would have to have it looked at by a professional. But for now, his amateurish bandaging would have to do. He gently and patiently swabbed the encrusted areas with hydrogen peroxide, softening and removing them to reveal his blue-black and red-peppered cheek. It didn't look so bad cleaned up. Cole covered it with a four-by-four sterile gauze pad and taped it around the edges. It didn't hold very well. Cole ended up making a cravat over the top of his head and under his chin to hold the gauze pad in place. His bandaging wasn't nearly as neat as Sylvia's but at least it covered the wound. One thing was for sure, anybody that saw him would remember the oversize bandaging and facial lacerations. For the near term, it meant that he had no disguise. He would have to be extra careful.

Cole wasn't sure when the pickup was going to be made, but he needed to be ready. He also wasn't sure what this afternoon would bring and decided to take his hunting knife. Cole used the medical tape to loosely, but securely, bind the knife's scabbard to his leg so as to conceal it within his pant leg. Cole loaded the handheld video camera and put it along with the binoculars back in the shopping bag. Before exiting the apartment, Cole checked the hallway; it was clear. He discreetly made his way to the first floor. On the first floor, he again had to pass all the unnerving little door peepholes, not knowing who was watching and committing his appearance to memory.

Cole exited the apartment building to find the building manager sitting in a chair, rocked up against the building. He looked at Cole strangely. Cole knew that his appearance had just been committed to a mental photograph that could link him to the apartment. He could never come back without wondering if that link would provide a trail to his extracurricular activities.

Cole pointed at the cravat and said, "Bad tooth," and then walked down the street. He could feel the building manager's eyes watching his every step and didn't cross the street until completely out of sight of the apartment building. As he worked his way back toward the minivan, he stayed close to storefronts and made every attempt to stay out of the manager's line of sight. But he wasn't sure how successful he had been.

Cole climbed into the minivan and began his surveillance of the convenience store. Traffic on Dresden was already heavy and it was only late afternoon. He felt like an obtrusive trespasser for all to see. The van didn't provide for concealment and the cravat on his head was an attention getter. He yearned for the coming of dark and the comfort of obscurity that it brought. It was a hot, muggy afternoon and a slight drizzle didn't provide for any cooling. Cole waited patiently for hours, watching every vehicle that passed until finally he spotted the armored car. It passed in front of him and then turned into the convenience store parking lot. Cole started the minivan and inched it toward the street to get a view down the block.

It was no more than five minutes until it re-emerged on Dresden. Cole pulled out just in time to see it make a right at the first corner. He mashed the accelerator to the floor, but the minivan only marginally responded. The armored car was well down the block when Cole rounded the corner. He realized he was going to have to stay a little closer if he was going to avoid losing it. Cole weaved his way through traffic to close the distance and was only a few car lengths behind the armored car when it signaled to get on the I-75 South on-ramp. Cole let the distance between him and the armored car increase as they got on the freeway, and then let the distance increase even further. The armored car was easy to see and there was no reason to crowd it. Traffic was heavy and Cole made a few lane changes, varying his cruising speed to advance with traffic for short periods of time, and then moving out of the fast lane to fall well behind.

Cole was well behind when the armored van positioned itself to go through the interchange onto I-20 West. Cole emulated the moves and found himself facing the setting sun on I-20. It was breaking through the overcast sky, illuminating the west with bright red brilliance and making the armored car more difficult to see. Cole closed his following distance. An accident brought traffic to a near standstill with everybody slowing and straining their necks in an attempt to get a glimpse of somebody else's misfortune. Cole lost sight of the armored car momentarily as it passed the accident and then accelerated back to freeway speeds. He worked to catch up and close on the armored car as it signaled to exit the freeway on Fulton Industrial Boulevard. He had to make two lane changes to follow, but did it methodically so that it looked planned. Cole was only a few car lengths behind as they exited the freeway but dropped back to a comfortable following distance when they merged into traffic on Fulton.

The armored car signaled and entered the left turn lane for Mableton Parkway. Cole tried to follow but couldn't get to the left turn lane and then got caught by the light. When the light finally changed, the armored car was out of sight. Cole mashed the gas pedal and worked his way through traffic. With a quick U-turn, Cole was back to Mableton. The Fulton County Airport was on his right, which meant that if the armored car had turned off, it had to have taken a side street to the left. Cole carefully studied each road to the right as he cruised down Fulton. It was an industrial area with large and small metal buildings spread out on a myriad little side streets. Some had fenced lots, others didn't. Cole passed Werkiel Drive and caught a glimpse of an industrial building down the street, not so different from the others, but surrounded by an eight-foot chain link fence with coiling serpentine wire extending its height another two feet. Cole guessed and made the first possible left.

As he made the left off of Mableton, he noticed a white sedan in his rear view mirror that made the left with him. For an instant, Cole thought it might be a cop—he had been speeding down Mableton. He realized he was in trouble when he studied the two men in the car; they were both clean-cut, suit-wearing business types and the passenger was putting on a headset. How did they know, thought Cole. I don't even know where the armored car went. It's impossible. Outrunning them in the minivan was not an option and Cole needed to know if they were really following him. Maybe they weren't after him; maybe they were just out on a patrol or something. He slowed and turned into the parking lot of a tool supply business and watched his rear-view mirror for the reaction of the white sedan. Cole stopped in front of the entrance at the same time that the sedan pulled up along the curb.

His options were limited. There was still enough light to see and there was no way he could outrun or hide from them. He decided on a little play-acting and got out of the van to test the door on the tool supply business. It was after business hours and the door was locked. He yanked at it a couple of times and turned, as if in disgust, to return to the minivan. The sedan was moving very slowly, into the parking lot. Cole walked back to the minivan and got inside with just enough time to back up a car length before the sedan blocked his rearward progress. They didn't move; they just sat there, as if to intimidate Cole into making his move. Cole mashed the gas pedal to the floor and pulled the shift lever into drive, chirping the front tires and bouncing the minivan over the sidewalk into the front of the building. The glass door and glass front on the tool supply shattered with an explosion and the van stopped, halfway in, high centered on the low lying window ledge. Cole jumped from the van with his shopping bag in hand and disappeared into the darkness of the unlit store.

He didn't waste time. The store presumably had an alarm system that would summon rent-a-cops or police and hopefully scare off his pursuers. Cole found a rear entrance to the store and swiftly exited.

This time things were going to be different. He wasn't going to be pursued; he was going to be the pursuer. From the corner of the building, Cole watched the sedan pull from the parking lot and make an immediate left back toward Werkiel. They had now seen him in the daylight and probably had the license number of the minivan. It would eventually lead them back to the used car lot. But then, nowhere.

     Brian David Simmons

He followed on foot, dashing across the street to find another vantage point behind a dumpster. A siren could be heard off in the distance. The sedan made a right on Werkiel and then disappeared from sight. Cole ran in pursuit, cutting diagonally across the street and then shortcut the corner by going behind a large industrial warehouse. From the back corner of the warehouse, he could see a large door just closing behind the white sedan.

The warehouse was a large, two-story, steel building with no windows. It sat on a large, empty lot surrounded by chain link and serpentine wire. The fence was impenetrable, and even in the dim light Cole could see surveillance cameras covering every possible approach. The best he could do was watch from a distance.

Cole relaxed for a moment hiding behind the warehouse evaluating his options. Soon police or rent-a-cops would be cruising the area looking for the owner of the minivan and he needed to be out of sight. He also needed a vantage point to observe the building across the street. Cole inspected every possible entry along the back of the warehouse but it had no windows and the back door was locked and wired for security; the warehouse was impenetrable from the rear. The roof was inaccessible except for a flimsy drainpipe. Cole tested it and it nearly came loose from the building; it didn't look like much of an option.

In the distance, Cole heard the squeal of tires. Police would be cruising soon and he was in plain sight at the rear of the building. He was out of options. Cole put the binoculars around his neck and the camera strap around his wrist, then grasped the drainpipe. Hand over hand, he rhythmically inched his way up the pipe. The climb required every bit of strength his over-sized hands could deliver. The warehouse was at least two stories high and he strained to maintain his grip with every advance. It was a four-inch diameter pipe and each hand hold barely grasped the diameter of the pipe. His fingers were near their limit when he reached the top and a bigger challenge. He lunged upward and outward to hook his fingertips over the edge of the gutter and then let go of the pipe. He swung freely along side the warehouse, in open view from Werkiel and the building on the other side. He pulled up to chin level and then, with a kick of his feet and the strength of his arms, propelled his body above the edge of the gutter. His momentum rocked him forward to rest his face against the metal roof and then slowly he brought his knee up over the edge of the gutter.

On top, he stood and walked to the front of the warehouse. It was a perfect vantage spot. He could stay slightly back from the edge and be virtually undetectable, especially with the darkness of night approaching. A police car cruised by with its driver checking left and right. Cole got some footage of it and the build-

     Brian David Simmons

ing across the street with the video camera in the diminishing daylight. Cole watched patiently, keeping his head motionless above the outline of the roof. The memory of his adversary's ability to see in the dark was forever with him.

A single floodlight automatically came on just before the last inkling of daylight disappeared. Cole watched for several hours. He could hear sawing and hammering going on in the distance. Probably the owner of the tool supply store making temporary repairs. Several small aircraft buzzed overhead as they made their approach to the Fulton County Airport. The police car made another pass and the surrounding area got quiet. Cole continued to watch, wondering if he was wasting his time. He knew there had to be at least one car and its occupants inside. What are they doing? Or have they left through some rear exit? He continued his surveillance.

The large roll-up door started to rise and Cole quickly aimed the video camera at full zoom. It was well lit inside, and he could see the back of the armored car. The white sedan was parked next to it. A chain link gate slowly began to swing open and a brown sedan emerged through the building door. With the video camera still rolling and pointed in the general direction of the action, Cole moved closer to the edge of the roof and peered through the binoculars. He recognized the passenger. It was the same clean-cut guy with the little mustache that he had seen two nights earlier. Another figure stepped into view: a tall and well-built black man wearing an immaculate tan suit. He stood with his feet apart in a firm stance and his hands behind his back.

The man maintained his stance as the roll-up door came down and closed in front of him. Cole slowed his breathing and inched away from the edge of roof. He was well back from the edge when the door began to rise again. As it started up, Cole could the see the brilliance of headlights breaking out from underneath the door. He got an uneasy feeling and intuitively knew that he had worn out his welcome.

Cole ejected the small videocassette and slipped it in his back pocket. He took a final look and saw two sedans, side by side, waiting for the door raise high enough for them to clear. The gate out front was start- ing to open and in moments, if he had been spotted, they would have him trapped. Abandoning the camera and binoculars on the roof, he ran to the back of the building and slithered off the edge to hang from the rain gutter. He grabbed the drainpipe and descended to the ground at almost free fall speed.

Using the building to block their view, he ran toward the tool supply. If they were really after him, they would first have to check out the rooftop. He crossed the little side street leading to the tool supply store and dove behind a fifty-five gallon drum along- side another building just in time to avoid a flash of headlights. Peeking around the drum, Cole saw a car slide sideways in the dirt, coming to a stop with its headlights focused at the back of the warehouse. The other car was still out of sight and Cole didn't stick around to find out where it went.

He gambled that the back of the warehouse and the rooftop would hold their attention and allow him to swiftly move across in front of the building. Ordinarily, nobody would have ever seen him, but memories of pursuit by night-seeing, gun-carrying hunters were still vivid. He made it out of view of the car and broke into a full run toward the tool supply store. He passed a fenced plumbing stockyard with a pickup sitting inside. He passed it up; the chances that it would be unlocked with keys inside were slim.

Cole turned to see a helicopter whirling over the warehouse, using a spotlight to inspect the roof. They now knew that he had eluded them and would soon be expanding their search. His knees and arms found the optimum rhythm and he sped past the tool supply place to hop a back fence into an adjacent business. Halfway through the lot, a guard dog realized his territory had been violated; Cole hopped the front fence before the dog could mobilize and attack, leaving it barking in frustration. Cole charged across the street and disappeared alongside another building. He was now two blocks away and thought he had made a successful escape.

He kept up the pace, making his way through the industrial park, but heard the whirl of the helicopter coming from behind. It was several hundred feet above the ground and moved into position directly overhead. Cole had been spotted, even though the helicopter wasn't using the spotlight he had seen earlier. He didn't know the area and had no ideas for escape, but he remembered the lessons they had taught him and the lessons of the compound.

It was their hunting ground and they knew every hiding place. They knew his movements and spotted him when no one could; they had eyes in the dark and he was blind. They were many and could mobilize to position themselves anywhere they thought he might go. The odds were against him whatever he did, but they also had weaknesses. They didn't like attention from the police. His stunt at the tool supply had driven them away. They hunted best when he was the only possible target and when they could hunt without being seen by others. They weren't prepared for surprise and, as demonstrated by his deception at Piedmont Hospital, they were gullible.

Cole backed up against a building, hoping that the overhang of the roof would shelter him from the eyes above. He knew the ground troops would be here soon. His options were limited and he searched his cunning mind for a plan of action. He could set off a security alarm to summon the police, which would arrive in, maybe, five minutes at best. In five minutes, he could easily be dead and, even if he eluded them, he would then have to elude the police as well. If they found him, his identity would become known and he would never be safe. Melvin, Ike, Laughlin or their army would hunt him down in Ogden, Boston, or Timbuktu. Either way, setting off alarms by itself was not an attractive option. Finding a crowd to hide in was unlikely. He didn't know where he was or where to find people. Deception would be possible if he had a few moments out of their sight. But with their night vision, helicopter, and numbers, deception would be extremely difficult. His options didn't look promising and his mind became desperate for a strategy.

He was a dead man if he didn't come up with something soon. Cole stepped out from under the overhang and surveyed the street. They would probably be coming by way of Fulton Industrial Boulevard. Down the street toward Fulton, Cole could see an overhead streetlight illuminating an intersection. On the corner, there was a small unfenced business. His pursuers preferred the dark; he would take them to the light. Cole set off down the street in a mild jog. The helicopter followed overhead. He had a desperate plan formulating in his mind. Cole crossed the street and found refuge under the eaves of the building at the corner. In the shadow of the building, he peered around its corner to watch down the street. He could see the traffic in the distance whistling by on Fulton, indifferent to his situation. Cole retreated along the building, staying under the eaves, and inspected the back of the building. He then returned to the front of the building to watch and wait.

It seemed like minutes but it was really just a few seconds before Cole saw the brown sedan turn off of Fulton and head his way at full throttle. Cole reached down, lifted his pant leg, and withdrew his hunting knife. Even in the shadows, its eight-inch, stainless-steel blade glimmered. Cole held it behind him, and as the sedan approached the intersection, he stepped out from the building to reveal himself. He glared at the oncoming car and when he was sure they had spotted him, acted as if he had been surprised. He returned to the cover of the eaves and the shadow of the building. He waited, listened, and then, at the calculated moment, showed himself once more before quickly returning to the shadows.

He raced to the back of the building and turned at the back wall. Still under cover of the eaves, he circled behind to the other back corner and, just as the car passed, rounded the corner emerging on the side of the building. With life or death in the balance, Cole exerted all his energy to force long, rapid strides from his legs to propel himself to the front of the building. He exploded from the front of the building at breakneck speed.

The sedan had pulled up curbside. Its passenger had just gotten out. His back was to Cole. He turned his head to see Cole's advancing charge and stepped sideways to swing his nine-millimeter silencer free of the open door. He wheeled the machine gun around to take aim at Cole but by then, Cole was already there.

     Brian David Simmons

With a slash of the knife, thrust with the great strength in Cole's arm and the forward momentum of his charge, Cole severed the man's trachea, esophagus, and carotid artery as he passed. Before the man hit the ground, Cole flew through the open door at the driver. The driver had withdrawn a .45 semi-auto pistol from his holster and managed to get off a shot just as Cole drove the knife deep into the man's neck, penetrating sternomastoid muscles and separating the medulla from the spinal cord.

The knife squeaked as Cole wiggled it free from the compression of vertebra. When the knife came free, Cole pushed the driver through the driver's side door, onto the street. He jumped into position behind the wheel, dropped the shift lever into drive, and mashed the accelerator, closing both doors with the force of the acceleration.

It had all taken only a few seconds and the helicopter pilot was probably still trying to find the button on his mic to make a report. Cole made a squealing U-turn and roared past the two dead men.

As Cole approached Fulton, a white sedan made a left and came down the road toward him. As they passed, the driver gave Cole a puzzled look. Cole slammed on the brakes and squealed around the corner onto Fulton. His abdominal muscles resisted the forward motion of his body and Cole realized he had a problem.

He accelerated as he made his way down Fulton toward the freeway. As he worked his way in and out of traffic, he reached his right hand across his stomach and around to his left flank. When his hand reached the warm wetness of his shirt, his brain registered the pain. He ran his hand down along his flank and found the cause of his pain. The .45 had hit him just above his pelvic bone and left a gaping hole through skin and muscle to the abdominal cavity. There was no entrance and exit hole; it was just one big mess. Cole pulled the cravat from his head and bandage from his face; he slipped them inside his shirt to fill the gap in his side. He pressed hard against his side with his elbow to slow the bleeding but he knew he had a real problem. How much blood was he losing and how long could he go before his injury got the best of him? Cole overcame the momentary woozy feeling to deal with his other problems.

He entered the eastbound freeway, toward I-75. Speeding, at least too much, had to be avoided. Getting stopped for a simple traffic violation meant detection, identification, and then potential death. Hospitalization was the same. Official record of his real identity could easily become information Ike could use to hunt him down and kill him.

The helicopter had no doubt followed him onto I-20 and would track his every move. By now, the white sedan was in pursuit, getting directions from the helicopter. Maybe the helicopter would call for help, and they would devise a plan to intercept and trap him. Cole had one hope for escape.

 Brian David Simmons

Cole pushed past the speed limit to stay with the fastest of traffic. Finally, he saw the sign for the Atlanta International Airport. He took the southbound interchange onto I-285 and headed toward the airport. He slowed to just barely stay with the traffic. The white sedan couldn't be far behind. Cole studied every car that approached and traced the lane change movements of traffic to the rear. He detected a set of fast-moving headlights way back in traffic making erratic lane changes; it had to be them. He pushed past the speed limit and moved back out into the left lane. The headlights kept coming.

When the white sedan approached Cole's rear bumper, he made an erratic maneuver out of and back into the fast lane to pass a car in front of him; they followed. Cole moved to the left shoulder to pass another car; again they followed. Cole moved back into the fast lane but kept changing lanes, clear across traffic to exit the freeway. The white sedan was too far downstream in the flow of traffic to make the exit. Cole headed due east on Camp Creek Parkway toward the airport. The helicopter was able to get away with low flying in the industrial park but not in the restricted airspace of the Atlanta International Airport. If he got close enough to the airport, the eyes above would be gone, and he would be free.

With the airport in sight, Cole again spotted the white sedan closing from behind. Cole spit out a curse. He had to shake them. As they closed to less than fifty yards, Cole slammed on the brakes and brought the car to a curbside stop. The white sedan also pulled up to the curb not more than twenty-five yards behind. The street was well lit. Cole could clearly see the faces of the men in the white sedan.

He attacked, moving the shift lever to reverse and flooring the car. It swerved and wiggled side to side as Cole worked to keep it next to the curb. Cars honked and flashed their lights as they passed Cole who was still accelerating toward the sedan. Cole saw the passenger hold his silenced nine-millimeter machine out the window only seconds before the impact. He never got a shot off. The impact made a horrific sound as the two cars crumbled. Both driver and passenger air bags exploded, forcing both men back into their seats; the passenger lost his grip on the gun and it dropped in the gutter.

Cole's air bag also exploded, but Cole was ready for it and sliced it free with his hunting knife. He pulled the shift lever back into drive, mashed the pedal, and accelerated away from the disabled car.

No telling how bad the back of the car really was. The taillights couldn't have survived; the first police car that saw him would surely pull him over. Cole made a right into the airport and followed the signs to "Passenger Pickup." It was late but he was hoping that there would be at least one die-hard cabbie waiting for a straggling drunk from one of many bars. Ordinarily, he would have never risked a cab, but he was in no condition to go jogging across Atlanta. He didn't have a choice. He was also in luck. There were two cabs in line, curbside. The two cabbies were sitting on the hood of the first car smoking a cigarette watching the door for potential fares. Cole pulled up and asked through the open passenger window, "One of you guys give me a lift? Some jerk ran into me and I can't get this thing home until daylight."

One of the cabbies replied, "Yeah, where you need to go?"

"North on I-75 near the Chattahoochee."

"That'll cost you a pretty penny," said the cabbie as he glanced at the damage to the rear of the car.

"I figured as much. Here's my down payment," said Cole and extended his hand with two twenties. "Follow me back out to Central where I can leave this thing." Cole's hand had dried blood that was clearly visible in the dim light, but the cabbie was tired and more focused on the twenties than Cole's hand.

"Right behind you," said the cabbie as he grabbed the cash and headed for his car.

Cole sped off and the cabbie followed. The airport was mostly empty and it was a fast trip out to Central. While looking for a place to leave the car, Cole slipped his hunting knife back into its sheath under his pant leg and checked the safety on the .45 that had injured him. Cole hated handguns. He had shot them a number of times but had never become very proficient with them, at least by his standards.

He worked the gun into the back of his pants and then concealed it with his shirt. When he did, he felt his blood-soaked shirt and pants. He knew the cabbie would never let him get in the cab if the cabbie suspected things weren't exactly as Cole had explained them.

The street was well lit and Cole was afraid the cabbie would suspect something and just speed away. Cole selected a parking spot between streetlights and turned off the car. The cab pulled in behind him as Cole got out of the car. Cole hustled past the driver and jumped into the backseat, startling the cabbie with the briskness of his movements.

The cabbie studied Cole in the rear-view mirror and Cole saw the questions forming in his mind. Immediately Cole withdrew the .45 and pointed it at the back of the cabbie's head. Cole shouted, "Drive." As the cabbie accelerated away from the curb, Cole explained the way things were going to be, "I got a thousand-dollar deal for you. All you gotta do is take me north and forget you ever saw me. You don't even have to call in the ride."

"Do I have a choice?" asked the cabbie, looking in the rear-view mirror.

"Not really," said Cole.

It was silent for several minutes and then the cabbie broke the silence, "A thousand dollars, right?"

"That's right."

"Let me see it."

Cole pulled the wad from his pocket and counted out ten blood-soaked hundred-dollar bills. He passed them forward and the cabbie snatched them.

"You all right, man?" said the cabbie as he inspected the bills.

"Fine, just fine."

"Okay, but I gotta call in and fix your fare."

"Do what you gotta do."

The cabbie picked up the mike and called in, "This is 401, fare with the bent bumper stiffed me. I've had just about enough tonight. I'll be heading in a half hour."

"Ten-four, see you then," came the reply.

"Now exactly where you want me to take you?"

"Just run up seventy-five toward North Atlanta. I'll tell you were to get off."

The cabbie did as Cole instructed making the right transitions to end up on I-85 North. Cole allowed himself to relax but wondered if he was going to live. He was feeling faint again. His wound was serious enough to have caused internal damage, maybe to his intestines, liver, or spleen. He wasn't sure which side things were on or what was where. It didn't matter because whatever it was, it was bad. When they passed the I-75 split-off, Cole instructed the cabbie to go to Dresden Drive Northeast. A few minutes passed and they were soon only a couple of blocks from the apartment building.

"How much is that radio up there worth?" said Cole.

"Huh?"

"Here's another thousand bucks," said Cole as he handed the cabbie a handful of bills. "Now rip that mic out and hand it back here."

The cabbie did as Cole instructed, handed him the mike and then reiterated their agreement; "I ain't going call this fare in, you know."

"Yeah, but when Sugar Ike comes to talk to you, you're going to talk."

"Hey, that ain't part of the deal, man. I don't want nothing to do with Sugar Ike."

"Then you'd better not tell a soul where you got that money or anything about me," said Cole as they passed the apartment building. "You'll be a lot better off if you just forget this whole night."

"I've heard stories about Ike. None of 'em good."

"What've you heard?"

"Just that he is bad. If there's something crooked going on in this city, he's involved. An' he don't play nice. He's the last person I want to meet. If you're on his list, you're in trouble."

"You sound like you're afraid of him."

"You ain't kidding. You better be too."

"I am, and I don't want him coming to find me. That's why I paid you two grand for this little ride. You gotta keep your mouth shut and pretend like this never happened. Hey, pull over here," said Cole pointing to a pay phone. Cole knew that eventually Ike and company would catch up with the cabbie and he would tell all. He needed to shake the cabbie and the phone call for help was the opportunity.

The cab pulled over at the pay phone and Cole stated instructions that he hoped the cabbie wouldn't follow. "We're ten blocks or so from where I need to be. But I gotta make a call first. You wait here. I'll be right back," said Cole as he stepped out of the cab and closed the door.

Cole made it to the phone booth before the cabbie floored the cab and made a wheel-screeching U-turn back down Dresden, just as Cole expected. Cole was only about two blocks from the apartment and the temporary sanctity that it offered, but first he needed to make a distress call. There was no phone in the booth; it was just a left over from days gone by. Cole needed Kevin; he was the only one who could help him, but there was no answer and a feeling of isolation grew. It started to rain. Not just a gentle rain, but a full downpour and Cole was soaked in moments.

Cole's attention now focused on his injury; the faintness he had been fighting all night became increasingly difficult to ward off. He began the two-block walk to the apartment, concentrating on each step, forcing each foot in front of the other. Traffic on Dresden was light but he had to avoid drawing attention to himself. Each step became harder.

Cole leaned against the front of a store with rain pouring down his head. In a daze, he looked upward

at the downpour and then collapsed to find himself lying flat on his back on the sidewalk. As the
rain pelted his face, he searched for the strength to
continue. He remembered a deer he had shot, clean
through the heart, that had mustered strength from
the depths of life's essence to conquer a hill at a dead
run. The deer died on his feet, fighting to the end,
to escape his hunter. Where did the strength come
from? Cole searched his soul for the ethereal source
of hidden strength within himself, but it was illusive.

He fought on, refusing to let go of the search for
inner strength. The rain beat down on his face as he
looked upward at the heavy black clouds overhead.
Dawn was approaching. He was out of time.

"You sniffling, whining wimp. Either get up on
your feet and move or all is for nothing. If you're
going to die, do it on your feet," Cole demanded. His
fingertips slid up the wall to find the recesses between
the bricks in the storefront. He commanded his body
to rise and stand. With a glance skyward, he took a
step forward, and then again and again.

Each staggered step brought more light to the
sky and more fear to keep moving. His vision soon
blocked out all that surrounded him to focus every
remnant of concentration on the sidewalk in front of
him. He plodded onward, losing the sense of where
he was and how far he'd come.

Then, he was startled by a familiar voice and felt
a comforting arm.

"Cody, my God, boy, we gotta get you to a hospital," said Joe who had just stepped out of the apartment entrance.

Cole fought to respond with clarity as Joe helped him inside the apartment building. "No!" demanded Cole. "If I go to the hospital, I will die. Please just help me upstairs."

"All right, but then I'm calling the police and an ambulance."

Joe took Cole's arm around his neck and carried the weight of Cole's body, leaving Cole to manage only the movements of his feet as they worked their way down the hall and up the stairs to his apartment. Cole found the key in his pocket and they entered. Joe took Cole past the video camera to the bedroom and gently set him down on the bed. Joe turned to look out the bedroom door to study the video camera.

"What's the camera for?"

"Nothing."

"I'm calling an ambulance," said Joe as he started to rise but Cole had a death grip on Joe's arm.

"You can't call an ambulance or I'm dead for sure."

"You're going to die if I don't."

Cole mumbled a delirious response, "Not you—Ike, Sugar Ike. And then with the last of his strength and mustered coherence, Cole reached up, grabbed Joe's shirt, and restated his command, "No ambulance. Ike is expecting me to show up at the hospital and I'll be dead before noon if I go. I'll take my chances here!

Now, you get the hell out of here and forget you ever met me, or Ike will add you to the list!" As the last of his energy fleeted, Cole dropped back on to the bed.

"Listen, you arrogant honky. Sylvia is only one step from the grave and I'm only two steps behind her. There's nothing this Ike can do to scare me. I'll do as I see fit!"

"Please, just let me ride it out. No ambulance," pleaded Cole with his last conscious breath.

Chapter Thirteen

VISITORS

TULEE COUNTY DETECTIVES MET TWO UNITS FROM the Ogden Police Department at the convenience store around the corner from Hamilton Cole Davis' house to formulate their plan. The detectives needed to question their suspect but didn't have any evidence for an arrest. The two police cars would take up a position at both ends of the block while the detectives approached the house. One officer from each car would approach the house on foot and gain a position at the rear of the house. If Hamilton Cole Davis was home, they would use any excuse to gain entry into the house and then the two units would move in to aid in a visual inspection of the interior of the house. It was a simple but effective approach that had worked in the past, and they expected it would work again.

The two police cars took their positions at both ends of the block. Officers on foot made their way to the house and then discreetly moved into position at the rear. The detectives watched their progress at a safe distance and then they idled the unmarked car down Twenty-Third Street toward Cole's house. They pulled in the driveway and got out. Advancing in a guarded fashion, they approached the front of the house. One of the detectives looked through the front window; there were no signs of movement. He signaled to the other detective, and they each took a position at opposing sides of the front door. One detective reached forward and pounded with a commanding knock. There was no answer and no sounds of movement inside.

He reached out and pounded on the door again, this time with more force. Still no answer. The other detective, with his back to the wall, extended his arm and tried the door handle. It refused to rotate. The first detective put his hand on his XDM .40, looked at the other, and whispered, "Probable cause?"

The other detective looked both directions down the street, shook his head and replied, "Too much traffic and too many eyes peering from the corners of closed drapes."

"What about the back?"

"We've already been spotted. Too late for that."

The first detective reached out and pounded on the door with huge, striking blows and yelled, "Police! Open up!"

They paused to watch a Toyota pickup truck with a camper shell that had just turned onto the street. It approached slowly and they studied the driver. He studied them as well. The left turn signal began to flash as the truck approached the driveway and then it quickly accelerated away.

Kevin, having made a heartbreaking sacrifice of the Porsche, had just returned from his California shopping trip in his new Toyota pickup and had almost turned into the driveway before seeing the action in front of Cole's house. He first thought the men on the front porch were salesmen, then Melvin's men, but he spotted the three little antennas on the roof of the car and he knew. As he accelerated past the house, he saw a uniformed cop near the rear corner of the house. *Where is Cole? Have they arrested him? Are they here to search the house? Or are they here to arrest Cole? Or me?*

Kevin had problems of his own. Most of the equipment in the back of the truck was illegal and he couldn't afford to be stopped or questioned; he sped on, passing a parked police car before finally reaching the end of the block and making quick a right turn out of their sight. The anxiety was building as his imagination created the worst of all scenarios: Cole had been arrested and hauled off to jail for the desert murders. The police had a warrant for Kevin's arrest for his computer transgressions, but because of his association with Cole, he was also a co-conspirator in the desert murders. They were there for him. He knew it had to be.

He pulled over to the curb; his hands were shaking and his breathing was rapid. "Why me?" mumbled Kevin in almost a cry. "What went wrong? Where in the heck is Cole? Oh Jesus. They're going to find everything." The anxiety continued to mount until finally he put his face in his hands and cried, "Oh God."

With a deep breath he regained some control. He rolled his eyes up, closed his eyelids, and then took three slow, deep breaths while counting: a relaxation trick he'd learned when faced with difficult people situations. As he counted, his mind went blank, his heart rate slowed, and his breathing returned to normal. Eventually, the counting evolved into rational thought.

If the cops were still outside the house, then one thing was of extreme concern: the house was full of incriminating information. In the house, there were probably at least $250,000, IDs of dead men, hotel and rental car paper work, and the .22 rifle that could link Cole to the death of the men in the desert. There were also computer equipment and tapes of recorded phone conversations that would link Cole, and maybe himself, to Callaway. It was all bad.

Kevin pulled away from the curb and made the first right on Twenty-Fourth Street. He tried to see between the houses to figure out what was going on, but it was too far and houses, out buildings, fences, and trees obscured the view. He continued on through the intersection and then circled back to find a vantage point on Twenty-Third Street.

He parked more than a block away and couldn't see the front of the house, but he could see the two police cars and the unmarked car in Cole's driveway. He opened the windows between the cab and the camper shell to retrieve a pair of binoculars. They were extremely powerful binoculars, 20X80, which Kevin had bought for just this purpose; it put lots of distance between him and anybody he was to spy on. They were military style, but didn't include range-finding features like the pair Cole took to Atlanta. It took some mastery to use the binoculars. With the high-power magnification, even the slightest movement left the picture jumping and jerking. The trick, Kevin learned, was to just let the binoculars rest on the dash and steering wheel and then peer through while gently holding them in position. He adjusted the tilt on the steering wheel to get the right elevation and then focused on the meeting taking place in Cole's front yard.

The police cars had now pulled up and were parked nose-to-nose in front of Cole's house. Four uniformed cops and two casually dressed men were standing in the front yard. The binoculars were powerful enough that Kevin could see their lips moving. One of the men turned and pointed down the street in Kevin's direction. The magnification of the binoculars made them seem like they were standing right in front him and he scrunched down in the seat, only to relax when the six men departed in different directions.

Kevin watched as they spread out through the neighborhood and began knocking on doors. Most doors remained closed even after repeated knocks. Those doors that were answered resulted in a short conversation with the officers taking notes. As they worked their way further and further away from Cole's house, Kevin knew what he had to do. There was no other way and it had to be now.

Kevin started the truck and pulled away from the curb. He made a left before entering Cole's block and then a right onto a parallel street to the rear of Cole's house. Kevin estimated the approximate location of Cole's house through the block and pulled up to the curb. He studied the front of the small house for a few seconds, then decided that detection didn't matter at this point. He got out and hurried up the driveway toward a detached garage at the rear. As he passed the house, the windows were open and he could hear a TV blasting inside. Chain link fence ran alongside the driveway and garage. The two-foot space between the fence and garage was filled with engine parts, open buckets of oil, and other discarded trash.

Kevin made his way between the fence and garage, accidentally knocking over a small barrel of oil. He created enough noise to wake the dead when he clambered over a muffler still attached to a complete exhaust system. It was a horrid obstacle course: a garbage can full of aluminum cans, an engine block, a discarded swing set, scrap metal, and a pyre of trash. It was a grand effort to make his way to the rear of the garage but when he finally made it, he could see the back of Cole's house. He climbed the wooden fence between him and Cole's backyard; it creaked and canted over as he jumped. He could see the unmarked police car sitting in the driveway and if they had been there, they would have seen him. At this point, though, it didn't matter; he was committed. It was that simple.

 Brian David Simmons

Trembling so badly that he could hardly stand, Kevin stumbled to the back door, took out his key, unlocked the door, and went inside. Quickly, he locked the door behind him and surveyed the interior; it was just as he remembered leaving it. First stop was Cole's bedroom. He tipped up the mattress on Cole's bed and let it rest against the wall. Cash, IDs, notes, hotel receipts were all there. The police hadn't searched the place yet; he was in time. Cole's sleeping bag was tightly rolled up at the foot of the bed. He pulled the tie string and jerked it open. He quickly raked the cash and other items into the sleeping bag and then searched out Cole's rifle. He found two rifles in the closet and shoved them both into the sleeping bag. He retrieved the third rifle, Melvin's rifle, from the living room and also shoved it into the bag, case and all.

Then he entered the living room and ventured a peek out the front window. No one was in sight. They were probably still questioning the neighbors. Kevin would have liked to take his computer, except that he already had more than he could carry. But the computer had to go, or at least its memory did, and it had to go now.

Kevin switched it on and slipped in a bootable disc. When it came up, Kevin went to format and started the process of wiping out his hard drive. While the computer clicked through the hard drive, Kevin boxed up his discs, zoom drives, and telephone recordings. They too found their way into the sleeping bag, which by this time was nearly full. With the computer still clicking, Kevin sneaked another peek out the front window. Still nobody in sight. The computer finished its formatting. Kevin inserted another disc and a game CD.

All of the information was still retrievable by anyone who understood computers. With a few lines of code in an executable file, Kevin set up a routine to repeatedly copy the CD files onto his hard drive. Each time the CD files were copied, the routine changed their saved names by incrementally increasing by one. This way, the entire hard drive would be overwritten and nothing other than the game files could ever be extracted.

With the computer at work, he dragged the sleeping bag to the back door, but momentarily paused to consider his actions; had he forgotten anything? He remembered Melvin's cell phone and quickly returned to the living room to retrieve it. Out front, he could see one of the uniformed officers standing at the driver's door of one of the units. It was time to go. He stooped to avoid making his presence known to the cop out front, as he hurried to the back door and exited the house.

Kevin closed the back door behind him and quietly, but quickly, moved to the fence, dragging the overloaded sleeping bag behind. If the officer out front took ten steps from where Kevin had seen him last, Kevin would be seen and it would all be over. It took

     Brian David Simmons

all of Kevin's strength to heft the bag over the fence, and it crashed down on the other side. He followed behind it only to crash down onto the narrow junk pile. He struggled through the junk, jerking and hefting the bag. Again, he stepped on the tailpipe attached to the exhaust system and the muffler jumped to echo more noise notifying everyone that he was there. He climbed on top of the garbage can full of aluminum cans and it tipped over, sending Kevin crashing down onto a bucket of discarded oil, creating even more clamor. He continued to fight his way toward the front of the garage, but the cop in front of Cole's house had been alerted.

Kevin could see movement between the cracks in the fence. The Ogden police officer had returned to Cole's back yard and, after a quick inspection of the back of the house, approached the fence. Kevin made it to the front of the garage just as he heard the fence creek behind him. He stepped around the corner of the garage and stood motionless, clutching the sleeping bag in his arms and praying that the cop would go away. The fence creaked again. Either the cop had stepped off the fence or he was coming over. Either way, it was time to go. Kevin hurried down the driveway only to be met by a repulsive woman with her head out the open window.

"What do you think you're doing?" she barked.

"Looking for cans," was the only response Kevin could think of.

"We don't have any! You get on out of here!"

"Okay."

And with that, she withdrew back inside, no doubt to continue watching her TV. Kevin hurried to the street and popped open the back window on the camper shell. The addition of the sleeping bag and its contents took up the remaining space in the back of the truck.

He jumped in the truck and quickly accelerated away from the curb. He stopped at the intersection and then turned left. Glancing back down the street, just before accelerating out of sight, he saw a police car enter the street at the other end of the block. Kevin didn't waste time proceeding to the next intersection, making a quick right turn, and then a left to lose himself in the maze of city streets.

Chapter Fourteen

REVELATION

LAUGHLIN WAS JUST FINISHED A MEETING WITH HIS accountants and Isaac Bartrum. Melvin Roberson sat on the sidelines and just glared at the accountants who were noticeably unsettled by his tormenting demeanor. Melvin blew smoke from his cigarette and squinted to intensify the effect. Laughlin concluded the meeting and Melvin didn't hesitate.

"Out. You two bean counters are excused. Out." commanded Melvin. "Close the door behind you." Then while scowling at the departing account managers, he advised David and Isaac, "I've got something from last night I want to show you." He walked over to the desk top computer and inserted a USB connection to the drive from the helicopter's camera system.

"You've heard the saying, 'Don't bring a knife to a gun fight?' You may re-think that after you see this." Laughlin and Bartrum both stared at the screen as it came to life.

"Watch this," Melvin said with excitement in his voice. "This is from the fixed camera on-board the helicopter."

The video started playing; it was an aerial view of the previous night's events. "This is absolutely incredible. Watch! Watch! Right here at the corner of the building he'll come running out," said Melvin as he pointed at the screen. "There, see that! And - and - one," said Melvin as he snapped his fingers. "And two," as he snapped his fingers again. "And then, we're gone. Ain't that something! Killed two of my best men and stole my car in less than fifteen seconds."

"Jesus Christ!" exclaimed Laughlin.

"That mutha doesn't mess around, does he!" added Ike with a hint of fear in his voice.

Melvin pointed at the car speeding away and declared, "That's the guy that's been snooping around. First this house and then Ike's warehouse. I think he's also the same prick that took the Saudi's money and did this to my hand!"

"I pay you to deal with this kind of shit, Melvin," blasted Laughlin. "How in the fuck? Were your guys sleeping or what?"

"Did you ever follow up on the sheriff in Cootie County?" questioned Melvin.

"I had the IT guys research it. Best they could come up with was some God damn nowhere place in Idaho. Ten years ago, the Kootenai County sheriff was sliced dick to chin right in his own front yard. The sheriff got off a shot before he died but that's about all they could get. It's still an open investigation with no real suspects and details on it are limited."

"It was the same mother fucker that did this to my hand," said Melvin as he raised his bandaged hand.

"He warned me that if I didn't back off, he'd gut me like the Kootenai County Sheriff."

"I don't want him around here, Melvin. I want him gone now!" declared David Laughlin with an alarmed tone. "What are you going to do about it?"

"I'm going to track that quick little sucker down and break every bone in his body, starting with his hands. And then I'll got to work with a knife."

"Do it soon. And find out who he's working for. I don't like this a bit, Melvin. I don't like being squeezed by this little problem of yours."

The meeting concluded. Isaac stumbled out the rear of the mansion to his car. Melvin followed, helping guide him down the hall and through the doorway with a shove. Isaac's chauffeur was waiting. Melvin got in a full-size sedan and set off for the airport; he had a lead to follow up on: a cabbie spending blood stained hundred dollar bills.

Chapter Fifteen

HIDING

THE HEAT WAS INTENSE. THE SUN WAS A TORCH THAT set the sand on fire. The beach sand was a heavy blanket, burning to the touch, and yet covering, entrapping and preventing all movement. Cole's commands to his arms and legs were met with the sand's crushing resistance and all movement was stifled. In the distance, a tropical setting with shade, flowers, and a gentle, flowing waterfall was in sight. The rumble of the little waterfall could be heard and relief from the intense heat was only steps away, but there was no escape from the burning sand. Down the beach, gentle waves could be seen crashing their cool waters onto the sand, just out of reach. Further down the beach, cliffs jetted from the ocean with cool caves offering shade and moist, cooling rock. Relief was almost within reach, yet life was still just an illusion for Cole's hallucinating mind.

A SENSE OF DEFEAT AND ISOLATION BROUGHT KEVIN to depression. Hamilton Cole Davis was now either arrested or a wanted man. However they had found out, it meant that there was no safe haven for Kevin. Sooner or later they would link him to Cole. Sooner if they searched Cole's house; there were enough personal belongings in the house to lead them straight to

Kevin. By association with Cole, or from his computer transgressions, he was now a criminal and envisioned himself on Ogden's Most Wanted List. But what did they know?

The computer was his avenue to information and, given a place and enough time, he knew he could figure it out. But where could he go? He had no relatives in Utah. And now, by circumstance, Cole was his only real friend. He couldn't ask anybody he knew to harbor him. Sooner or later, if they really wanted to find him, that would lead them to him as well.

Kevin found himself aimlessly driving around. "What would Cole do?" was the question he kept pondering. "He would survey the situation, formulate a plan, and then act on it. But what would he really do?" Maybe it wasn't so much what Cole would do, but rather what he, himself, could do. His computer was his strength and the things he could do all revolved around it. That took him back to needing time and a place.

Kevin stopped at a convenience store and picked up a copy of every Salt Lake, Ogden, and northern Utah paper with a classified section. He scanned each one looking for something more than an apartment, something with isolation and low probability of detection. He found what he was looking for: a seasonal cabin at Bear Lake. If the owner would take him without references and credit checks, it would work. He made the call using a newly acquired cell phone, complete with encryption capabilities.

Kevin got the right answers to his questions and, with the promise of a photo review, agreed to rent the cabin through December. He represented himself as Casper Johnson and concocted a story about writing a book on computer technology and Internet indiscretion that justified his need for isolation. He sounded like the ideal tenant. They arranged to meet in Salt Lake to make the necessary arrangements. The directions given to Kevin were clear and he drove straight to the owner's neighborhood. As it turned out, the address wasn't very far from Callaway's mansion. Kevin wondered who really killed the mayor as he neared the address.

Kevin was met at the door of the stately residence and granted immediate entry after identifying himself. Introductions were short, and he and the owner got right down to business. She was a very businesslike woman in her mid-fifties, who obviously managed the household affairs, including the summer cabin.

"Do you still think the cabin is acceptable for your purposes? You realize we can get the rental rate we ask because of its location and complete furnishings."

"Yes, I like the looks of the cabin," said Kevin, reviewing the photographs. "I think it will do fine and your rate seems fair to me."

"You realize December can be a little rough up there. You may not be able to get up and down the road. There is no snow removal."

"That's all right. I may just stock up and camp in."

"Well, that will certainly provide the peace and quiet you asked about."

"How would you like me to pay you? Can I just give you the four months rent up front?"

"That would be quite a bit of money and we usually do a credit and references check before we accept any money."

"I'm actually pretty anxious to get started on my book. I've got some thoughts I'd like to capture as quickly as possible. If I paid cash, do you think I could drive up there tonight?"

"I don't like to turn my property over to anyone without knowing something about them."

"How about I fill out the big items on your application, pay you cash for the security deposit and full four months and then send you a full list of credit references, employment history, or any other information you need over the Internet?"

"I don't know. It might be all right, I suppose, but..."

"But what?"

"I'm a little embarrassed to ask. My husband has the Internet and I have instructions, but I just feel so uncomfortable with it. If you sent me your references, could you show me how to get it?"

"Sure, where's your computer? I assume your husband set you up with email."

They proceeded to the study and she inquired further, "Could you show me how to find some of the friends I went to high school with? I'm just not adept with computers, and my husband never seems to have the time to show me."

With an hour tutorial on searches, email and websites, Kevin, or Casper as she knew him, had a new friend. He helped her find long-lost high school friends, bookstores, and auctions. Kevin left her his cell phone number and assured her that she was his special student and could call him anytime. She felt good about Casper and the rental arrangement. So did Kevin; now he had a place. They parted with a handshake and Kevin was on his way with the keys to the cabin in his pocket.

He had two more stops to make before heading for Bear Lake. At the first stop, he replaced his computer, or at least a basic variation of it. He would have to make some internal additions and modifications with cards purchased in California. What he had in mind had never been tried before, at least as far as he knew.

He settled for an unsatisfying Pentium 4GHz processor, boostable to 4056 MHz with software, and 512Kb SDRAM at 100MHz. It came with a massive hard drive, and other miscellaneous cards and features, all of which were also very substandard for him.

The computer rested in its box on the seat next to him. The monitor and keyboard, along with other peripheral equipment and software, sat on the floor. Now the entire truck was full, leaving only enough space for a driver. Kevin drove west on I-80 to the airport exit. He exited the freeway and followed the signs to long-term parking.

On the chance Cole was returning from Atlanta, Kevin had to warn him. He made pass after pass down the rows of parked cars looking for the Sun Fire. Eventually, he found it. A film of dust had settled on the car and its long-term stay was obvious. Kevin wrote a cryptic note to warn Cole of their predicament. He also left the number for his new cell phone. The unsigned note read:

> One-Eyed-Jack rescuers have found your house. They want to recognize you for your efforts. If you don't want that, call 555-7626 before you go home.

It wasn't all that well written, but it was enough to let Cole know he had a problem. Kevin pried the driver's window out just enough to slip the note through. The note dropped through onto the seat.

Kevin exited the parking lot and made the four-hour drive to Bear Lake. It was late when he got there and he had trouble finding the turn off to the cabin. After several wrong turns, he finally found it and promptly moved all his equipment in. The first order of business was to get the computer up and running. Kevin loaded a few of his specialty programs and hotspotted his cell phone to get an Internet connection. Warning Cole was his first priority. A hand-delivered Western Union telegram delivered directly to Cole's apartment was direct and fast. Kevin sent the same cryptic message that he had left in Cole's car. Since anonymity was not important, he charged it to his own credit card. Assuming Cole was still in Atlanta, Kevin expected a reply by tomorrow evening at the latest, and then the two could make plans for the future.

It wasn't to be; Kevin waited the whole next day for a reply from Cole, and then another. Kevin relied on the media to do the scanning of police reports and regularly, sometimes ten times a day, checked the API web site for any news from Atlanta or Salt Lake. The Salt Lake and Ogden papers had small follow-up articles on the desert murder investigation, but Cole's name was never mentioned. It would have contradicted other, earlier reports that had suggested Callaway was involved and besides, Cole wasn't nearly as colorful a subject as Callaway.

Kevin upgraded his hotspot connection with a dedicated UPG satellite box. It was faster than his cell phone, but still only 100 Mbps. He spent his days and nights working with his electronic equipment, exploring the bounds of cyberspace and waiting for word from Cole. He created new identities for Cole and himself, starting with social security numbers from people who had recently died and finishing with records of legal name changes. Kevin printed up new identification, including driver's licenses, using his computer and laminating equipment brought back from California. He became Casper Johnson and James Que Bond. Kevin thought a cross between James Bond and Que was appropriate, since he fantasized about the role he thought he was about play in the underworld of intrigue and deception. Cole became Cody Calhoon and Jason West, which Kevin also thought had appropriate mimicry. FBI identification was also created for each fictitious character. Via the Internet, Kevin applied for personal and company credit cards for each character. The company cards were in the name of each character with payment guaranteed by IAB Food and Liquor. The billing address was a post office box in Lakeview, about twenty miles away.

With still no word from Cole, Kevin sent another telegram, but more days passed with still no response. Kevin engrossed himself in his work, integrating incongruent electronic equipment, computer hardware, and software. His computer grew into what he referred to as his "4056." The 4056 had as much capability as technology permitted in a personal computer.

As an expert in data storage and manipulation, his second project was to develop a new path of intrusion into high security computer systems. For systems that coupled physical surveillance, video cameras, and the computer, he would simply follow the data. His approach was unique. To Kevin, it was just simple data compression and storage, an artifact of his past life at Omage. Kevin had pioneered laser read and write of digital information that was integral with complex cloud based servers and interfaces. The frequency of a laser beam is over a million times shorter than other wave frequencies, making it possible to carry thousands of bits of data and transmissions on a single laser beam. This expertise with data and lasers provided him with the basis to expand his thinking beyond the simplicity of fiber optics and data storage.

His hypothesis led to development of the system that he set up in the living room of the cabin. At one end of the room, he had a video camera hardwired to his 4056 computer for recording. It simulated security systems like the one at the Grand Hotel in Ogden. Kevin set up a low-power laser with a high-power riflescope mounted to its top. The semiconductor laser was contained in a three-inch diameter tube two feet long. The laser, although similar to a light-emitting laser, emitted a shorter wavelength in the infrared radiation range. It was well below the visible light spectra and except for faint glow of non-coherent diffracted light, was invisible to the human eye. An interface for the laser system was created so that it could communicate with a laptop computer through hardwired connections.

When he was ready to test his equipment, he turned on his 4056 and programmed it with security measures used to prevent hacking by typical means. With the video camera connected to his 4056 and transmitting its signal to the computer, it was now taking digital video data that was impenetrable from normal front-end hacking or backdoor access.

    Brian David Simmons

At the other end of the room, Kevin switched on the laptop, pressed his cell phone into a cutaway pocket and then sighted the laser at the camera aperture using the rifle's scope. He switched on the laser and executed his program, "breakin," on the laptop.

Fast as light, the semiconductor laser fired the modulated signal feed from the laptop into the aperture of the video camera. The vidicon tube in the camera received the infrared signal, processed it through the chrominance mixer, converted to it digital output, overlaid it with digital image bits, and processed it through to the CPU on its way to the laser read/write drive. But the drive never got the overlaid digital instructions; instead the CPU picked up the instructions and commanded its extremities as directed. Less than a fraction of a second later, the unhackable 4056 dialed the cell phone number, screeched momentarily, and then began transmitting to the cell phone and openly communicated with the laptop, thus completing the communication loop.

With the technical challenge mastered, Kevin felt it was time to see what he could find out about Cole. Media reports were still no help and he was becoming increasingly impatient. Kevin scheduled an afternoon flight out of Salt Lake to Atlanta. He would take his new development with him and give it a real challenge. If he could get into Laughlin's computer system through its security cameras, maybe he could find the answers to Laughlin's financial dealings. Maybe he could find out what Cole had gone to Atlanta to learn in the first place: how to hurt Laughlin financially and expose him to the world for what he is.

But first his new creation needed a field test. In route to the airport, Kevin parked across the street from the telephone company. It would be a good test. He had no idea what kind of computer system they were running or what kind of data storage medium they were using. It was midday and they would be using the computer to post accounts and survey telephone system operations. Their mistake was that they had video surveillance of the front entrance. With a pair of c-clamps, Kevin secured the laser and its scope to the steering wheel and adjusted the window height to get the right elevation. He connected the laser to the laptop and inserted his cell phone into its cutaway pocket. He turned on the laptop and brought up "breakin." He executed.

A few seconds later, the phone company computer called Kevin's cell phone, the laptop buzzed and the loop was closed; he was in. With a little fumbling around, Kevin figured out the system configuration and began compressing, sending and downloading all billing records for August. He would sort and filter the data later. It would provide all the to-and-from links to phone conversations he had recorded. Transmission was slow, but Kevin compressed the data before transmitting, making the process as fast as possible.

     Brian David Simmons

Kevin tried another field test at the Grand Hotel. It was daylight, and he kept his distance from the front entrance. He found a parking space that was about a hundred yards from the video camera over the front entrance. He was also at an angle to the camera, another good test. Kevin set up the laser, laptop, and cell phone and then fired his weapon again—another success.

Kevin was elated with the success of his system and drove west to the airport. He paid cash for the flight to Atlanta and used the alias of Casper Johnson. His luggage consisted of an overnight bag, his laptop, and a large briefcase with his laser, cell phone and miscellaneous connection cables. It caught the attention of the TSA security guard at the carry-on baggage inspection, but was allowed to pass after an inspection of the contents of the case and assurances from Kevin that the laser was a telescope.

The flight seemed to take forever, but it gave Kevin time to think through how FBI agent Casper Johnson would track down Cole. The flight arrived on time, and once through the formalities of a getting a rental car, he proceeded directly to Cole's apartment building. He entered through the front, passed the building manager's apartment, and went down the hall, up the stairs, and then to Cole's apartment. He pounded repeatedly on the door but there was no answer. He returned to manager's apartment and by displaying his leather cased FBI identification, convinced the manager to let him into Cole's apartment.

The building manager was a little puzzled by Special Agent Johnson's request and quizzed Kevin, "You know you're the second fed to ask to see the apartment. Didn't you guys find what you're looking for the first time?"

"Just following up," replied Kevin.

"What do ya want him for, anyway?"

"He's just missing. That's all."

"Well, okay."

The building manager let Kevin into Cole's apartment. It stank; the putrid smell was overwhelming and made Kevin nauseous. Kevin and the manager searched out the source of the odor and found it in the trash can: bed sheets soaked in blood had been left to cook in the Georgia heat and the air conditioner hadn't been run in days. The apartment was a like a broiler cooking rotten liver and onions. Kevin found nothing in the front room and went toward the bedroom, only to be met with the most horrid of scenes. Flies swarmed throughout the room and the smell was overpowering; Kevin felt his stomach come to his throat, but managed to hold it down.

"Jesus, that crap head's ruined my bed. Nobody will ever sleep on that again," said the building manager as he inspected the ripened mattress.

"When did you say the other agent came by?"

"A couple of weeks ago. But I never came in here. And the place didn't stink like it does now."

"Did the agent come back here?"

"Yeah, I think he did."

"Did he take anything?"

"Nope, it was as empty then as it is now. Hey, do you think I can rent this place?"

"Is the lease up?"

"Well, no, but if he ain't coming back, why can't I rent it?"

The shock of the possibility that Cole was dead had never occurred to Kevin and he wasn't ready to accept it. "How do you know he isn't coming back?" he asked.

"Well, I don't, but just look around."

Kevin's mind strayed and he didn't hear the manager's response. Instead, his imagination created its own scenario: Melvin and his buddies had watched the apartment until Cole showed up and then knocked him unconscious. When he awoke, his hands and feet were tied and he had a pair of socks stuffed his mouth. They beat him, cut on him with knives. Cole choked and gasped for breath as they cut on him some more until finally he bled into unconsciousness and then death. They waited until late at night, joking and laughing at Cole's mutilated body, and then tossed him into the trunk of a car. By now Cole's body was decomposing in a ditch somewhere. Kevin's pale skin turned bleach white and he ran to the bathroom to unload the contents of his stomach.

When Kevin recovered, he and the manager left Cole's apartment and returned to the front entrance of the apartment building. Kevin was in desperate need of the fresh air. It was hopeless, but Kevin provided him with an official-looking business card with his cell phone number anyway. For which, Kevin got a cynical, "Yeah right, FBI," from the building super and was compelled to give him a hundred-dollar bill with the promise of another if he would call when or if he ever saw Cole. Kevin was relieved to get away from the super, but the stench that clouded his mind wouldn't go away.

He thought about finding a hiding place and crying; maybe that would relieve the pain. For while, he just drove aimlessly around. He drove by many of the historical sights, including the governor's mansion. He paused momentarily to try and gain some inkling of appreciation for its grandeur, but he had nothing to appreciate tonight and his emotional loss sunk to new depths. He wiped a tear from his eye. What good is that going to do? Screw it all. Quit worrying about Cole, you better worry about yourself. If Melvin got Cole, he's sure to find me. I'm next. Then what the heck. Better to die trying than crying.

Kevin's stay in Atlanta was going to be brief, especially now that Cole was dead, but he had come with the intention of testing his new apparatus and he might as well go ahead. Kevin drove toward Laughlin's house at about eleven o'clock. He made a single pass by the front of the mansion that told him what he needed to know - it had video surveillance cameras. He selected a safe distance down the street at the corner and got out his laser. He set it up, made the connections to the laptop, and sighted it in on a camera over the front door. He switched on the laser and re-sighted it while he waited for the laptop to boot up. He brought up "breakin," executed, and the laser fired its instruction-packed wave perturbations.

Nothing. The cell phone didn't receive a call; the laptop was silent and its screen was blank. Kevin re-sighted the laser and tried again. Again, no response. That meant one of two things. Either the residential security system was archaic and not connected to a computer system, or the computer wasn't connected to a phone line. He didn't know and at the moment; in comparison to the heartfelt loss of his friend, this was just a mere temporary technical setback. Kevin put away his laser and drove off.

Consumed in reflection, he continued to drive aimlessly about the city, eventually finding himself back at the airport. It was still a couple of hours before the ticket counter opened, but a coffee shop was open. Kevin ordered breakfast and coffee and put his mind to work on the problem with the laser. It was a desperately needed technical distraction that took his mind away from the loss of his friend.

The laser was useless unless he could close the loop. Just sending information to the camera wasn't enough if it wouldn't respond. Video cameras don't emit any signal, either for focusing or zooming. Internally, it's a dumb device. By manual commands or automatically, a focusing coil balances image brightness with the charge density pattern on a photoconductive layer within the vidicon tube. The only output signal produced by the camera is that which is sent to the data storage media and, for handheld cameras, the electronic view finder. Laughlin's surveillance cameras weren't going to have that feature and so it wasn't worth the mental deliberation. So much effort went into the laser system that Kevin couldn't just drop it. "Why didn't it perform its intended purpose?" he continued to ponder.

Five o'clock came sooner than Kevin expected and he bought a ticket for the early-bird flight out of Atlanta. He would have to change planes in Dallas but that still got him into Salt Lake before noon. Masks were everywhere; was the whole world going to hide behind masks forever; how long could this last? Kevin pondered. He was asleep soon after boarding the plane, and after making the transfer in Dallas, slept on the remaining leg of the flight as well. The airport was busy and Kevin was relieved to get outside. He really wasn't a people person and felt claustrophobic in crowded places. The truck was in short-term parking near the exit and he made a fast departure from the parking lot.

He circled around the parking lot and returned to the long-term parking. Cole's car was still there, but there was a ticket on the windshield indicating that the car would be towed off in less than a week.

     Brian David Simmons

Downhearted, he left the parking lot to return to the security of the cabin.

In route to the cabin, Kevin recounted and analyzed his inspection of Cole's apartment. One piece of data didn't fit his conjectured summation of Cole's fate. The building manager had said that the apartment was clean when he let the other FBI agent in. That meant that Cole's personal belongings were removed before the man was let into the apartment. Could Cole have packed up and left? Before or after leaving buckets of blood? Was it even Cole's blood? Maybe Cole was still out there somewhere. Why hadn't he called? Maybe he couldn't. If he was out there, how would he know to call the cell phone or where to find the cabin? Things weren't at all like they planned, but maybe they weren't as bad as Kevin imagined.

Back at the cabin, Kevin found company in the Internet. He visited a few chat sessions to fill the void left by his friend, but eventually went back to work searching for information on Laughlin. "Wall Street Laughlin" was how Melvin had described him. That's where Kevin concentrated his search.

THE TASTE WAS FOREIGN BUT IT CAME WITH delight. The sensation had a slight hint of spinach and then it switched to liver—not fresh deer liver that he loved so well, but more like overcooked beef liver with no substance. It sat in Cole's mouth with its juices dissolving and eventually disappearing to the depths of his stomach. It was followed by a cool liquid with a sweet apple taste.

The sweet liquid cooled the fire inside, but the heat was intense and there was no escape from the furnace. Every pore in his body worked to extinguish the fire outside, but there was no breeze to cool the burning skin, instead the body was just suffocating in its own sweat. The mind registered a torturing desire to scratch the body's abdomen, but it couldn't muster the commands to move its arms; the mind was on a journey of its own.

The thoughts refused to focus as they passed through intermixed mirages and voices from his mother and father, racist Patriot Rebirth Society chants, compound experiences, his grandmother, Carol, Kevin and then the slowly spinning chasm of black and white. His state of delusion was timeless and boundless and continually shifting without control or direction, but always bordering on the great, dark, blackness.

Chapter Sixteen

Potato Soup

Consciousness came to Cole with a swirling blur. The room, obscured by distortion, revolved around him, slowly coming to a stop. His focus developed on a picture on the wall. Vivid yellow flowers in the forefront of a watery glen were the first things that activated his mind. In the background was a small waterfall surrounded by lush, green vegetation. The creek emanating from the waterfall trickled over moss-covered rocks to run past lobster claw-shaped flowers. A painting on the wall portrayed waves crashing onto a white sandy beach. The artist had captured the realism of the waves with curling streaks of cool white wrapping underneath divisions of billowing, pure blue water.

Another framed photo on the wall portrayed a rugged cliff towering to heights above the ocean waters. Within the rock structure was a cave with water crashing into its opening. The walls had a wonderfully cool, shining semblance. Cole shivered, but was warmed with a frilly white bedspread that weighed heavily on him and shielded him from the air currents of a window mounted air-conditioning unit.

Cole struggled to get up, but his body refused cerebral commands and the best he could do was moan with each successive attempt. Over the hum of the air conditioner, through the open bedroom door, he could hear singing. It was the sweet tune of a Southern woman that lulled him into a state of comfort and security. Warm, comfortable, and secure, he dozed off into a dream state.

In the next room, Sylvia Atkinson was going about her daily preparations, which had now become routine. She stood at the stove singing a religious tune, breaking occasionally from humming to outright singing. Mid-morning was soup. Today it was potato, but each lump had to be mashed and dissolved to be sure her patient wouldn't have trouble with it. Mid-afternoon, it would be puréed beef stew and strained spinach. She had each day carefully planned and looked forward to the careful preparation and serving of each meal.

As the potato soup simmered, she prepared bathing and bandage supplies: antiseptic soap, washcloth, towel, clean underclothes, toothbrush and toothpaste, sterile packaged gauze pad and tape. Sylvia dished out a full bowl of soup and, with a baby spoon in hand, went to see her patient. She set the bowl on the night table and gently positioned Cole's head atop another pillow.

She began to hum as she sat on the bed next to Cole and prepared to feed her patient. With towel in hand to guard his chin from spillage, she carefully loaded the spoon, checking for consistency. The delicate touch of the spoon to Cole's lips opened his mouth and she delivered the contents of the spoon only to be startled when Cole's eyes opened.

Without saying a word, she hurried off to the other room and made a phone call to Joe. A few minutes later, she returned to peer at Cole from the doorway.

"Are you hungry? Can you hear me?"

"Yes, ma'am," managed Cole in a feeble voice. "Soup's good."

She returned to take her place next to Cole and resumed the feeding operation. Cole, taking each spoonful with increased vigor, felt the warmth of the woman's love. Her presence made him feel a comfort and fulfillment that he had never known; radiance of her maternal love penetrated his very soul.

Soon, a towering figure appeared at the foot of the bed. It was Joe Atkinson. He recounted the last weeks with excitement, "I see you've returned from the dead. I wasn't sure, but Sylvia never gave up. I didn't think a man had so much blood to lose. It's amazing! Sylvia sewed you like an old pair of pants and you're going to live. I never saw such a mess in my whole life. I mean nothing but hamburger to stitch, but this old gal just pulled the pieces together and stitched 'em up. Outside's pretty ugly and I ain't saying what's inside. The whole time she was plugging me in to ante up some of my good-ole O-negative blood. You probably got a gallon of negro blood in ya now."

"Hush," interrupted Sylvia. "He doesn't want to hear any of that. Do you?"

Cole mustered a question. "What day is it?"

"Why, it's Friday," said Joe.

"Then I'm late."

"I should say. You been here almost three weeks."

"How long?"

"Almost three weeks. We moved you over here after I got a visit from the FBI over at the store. He walked in, flashed his ID, said all the right words, but when he spoke your name I could see the fire in his eyes. He was a pushy, mean-looking character and I didn't like him a bit. When he tried to intimidate me, I doubled up my fist and came close to taking a swing. If I had been twenty years younger, I'd have decked him. That afternoon we moved you over here. Good thing, too. Later that day he got the building manager to let him into your apartment."

"What did he look like?"

"He was tall and thin, nasty-looking eyes. Maybe forty. He had done something to his hand. It was bandaged. We think maybe -"

"He worked for Isaac Bartrum," inserted Cole. "His name is Melvin Roberson. He 'cleans for Ike,' as he puts it. His job is to torture and kill anyone who cheats or crosses Ike. You are in jeopardy just having me here. I need to leave."

"No way," asserted Joe. "You just lay right there. Sylvia and I already talked about it. Our life doesn't have much purpose anymore and for a short time here, you give us purpose. Sylvia's a pretty good judge of character and she figures you're okay. Besides, if helping you hurts Isaac Bartrum, then so much the better."

"You don't know. Who do you think smashed Melvin's hand? I might be worse than Melvin."

"No, I don't think so," said Sylvia as she took Cole's hand and caressed it.

"Something else, too," said Joe. "They're still looking for you. The building manager has been questioning everybody about you. He got a visit from another fed and ever since then he's been out banging on doors trying to find anybody that's seen you."

"What'd he look like?"

"I only saw him from across the street and I'm still not sure it was the fed. I only watched him because he was a skinny little whitey in the neighborhood; kind of like you. He and the super stood out front for a while. It looked like he passed the super some cash and I figured the neighborhood was going get more integrated, at least until the super started asking questions."

Sylvia recognized the signs of fatigue and took command, "All right, that's enough. Whatever you boys got to talk about can wait. Now Cody, I want you to get your rest. You just close your eyes and everything will be fine." She took his hand and with her other hand closed his eyes and remarked quietly to herself, "After dinner, we'll change that dressing and get you all cleaned up."

Chapter Seventeen

Impenetrable Intrusion

Melvin had described Laughlin as "Wall Street Laughlin," inferring that he was somehow involved with stocks, bonds, or futures. Kevin viewed the financial world of Wall Street with irreverence, as an activity where no product is actually produced and therefore immoral. Money just feeds on itself to create more money, while providing no benefit, service, or commodity, except for those who have money to create money. Those who play aren't interested in buying a piece of a company and then helping it to expand, improve, and prosper. They aren't interested in nurturing it to maturity and then reaping benefits of their efforts. Instead, they're only interested in multiplying the dollar through trades, exchanges, scheming, and wagering.

The financial world has an infinite number of databases to record the activity. Regulatory agencies, such as the FCC, only monitor large transactions or major single party acquisition of large blocks of shares. Intrusion into one of the many sources for information would have been possible given enough time to hack through computer barricades, but to hack into hundreds of databases would have been a ludicrous undertaking. Besides, somebody was already monitoring, analyzing and policing large-scale money laundering activities. This was the database he needed to access.

A branch of the Treasury Department, known as the Financial Crimes Enforcement Network (FINCEN), is the focal point for tracking financial transactions. They are given computerized access to brokerage, exchange, IRS, real estate, bank and almost all other databases dealing with financial transactions. They are also given direct access to FBI, CIA, Secret Service, NSA, Defense Intelligence Agency, and Bureau of Intelligence databases. Kevin's best chance of establishing Laughlin's financial activities was hidden within the FINCEN databases. Gaining access meant violating the integrity of the United States, the law, and national security itself. It also meant taking on the impervious, anti-hacking safeguards designed to protect computers of the United States.

Morally, ethically, and legally it was wrong - but what a challenge! He struck an ethical compromise with himself: if he were successful in getting in, he would limit his data acquisition mostly to Laughlin's financial records. He would go no further and extract no unneeded data. After getting what he needed, he would lock the access door behind him so others could never gain access. This was the superficial promise he made to himself.

Kevin started his attack with simple surveillance of his adversary. FINCEN likes to toot their horn and advertises on the Internet. Kevin clicked on www.

treas.gov and then followed the links to FINCEN. According to FINCEN, they are the champions of the criminal investigation world, keeping banks and depositors in check, defeating international money launderers, exposing tax cheats, squashing drug lords, and conquering illegally encrypted cyber transactions. Kevin went to work.

He called up his search engine and put it to work activating Yahoo, Lycos, and other common search engines, as well as reaching out into local and clandestine servers for references to FINCEN. He disregarded all results returned by the common search engines and concentrated on local server hits. He found two hundred and sixty-seven sites that fit his criteria, but eliminated all except two that resided at USTreasury. FINCEN. Kevin tried the first site. He got no response. His computer simply told him that it could not open it. Kevin exited his program and tried accessing the site directly, as if it were a fax machine, but to no avail. It was not accessible, at least through the Internet or external unencrypted lines. He tried the second site but got the same result. He couldn't even communicate with the server much less try to hack through the defenses and gain access to the sites and what lay beyond.

He tried another avenue. He searched and obtained a list of six phone numbers for FINCEN and dialed each one. In each case, he got the after-hours voice mail for a receptionist at FINCEN. Kevin selected a receptionist and tried to dial past the recorded greeting and enter her private recorded messages. He was stopped by phone system password requirements. But the phone system had no block on the number of access attempts and was easily overcome with an iterative search routine. Once inside the receptionist's voice mail system, Kevin crawled deeper into the FINCEN phone system scanning inward to find a communications relay with seven hundred twenty-seven access lines. He retreated back into voice mail and identified only six hundred six possible phone numbers, leaving one hundred twenty-one unaccounted for lines. He crawled back into the communications relay and ventured down one of the unaccounted for lines to encounter a terminal server.

Kevin reached into his computer bag of tools and resurrected a program to speak in the almost forgotten, yet most fundamental of all computer languages: the machine code of zeros and ones. He bounced his instructions at each service entrance of the terminal server until he found the programming access. He needed access through the terminal, but couldn't afford to perturb its existing programming if he was to avoid detection. Kevin bounced his program against each microchip, testing its setting and reporting results back to the 4056, thus creating a mirrored image of the server configuration and programming.

Kevin lost track of time, evening transitioned into morning, and his connection was abruptly interrupted by an outgoing phone call. If the receptionist had been paying attention, she probably would have detected Kevin's intrusion; but she wasn't and Kevin quickly retreated from the system leaving the receptionist momentarily confused by a dead line.

Cole was on his feet, but just barely. He struggled to make it out of the bedroom, using the doorway and walls to stay upright. The hallway, as well as the bedroom, was decorated with pictures and paintings of the Caribbean. He was careful not to knock any of them down as he struggled, bouncing from wall to wall, down the hallway.

Sylvia heard him bumping back and forth and went to help. She had bound Cole's left arm above the elbow and across his chest to keep him from stressing stitches in his side. Cole only had one arm to keep him off the walls and Sylvia's help was welcomed. She escorted him to the living room and he dropped into Joe's oversize chair.

"You're looking a lot better," she said. "The color's coming back to your face, and the scars on your check are hardly noticeable. I think you're going to be as handsome as ever."

"I don't feel very handsome. I'm so weak."

"It'll come with time, son."

"Why did you do it?"

"Why did I do what?" she replied with confusion.

"Why did you take me into your home, nurse me, feed me, clean me, and put yourself in danger?"

"Joe has a got a thing for knowing what's right. He knew you were right. When he figured that, that Isaac person did this to you, then he was sure."

"I sure appreciate all you have done," said Cole and then paused. "I thought the store belonged to Ike. Didn't you tell me that you and Joe work for him?"

"That's our store. That man swindled us out of it when we needed money. Joe hates him with a passion. Bartrum's a drug dealer, you know. As soon as we get enough money, we're out of here." She sighed and then continued. "We have such dreams. Run the store for a few years, scrape by on nickels to save pennies, and then go to the Caribbean and bathe in the warm clear water on a sandy beach. Replace this God-awful humidity with cool sea breezes, and just live a life of leisure. But that's all just a dream; right now we are so far behind that it'll take forever."

"I owe you. I'd sure like to help."

"We wouldn't expect that. Besides, I don't know what there is you could do. It is what it is."

"Let me think on it," said Cole before changing the subject. "I need to get to a pay phone - somewhere on the other side of town - and I need to get there without being seen."

"Ask Joe. He'll go for you."

Cole thought it through. It would work. He would work with Joe to decide what key words would clue Kevin in. "Poor kid," he thought as he realized that Kevin might have been identified. If they found him, they could find Kevin. The phone call to Kevin became all that more important. He would get Joe to make the call at his first opportunity.

Joe did as Cole requested, but returned with disappointing news. There was no answer at Cole's house, Kevin's house, or his cell phone. Where could Kevin have gone? Or, what may have happened to him? Cole needed to regain his strength and return to Utah. He would accelerate his physical recovery with resolve, working his body as many hours of every day as he could muster.

With the receptionist's interruption, Tuesday morning had come all too soon. Kevin hadn't gotten close enough to the FINCEN computer to know if he was going to be able to get in. He had a day's work cut out for him and went about developing a program he could download to the terminal server. It would give him access to the FINCEN computer just as if he were sitting at a desk in Washington, D.C. With the interruption of the receptionist, he recognized the need to jump from phone line to phone line and added that to his list of things to do.

Kevin wrote his programs and added them to his bag of computer tools. He had been without sleep for over thirty-six hours and took the opportunity to nap before re-entering the FINCEN world.

He slept until nearly seven o'clock, Eastern time. By now, the FINCEN offices were empty and their

     Brian David Simmons

computer would be left to run overnight batch jobs, guarded only by its interface and software defenses. Kevin dialed his receptionist. Again, he mentally crawled into the voice mail system, through the communications relay and then onto the terminal server. He commanded a reset and then downloaded new instructions for the terminal server from his 4056. The terminal server responded, and Kevin accessed the external interface.

The interface asked for name, host, job number, classification, and password. He backtracked to the voice mail system and retrieved the list of FINCEN employees along with their phone system passwords. At least one of the employees had to have the same password for voice mail and computer. Even if it wasn't exact, he could still try several variations before the interface locked him out after too many failed attempts. Of course, he had two hundred and six employees to try before he was completely locked out.

With the 4056 linked to the FINCEN computer, he updated his random search routine. It was almost done processing the employees when he was sensed the probing tentacle of electrons. Kevin recognized the pattern and broke away from the interface. It was too late; he had already been questioned by a Gatemaster that was probing and patrolling for unauthorized computer access.

The Gatemaster's mission was to randomly interrogate all users, identify unauthorized use, trace it back to origins, and then drive a spike all the back to and into the source. It would kill any offending computer and leave communications lines open for its human masters to follow.

Kevin backed out of the terminal server and communications relay. With electronic speed, the Gatemaster's spiking tentacle followed him to the voice mail where, with the punch of a key, Kevin switched phone lines. The Gatemaster was momentarily befuddled and Kevin escaped with only nanoseconds to spare, quickly closing all communications lines behind him. The Gatemaster was a formidable adversary, and Kevin had a new challenge.

Mentally exhausted from a night's work and his flight from the Gatemaster, Kevin put away his programs and turned off his computer. This would require some work and he wasn't going to solve the Gatemaster problem tonight. Kevin went to bed to regain his strength, gather his wits, and sharpen his mental keenness. It would take all his skill to beat this Gatemaster.

Kevin's subconscious worked the problem while his body and conscious mind rested. He awoke the next morning with the solution to the Gatemaster problem. He would tantalize its electronic tentacles, feed it, befriend it, and then defeat it. He went to work writing the lines of code to defeat his adversary. By midday he was ready, but he had to wait for the offices at FINCEN to empty before he dared make his intrusion.

     Brian David Simmons

Kevin returned to the problem of the trying to complete the communications loop between a remote computer and one taking digital feed from video cameras. He had not been successful at Laughlin's. If the computer was not connected to the telephone system, then his laser-sent instructions couldn't close the loop. It didn't mean that the computer hadn't gotten his instructions; it just couldn't comply.

He set up his laser, video camera and the 4056. Without a telephone tie-in, the only output from the computer was from the monitor. But from hundreds of yards away, anything on the target computer's screen is useless. Or is it?

Maybe the solution was simple. Rather than transmit data and computer files, just extract data directly from the computer CRT. The surveillance camera connected to the 4056 could receive, and so could another camera connected to the laptop. Kevin set up another digital video camera on a tripod next to the laser. He connected the digital camera to his laptop. Then with two computers, two video cameras and the laser set, he sent a simple command through the laptop to the laser, which fired at the video camera and relayed the instruction to the 4056. The target CRT flashed, cleared its screen, and then displayed Kevin's spyfile directory. Kevin clicked the button on the digital camera to capture the zoomed image. The image was then transferred to the slow laptop. The image developed, from top to bottom. With a few keystrokes, he enlarged the window, converted its contents to a text image and saved it as a file. The process was terribly slow but it would close the loop; it also required that he be close enough to capture text off the target computer's screen. This wouldn't work at Laughlin's; he would be too far away and only speculated that the computer was in the attic, which might be visibly accessible through the strange looking dormers. He needed other options.

If he couldn't read the screen, at least he could record feedback from a flickering screen: the machine language basics of zeros and ones. He tested it and it worked, but it was far too slow for any serious communication with a remote computer. At best, it would get him into Laughlin's computer but once in, he would have to figure out another method of downloading information.

The system was complete except for a high-power lens for the digital video camera. That would be first on his next shopping list. Time passed quickly and by now the FINCEN offices were again empty. Kevin set up his 4056 and checked his tool bag of programs. He set an alarm clock to ensure that he would be out before business began in the offices. He set it for six A.M. Eastern Standard Time.

Before dialing, he thought through each step of his mental journey into the electronic maze. Like a spy going deep, far beyond the bounds of safety, he realized this could be his final moment of peace, security, and serenity. He dialed his FINCEN receptionist.

     Brian David Simmons

With the password already established, Kevin mentally strolled through the voice mail system and onto the communications relay. His attention intensified as he touched the terminal server with his machine language instruction. He cautiously approached the interface, scanning for his nemesis, the Gatemaster; it was disguised in the software, hiding, waiting and watching for the unauthorized user. Kevin was about to intrude. He knew that as soon as he probed the password interface, he would alert the Gatemaster and all his cleverness would be put to the test.

Kevin's program "enslaver" sensed an approaching electronic tentacle of the Gatemaster; it inquired, "user authenticity" and then shot a traceable electronic spike toward the communications relay. The "enslaver" software intervened, temporary locking up the system and sending Kevin scrambling for more code. He added a retractable virus and gave it the ability to clone its sixteen-bit platform to fill any electronic void it encountered.

Kevin freed up the system and again commanded his "enslaver." This time, as the Gatemaster struck with its tentacle, the "enslaver" attached itself and the code immediately began modifying the Gatemaster programming; its user search slowed and became rhythmic. It began a timekeeping function iterating between initiate and cancel user search.

Kevin now had unfettered access to the password interface and was met with five questions: name, classification, password, job number, and host. Kevin assumed a host name from the inaccessible Internet site: FINCEN.Hueyportal.sec@USTreasury.FINCEN. Programmers like to name their computer children after comical characters and Kevin immediately recognized Huey. There was probably also a Dewey and Louie around somewhere. For the job number, Kevin knew his job was new and assumed the computer would assign one. For classification, Kevin assumed it would default to the lowest clearance and left it blank as well. That left name and password.

Safeguarded systems don't allow multiple iterations of name and password. They only allow a limited number of attempts before locking the user out or triggering an alarm that shuts down the entire system. Kevin estimated that he had up to five, maybe four, logon attempts before he would be locked out of the system.

With the two hundred six employee names and voice mail passwords and four slight variations for each, Kevin had more than hundred shots. He thought his chances were pretty good. He put the 4056 to work with a short iterative routine and got an instant hit: Stanley Belmont with "LoveToSki4$" for a password and "Confidential" for a clearance.

He was in. He had intruded into the impenetrable but he still had more challenges. The computer beyond talked to Kevin in a strange, yet somehow familiar tongue. He probed and tested, but failed to get a coherent response until he emulated one-hundred-twenty-eight-bit parallel processing. Huey was a hopped-up Super-Cray. Once Kevin established a common language, he found two other Crays: Dewey and Louie. The instantaneous gigabyte computing power of the triplets was phenomenal.

In a fantasy state, Kevin explored the databases, examining only a fraction of their records to gain an understanding of their contents and then moved on. Many of the databases he tried to access rejected his attempts returning messages "Secret Clearance Required" or "Top Secret Clearance Required." He was locked out based on his initial logon. This wouldn't do.

Kevin explored the logon interface from the backside. It placed shackles on the user at logon that were detected by sensitive databases and programs. When the shackles were detected, an insurmountable wall went up, preventing Kevin from gaining even a glimpse of the world beyond. He could explore, but was inhibited from full freedom within the computer system.

The alarm clock rang, alerting Kevin that it was time to leave. He quickly downloaded several files and exited through the password interface. The Gatemaster was still keeping time; Kevin extracted his "enslaver" virus program and reset the Gatemaster. He withdrew from the communications relay and left the system without leaving a trace.

The intensity of the night subsided when Kevin's consciousness returned to the comfort of the cabin. He rested from his adventure during the day, but all the while he was planning his next reconnaissance mission.

The FINCEN offices were quiet the next night. Unbeknownst to those who normally fill the offices, the telephone rang and an electronic umbilical was established through the phone system to the heart of their computer. Thursday night was similar to the previous, except he modified his log on approach. He let the 4056 sequentially search for a name and password with "Top Secret" access. He found none and went back to "Confidential" access. Kevin became Sally Stromberg with the password "21VIRGINISLANDs." Again, he ventured into the FINCEN computer world exploring its databases, programs, and capabilities. This time he found an access to IRS-related files and personal databases on U.S. citizens.

He was shocked at what he found. They had electronic information on every working person in the U.S. with a social security number: tax returns, bank account records, automatic teller transactions, credit card activity, property tax, vehicle ownership records, stock market transactions, and more. They were spying on the general population. Then, was it really any different from what Kevin was about to do to Laughlin? Kevin had almost forgotten the reason he had violated the FINCEN computer. Instead, he had become entranced with the challenge and was fulfilled with his successes.

     Brian David Simmons

If "Confidential" allowed access to such detailed information, what did "Secret" have to offer? He decided to explore beyond this shackled, security limitation.

Kevin implemented a plan with alternate strategies. Once entering the computer with a designated security classification, he was tagged, shackled, and restricted from access to "Secret" databases and files. He had to live with the shackles, but devised a software cloak to conceal his shackles to Huey. He called his program "incognito." But with multiple and iterated tries, he couldn't get through security classification firewall.

Kevin returned his focus to Laughlin; after all, that was why he was here. He built several batch runs for the Cray to crunch, correlating Laughlin's personal stock market, futures, and bond transactions; real estate and other property acquisitions; bank deposit amounts; domestic and foreign travel; shipments documented through U.S. Customs; income and property tax amounts; and generalized and specific stock, bond, and futures markets activities. He submitted the batch jobs, and while waiting for results, went snooping. He downloaded Laughlin's tax returns for the last five years, some U.S. Customs records, and other easily identifiable Laughlin information to the 4056.

When Huey finished crunching Laughlin's data, those files were transmitted to the 4056 as well. Kevin now had gigabytes of data to investigate.

Chapter Eighteen

MALEVOLENCE

"The super just doesn't give up," said Joe as he walked through the door. "He's still asking questions about you. He offered to split a thousand bucks with me if I had seen you. He said he had a name and number for a dude that was willing to pay, maybe even more than a thousand bucks with negotiation."

Cole was intensely worried Melvin, Laughlin, or Isaac would deal with Joe and Sylvia in the most horrid manner possible if they ever discovered the role Joe and Sylvia had played in saving his life. Cole pleaded with Joe, "It's worth a thousand bucks just to get him to quit asking. I have to get out of here, Joe. He wouldn't hesitate a moment to turn us both over to Ike for a little cash. You and Sylvia can't afford to have me around."

"Ain't no thing as long as you stay out of sight. You just rest up till you're good and ready. The super can just ask all the questions he wants. And as for that scrawny little white dude, even I could take care of him."

"Scrawny little white dude?"

"Yeah, I think it's the runt I eyeballed couple of weeks ago. Not many white boys come calling in this neighborhood unless they're looking for drugs or a hooker, even then they're taking their life in their hands. You got a firsthand taste of that, didn't you?"

"What'd this 'scrawny little white dude' look like?"

"I really don't recall too much, other than he was a skinny kid," said Joe as he shook his head.

"Do you think you could get his name from the building super?" questioned Cole as the thought of an optimistic similarity entered his mind.

"Hey, if it's important to you, consider it done. You think you know this dude?"

"I don't know. I'm not sure it's worth the risk to find out."

"Money buys just about anything. Probably cost me a couple hundred bucks, but I'm sure I could get it."

"Could you do it without generating any suspicion? Could you do it without implicating yourself?"

"Yeah, maybe later this afternoon. The super's always scamming to get an easy dollar. I could tell him somebody came into the store willing to pay big bucks for your whereabouts. Then, offer to share sources with him. He'd jump at the chance to get tied into a name with big bucks. I could make a name up and trade information. Maybe it wouldn't even cost me any money."

"Might work. You think he'd trust you?"

"Maybe I give him a hundred bucks. Maybe two hundred. Then even if he thought I was lying, he'd bicker a little bit, but in the end he'd still grab the easy money."

Cole put his hand over his mouth and breathed through his fingers as he analyzed the risk and asked for reconfirmation of his feeble premise of a coincidence, "Skinny white dude, huh?"

"Yeah."

"Okay. How much money you need?"

"Let's try two hundred."

Cole handed Joe three hundred-dollar bills and Joe departed. Time passed slowly as the unlikely coincidence developed into hope of finding Kevin. Cole paced the floor, did his exercises, and then paced some more until he was physically exhausted. Collapsing in Joe's oversize chair, Cole's eyes closed but his mind continued to build the expected outcome of Joe's inquiry.

Sylvia woke Cole for dinner; still no Joe. After dinner, Cole resumed his pacing and Sylvia went to relieve Joe at the store. He was alone for what seemed like hours. Then, Cole heard the door lock mechanism click and watched the door handle turn. Joe stepped in with a big smile on his face.

"Got it," he boasted and then looked down at the business card. "His name is Casper Johnson and he's with the FBI."

Cole's heart soared. "His real name is not Casper and he's no FBI agent, but I love him just the same. Let me see the card."

It was a professionally done card, or at least it looked that way, with Special Agent Casper Johnson's name in bold and a phone number.

"He learns fast," said Cole as he examined the card. "Let's give it a try."

"Don't you have to worry about a trace or something?"

"Not with this guy. If he's advertising a number, there is no way."

Cole picked up this cell phone and dialed the number. He waited in anticipation as it rang several times.

"Hello," said a familiar voice.

With contained excitement, Cole asked, "Is this Special Agent Casper Johnson?"

"Ah, yes it is."

"I have some questions to ask you about illegal Internet activities, wire tapping, eavesdropping, and impersonating an agent of the federal government. First question I have is: do you know who this is?"

The line was silent. Then came the reply with a burst of excitement, "You prick! Where have you been? You just up and disappear for a month and then call out of the clear blue. What makes you think I want to talk to you? Jerk!"

"Aw, come on, you love me and you know it."

"The hell I do!"

"By the way, who's listening in on this phone call?"

"Half the world for all I know, or care. Dickhead."

"You wouldn't say such terrible things to me if I was there to give you a big hug and a kiss."

"What did you expect? You need to call once in a while, you know."

"It hasn't been that easy. You and I need to have a serious talk. How do we do that without half the world listening?"

Kevin's cryptic mind went to work and he set up a meeting, "Get a pencil and paper. Just write down the answers to the questions I ask. Don't respond. Okay?"

"Got it."

"Subtract one from the day of the month you arrived. That's the day we will meet. You named an ugly man one time. Add four to the number in his name for the time. Write down the seventh, then the seventh again, letter in the name of the other man and then the first letter of my pride and joy for a letter in the middle. That's the location. Where did you first see me? What direction from your house did you last see my pride and joy? Write down the third, which is same as the fourth, letter of another man's name. Bye, see you then and there," finished Kevin and then hung up.

Cole looked at his notes. He had arrived on September 8; tomorrow was October 9. One-Eyed-Jack plus four was five o'clock. Letters from Mr. Muddy-Face and Kevin's "pride and joy," his Porsche, yielded AAP—Atlanta Airport. Cole had first seen Kevin in the Grand Hotel bar and Kevin's Porsche was last parked west of Cole's house. The third letter was "D." Kevin would meet Cole tomorrow at five o'clock in the West bar just outside the "D" terminal at the Atlanta Airport.

     Brian David Simmons

Joe, who had watched the cryptic communication, inquired, "You guys are pretty secret. Are you some kind of super-cops or spies or something?"

"Something like that, but we're not the real kind."

"You seem real to me. Spying on Ike, gun shot, secret meetings - that's some kind of real."

"You ever thought about getting even with the bad guys, the guys that always seem to win at the expense of everybody else?" questioned Cole.

"Get even or get shot at? Heck no. I'm too old for that. I had my share of tough times when I was younger, but only to survive, not as an occupation. When I was driving trucks, I had run-ins. Couple of times I faced down punks looking to rip off televisions or cigarettes I was hauling. Back then, it was my tire iron against their knives; they always lost, but I was a lot tougher back then. It's different today; the knives have been replaced with semi-auto pistols and assault rifles. Every punk in America's got one. And I sure ain't what I used to be. I'm just an old fart growing weaker by the day."

"My partner, Kevin, is nothing but a 'scrawny little white boy' that couldn't fight his way out of a paper bag. But let me tell you, I would hate to go up against him. He would kick my butt with genius and computer smarts. Without ever leaving his PC, he could turn me into America's most wanted and make sure I got convicted. He could re-arrange my life so that I couldn't get a driver's license, job, or airline ticket. He could screw it up so bad even my phone wouldn't ring any where except the police station. Then, he would destroy my finances and any financial future I might have had. With that PC of his, he could sic the IRS and every debt collector in the country on me. Everybody's got his or her own strengths; I got mine, Kevin's got his, and you've got yours. Don't fool yourself."

Cole owed Joe and Sylvia his life. He would repay them someday, somehow. He could just hand them cash but that would be an insult to a man who believed in nothing but hard work. Joe was a man who earned every dollar he ever had through years of long nights behind the wheel of an eighteen-wheeler. Even now, in what should be retirement, Joe logged the long hours necessary to run the store and provide for Sylvia. He was a man of integrity and hard work; cash was not the answer. It would have to be more than that.

Cole thought it through as he led the conversation, "I've got a problem that I don't have an answer for. It's a matter of trust. Kevin and I are pretty much homeless. We've got Laughlin, Ike, and probably the cops after us with no place to hide or ever get a good night's sleep. It's like always sleeping with at least one eye open. Maybe it's the way it's supposed to be; no rest for the wicked or something like that."

"You're always welcome here, Cody. I probably shouldn't tell you this, but even the pale color of your skin can't keep Sylvia from thinking of you as her son. That old woman loves you like you were her own."

     Brian David Simmons

"Wow, I appreciate that."

"She's quite a gal. She slaved over you day and night for three weeks, always knowing you would live. I wasn't so sure. All she had was first aid training from years ago, a medical book, old wives tales, and penicillin and other stuff I conned a vet friend of mine out of. For the visible wound, she just used needle and thread sewing the pieces of mess back together. For internal diagnosis, she was feeding you onion soup twice a day and then sniffing around your wound to see if your innards leaked. For infection, she was shooting you with horse-size doses of veterinary penicillin. She's not about to let you go."

"I owe her my life. I'd like to do something for her. Sylvia said something about living down on the coast or in the Caribbean. Maybe we could get Sylvia away from this place and I could get a safe hiding place at the same time. I've got a little cash stashed away and maybe we could work something out."

"Maybe," conceded Joe. "What kind of something are you talking about?"

"How about setting up a safe house? Somewhere out of the country where Kevin and I can hide if things get bad."

"No, I don't think so."

"Joe, don't reject the thought off-hand. Just think it through. Retire and live a life of leisure. Talk to Sylvia before you decide. I've got cash that I don't need or want; it's nothing to me, but it might mean the world to Sylvia. You don't have to answer. I think Sylvia will convince you. After I leave here tomorrow, even if you don't here from me personally, don't hesitate to do exactly as instructed. Seriously! You won't regret it. Minding Ike's store is no life for Sylvia. Talk to Sylvia and think about it, Joe."

"You can't just walk out of Sylvia's life. That would tear her up."

"Then consider my offer."

"You make it sound awful sweet. I know what Sylvia would say. She has had a Caribbean fantasy for twenty years." With an air of disbelief, Joe conceded, "When the time comes, we'll see. Just keep it between you and me. I don't want Sylvia anticipating something that may not happen for a while. Just don't tell her you're leaving and never coming back."

With good-byes said, Joe hurried out the door, back across the street to the IAB Food and Liquor; Sylvia had been left alone too long. Cole continued his workout with new enthusiasm, exercising his mid-section as much as he dared; his left side was terribly weak and the wound could easily reopen. He knew Sylvia would be extremely upset with him if he reopened the wound and he couldn't have that. He did leg squats, partial sit-ups, leg lifts, and then repeated the exercises all over again. He exercised his arms, lifting cans of beans over his head as high as he could without over stretching his side. The exercise made him feel like part of the living once again.

    Brian David Simmons

When Sylvia returned from the store, the two spent a pleasant mother-son evening together talking about Joe and Sylvia's life together and some of Cole's high school experiences. Before bed, Cole worked through his routine again and then waited for Joe to close up the store. The older man was noticeably tired when he stepped through door, which strengthened Cole's resolve to do something for the couple. They said their final good-byes and went to bed. Cole knew he had probably spoken to Joe for the last time.

Joe was already across the street at the convenience store when Cole rose from a peaceful night's sleep. Cole packed his bag and said his good-byes to Sylvia, which of course included the promise to stay in touch and visit soon. He left the apartment for the first time in weeks, sneaking down the stairs, passing all the door peepholes on the first floor, and then eagerly venturing out into the sunshine. He waved at Joe across the street as he walked down Dresden, watching over his shoulder for a cab. None came by and he ended up calling for one from his cell phone; as it turned out, he'd walked to the same empty pay phone he had been deserted at weeks earlier. Wouldn't it be a calamity if it turned out to be the same cabbie, thought Cole, amusingly.

It wasn't. A cab showed up in short order. Cole put on his face mask and glasses before climbing in the cab. The driver was a gabby little man who kept trying to foster a conversation with Cole, but the less he said the better off he was. He was out in the world again and subject to the risks of identification. Ike had probably put out some kind of contract on him. Maybe they had his picture and were circulating that as well. The world was now a fearful place that required every action to be inconspicuous, even a taxi ride. Midday traffic was light and the ride to airport was short. Cole left the cabbie with a bloodstained hundred and collected his change in twenties and a ten.

Cole went directly to the TSA security check point for the "D" terminal, glancing briefly at the flight arrivals. A Salt Lake flight was arriving at four-twenty at Gate D-22; he assumed that was Kevin's flight. Cole found the bar and found a vantage point for people exiting the security area. Cole blended in with the hundreds of indistinct and partially covered faces suffering from airport travel. Hundreds of people passed in the aisle never speaking a word to, smiling at, or even acknowledging their fellow travelers. Even eye contact was avoided. It was a perfect place to hide, except for the ever penetrating security cameras.

Passengers began emerged from the security area in waves, most probably corresponding to arrival of underground trains. Cole studied every set of eyes emerging from the exit. There were all the normal greetings and hugs from waiting relatives and friends, business types scurrying off to catch a connecting flight or find ground transportation, and then there was Kevin. He strolled out of the gate with a tubular

     Brian David Simmons

shaped carry-on bag and into the main pedestrian thoroughfare. The inattentive Kevin walked right past Cole. Cole watched each passenger carefully and categorized his or her threat potential; nobody was watching or following Kevin. Cole pulled the strap of his duffel bag over his shoulder and merged into the flow of pedestrian traffic, always keeping Kevin in sight.

Cole was out breath with exhaustion when he caught up with Kevin. He quietly spoke to him from behind, "Keep walking."

Kevin turned, resisted the urge to hug to Cole, and responded. "You always sneak up on people, don't you?"

"Just keep walking," said Cole as he moved alongside. "You have a pleasant trip?"

"You look like crap. You need some sunshine."

"Yeah, I look like you. Think anybody will mistake me for a computer geek?"

"I doubt it. It's obvious you don't even know how to log on."

"Where are we going?"

"Baggage claim and then the rental car counter."

"Slow down," said Cole, struggling to keep pace. "What's the hurry?"

"You look sick," said Kevin, giving Cole a once-over with a glance up and down. "You haven't been taking your vitamins, have you?"

"Screw you."

"Oh, you missed me that much, did you? You know, if you really wanted me, you wouldn't have waited a month to call."

"Yeah, well, not my choice."

"I suppose not," said Kevin, giving Cole another interrogating glance. "I've been busy. We've got lots to talk about."

At the baggage claim area, Kevin retrieved two suitcases while Cole waited near the rental car counter. Kevin returned and set the suitcases next to Cole and then started the formalities of getting a rental car. The exertion of the day was affecting Cole's concentration and he just barely caught the parting comment from the rental car agent, "Y'all have a nice day now, Mr. Johnson."

"It's Casper Johnson now, is it?" commented Cole upon Kevin's return.

"Yeah, and let's rock and roll, Mr. Calhoon. Let's get out of here."

Kevin had rented a full-size Buick and had hotel rooms reserved at the Budget Deluxe. In the car, Kevin handed Cole a packet with driver's license, credit card and FBI identification. The photos even resembled him. Cole was now Special Agent Cody Calhoon from Tupelo, Mississippi.

"I like the badge. Why Mississippi?"

"Mississippi doesn't have computerized driver's licenses yet. They still file everything by hand. In fact, they don't even print their own licenses; they contract with Alabama. If anybody tries to check on a Mississippi driver's license, it will take at least a day before Mississippi can respond. Speaking of checking up, why didn't you call?"

"I was a little incapacitated. I took a bullet in my left side." Cole pulled up his shirt. The indentation in Cole's side was apparent even with the bandage coverings.

"You going to be all right?"

"So far, I think so. The diagnosis of my insides says I'm going to be okay."

"I checked hospitals. There was no Cole Davis registered. What name did you use?"

"I didn't go to a hospital. If I had, Sugar Ike would have had an easy time finding me and I wouldn't be here talking to you. Instead I rode it out with the help of some friends."

"I didn't think you had any friends."

"Well, I do now. I owe them big time. They're an old couple that took me in, hid me from Ike, and took care of me. Now it's my turn to take care of them. With some of the cash I've got stashed, I'm going buy a beach house somewhere and set them up in it."

Kevin pulled into the hotel driveway. Two rooms at the Budget Deluxe were reserved under Kevin's name and he proceeded to check in while Cole stayed in the car. With check-in complete and Cole rested, Kevin suggested they find a beer and continue catching up on recent events.

The nearest bar was a strip joint. It was in harmony with the neighborhood: lower class, rough clientele, attractive dancers, at least as much as could be see in the dim light. Just inside, they encountered a heavyset bouncer who demanded a ten-dollar cover charge, which Kevin paid. He had never been in place quite like this. They walked past a bar counter full of scary looking patrons. With malison glares, a couple of them took notice of the geek and his sickly friend.

The out-of-place pair stepped into the darkened burlesque lounge to the blare of loud music. Cole's eyes adjusted and he studied the patrons, each interrogated as a potential threat. A stage was in center of the lounge. Candy, as announced by the DJ, was center stage and had the attention of patrons sitting on the edge of their chairs clinging to the edge of the stage, each with a dollar bill in their hand. Small tables along the walls, each with only two chairs, were only partially occupied.

Cole and Kevin slowly moved past the stage. Kevin couldn't believe what he saw; he stared intensely and his mouth hung open. Candy moved into position over a dollar bill, creased in the middle standing lengthwise on the dance floor. Kevin tilted his head to get a better view and lost his balance, stumbling into Cole. Cole gave him a gentle shove toward the stage and shouted, "Take a front row seat." Kevin resisted. Candy smiled at them and beckoned them to the front row with a seductive look, gesturing with her finger.

    Brian David Simmons

Cole continued with his torment, "Go ahead. She's a woman like any other. I think she wants you. Go for it." But Kevin was overwhelmed and couldn't speak. A heavyset man put a folded dollar bill in his lips and summoned her over. Cole smiled maliciously, gave Kevin another shove, forced a ten dollar bill into his hand and then shouted over the loud music, "Your turn." Kevin nervously declined.

They found a table far from the dance stage. The music was irritating; Cole and Kevin could hardly hear each other, even in the distant corner of the bar. A beautiful blond approached Kevin and alluringly tried to excite him. She did a seductive little dance just for Kevin and then stroked his cheek. She set the price for a more personal lap dance in the corner. Kevin's blushing was visible even in the dimly lit lounge. This was all to Cole's amusement and he smiled at Kevin's awkward attempts to ward her off. He tried repeatedly with gentlemanly objections but they weren't enough to send her away.

Finally, when Cole decided Kevin had had enough, Cole abruptly terminated her advances with the suggestion that he and Kevin were gay. It further embarrassed Kevin, also to Cole's amusement, and word spread quickly amongst the other dancers. Whispers of queers amongst their midst circulated through the entire bar and Cole and Kevin soon were drawing squinty-eyed stares. Except for competing bar maids ensuring everyone had a fresh beer, Cole and Kevin were left alone in the corner of bar to do their own thing, which was to catch up on a months' worth of activities.

Cole told Kevin what he knew about how Ike's money laundering operation worked and then moved on to relay his experience at Laughlin's house.

"It was quiet the first time I drove by so I went back for another look. I spotted all the video cameras and was trying to figure out an approach to get to the rear of the house. I went back a fourth time with my video camera running and a car cut me off—"

"What'd you expect? You laugh at my undercover skills. You just drive up to the front of the house four times and expect nobody to notice."

"Hey, the street is seventy-five yards from the road. There's no way they made me."

"What'd you say when they cut you off?"

"Nothing. Another car was coming up from the rear and I made a run for it. That really piqued their interest. They called out a small army and turned it into a hunt."

"How do you know they weren't cops? Maybe they just wanted to check your license and registration."

"Right. They don't check license and registration with nine-millimeter machine guns. They started blasting first thing."

"Is that when you got shot?"

"No, I got shot when I went to take a look at Ike's operation. Some of the same guys, though. These guys

 Brian David Simmons

were good. They had night vision equipment and there was no way to hide. I'm thinking it might be thermographic rather than infrared. These guys could see me hiding in a thicket in total darkness. And they could see me from two hundred yards away. The worst of it was a sniper with a clear view of the park. It was like they had rehearsed the whole thing and I fell right in to the pre-planned hunt."

"And all you did was drive by?"

"Yeah, at that time, all I was guilty of was spying on Laughlin with binoculars and hanging a video camera out the window. Nothing more!"

"These guys obviously know more than you give 'em credit for. What about Ike?"

"Same kind of deal. I was just one of a million cars driving around Atlanta. I followed the armored car, sure, but there is no way they could have made me. I bought the ugliest, most common car I could find, a minivan of all things. I stayed way back and never got anywhere near 'em, except maybe a couple or three times. And that was over a forty-five minute period. There is no way."

"Then how did they make you?"

"Heck if I know. I never even drove by Ike's drop-off. I missed the turn. But those guys still found me and summoned up the army. I pulled up in front of some tool supply to look like I belonged in the neighborhood and one of their sedans pulled in behind me. With nowhere to go, I ended up on foot again."

"They hunt you again?"

"You know it. Sedans, helicopter, and foot soldiers," said Cole before pausing and then stuttered as he continued. "I had to kill a couple of 'em. That's when they shot me."

"You're not making any friends, are you? I had some good news for you, but it doesn't sound like it will matter much. I did a little research and figured out how the local cops got your name. You won't believe it. The CIA investigated Beech and tried to link anybody in the rocket industry that might be involved with him. They linked you because you took vacation from work and then went AWOL. That's all they got. They have nothing. They just want to talk to you. If it wasn't for Ike and company, you could just walk right back into your life."

"Maybe. If they really wanted me, they could match dirt or something from the desert. And then they could confirm their findings with some hair or blood samples and do some DNA or other high-powered test to strengthen the connection."

"Probably not. Somebody sent you a little message right after the cops visited. The same day, not more than eight hours after the cops first visited, they fire-bombed your house and it went right to the ground. There's nothing left. It burned your house to the ground and half the house next door. Look, Cole," insisted Kevin. "They've got nothing. All they've got is a wild guess and that isn't going to tie you to anything. Our only worry is Ike."

"You know, Melvin made a visit to the apartment on Dresden."

"Well, he's a good a friend of yours. By the way, it's time for true confessions and I got a little confessing to do. I spent the last couple of weeks hacking into a few government computers."

"Why am I not surprised?"

"I got into the FINCEN computer system and from there figured out how to get into whatever government computer I want: FBI, CIA, all of 'em. Well, almost all of them; I can't get past Confidential clearance. And the NSA is real one-sided - they can get out, but nobody else can get in. Reports classified 'Confidential' are where I got the CIA data on you."

"Well, it's good you haven't been sitting around watching TV."

"You don't understand! I mean I broke in. If you want it, I can get it."

"Why would you think about stuff like that?"

"I don't mean to. I'm really not after access to government information, but you have to admit it's a little bit tempting. The stuff I got just came along with the financial data on Laughlin. Besides, the only thing I stole was the report on Beech with your name in it. It looks like your name was given to the FBI by the CIA and then the FBI gave it to the local cops."

"So, did the CIA, FBI, or local cops give my name to Ike and company?"

"Probably not the CIA or FBI. It's also strange that the CIA missed the punch line. They figured out all the foreign activity but completely missed the domestic side, Laughlin included. Your name easily got back to Ike once the local cops had it. Your name becomes publicly accessible once the local cops get a hold of it. Where do you think the media gets their information? You know, Cole, we're both dead if Ike or Laughlin ever catch up with us and sooner or later -"

"We kill 'em," interrupted Cole. "Either we mess 'em up so bad they forget about us forever or we kill 'em."

"What is this killing with you? You are not a good person. You are an evil person and I don't like it! Are you some kind of angel of death or something?"

"If it's right, then that's the way it is. If they do harm to others, I do harm to them. That's the way it is," replied Cole and then paused, "I recollect you ain't so pure yourself. Remember Callaway."

"I remember," mumbled Kevin.

"Then let's get on with it. What more do you know about Ike and Laughlin's finances?"

"I downloaded a bunch of batch run data from the FINCEN computer, but I haven't had a chance to look at it." Kevin paused and then added, "Want to go back to Laughlin's?"

"Not without a little diesel fuel and ammonium nitrate. Why?"

"This isn't Oklahoma City. I just want another look. I brought a new toy I want to try out. Last time

I couldn't get into Laughlin's computer system. This time I will."

"You've been there?"

"Yeah. I've been there. You think you're the only spy around?"

"When?"

"Maybe tomorrow, early."

A brunette in tight, tight shorts interrupted to check the level of Kevin and Cole's beer. She was followed by two large nefarious bar patrons with full beards. One of them pushed her aside and then deliberately knocked over Cole's half-full beer.

In a deep-down Southern drawl, the other man confronted Kevin, "We all understand you like a different flavor. You cock-sucking queers ain't welcome here."

Kevin's reply was meek. "We'll go. No problem here. It's okay. It's okay."

"Yeah, you'll go all right. I'll show you the door."

The second man spat on Cole and added to the harassment, "I ain't touching this sickly lookin' thing. He's probably got AIDS."

Cole didn't move: didn't even flinch. He just locked his eyes onto the man with a demonic glare that brought a chill to Kevin. The man took a step backward and turned his palms upward as if to say: "I'm done - enough."

The first man grabbed Kevin's arm and pulled him from his seat, "Let's go, boy." Like a striking rattlesnake, Cole brushed the table aside, sprang from his seat and latched onto the man's neck with his right hand. He tightened his grip, bringing the man to his knees and shouted, "Listen, you dumb redneck. I'm going rip to your lungs out through your neck and then stick them down your friend's throat." Cole pointed at the other man and continued, "You want your friend here to live, back off. Back off!"

The DJ stopped the music and the dancer, abashed by the violence, covered her chest with her hands. All conversations in the bar stopped and all ears strained to eavesdrop on the conversation.

Cole stared deep into the man's terrified eyes and pierced his very soul. He tightened his grip as the man used both his hands in an attempt to free the crushing hold. Cole lowered his voice to a whisper, "We're leaving but understand this: at this moment, I decide if you live or die. When you bully somebody, you take that risk. Should I kill you now?" The man saw horror; he tried to close his eyes but Cole's focus hypnotically prevented it. His very soul was exposed and there was no escape.

The bouncer came charging over, but stopped short with a glare from Cole. Cole looked down at the man in his grasp. "What should I do? What do you think? Live or die?" said Cole as he bent over to come face to face with the man. He paused and then continued, "I think today I'll let you live." Cole pushed him to the floor and then stepped past. Kevin followed as they

     Brian David Simmons

headed for the door. All eyes in the bar were upon them as the bouncer stepped aside and they exited. Not a word was said.

Once outside, Kevin exploded, "What do you think you're doing! None of that was necessary. You just couldn't resist beating up on that ugly jerk. You enjoy it, don't you? Admit it. I could see it in your eyes. You wanted to kill that guy just because he was a jerk. That isn't the way it is. You give and take in this world. You don't just kill. Didn't your mother teach you that?"

"My mother certainly didn't teach me to turn the other cheek."

"Well, she should have!"

"She died when I was twelve."

"Sorry, but it doesn't matter. You just don't do that."

Cole checked back toward the bar as they retreated toward the hotel, "I got us out of there, didn't I?"

"I'd have gotten out of there. I'd have swallowed my pride and gotten out of there without any violence. You, on the contrary, are so weak you can hardly stand yet you couldn't resist the opportunity to beat up on somebody. You need to get your head examined. You probably killed those men in the desert for sport. Maybe you were just out having fun. No wonder Laughlin's boys came after you. You probably picked the fight. Did you?"

"No," asserted Cole as they walked around the corner into the hotel driveway.

"Bull. I don't know what to believe. This whole thing is out of control. You can't just go around beating up and killing people. It isn't right. There is something essentially and fundamentally wrong with you. You're a maniac."

"Slow down, Kevin."

"Shut up! Four A.M. Don't be late!" finished Kevin and then marched toward his room.

Cole hung out in the shadows for a few minutes to be sure they weren't followed and then discreetly went to his room. Kevin was just upset and he would get over it, surmised Cole. Tomorrow would be a new day.

     Brian David Simmons

Chapter Nineteen

THE ARTEE

EMERGING FROM HIS HOTEL ROOM AFTER ONLY FEW hours of sleep, Cole was still tired. He was in no shape for another jog in the park. Kevin privately evaluated Cole's struggling physical condition and knew he would overcome. Kevin had a new toy to test and could have done it without Cole, but then he wouldn't have anybody to share his success - or failure. It was better this way; they were partners.

It was an easy early morning drive across Atlanta with the almost non-existent traffic. Kevin parked the car on Garden Street at the corner of the narrow lane leading up to Laughlin's house. He had failed to gain remote access to Laughlin's security system, but this time he came equipped to hopefully close the loop. Cole got in the back seat and followed Kevin's instructions. He set up the digital camera with two tripod legs resting on the floorboard and the third leg resting in the inter-section of the rear window and rear shelf. Meanwhile, Kevin sighted-in the laser on the video camera over Laughlin's front door. Under Kevin's direction, cables were run from front to rear and across Kevin's lap to the laptop computer on the passenger seat.

Only Kevin understood the cable set up running throughout the car. As Kevin plugged things in and warmed up the laptop, he explained the system's operation in technical terms, as if giving a dissertation on the internal operation of each component and their interconnected interactions. Cole grasped the overall concept of what Kevin was about to attempt, but the technical electronic and computer narration escaped him.

"And now we're ready," said Kevin as he concluded his technical dissertation. "Set the camera to wide angle so you just get the front of the house in view finder. Stop moving. You're messing up my laser target."

Cole adjusted the camera and replied, "Ready, captain."

"Don't move. Don't even breathe," said Kevin as he fired the laser. "Just a moment now. Come on, baby. Come on."

"What are we waiting on, captain?"

"Shut up!"

"How -"

"All right," interrupted Kevin. "Looks like we got it. I sent it a command to refresh the CRT screen and it talked to me. Zoom that camera in on the upper right hand dormer."

The dormers had caught Cole's attention before. Not that dormers themselves were unusual, but they looked out of place sitting atop the mansion. They were somebody's non-architectural afterthought. Cole zoomed the camera in, squaring its picture on the dark window.

     Brian David Simmons

"Ready, captain."

Kevin fired the laser again and monitored the laptop. Oblivious to the physical world, his mind followed the laser through the laptop and visualized his signal passing through the vidicon tube and chrominance mixer, and then overlaying itself with the intended digital image. His digital signal entered the CPU and it responded with a flash from the CRT screen that appeared as a momentary light, emitted from the dormer window. The flash was detected by the digital video camera and Kevin had his loop closure.

He touched the space bar, paused, typed in "breakin8," and then began typing as he mumbled to himself: "What are you telling me? Why won't you let me in? I'm friendly. Oh, I'm not. Then what am I? Intruder? No. What are you? You are. You sly devil. That's why you wouldn't let me in before; you don't allow non-catalogued files."

Kevin continued with his seduction, rattling the keyboard and firing inputs through the laser probing for answers. The inquisition manifest itself with continued mumbling, "Can't I be catalogued, too? Not allowed. That's not fair. Why not? How clever. Okay then, I'll be Mickey Mouse and we'll be a hidden file."

The keys on the laptop rattled as "mickmose" was constructed and then buried deep on the host hard drive. Cole watched and listened as the strange communication continued. At times, it sounded like a lover's quarrel. At other times, Kevin was charming it with affection. It was nearly an hour before Kevin finished, "Okay, baby, we're friends now, just don't forget me."

"You aren't going to believe it," exclaimed Kevin as he began shutting equipment down. "They've got an Artee."

"A what?"

"An Artee. You know, an artificial intelligence routine. These guys are good. Real good. It also explains a few things. It processes more obscure pieces of data than the human mind can possibly assimilate, makes comparisons and correlations, evaluates, adapts, and then decides."

"Decides what?"

"You name it. If it decides I'm a possible threat, it shuts down my attempts to hack in. When I change my approach, it adapts and counters to block me out. It also means that it's evaluating video surveillance data. In fact, I'll bet it's why they figured you out. Just think about it. How else could they have tagged you after your drive-bys? It's so simple, I don't know why I didn't pick up on it sooner; all the signs were there."

"All right, Kevin. I don't get it. Tell me, but keep it simple."

"It's an Artee. It takes data, categorizes it, analyzes it, and then makes decisions. You drove by taking pictures and using binoculars to spy on Laughlin. You did it late at night. You did it three times. The Artee probably processed this data as a possible threat and triggered a yellow alarm. Then you drove by a fourth time with a weapon—in your case, a video camera hanging out the window. It triggered a red alarm and dispatched its human servants to squelch the perpetrator. It's so simple.

"When you followed the armored car, it probably registered the minivan and its license plate three times. Three times is the charm, and again it sounded a yellow alarm. It dispatched its servants to investigate and you were had. You didn't have a chance. All that cloak and dagger stuff doesn't work against an Artee."

"That means Sugar Ike is somehow tied into Laughlin's home computer, doesn't it?"

"That it does. But it's a little more than a home computer. I'm still not sure what I was talking to. I suspect its just a remote computer station in the attic"

"So if this artificial intelligence thing is going to spot us coming from a mile away, how do we get close?"

"We'll just counter their Artee with a Mickey Mouse."

"Okay, I'll play. What is a Mickey Mouse?"

"Not just any old Mickey Mouse, a friendly Mickey Mouse who is everybody's special friend, especially the Artee's. Mickey Mouse can do no harm to Artee."

"Enough. Enough. I give. I suppose Artee's going to become a mouseketeer or musketeer or whatever."

"Absolutely, and they're going to chat tomorrow at four a.m."

"For crying out loud, Kevin! What are you talking about? Sometimes I think you're on drugs."

"Okay, Mr. Tech-_no_-crat. It's real simple. I just sent it a little program that will allow me to call at four o'clock in the morning and tie in through its router. I can call any day I want and it will recognize me as non-threatening, i.e., Mickey Mouse."

"Why didn't you just say so?"

"I did one other thing."

"What's that?"

"Mickey Mouse is everybody's friend, you know. He's even Artee's friend, now."

"Did you ever do LSD! No, no, don't answer," said Cole, waving his hand. "It's okay. I can't take anymore of this Mickey Mouse/Artee stuff! Let's just get out of here."

They unplugged and coiled cables, neatly packing them along with their electronic components back in their suitcases. In the names of Casper Johnson and Cody Calhoon, Kevin had tickets for the eight-fifty flight to Los Angeles with a forty-five-minute layover in Dallas. He had another set of tickets from Dallas to Salt Lake for James Que Bond and Jason West. Even though when it was time to go, Kevin wanted to complete one more test.

In route to the airport, Kevin stopped in front of a sleazy frontage road motel and let Cole out. Following Kevin's instructions, Cole went to the motel office and pounded on the door until he gained attention. An older, heavy-set woman choking and hacking on the morning's first cigarette came to the security window. She looked like warmed over death that had just crawled out of bed, and was just as pleasant.

"What do you want?"

"How 'bout a room, ma'am?"

"You gotta be out by ten or pay two days, you understand."

"Yes, ma'am, I'll take two days. You take credit cards, right?" Cole slipped his VISA card through the slot under the security window. It wasn't a card with Cody's or James' name on it; it was his own personal credit card. It was the test.

"I'd like a room with a view of the street, if you don't mind."

"I don't mind. All my rooms got a view."

With the transaction complete, Cole headed in the general direction of his room until he saw the light in the office go off. He then turned and hurried back to the street where Kevin picked him up. They circled the block and found an inconspicuous parking place in plain view of Cole's newly rented room. They didn't have very much time before their flight, but it didn't take long for Kevin's test to have results.

Two cars pulled into the motel parking lot and Kevin sighed, "Dang, that's what I was afraid of. They not only know who you are but they also have access to credit card transactions. No doubt from the Artee."

"We're screwed."

"There's no going back. That's for sure."

Cole and Kevin watched as two men got out of

the first sedan and demanded service at the security window. Some sort of transaction took place and one of the men signaled the occupants of the second car. Two more men joined them and all four advanced on Cole's room. Their movements were police-like, being careful not to approach the door front-on. With two men on each side of Cole's door, one of the men inserted a key.

Kevin sighed as all four barged in, "I don't know what kind of machine they've got, but it's gotta be a monster. My frail little door to the Artee isn't much."

"I'm more worried about the goons. We ain't ever going get a night's sleep."

Kevin started the car and they pulled away. It was after six and they went straight to the airport. Traffic was picking up which slowed their trip back across the city. The trip was mostly silent as both contemplated the ease at which Laughlin could track them down. They made their flight with only minutes to spare after handing off Kevin's luggage at the sky cab and leaving the rental car curbside.

Kevin relaxed in the comfort of the first class seat but his test had made it clear that they could never quit, at least as long as Ike and Laughlin were around.

Kevin and Cole made the second flight in Dallas and were in Salt Lake shortly after one. It was unusually early for snow, but the whole valley had a beautiful white frosting. It slowed their long trip to the cabin at Bear Lake, but the time was well spent as they began to lay out their strategy.

     Brian David Simmons

Chapter Twenty

WASHING MACHINE

COLE THOUGHT THE CABIN WAS PERFECT. IT HAD NO neighbors and a clear view of anybody approaching. Kevin had done well. He had even stocked the food supply like a mountain man expecting to winter in the high mountains. Cole instantly felt comfortable with the cabin, but he didn't have time to be comfortable. He had work to do.

Cole was in terrible physical condition and only hard work could return the vitality he once had. Every day started with push-ups, sit-ups, and a short jog down to the main road and back. When he completed his routine, he started all over again, and then again.

Kevin made his call every morning at two A.M., Mountain Time, to Laughlin's Artee, but it was unco-operative. No matter how much Kevin sweet-talked it, it was still evasive. He couldn't even figure out what it was; it acted like a common PC, but only at its extremity. It wouldn't let him inspect its hardware configuration, much less touch any of its software or data. Even time was limited; two A.M. Utah time was four A.M. in Atlanta, and its human masters might get wise if he talked too late in the morning. During the day, he concentrated on the downloaded FINCEN data.

Cole worked harder and harder every day as Kevin sorted and analyzed his data. Little was said between the two throughout the day, both contemplating elements of the plan individually. Evening breaks were spent merging their ideas and formulating the details of their strategy. The overall plan was simple: confusion, distraction, turmoil, bankruptcy, and incarceration or death.

In the end, Ike, Laughlin, Beech, and as many of their associates as possible would be broke and either dead or in jail. Kevin's preference was jail; Cole didn't care.

The key was understanding how Ike and Laughlin laundered their money. It was obvious from Cole's reconnaissance that Ike's chain of convenience stores, by itself, was a big loser. Yet, income tax reports revealed that Ike was reporting tremendous profits. It was supposition, but reasonably conclusive, that Ike was supplementing his semi-weekly convenience store bank deposits with drug money. The armored car stop at the warehouse on Werkiel was probably where they augmented the collection from the stores with the drug money before making bank deposits. It was simple, straightforward money laundering. Each store having sales of a couple of thousand per day mixed with dirty money of thirty-five thousand dollars per day made it all look clean when deposited.

Laughlin's finances were far more difficult to figure out. It was only with help from the FINCEN

Super-Cray's correlation runs that Kevin began to sort it out. The Cray established a weak relationship between Laughlin's futures market trades and activity in four Futures Commission Merchants (FCM). Kevin didn't understand the futures market, much less the complexity of Laughlin's finances.

It was a learning experience for both Cole and Kevin, and through the Internet, they learned the ins and outs of the futures market. It really wasn't that complicated when they reduced it to an analogy. Kevin created the basic analogy and then they built on it as they learned more.

A futures contract is like buying stock on lay-away. A purchase contract is established based on today's price with delivery and final payment due at a specified future date. Initially, only the lay-away, or margin, price is required to purchase the contract, even though it locks the buyer into an obligation for the full contract price.

If the price of stock (commodity) increases during the term of the contract, the contract can be sold at a profit. Similarly, if the price of the commodity decreases, the contract is sold at a loss. For the margin price, a contract can be sold, or someone else's contract can be bought, before a given contract expires.

If the commodity is not wanted and the contract was bought strictly for the purpose of profit, then sometime prior to contract expiration, the contract is sold short.

In simple numbers, if a commodity contract with a delivery date of 6 June is selling for $50,000 on 6 April and a single contract is purchased at a margin price of $5,000, the contract can be sold before 6 June at a profit or loss. If on 6 May, the price of the commodity contract has a value of $60,000, then the contract can be sold for a $10,000 profit with only the original $5,000 investment. Kevin equated it to a highly leveraged form of gambling.

The gambling was further complicated by options. A call option could be placed on the commodity contract that provides the buyer an opportunity to buy the contract at a later date. The option price, or option premium, provides the buyer the opportunity to buy the contract at a pre-established strike price. Options to buy, call options, or options to sell, put options, can be bought or sold just like futures contracts. It also meant that commodities can be sold even though the commodity isn't owned, which further enables the level of gambling.

Futures and options are sold through a futures broker who places automated orders to buy or sell in the trading pits of futures exchanges. All brokers must work through a FCM who keeps all records of trades, holds all margin funds, and files tax information. FCMs are members of clearing corporations to guarantee the commitment of buyers and sellers of leveraged contracts.

Laughlin was a futures broker. There was dirt in Laughlin's financial data, but it continued to elude

     Brian David Simmons

Kevin. The downloaded data from FINCEN showed that Laughlin had unusual success in the futures market, yielding phenomenal daily gains, but it was all legitimate. He surmised, assumed, and guessed at possible scenarios, supplementing Laughlin's profit/ loss data with actual market data and then trying to back into something irregular. He found nothing and could only surmise that Laughlin was doing extensive day trading, probably Artee directed. In early morning phone calls, the Artee wouldn't tell him anything about the financial data and the FINCEN data he had wasn't enough; Kevin decided to go after one of the FCMs used by Laughlin.

The context and address of Laughlin's data transactions were included in the FINCEN data: it was the location of the Artee in a cyberspace cloud server. Address alone wasn't enough; Kevin anticipated the complexity of data encryption and the weeks, months or years it might take to crack.

In concept, encryption and decryption is simple. A mathematical algorithm, in the form of a "key" is used to encrypt plain text characters. The simplest of algorithms, or convention cryptography, simply substitutes or offsets characters. ABCDEF could become ZBCDE or CDEFGH. But with today's computer technology, encryption keys are extremely complex, turning plain text into mathematical nightmares of gibberish. The key that is used to encrypt data is typically known as a public key. The key that is used to decrypt data is held by the recipient of the data and is undecipherable from the public key. Kevin understood this complex world of encryption and was fully aware of the challenge that awaited him.

Encryption is further complicated by a gambit of encryption standards and techniques. The combination of encryption complexity and encryption variants made deciphering Laughlin's data an almost impossible task. Kevin continued to ponder his dilemma.

Given a variety of encryption techniques, deciphering the method alone was highly unlikely. Would the encryption method be based on a standard technique, such as the Federal Data Encryption Standard (DES) or would it be some new technology? If it was CAST, Triple-DES, IDEA, or other high-power technology operating with cipher feedback, a conventional cryptanalysis attack was out of the question. A million computers processing data at a billion bytes a second would take until the turn of the century to crack a single file. Kevin needed an angle.

He devised a multi-pronged approach based on key assumptions. The financial industry is highly regulated and therefore probably had all of the FCMs using DES. This was a key assumption that greatly simplified the task at hand. But it still required that he obtain a decryption key.

The second assumption was that public and private keys were used. The FCM having the Artee's public key and the Artee, of course, having a private random pass-phrase key.

 Brian David Simmons

Kevin also assumed that the Artee would randomly change the key with each day's transmission. It's simple to do so with a random number generator or time and date updates. It was a logical assumption given the complexity and abilities of the Artee. With the encryption key changing on a daily basis, each data set captured would require Kevin to repeat the task of ascertaining the correct key. It was irrational to expect to crack a single key, much less a new key for each data set. A different approach was required and Kevin had to formulate some cyber-espionage tactics.

The first step was to get a data sample. In cyberspace, knowing where the data was headed made its capture a relatively easy task. Kevin assumed that accumulated FCM data on a day's activity would be downloaded via Laughlin's T-1 line to the Artee after the commodities markets closed. Kevin would simply disguise the Artee's address, leaving a dummy in its place that rerouted the data to an alternate server and then on to his computer. This was similar to the way Kevin emulated Councilman Hubbard's website; Kevin would just grab the data from the Artee before it arrived, make some very special changes and then send the data on.

Kevin wrote a program named "mailbox" and test-ran it with several different scenarios on the 4056. Speed was a problem; the phone lines only marginally handled a 56K modem, even though the 4056's capability had been boosted to 256K. If the data set was large, the delay might attract the attention of FCM computer or the Artee, especially if they had additional security features.

Kevin wrote two other programs: one called "wormboy" and the other called "vrtlgrab." "Wormboy" was a unique form of virus. It was to accompany data that Kevin passed on to the Artee and then capture key and pass-phrase information. "Vrtlgrab" went the other way; it went back to the FCM computer to look for unencrypted data still residing in the scratch pad area of the disc or in a swap file. With his three codes prepared, he was ready to enter cyberspace. This trip would take all his energy and skill. The last thing he needed was distractions; he needed to get rid of Cole.

Kevin made out a list and then sent Cole on a shopping trip to Salt Lake. The list included proximity sensors used in conjunction with plumbing and electrical fixtures. Proximity sensors are commonplace in commercial urinals, water saving faucet systems, and outside lights. The list was simple enough, but essential to their plan. The sensors would enable them to monitor activities at the cabin from thousands of miles away. Just as important, Kevin needed the cabin to himself at three o'clock, five o'clock eastern, when most commodity markets closed.

The cabin was quiet. The only sound was that of the humming computer. He opened three windows and thought through his attack one more time. Kevin took a deep breath to mentally prepare himself for the frantic moments that would follow.

     Brian David Simmons

He verified server locations and addresses for the Artee and FCM, then he waited. Timing would be critical. Too soon and he might draw attention to himself, too late and he might miss the data. Three o'clock came and went; still he waited. Then, when it felt right, at 3:04, he hit "enter" and commanded his "mailbox."

Thirty-seven seconds later, data from the FCM computer began to flow into his "mailbox." As it flowed in, it was forwarded to the 4056. Simultaneously, "vrtlgrab" was launched at the FCM's virtual memory scratchpad. "Vrtlgrab" scored multiple hits and also began transmitting data. "Vrtlgrab" didn't wait for complete files; it transmitted every byte as quickly as it could grab them. Files, some complete, began to assemble on Kevin's e-mail server. The data flow lasted three seconds before the FCM computer began overwriting its virtual memory. "Vrtlgrab" continued to snatch data even with the onslaught of bit-dissolving electronic rain.

As the last of the encrypted data flowed into Kevin's artificial mailbox, he attached his "wormboy" software to the data file. The process was incredibly slow; seven minutes had expired before the data was ready to forward on to Laughlin's Artee.

The Artee was already inquiring, "Where's my data?" It was temporally satisfied when it began receiving data from the "mailbox." The Artee loaded the data into its file structure where the routine virus check was performed. "Wormboy" was already at work and had located the Artee's private key. At the moment of capturing the key - bam! The Artee's anti-virus protection smashed "wormboy." "Wormboy" had failed.

The Artee fired an immediate message to the masters of the FCM computer to diagnose the problem and eradicate the virus from their system. They confirmed and the Artee was satisfied.

Kevin withdrew from the expanses of cyberspace bringing his mailbox with him. He had something, but he didn't know what. As Kevin had suspected, the Artee's data file was fully encrypted, appearing only as jumbled symbols. "Vrtlgrab" had snatched two hundred and eighty-one partial files containing something. Maybe it was enough.

Kevin's challenge was to reconstruct the Artee's private key. By comparing the encrypted data to plain text stolen from the FCM computer's virtual memory scratchpad, patterns could be developed into a key to decrypt the Artee's data. He built an iterative routine based on an initial set of assumptions. It was going to be colossal task for the little PC; each plain text character, or element, has 3,628,800 possible permutations, each making sense only when combined with adjacent characters, or elements. Each hit, or potential pattern find, could then be combined to verify the mathematical relationship between encrypted elements and plain text elements to build the key. Kevin built his iterative routines and put the PC to work. He went to bed before Cole got back to the cabin. Tomorrow, he would send Cole back to Salt Lake for a few more PCs.

     Brian David Simmons

The 4056 was still cranking the following morning, humming and clicking away as the virtual memory flowed in and out of swap files on its hard drive. Kevin monitored his 4056 throughout the morning, but nothing converged. He and Cole were reduced to watching cartoons on TV while the computer hummed in the background. They prepared another shopping list for Cole. He would leave before three, giving Kevin the isolation he needed. Cole left and as three o'clock approached, Kevin suspended the "4056's iterative interrogation and brought up "mailbox" and "vrtlgrab."

Today, the Artee would use a new encryption key and the challenge would start over. The Artee was too clever for "wormboy," and Kevin decided not to try it again. He would have to rely on "vrtlgrab" and hope that that his iterative routines would eventually yield encryption keys.

Kevin waited until precisely 3:04 and then slid his "mailbox" into place. Almost instantly, data began to trickle in. Again, he launched "vrtlgrab" concurrently with the capture of the encrypted data. This time it only took five minutes for the "mailbox" to reroute the data. But when it was finished, the Artee was already asking for its data.

As before, the human masters of the FCM computer were summoned, but Kevin detected no action. Kevin now had two days of something. He saved the file and the 4056 went back to work searching for the key.

Kevin was waiting for Cole when he arrived at the cabin. Greeting was non-existent. Kevin immediately unloaded the first PC and began the assembly process before Cole had unloaded the other two. All three had 2GHz processors with 512 SDRAM at 100MHz and a 206GB hard drive. As Kevin finished assembling the first one, he dubbed it "R2." Cole helped assemble the other two and then Kevin loaded his software to boost their processor speed to 2028 MHz. He named his other children "D2" and "CP3O." With all four computers humming, Kevin routed cable and loaded software to establish his own little intranet.

Kevin divided the work on the first data set captured evenly between 4056, R2, D2, and CP3O. All four hummed and crunched. Kevin admired his children, all in a line, each with data streaming across their CRTs as they slaved away for him. He said good night to his children and then went to bed.

Kevin woke early to check on the progress of his children. Data had stopped streaming across their CRTs and they just hummed idly. Except for the DOS prompt, the CRTs on R2, D2, and CP3O were blank. The CRT on 4056 displayed the history of the four-some's final actions: encryption key had been recovered, the data set had been decrypted and then copied to a new file. Kevin was elated.

He howled as he burst into Cole's room and then jumped onto the bed. He continued to jump, bouncing Cole left and right.

"What's the matter with you? You're losing it. Go away."

"I'm not losing it. I got it. Come see. Come on. Get out of bed."

"Go away."

"Get up. You're awake now. Come on. Come see."

"I'm asleep!"

"Let's go," insisted Kevin as he tugged at Cole's arm to get him out of bed.

"Let go of me! I'm coming."

When they entered the living room, Cole lambasted Kevin, "What!"

"Look, see that? They converged."

"See what?"

Kevin pointed at the 4056, "See."

"You got me out of bed for that," concluded Cole and went in search of cold cereal.

Kevin skipped breakfast, brought up the decrypted data set and delved into the world of Laughlin's finances. The data included Laughlin's personal transactions as well as that of fifty-one customers. Kevin was not a futures expert, but something was wrong. Many of the trades were just plain stupid; it was as if some of Laughlin's customers were intentionally losing money. It made no sense whatsoever. Kevin's elation turned to depression as morning turned to afternoon.

Laughlin's personal trade data for the single day showed that he traded continuously and racked up a tremendous volume, sometimes trading a single commodity more than twenty-five times. In contrast to his clients, Laughlin never lost on a trade; every short sale resulted in a gain, and they were legitimate. Kevin hammered the keys until three o'clock approached.

This time at 3:03, he put his "mailbox" back to work. The result was as it had been the previous two days. Kevin captured a third data set.

Before bed, Kevin put his children to work, and overnight, they provided him another legible file. The data was still confusing: Laughlin and some of his clients won; other clients lost miserably. It just made no sense. Maybe Laughlin had idiots for clients that didn't mind dropping hundreds of thousands of dollars.

Kevin captured Friday's data at 3:03 to give him four days' worth of trading activity. He decided to broaden his analysis. First, he would decrypt the remaining data sets. Then, he would combine the four days' worth of data. He would run a correlation analysis and establish trading patterns to try to understand the insanity of the Artee's trading logic.

As the computers worked, Cole and Kevin speculated. Could Laughlin be using the futures market to launder money? If so, how? All they had was Laughlin's presumed guilt. If Laughlin was laundering other people's money, it meant that he would have to control the money that wasn't his, and the path was obscured by the complexities of dozens of customers with multiple futures trading accounts in different self-service brokerages. For the correlation to exist, the Artee had to be orchestrating long and short contract purchases for hundreds of individual traders, each with hundreds of trades. Laughlin's trades could just be money skimmed for his services.

In concept, it made sense: dirty money in and clean money out. But in order to make it work, a lot had to happen. The trades had to be made at the right time with the right direction of the market. Otherwise, you could just as easily turn clean money into lost money. The futures washing machine was easy enough to conceptualize, but the details were complex, and deciphering the money trail and mechanics of the trades was a horridly convoluted undertaking.

Kevin spent the weekend working with the data. Thousands of trades were analyzed, focusing on large, simultaneous investor trades with parallel personal trades made by Laughlin. It was as if hundreds of day-traders, making thousands of trades through multiple exchanges were somehow orchestrated for some indecipherable outcome.

It finally came together when Kevin came across two traders playing two exchanges in parallel. The two traders, Tiziano Vecelli and Casey Neller, deposited five hundred thousand dollars in self-service brokerage accounts. The futures contracts were highly leveraged at twenty percent, which gave each trader two-and-a-half million dollars of purchasing power. Tiziano Vecelli bought approximately one hundred contracts of live cattle futures on the Chicago Mercantile Exchange, CME. At the same time, Casey Neller bought futures contracts for Asian Import Crude on the New York Mercantile Exchange, NYMEX. Each of the traders were then leveraged in the futures market for two-and-a-half million dollars with five hundred thousand dollars of presumed dirty money. But the real key was that conceptually for the first time Kevin could see how dirty money had been lost in the market and new, clean, traceable money had emerged in the form of commodity gains.

Kevin summarized the washing machine mechanics for Cole. It took a spreadsheet to summarize the trades and end results. He was elated with his find as he explained it to Cole. "These two traders held their contracts for two days, letting the market take its natural course until the final day. Sometime during the day when the live cattle and oil futures were up, Tiziano Vecelli sold his live cattle futures, short, taking a loss. The same day, when the oil futures were up, Casey Neller sold his oil futures, also taking a loss. To offset their trades, Casey Neller exercised options to buy cattle futures and Tiziano Vecelli exercised options to buy oil futures."

"Then it's a push. Both lose, but at the same time they both win. Cool."

"That's my name, Kevin Mc-Cool" bragged Kevin. "Pretty incredible, considering Laughlin's doing this for at least a hundred dirty people."

"What a convoluted mess."

"Exactly! That's why the Artee is the master of ceremonies."

"How much money does that mean it's manipulating?"

"I don't know yet. Total money out there at any given time is somewhere between twenty-five and seventy-five million. But that's just straight money; leveraged it could be worth five times that amount."

"Wow! I think you just hit pay dirt."

Chapter Twenty-One

Contact

Except for the simple Casey Neller and Tiziano Vecelli futures contract exchange, Laughlin's trading activity involved so many variables that it was impossible for Kevin to decipher which of Laughlin's clients traded what to whom. Yet, the trades had to work out even at the end of each day for each trader. Algorithm after algorithm failed and Kevin became increasingly frustrated with the futures quagmire.

The frequency of Kevin's breaks from his data analysis increased and he found more time to help Cole with cabin preparations. Cole retrieved specialty supplies from Salt Lake and collected other items en route. He picked up Kevin's orders for combat and electronic gear, some of it legal, some of it not. He made small cash purchases for ammonium nitrate fertilizer from every farm supply store between Salt Lake and Bear Lake on each trip until he had a massive supply. He had bought an aging four-wheel-drive pickup with a snowplow blade on the front, which made him look like a typical customer at the feed stores. He also purchased three fifty-five-gallon drums of powdered aluminum from a scrap yard and stockpiled it with his fertilizer.

Kevin and Cole gave the cabin "eyes" for events to

come. They mounted surveillance cameras under the eaves of the cabin to provide for panoramic surveillance. They also mounted cameras inside to cover the interior of the cabin. Cole selected locations for motion detectors and Kevin designed the wiring.

Kevin's best attempts at satellite link eavesdropping and decoding the distant phone conversations were as unsuccessful as his futures perplexity. He just didn't have the computational ability needed; his homegrown system was nothing in comparison to the rumored NSA "Echelon" system that scans the airways for key words and then locks in on conversations, personal or other. And then with its banks of super Crays and keys to common encryption, it exposes, interrogates, and analyzes each call.

For the first time in Kevin's life, he had been defeated, not just on one front, but two computer fronts. Depression was setting in, only this time, he had no solvable technical problem in which to absorb himself. He turned to Cole instead, "I can't make it happen, Cole. What's the matter with me? It's just data, bits and bytes, nothing more, but I can't make it happen anymore."

"Maybe you're trying too hard."

"I'm trying as hard as I can," replied Kevin almost tearfully.

"That's what I mean. Slow down and just ask yourself: what do I really want?"

"I am!"

"No. Let's take them one at a time. What do we really want from Laughlin?"

"Well, we want to decipher his data and understand how he does his trading."

"No, we don't."

"What?"

"Sure. What we really want is to interfere with Laughlin's trading so bad that he ends up owing every murdering, drug-dealing gangster in the country. They take care of him and our problem goes away. Simple."

"Yeah, and that takes us right back to deciphering the futures data."

"No. You're working too hard again. We don't need to know where every dollar went. We just need the Artee to do the opposite of what it's doing now; instead of turning their dirty money into clean, we need it to turn their money into our money. What if the Artee just kept on doing what it does, only it did it for us? Do you get my drift? Do you think you could just slip the Artee a virus of some kind that would do that?"

"I don't know, maybe. Not a virus though," replied Kevin as his eyes lit up and the wheels started spinning.

"Okay, but something."

"You know that just might work. Multiple accounts, siphon it off with every transaction. Yeah, I'll try a different approach. You know, that might really work!"

Kevin went back to his 4056 and the keyboard hummed. He pounded on late into the night until he was mentally exhausted and collapsed on the keyboard. Their plan for Laughlin came together the next morning: phase one would irritate and distract; phase two would confuse and create customer dissatisfaction and mistrust; phase three would destroy Laughlin's wealth; phase four would create total mayhem and bring an army of FBI, IRS, and FINCEN agents. Kevin objected to phase five, but eventually partially conceded. Laughlin would have to die.

Late into the morning, Cole and Kevin continued to work on the details of their scheme, defining contingencies, evaluating actions and possible reactions, setting up and de-bugging computer programs, double and triple checking transportation reservations, and getting final supplies. It was almost time. Christmas was rapidly approaching and they had a special present for Laughlin.

Chapter Twenty-Two

It Begins

Kevin and Cole had planned enough; it was time to start Phase I: harassment. Kevin positioned himself at his computer with the anticipation of an athlete waiting for the starter's shot. Then he began. The keyboard rattled and the mouse swirled, clicked, and swirled some more as he went into his special passport. Anonymity was still important. He would start by ordering some special gifts for Laughlin. Of course, Laughlin would have to pay with his own credit cards.

Kevin loved his game and congratulated himself with every move. First, Laughlin needed some small stuff. The Internet and a few credit card numbers would take care of Laughlin's needs.

Laughlin didn't get out much and he probably ran out of things to read. Kevin took care of that problem. He ordered twenty-two books from Amazon.com, seventeen more Barnes Books, and a final fifty-eight from Banum Books. He thought Laughlin might really enjoy the order for fifty-eight books so he paid the premium shipping as well. Kevin was also sure that Laughlin was in need of a pocketknife, but he wasn't sure which kind he would really like. So instead of guessing, Kevin just randomly ordered thirteen different styles from eight online companies. Next, Kevin was off evaluating sex toys and lingerie. These were things Laughlin really needed. After ordering Laughlin an array of sex toys, the rest was anticlimactic. Nonetheless, Kevin went on to cameras, kid's toys, dishware, toasters, towel sets, antique and custom car parts, clothing, shoes, perfume, jewelry, and lawn equipment. Kevin made a final stop at eBay and made some outrageous bids that he was sure Laughlin would appreciate.

In the process, Kevin maxed out all three credit cards. He made as many purchases from as many different companies as possible. It would be a massive task for somebody to sort out all the deliveries, argue with the senders and credit card companies, and return all the merchandise - of course, only if Laughlin didn't like Kevin's selections. Kevin was proud of his selections and openly gloated, "There now - all gone. No more credit for you."

"You really enjoy messing with people, don't you?"

"Yeah, and I'm just getting started," laughed Kevin. "Now that he's spent all his credit, we'll fix his credit rating. How many late payments on his house in Florida do you think he should have?"

"Well, not as many as you think, I'm sure."

"All right then, I'll decide," said Kevin as he continued to alternate between driving the mouse and hammering the keyboard. "I think he should have sixteen. He has so much money he doesn't need an eight hundred credit score."

With the payment record fixed, Kevin went on to mail-order lists to ensure that Laughlin would get every piece of junk mail he was entitled to, and then some. Kevin didn't stop there. Laughlin might miss an important offer from the telemarketers and that was just unacceptable. Kevin inserted Laughlin's name right at the top of every sucker list he could find. In the process, Kevin almost forgot about magazine subscriptions. It was a good thing for Laughlin that he remembered.

Kevin broke into a sweat as he went into the Press International headline database to plant the first of several incriminating stories about Laughlin. In Kevin's first story, Laughlin had been witness to, and a participant in, the brutal beating and killing of two black men in Atlanta:

> "…Informed sources say that Laughlin watched as the two men were severely beaten and then inflicted the final blows himself. One man was struck in the head from behind and the other had his face caved in with a two-by-four. The two men had attempted to cheat Laughlin in a drug deal and were being questioned by Laughlin, torture style, when they were killed. Friends close to the victims say Laughlin routinely conducts business with torture. They refused to identify themselves in fear of Laughlin."

     Brian David Simmons

In Kevin's second story, Isaac Bartrum had agreed to turn state's evidence against Laughlin for running a money-laundering scheme using his chain of convenience stores. Kevin provided the facts and figures and explained the scheme in detail.

The stories didn't have to be run; they just had to prompt questions for the Atlanta police to confirm. Laughlin was going to have some very enjoyable company. Kevin suspected he would get visits from both the police and the media.

Next it was time for the IRS to investigate. Kevin dialed up FINCEN and went directly to the password interface. He greeted the Gatemaster, shook hands with its electronic tentacle, then left it rocking in perfect time. He went in under the user name "Presidential Access" with the password "BIGDUDE" and then went to work. Huey helped Kevin connect directly into the IRS computer system with unlimited access. First step was to delete all past records of income tax returns. Then he deleted all record of Laughlin's quarterly tax statements. Kevin got all Laughlin's files; he even had the back-up tapes mounted and then deleted every record of Laughlin's existence. He topped it off with a short e-mail from the IRS director to the regional office:

Please investigate recent tax history for David Laughlin, SS 123-01-2010, and initiate immediate on-site audit. Assets indicate seven-figure income with no tax records. Expect a multi-million dollar recovery.

"That ought to get the attention of every tax examiner in the Atlanta office," gloated Kevin as he backed out of the FINCEN computer. "Anything else for Laughlin?"

"No, Kevin," replied Cole. "I think you have taken excellent care of him."

" I haven't even gotten to Twitter and Facebook yet."

"I think you've done enough, Kevin."

High on his accomplishments and the spirit of his game, Kevin pronounced his vision with the enthusiasm of a Roman conqueror, "Yeah, it sure beats programming for Omage. You know, I have kind of a fantasy. This is the ultimate game. We could do this again and again whenever we run low on pocket money."

"A new profession of sorts?"

"Yeah. Take a vacation. Have some fun. And then pick another target. Go into business stealing from the bad guys. What do you figure our chances would be?"

"Not good," hesitated Cole. "The way we have it planned, we gotta have things fall into place perfectly. We're relying on all this electronic gadgetry with too many unmonitored timed events. We have to split up and be too many places at too many times. All it takes is one little screw-up and we're done. The plan is too complicated for just the two of us. Our chances aren't good."

"Want to back out?"

"No. That's not what I mean. I just mean we'll be lucky if we get away with this just once, much less if we try it again."

"Ever think about God?"

"Where'd that come from? Godly things don't apply to you and me."

"You ever think about what happens when you die?" questioned Kevin. "Do you think you go to heaven or hell or just blackout for ever?"

"Well, you and I already have our passports to hell. It's too late. We're for sure going to get an entrance stamp to hell with no possibility of an exit visa."

"We don't have to kill any more people."

"They're not people. They're bad guys. They deserve anything they get. Just think of it as self-defense. They came looking for us, now they die."

"You're spooky."

Kevin made a check of motion detectors and surveillance cameras. They all worked as planned. The final preparation for the cabin was prepare its walls and attic for events to come. Cole and Kevin dry-blended the ammonium nitrate fertilizer with the sawdust and aluminum powder. Then packed it in the walls of the cabin. Insulation in the cabin walls was poor, so it was a simple matter of drilling two-inch diameter holes in the sheet rock and then loading spaces between studs with the explosive mixture. The remaining mixture was hauled up to the attic in buckets and spread to layer the entire attic.

Chapter Twenty-Three

FLIGHT

JACK CROSS AWOKE TO THE INSISTENT RINGING OF the telephone. Drinking the night before, coupled with the irritation of the ringing phone, brought consciousness with a headache and severe abhorrence for the caller. Bobbling the phone, he managed to get it into position and lambasted the caller, "What!"

"I got a job for you," came a controlled response from Richard Hoecker, the CEO of Friendship Aviation.

"Tomorrow. It's two A.M."

"No, today, right now."

"Get somebody else. Come on, man."

"Nope, the fare came with a premium rate and conditions. It's you or nobody, and it's seven A.M. Mountain Time in Salt Lake, now or never."

"It's two. How many hours? Five, midnight—that's seven hours. I can't get there."

"Yes, you can. Cab is on its way to your apartment and they're rolling out the GIII as we speak."

"No way, man. Why me?"

"I don't know. They knew you by name and made it clear that you were it. I hit them with a premium-plus rate and I think I could have gotten more. There's an extra thousand bucks in it for you and this is a tipping fare. Treat them right and it's probably worth at least another thousand."

"I wasn't scheduled to drive for another couple of days and I won't pass a blood-alcohol test."

"Just don't make a mistake and nobody will know the difference. By the time you get to Salt Lake, you'll be plenty dried-out."

"Who's the client?"

"Microware. The corporate jet had landing gear problems on arrival in Salt Lake and they're stranded. They need to be in Dallas for an afternoon meeting, in Atlanta for dinner, and then on Dulles first thing in the morning. You need to be on standby for wherever they want to go, whenever they want to go, until their corporate jet gets back on line."

"You owe me, Hoecker. Who's in the right seat?"

"You fly solo to Salt Lake. You'll get one of their pilots there."

"Great. Put the coffee on."

Kevin's ability to get information about almost anybody never ceased to amaze Cole. Cole and Kevin chose Jack Cross because he regularly flew charter flights for Laughlin, and had gotten his flight training from the Navy bouncing F/A-18s onto carrier decks. He had a criminal record for assault and other sordid incidents in his background. All-out tail hook parties, including pass-out-fall-down binges and fraternization with demimondes had gone underground -but not far enough for Jack. He had been caught on videotape by a Department of Defense sting operation and then made an example. All he had really done was get incredibly drunk, chase hired dancers with his pants down like a schoolboy game, and got caught on videotape. It looked worse than it really was but it ruined his career.

After the Navy, bad went to worse. He was convicted of assault for slapping a haughty motorist who ran a stop sign and smashed his truck. Since then, he had taken whatever flying job he could get. Cole and Kevin were really satisfied with their choice. With Jack Cross's sordid background, he was the perfect pilot for the mission they had in mind.

As morning approached, Cole loaded the four-wheel-drive pickup and then plowed the driveway one last time before he and Kevin headed over the mountains to Brigham City. In the moonlight, he found his little road up into the canyon where he and the Sun Fire had navigated deep into the canyon. The road was now covered by several inches of snow, but with the four-wheel-drive pickup it was much easier to travel. The elevated snowplow blade hammered the ground a few times as the truck bounced in and out of snow-covered ruts. It made a horrendous racket. Cole carefully watched the terrain as they bounced up the narrow road, sometimes spinning all four tires, until he spotted the familiar geographic features.

Cole recognized the surroundings defined by the two intersecting vectors he had ingrained in his mind months ago. He stopped the truck and walked to the spot where the vectors intersected: one extending through points at a distant mountain peak and the saddle of the ravine, and the other through two large and irregular rocky outcroppings on the hillside above.

With pick and shovel, Kevin and Cole exposed and chipped away the concrete covering the cache. The bundles of hundred dollar bills were fresh and dry. They packed the bundles in an unpretentious duffel bag and were soon heading down the mountain road, leaving pick and shovel behind.

The trip to the airport was noisy in the aging truck, making conversation difficult; but then, enough had already been said. Kevin dropped Cole at the private aircraft terminal side of the airport and left to make shipping arrangements for the rest of the gear in the truck. Kevin then had a commercial flight to Atlanta.

Cole was early and had breakfast while waiting for his ride. He got an uneasy feeling when Friendship Aviation wasn't there at seven. He watched and waited and finally at seven-fifteen spotted the Friendship plane coming in for a landing.

The plane taxied to the private terminal and Cole, with the duffel bag over his shoulder, greeted Jack on the tarmac. Jack was a very fit, broad-shouldered man, just under six feet and two hundred twenty pounds; he looked like he could take care of himself. Cole went straight to intimidation as the means of establishing their relationship.

"You're late."

"Yeah, The winds aloft were against me."

"You're still late," snapped Cole. "Gas it up and let's get out of here."

"Sorry, that's the best you get when the jet stream is against you. I ordered the fuel truck while I taxied in."

"The luggage is sitting by the office door."

"I thought I'd get a little breakfast."

"No time. Get the luggage, get it gassed, and let's leave," blasted Cole and then walked past Jack on his way to the plane. Cole cautiously boarded the plane, finding it empty. It was a Gulfstream GIII with comfort for ten passengers. Its interior was plush, complete with a stocked galley, video conferencing system, and other amenities to make its elite passengers comfortable.

Cole stood back from the window and watched as Jack followed his instructions. Jack was making his second trip with the luggage when the fuel tanker showed up. The tanker crew went right to work. Cole monitored the methodical fueling activities and Jack's movements, questioning every action for signs of trouble.

Jack brought the final load of luggage and again requested the opportunity to make a quick run for breakfast. Cole declined the request and instructed him to make ready for flight. Cole continued his watch of the refueling crew. He listened as Jack made contact with the tower and readied for takeoff; everything seemed normal.

Jack turned to Cole and inquired, "Are you it?"

     Brian David Simmons

"I'm it."

"You're not Microware, are you?"

"Nope, just got a little business to do for Laughlin."

"Why the charade?"

"When we're done with this flight, it's better for everyone if it's remembered as a Microware mission. One other thing; I am authorized to slip you, personally, a cash bonus if I make my appointments."

"This isn't drugs, is it? I don't fly drug runs."

"No, it's definitely not drugs."

"What's in the hard-sided gun case?"

"Just a souvenir I picked up a while back."

"Look, I don't do drugs. I don't do guns. I don't any of the stuff you guys do. I think you'd better get off my airplane."

"I can't tell you what I'm doing is exactly legal, but I can tell you that you aren't part of it. The duffel bag is money and the rifle is just for its protection. The money just has to go from point A to point B. That's it, nothing more. Nothing you haven't done a hundred times in the past. All right. Can we go now?"

"What kind of cash bonus?"

"Trust me. If everything goes like I expect it to, you'll get the biggest bonus you've seen in a long time. Something in the four figures range."

"Must be a lot of money in that bag?"

"It's enough, and so am I. I don't mean to make a big deal about this, but I've got a schedule to keep and so do you if you want to earn that bonus."

"You know I can't legally fly all night to get to Salt Lake and then fly you on to somewhere else. I need a copilot."

"No copilot. This is a special flight and we don't want anybody else involved. We don't even want you checking in with your home base."

"It'll mean falsifying logs and I'll have to dummy-up another pilot."

"I doubt if you'll need logs where we're going. But you do whatever you need to do."

"What's the final destination?"

"You'll get the final destination after we get to Houston. For now, just assume the final destination is Houston. Your flight plans have already been filed."

They were soon airborne, climbing to twenty-five thousand feet and in the lane for Houston. Cole relaxed.

Two hours into the flight, Cole brought Jack a cup of coffee. "It's time for a detour."

"I figured as much. Where to?"

"Tobago."

"Never heard of it."

"South tip of the Windward Island Arc - Robinson Crusoe's Island. Look it up on your chart."

"I don't know if I've got enough fuel."

"You do, even with the pedal to the metal. This thing's good for forty-two hundred miles."

"How much did you say that bonus was worth?"

"Minimum of ten grand."

"All right. I suppose you want me to get off radar?"

"That's how you earn the bonus. What'd you suggest?"

"Call Houston, announce a detour to New Orleans, circle out over the Gulf, descend to disappear for awhile. Then shoot back up and skirt the edge of radar fields."

"Do it. I'll arrange to have a record of our landing logged in New Orleans."

"That's a trick. How are you going to log me in at New Orleans?"

"Just a little electronic magic by a friend of mine."

"I still want breakfast."

"How about dinner, on me, after my appointment."

"I guess that'll have to do."

Jack was an expert at jumping out of the flight lanes. He had lots of practice flying for Laughlin. This is what Kevin and Cole were counting on. Soon, Jack had cleared the Houston radar by skipping out across the Gulf at near sea level and then climbing to forty thousand feet, which was above commercial traffic. He disabled GPS and black box transmission and recording functions. He pushed the plane to an air speed of five hundred seventy miles per hour and navigated a flight path that skirted Cuban airspace. He dodged air traffic control and radar fields in the Dominican Republic and Jamaica and then descended to Tobago. It was late afternoon when Jack contacted the airport at Crown Point, Tobago and gained clearance to land.

Once on the ground, Jack ordered fuel and, at Cole's request, a taxi.

As Jack exited the cockpit, Cole handed him a .45 semi-automatic pistol and asked, "You know how to use this?"

"Yeah, but remember I ain't going to have any part of your business."

"You all ready have. You exited the country illegally. You transported God knows what. You're part of it!" Cole jabbed his finger in the center of Jack's chest. "All I need is for you look mean and provide a little bodyguard help. Shouldn't be any trouble. I just want you armed in case there is."

"I told you no drugs."

"Just a little trip to the bank, nothing else," said Cole as he displayed a handful of cash from the duffel bag.

"Bonus better make it worth my while."

Cole didn't need a bodyguard. He just didn't want Jack out of his sight and the bodyguard requirement made sure that wouldn't happen.

The taxi arrived and they departed for the First Republic Bank. The island was small and it was a fast trip. Cole went inside with his duffel bag, leaving Jack standing guard at the door. Cole went directly to the bank manager's office and he and the bank manager counted the deposit together. Kevin had previously arranged for the account and was standing by, waiting to begin a series of complicated electronic transfers.

His job was to obscure the source of the funds from anybody who might be electronically snooping. First the money would be transferred to Colombia, then France, and finally Switzerland.

As previously agreed, Cole rewarded the bank manager's cooperation with a personal payment to his own fund. With business concluded, Cole and Jack departed. They stopped for a few moments for a snack on the way back to airport. Jack protested about lack of sleep and decent food when Cole mandated that he get back in the pilot's seat. Cole won out. He had another appointment.

They were quickly back in the air again, pushing the limits of the airplane. At better than five hundred miles an hour, the plane's range would only marginally allow them to make Atlanta.

Chapter Twenty-Four

MISCHIEF

KEVIN HAD SET UP AT THE GARDEN STREET INTERSEC-tion just barely in sight of Laughlin's Atlanta mansion but through the eighty-power lens of the video camera, things were as clear as if he were standing on the front yard. With distance between him and potential danger, Kevin was comfortable and settled back to enjoy the product of his creation.

The circular drive in front of Laughlin's mansion had exploded with chaos. Berger's Furniture delivered a couch and love seat. The purchase was rejected at the front door, which sent the driver into an arm-waving, finger-pointing tirade. He and his help tossed the furniture onto the front yard and then returned to the front door to continue the verbal confrontation, but they weren't alone.

A UPS driver was competing for attention at the front door. He had sixteen packages neatly stacked on the front porch and was seeking a signature. He extended his clipboard over the heads of two elderly women carrying small Confederate Flags; it had to be the Daughters of the Confederacy coming to collect the substantial donation offered by Laughlin.

Kevin imagined that the UPS driver was only asking for a minute of time, but his voice was drowned out the many screams and shouts. The most prevalent was that of four IRS agents demanding an immediate audience with Mr. David Laughlin. At least that was Kevin's conjecture; their funeral-like attire was a dead giveaway. The shortest of the bunch was yelling the loudest and waving a folded piece of paper, presumably a warrant of some kind. A driver for Alstar TV and Appliance stood back a few steps, no doubt afraid to get to close to the IRS agents. A siding salesman and a vacuum cleaner salesman had joined forces in the background and were yelling just for sport and just because everybody else was. Kevin laughed so hard he could hardly hold the video camera.

One of the Daughters of the Confederacy hit the short IRS agent with her umbrella. He retaliated with a verbal assault and she hit him again, and then again. He retreated from the porch, but she followed, getting in a few more good whacks before he reached the safety of his car. He jumped in the passenger side door and frantically scrambled for the door lock button. She smacked the side of the car with her umbrella and he cringed down below the window. A Yankee taxman ought to know better than to pick a fight with a Daughter of the Confederacy, thought Kevin.

Having seen the defeat of their leader by this ferocious old woman, the rest of the agents weren't about to suffer the same humiliation. They slinked off the porch giving wide passage to the woman. Their business could wait until tomorrow. Kevin was sure they would be back when the competition wasn't so tough. Maybe next time they would bring the local police; of course, the southern cops would probably just cheer the old ladies on. The BLM had been invited to the party as well but hadn't made an appearance yet. Kevin eagerly awaited their arrival – what a mixture of counter viewpoints! How much would the Daughters of the Confederacy enjoy mingling with the BLM? He was so excited he could hardly contain himself.

Cautiously, when the old woman was far enough away from the car, the short IRS agent unlocked the doors and let his co-conspirators in. With everyone buckled in, the driver received a plenitude of instructions from the leader and obediently nodded his head and pulled the shift lever into reverse. He then turned to maneuver the car down the narrow drive and discovered a Mid-Atlanta Gas pickup approaching from the rear, but not soon enough. They collided.

A big, burly black man stepped out of the truck and another verbal confrontation ensued. Back on the porch, the driver for Alstar TV and Appliance made his way to the front of the crowd and was presenting his demands to a plainclothes security man just inside the front entrance. He was interrupted by a mailman carrying a large mailbag. The mailman, undeterred by rain, sleet, snow, small mailboxes or other, forced his way to the front of the pack and dumped his sack just inside. Some of the junk mail and magazines spilled out on to the front porch. The security man

     Brian David Simmons

lost his temper and pushed the mailman back. He attempted to close the door but couldn't get it past the pile of mail. He kicked at the pile of mail, launching miscellaneous pieces at the group on the porch. A magazine struck the driver from Alstar TV and Appliance in the groin and he doubled over. When he recovered, he responded with a snapping right to the security man's nose and blood gushed immediately. The security man stumbled back into the confines of the hallway and beckoned for help. He was joined by two more security men who managed to get the door closed, further angering the crowd on the porch. Their shouts grew louder. Kevin had never laughed so hard in his life. And just as good, he got it all on video and couldn't wait to share his accomplishment with Cole.

Afternoon was wearing on, Kevin had laughed all he could and he began to feel nervous. It was best to avoid the darkness and return to his hotel room as quickly as possible.

Elated with his accomplishments and back in the safety of his hotel room, Kevin went on to implement the next phase of the game. CP3O's keys hummed as Kevin created and submitted an API story to the FINCEN director via interoffice e-mail. The FINCEN director received the e-mail from one of his civil servants. Kevin located just the right employee by searching voice mail greetings until he found someone on vacation. The urgent e-mail consisted of a simple cover letter and attachment:

The attached story may run nationwide. Videotapes that show business activity and substantiate the story will arrive addressed to you by FED-EX. How do you suggest we proceed?

"ATLANTA—In one of the largest money-laundering schemes ever uncovered, FINCEN sources confirm that Isaac Bartrum will be taken into custody today. He has agreed to turn state's evidence against long time Atlanta businessman David Laughlin. Bartrum has linked Laughlin directly to U.S. drug trade kingpins.

Bartrum confessed to widespread heroin and cocaine sales in the Atlanta area and nationwide distribution. Money derived from nationwide drug sales has allegedly been laundered through IAB convenience stores. Informed sources from inside the Laughlin organization report that overstated receipts from each of the stores in the IAB chain were funneled through a secret accounting operation in the industrial district. Armored cars picked up cash receipts from the each of the IAB stores and then supplemented weekly receipts with drug money before bank deposits were made.

Estimates put the laundering operation at over fifty million dollars per year. Annual cash flow for the six IAB stores in the Atlanta area is in excess of eighty million dollars. The overstated cash flow is confirmed with video surveillance and monitoring of sales.

In a related investigation, it has been confirmed that IRS agents are conducting a week-long audit at the Laughlin mansion in Atlanta. They were denied entrance to the Laughlin estate on Monday, but returned today with a court order. Indictments are expected..."

With a few clicks of the mouse, Kevin also placed the story in the API database. Kevin was amused with himself, How long would it take before FINCEN, the IRS, and Laughlin's residence started to get phone calls? He laughed. Even if his story didn't run, some variation of it would show up in the evening paper. It might even make the TV. He could hardly wait.

Unrevealed Winners

It was almost two o'clock when Jason West checked into the Siloxi Motel. It was a two-story motel frequented by call girls with their clients from the neighboring white-collar businesses. It was clean and free of gang and drug activities, but it was a far cry from the Ritz. Kevin had selected it because of its central location and lack of police attention.

Kevin watched as Cole parked the car and got out; soon he would be able share what he had learned. In the meantime, Kevin had been verifying his connections in preparation for events to come. CP3O was connected to the 4056 and all its surveillance equipment back at the cabin in Utah. He checked on perimeter security, displaying images from each of the external surveillance cameras. The cabin was undisturbed and a fresh layer of snow covered his Toyota pickup.

The phone rang just as Cole stepped through the door of his motel room. It was Kevin.

"We need to talk," were Kevin's urgent first words. "Come over right now."

"I'm tired, Kevin. I need a half-hour rest."

"Rest later. This is important."

"All right, Kevin," said Cole and he proceeded to Kevin's room where the conversation continued.

Kevin was also noticeably tired: his eyes were bloodshot and his speech was lethargic. Cole briefly filled in Kevin on the success of the trip to Tobago, but Kevin already knew; he hadn't slept since he had last seen Cole and had filled the time with his computer. Word was out in Washington that something big was happening and the Internet was buzzing with misinformation and speculation. Media hounds were pressuring every source and had posted several erroneous stories on the API database. Even the Dow Jones had reacted; it was sharply down.

"I wanted to tell you. Mickey Mouse is doing his thing and up about twenty grand," continued Kevin. Kevin filled Cole in on the API news story plants, FINCEN communication, and progress planting the cash delivered to Tobago as the hours of darkness moved on. Kevin and Cole eventually both crashed on the lumpy hotel mattress. Several miles away another man was just getting up from a very disturbed sleep.

David Laughlin entered his office and walked past Melvin, going directly to the bar. Melvin commented, "Good morning to you, too."

"Fuck off, Melvin. What is going on around here? Huh? I'd like for somebody to just tell me!"

"I'd say somebody's jerking your chain. Who'd you tick off?"

"Nobody. Not a soul. Every client I have is as pleased as a fat woman in a candy store. I've made every money-grubbing politician in the county happy with contributions. I went skeet-shooting with the governor. I had breakfast with the police chief and his pig of a wife. I'm sponsoring a training weekend at Lake Pickwick for the God-forsaken city council. I just don't get it, Melvin. I just don't get it."

"Then maybe it's somebody you don't know."

"Do you know what happened when House Rep Fredrickson called? Do you? His call was re-routed to a whorehouse in DeKalb. My own personal line. Can you believe it!"

Then as Laughlin tried to light a cigar, he knocked over his Bloody Mary and it splashed all over the front of his robe and exposed stomach. "Aw, cripes!"

"Not exactly your day, is it?"

"I didn't ask you, Melvin. I want you to find out what's going on and kill somebody!"

Just then, a security man opened the door and interrupted, "I think you'd better turn on the television. It sounds like we have a problem."

"We have a problem all right," snapped Laughlin as he threw his empty glass at the security man, only hitting the closing door. Melvin turned on the TV and the news anchor was just summarizing the recently completed news conference:

"In a brief news conference, FINCEN director Humston has just announced a full-scale investigation into the financial affairs of convenience stores operating in the greater Atlanta area. He said this action is being taken in response to rumored drug sales and money laundering through the convenience stores. Independent of the news conference, Channel Three's 'Eye On Crime' reporter Lester Monaghan has learned that Isaac Bartrum's stores will be the focus of the investigation and it is suspected that he may turn state's evidence against a larger racketeering organization."

Laughlin downed a straight shot of vodka and exclaimed, "That's it! He's gotta be the winner; that little prick friend of yours is only answer. Why can't you kill him? I want him taken care of, Melvin."

"I'm working on it. He's here in Atlanta and this is our playground. I've got every street punk, ganger, doper and whore on the look out. He'll turn up and when I find him it will be my pleasure."

COLE WOKE FIRST AND ROLLED OFF THE BED. HE turned on the TV to take his mind off it and drown out Kevin's obtrusive snoring. The CNN story wasn't very interesting:

"The chaotic stock trading of yesterday was followed again today with all-time records in both Dow Jones volume and high. Uncertain investor concerns about the new Corona virus strain, Demonicron, over taking Armicron, Omnicron and Delta coupled with rumored military action in Yemen and Fed rate increases resulted in a 2,178-point drop in the Dow Jones industrial average. The CDC came out with a ominous warning about expected Demonicron hospitalizations that contradicted a report from the UK, which left the market with uncertainty and resulting in never before seen volume. Then, just as unexpectedly as the fall of the Dow, it rebounded to new highs. By mid-afternoon, bargain-hunting buyers had pushed the Dow to its new record high. Prices continued to fluctuate throughout the afternoon in a wild roller-coaster ride that left the Dow off by only 52.79 at closing. Wall Street will watch this morning very closely as the opening bell rings. Analysts are predicting it will be another wild ride.

Coming up later this evening on Business News, we will have an in-depth report, 'Stock Market in Chaos.' What does it mean? What is happening? What do the analysts say about the future?"

The next story started and Cole immediately woke Kevin. CNN showed the first twenty seconds of the FINCEN press conference and then imposed their own interpretation, including a link to a recent IRS investigation. They put the finishing touches on their story with a live interview with IRS field agents. CNN had dispatched a film crew to Laughlin's estate and interviewed the lead IRS agent on the front lawn. Kevin had seen him on film before. He was great; his second performance was as good as his first.

The performance inspired Kevin to share his video with Cole. On the video, a car with a Daughters of the Confederacy banner across the deck lid pulled into the circular drive to block a furniture truck. Kevin could hardly contain himself and fast-forwarded to the assault on the IRS. Cole and Kevin laughed and laughed, and then rewound the tape to see it all over again. It was a great diversion from the momentous events developing.

The jovial mode returned to serious as the day wore on. Kevin just hammered away at his keyboard doing who knows what. Cole could only contemplate the future in agonizing silence. What would today bring?

Eventually Cole broke the silence with a thought had bothered him for months. "Hey. Why didn't the police respond when I drew fire at Laughlin's mansion? Why didn't they send an army of cops to the industrial park? You'd think Atlanta didn't have 911?"

Kevin ignored him and continued at the keyboard.

"Hey. did you hear me?" Cole asserted.

"Huh," mumbled Kevin and looked in Cole's direction.

"I crashed cars, caused all kinds of gun fire and commotion both at Laughlin's Mansion and the industrial park. Why didn't the police show up at Laughlin's? Why did they just send a lone cruiser to the industrial park?"

"It's the Artie."

"What?"

"It's the Artee. I haven't concentrated on it, but it's apparent that the Artee has the capability to direct police, intercept 911 calls, re-direct traffic, and control whatever situation you created."

"It can't do that? Can it? How would it do that?"

"Listen, I'll put it in simple terms even the computer illiterate can understand. The Artee and I play a friendly game of chess every morning. I move a pawn; he moves a pawn. I move another; he moves another one of his. It goes on until I take one of his pawns. Then, since the rules are all his, he replaces the pawn with two more. I attack with my knight; he positions his castle. I declare check with my bishop; he knocks over my pawns and declares checkmate. And then we start all over. I can't get past his defenses because they are constantly changing and adjusting to my every move - just the way he adjusts every situation, just the way he adjusted the situations you created."

"Holy shit. Then how are you going to feed it code? That's the heart of your game."

"The best I can do is leave a little crumb of code on the chessboard and hope he doesn't find it."

"What about your back door?"

"The laser-surveillance camera approach is too limited. I only downloaded a few lines of code. It, along with my few crumbs of chessboard code, are so limited that the outcome of our crude accounting game is absolutely unknown. And if the Artee finds any of it, he will stamp it out like a virus."

"Last night you said Mickey was up?"

"Yeah, Mickey has been posturing for growth. Activity should have been accelerating."

"How much?"

"Good question. It depends on the number of trades the Artee makes, the exchange volumes, and the value of the futures themselves. We've got oil, beef, corn, oranges, and a dozen other futures markets out there all pressured up or down for any number of unpredictable reasons. Ultimately, that will predict how big Mickey wins. How big Laughlin and his clients lose, however, will be approximately Mickey's gains multiplied by five. Remember, the Artee is making our gains by selling futures short. He is offsetting our gains by booking and buying the client's losing shares long. What he doesn't understand is that every buy he makes to offset us selling short, he's leveraging the maximum for the buy, sometimes five to one. Every offsetting loss is booked as a one-to-one loss when in reality it's a five-to-one. The Artee will continue to keep his books balanced so that at the end of each day, each client's under-calculated loss is offset by gains. With our random sales programmed to accelerate exponentially, more and more dirty money will be lost than is replaced with clean earnings. Client losses will pile up exponentially until the whole thing crashes or the Artee gets wise. Laughlin and his clients' losses will be somewhere between insignificant and astronomical. Only time and the market will tell."

"What about us?"

"We'll find out tomorrow. It is so complex and unpredictable that our dummy, Joe Anonymous, account may turn out to be the winner. All of Mickey's initial gains go into accounts with Joe's name on them. It's only the second-tier trades that make us winners. If the first-tier trades work and the second-tier trades don't, Joe is the big winner, in which case the money is out there in never-never-land. So as the Joe Anonymous account gains, the Artee has to play his dirty-to-clean transformation, leaving Joe's accounts empty and ours full. Joe leverages each dollar to buy five dollars worth of futures, long. Then the Artee intentionally sells his shares short at a loss. At the same time, our leveraged accounts buy long to offset the losses. With five-to-one leveraging and Joe's loss on his short sales at twenty percent, he loses his original investment and we win with clean money. And with five-to-one leveraging on top of five-to-one leveraging, we could be making twenty-five to one. This thing is so complicated that my feeble few lines of coded logic may do just the opposite. I don't know."

"I hope you know."

"Assuming the Artee does his thing, Joe Anonymous will be the only identifiable player, and he'll look like a winner. Just as the Artee orchestrates the transition of dirty money to clean without a trail, the trail to our accounts will be untraceable. Only the original first-tier trades will be identifiable."

"You hope."

"You're right. I do hope. Tomorrow will tell. In the meantime, we just wait."

"I can't stand the wait," commented Cole. "Can't you just check?"

"No, we are better off to just leave it alone, for better or worse."

"I guess if it doesn't work out, we're going to take care of Laughlin and Melvin anyway. The money is just secondary."

"You call it secondary. I think it's your primary. You and your diseased need to kill make me sick."

As morning wore on, Cole and Kevin baited the trap. Use of Cole's personal credit card months earlier had brought a quick response from Laughlin's goons, but were they still monitoring credit card usage and would they react so far from Atlanta? Cole and Kevin counted on it.

Cole called the mini-mart in Lake View to place an order. The mini-mart offered grocery delivery in the Bear Lake area. Of course, the price included a premium delivery fee. Cole placed his order and charged it to his personal credit card. The address of the cabin and special delivery instructions were given. The delivery boy was instructed to enter the cabin through the rear entrance and leave the groceries on the counter.

Cole made a second call to Electronic Specialties. He placed an order for a computer printer and charged it to his credit card. Again, he provided the address of the Bear Lake cabin. Cole turned down premium shipping and gladly accepted a fourteen-day delivery promise. The Christmas season compounded by supply chain issues had slowed down all shipping. To Kevin and Cole, fourteen days or forty made no difference.

An hour later, Kevin's CP3O computer beeped; the 4056 at the Bear Lake cabin was indicating a perimeter violation. Kevin rattled at the keyboard to link the two computers and then began transmitting surveillance camera footage of the perpetrator. It was the deliveryman from the mini-mart. Kevin and Cole watched as he carried in three loads of groceries. He didn't leave immediately but instead conducted a cursory search of the cabin. He searched until he found a small stash Kevin had planted in a cookie jar. He took two of the six hundred dollar bills in the cookie jar and quickly departed. Cole and Kevin captured it all on video.

     Brian David Simmons

It was time see if Laughlin had taken the bait. Cole called Friendship Aviation. With a little deceit, Cole was able to confirm that Melvin had reserved a small six-seater. It was scheduled to take off in thirty minutes. Kevin estimated the flight time to Lake View at six hours and then another half an hour to find the cabin. Whoever was going to Bear Lake would probably find an observation point and watch with binoculars. With Kevin's new truck still in the driveway, the obvious assumption would be that someone was home.

If the test Kevin had run at the motel three months earlier was any indication, they wouldn't wait very long; they would wait until nine or maybe ten o'clock. Then they would sneak up to the cabin and burst in. Cole and Kevin would be ready.

Cole hadn't spoken to Carol for months. Kevin helped him get the 911 Salt Lake City dispatch through the satellite system and into local cell phone service. It took three tries before he finally got the right 911 operator.

Her voice was professional, with only a hint of southern accent, but Cole recognized it immediately. "911 emergency. May I help you?" she asked.

"Hello, Carol. I just wanted to hear your voice."

"Yes, sir, can I have your name please, starting with last name first, then first name," she said without even a pause.

"You don't know who this is, do you?"

"Yes, sir. You are calling from cell phone 555-2790? Are you hurt?"

"Yes, my heart is aching for you."

"Cole? Is that you?" she whispered.

"Yeah."

"Where are you? You can't call me here. This is 911. You can't make personal calls on 911."

"In a few hours or days it won't matter."

"I'm not sure I want to talk to you. This is being recorded, don't you know? You'll have to hang up now. "

"Okay."

"No, wait. Call me again at home tonight."

"We'll see. Maybe in a week or two if things work right. You watch the mail and don't be surprised by anything you get. It's yours. I love you." Cole ended the phone call.

The hours passed. Cole wanted action, any action. Kevin just kept hammering the keyboard. How could he just do that for hours on end? He interrupted Kevin and declared he was going to pay Laughlin a personal visit, go to the press, do something, do anything but sit and wait.

Kevin was also noticeably on edge.

Cole inquired, "How about checking on our account?"

"You mean Mickey Mouse or Joe Anonymous?

"Mickey this and Mickey that. Maybe you should talk to Artee, too. How about having the Enslaver get it on with Mickey? Hey, what about Minnie Mouse? She's missing all the fun. It's always a game with you. When are you going to grow up and learn to talk?"

"Screw you."

The conversation was over. It was early but Cole pulled a beer out of an ice bucket and turned on the TV. He flipped through the channels finally settling on a Mighty Morphin's cartoon. It wasn't enough of a distraction, but it was something. Kevin again retreated to the comfort of his computer.

Markets wouldn't close for hours and daily futures trading activity wouldn't be posted until after 5:00. All told, Cole and Kevin had created six investors, each with eight accounts. Cole's two million dollars had been spread evenly across the forty-eight accounts to open each one with a little more than forty thousand dollars. Market closing was time for Kevin to check on the accounts. But he couldn't stand the wait and took the risk. He checked on a Mercantile Exchange account and studied it with confusion.

Cole was on his third beer and now watching Superman. Kevin was still off in his own world of cyberspace. Neither had spoken in hours but the tension had faded. But, a new realization was emerging in Cole's mind. This was all wrong. His training at the compound had never included re-act, it was always act. Whether it was MCMAP hand-to-hand combat, shooting, or pursuit training, the fundamental premise was always to act first. Don't give the enemy a chance to think and keep them on the defensive were essential, especially when out-manned, out-gunned, and in enemy territory. Another realization was also stirring Cole's senses. He and Kevin were trapped. The second floor motel rooms, clearly in enemy territory, had no escape route.

Cole ventured to the window and peered out through the edge of the curtain. He studied every car in the parking lot, traffic on the street, and every conceivable hiding place for a potential assailant. It all looked normal, but it wasn't. The illusive ethereal sense of knowing he had felt in the desert months earlier returned with a vengeance. The eyes were out there, hidden from sight, but they were out there. Cole searched every vehicle in the parking lot, straining to peer into the shadows of the passenger compartments. His senses screamed at him.

Kevin never spoke when he delved into cyberspace and he got Cole's attention when he mumbled, "Something's wrong."

"What?"

"This Mercantile Exchange account. It's got too many shares."

"That's fine. Shut it down. We're leaving!" commanded Cole.

"We can't. I've got to figure this out."

Cole slammed the screen on the laptop closed and shouted, "Now!" He grabbed Kevin by the arm and lifted him from the chair. "Take all your IDs and whatever you can carry. We're leaving."

Kevin complied taking only his brief case, laptop,

cell phone and jacket. Cole peered out the door. It was quiet, but his senses told him the eyes were out there. They crept down the stairs and then across the parking lot to the Buick. Cole had taken the case containing Melvin's rifle and binoculars and tossed it into backseat.

As Cole accelerated out of the parking lot and onto Weston Lane, Kevin forcefully inquired, "What the Hell Cole? I need to get on the computer. This isn't what we planned."

Cole was silent for a moment as he entered the freeway on ramp and then softly said, "Just trust me. I should have realized it earlier. We're in enemy territory and they'll find us sooner rather than later."

"What are you talking about?"

"Just trust me," said Cole as he studied the rear-view mirror and accelerated passed several cars to gain access to the fast lane.

"Where are we going?"

"You're going to the airport."

"What? I need to get on the computer. Something's wrong with the accounts. The Mercantile Exchange account was up eleven million and that's impossible."

Cole dropped back into the left lane and slowed to just under the speed limit. He studied the mirrors. Maybe, just maybe, he thought he might have seen a car far off in the rear imitating his traffic maneuver.

"Why isn't that good?" Cole said.

"It can't grow that fast, unless..."

"Unless what?"

"The daily limit on future contract gains and losses won't let it move that fast. Single trade loss or gain shouldn't be more than ten percent. That kind of growth could only come from an incredible number of fluctuations in the market. The market would have had to drop then rebound at least a hundred times during the last two days. I need to get back on the computer. Why in the hell are we going to the airport?"

"You're going to the airport and that's the way it is."

"What the Hell?"

"Look Kevin,"calmly stated Cole. "The money part of the plan might have worked, but we'd be dead. Just sitting in a motel room in enemy territory waiting for things to play out was an invitation for Melvin, Issaac, Beech, the Arabs, Laughlin's clients or who knows to pay us a visit and where would that leave us? Dead, that's where."

"Bull shit. Nobody knew we at the motel. Are you going paranoid nuts?"

"They were there. They had eyes on us. I felt it."

"You what? You felt it! You psycho retard. I'm not getting on a plane. Why would I get on a plane?"

"Because that's the only way you can be somewhere safe while I go deal with it."

"Oh, now I get it! You just want to get on with killing somebody and you don't want me around. You just can't resist the psychopathic calling, can you? Your head is so full shit; you should go put your head in the toilet and flush. You have some kind of bizarre addiction. I think you're a God damn serial killer."

"Yes and I love you too," said Cole as he signaled to exit the freeway. The car he'd seen ten back earlier signaled as well. "And you're going to have learn to appreciate this psycho retard serial killer. We're being followed."

"What?" exclaimed Kevin as he swiveled around to peer out the back window.

"Third car back. The gray sedan. We don't have much time; so listen. Let the plan play out at the cabin. The FBI gets Isaac and his operation, FINCEN gets the computer and all the financial data on Laughlin's clients, and I'll get Laughlin. Laughlin and Isaac won't rest until we're dead. It's just the way their world turns. And I'm not waiting for them."

Kevin meekly inquired, "Okay. Where do you want me to go?"

"It doesn't matter. Just get a ticket to somewhere with a lot of layovers. Make sure you have an arrival or layover window and are available between probably 8:00 and 11:00. The cabin is yours; Melvin is yours; you're going to have to do it. When you get off the plane at each of your layovers, run like hell, like you're about to miss a flight and see if anybody follows. If you think somebody is following, buy another ticket to somewhere else. Just don't leave the secured areas of the airport until you're sure nobody is following you. As a last resort for somebody following you, run to airport security and tell them a fake FBI agent wanted you to plant a bomb and is trying to kill you. Make some shit up. Give them a description of whoever is following you."

"I'm not doing the cabin."

"You have to! Do it from an empty boarding area, corner stall of a bathroom or wherever there's the least background noise. Just do it."

"That kind of thing is yours."

"It's just the two of us, Kevin. I do it; you do it. It doesn't matter. We're both in this and you don't need me to push the button."

"You're wanting me to join in on your psychotic bestiality. Don't you? You fucker! Shit! I'm going to be sick."

"Just wait to be sick until after you do it."

Signs at the entrance to Departures warned of parking too long and leaving a vehicle unattended. This was going to be a quick stop. Cole pulled up at the departure curb and studied the gray sedan as it passed them by. The two occupants of the car were thirty-somethings and looked like business types.

Kevin inquired, " Is that them?"

Cole wasn't sure it was Laughlin's men, but caution was better than complacency. "Yes. Now get out and get going."

He watched as the car drove far down the lane before pulling over to the curb. Cars at the curb and people on the move obscured Cole's view, but somebody always got out at the departure curb. Cole waited until the sedan pulled back out into the through traffic lane and then slowly crept out to follow. He watched Kevin enter through the departures sliding door and hoped Kevin was up to the challenge.

Cole followed the sedan at a distance, only getting close enough to verify one remaining occupant of the vehicle. He considered the possibility that the airport drop off was innocuous and he was wrong, until the car signaled to turn into the industrial park at Fulton. Cole didn't follow; instead passing the Fulton Industrial Boulevard turn off and heading north. He had hours to kill while the sun illuminated all. Tonight, darkness would be his friend and drove aimlessly to eventually encircle the entire city of Atlanta. He thought of Joe and Sylvia Atkinson. Sylvia's touch was so soft and delicate, even when she was working with needle and thread on his face. His mother had never touched him with so much love; it was a strange feeling of warmth that melded into his very soul and conflicted with everything he'd ever known. Carol's touch was pleasant yet different. What was she doing at this very moment he pondered: reading to Tamera, doing dishes, doing laundry, or just relaxing in front of the TV? Would he ever be able to see her again? Would she even have anything to do with him again? The hours passed.

WHILE KEVIN WAS IN THE AIR HEADED FOR NEW York City and over two thousand miles away, the 4056 computer sitting on the table in the Bear Lake cabin dialed a direct phone call to Laughlin's Artee. Communication was simple and undisguised; the 4056 requested a download of today's activity and current balance for Laughlin and each of his clients' accounts. The guise was under the friendly request of Mickey Mouse and the Artee complied with the request from its contrived friend.

     Brian David Simmons

Chapter Twenty-Six

BEST OF PLANS?

Cole made his first stop of the night and took up position in the park just beyond sight of Laughlin's mansion. It was chilly and Cole put on his gloves, but not just for cold. Hopefully, there was still some fingerprint still on the rifle from Melvin. Cole assembled the elements of Melvin's rifle and verified the night vision capabilities of the scope. He dialed in the range at one hundred yards, which he figured would be good for any shot he would have to take. The rifle had only come with six rounds of ammunition and he knew his adversaries would come with much, much more.

The phone vibrated in his pocket. Cole glanced at the screen and answered, "Where are you at?"

"New York," Kevin replied.

"Anybody follow you?"

"Maybe, but I got it covered. I did like you said and ran like hell when I got off the plane. I found cover in the bookstore and got a good picture of some business type that might have been following me. I'll forward it, along with the bomb story, to TSA just before I leave the airport. Right now I'm in the bathroom checking out the accounts. This is freaking bizarre."

Cole envisioned Kevin swirling at the key pad and driving the computer keyboard faster than it wanted to go."What is?" he asked.

"The Artee that's what. It would have had to keep up; that's like instantaneously keeping the books balanced on five thousand factorial - incredible."

"Just tell me. Did it work or didn't it?"

Kevin mumbled something and spoke gibberish until he got to a point of conclusion. "I counted seventy-nine buys and corresponding sales for the day. Each buy was leveraged to max. And that's just one account."

"So did it work or didn't it."

"I'm checking. Shit – checking – what the fuck – how? You ain't going to believe this."

"Just give me the punchline."

"Results are mixed but all are up, way up. Currency, wheat, oil, soy beans, oranges, corn, beef, pork, coffee, sugar, cocoa - all of the markets set record volumes on futures contracts. I'll have to add it up. But I'd say it more than fucking worked!"

Just out of sight from Cole's hiding position, David Laughlin pounded the computer keys, searching for anything other than accounts with a negative balance. His accountant and computer programmer stood by, receiving periodic reprimands. He screamed at them then went back to the computer, pounding the keys ever harder in an attempt to make the money reappear. Then, in language only a madman could understand, he screamed something at his accountant.

Receiving no satisfaction, he re-focused his anger at his programmer to point and spit as he screamed. The screaming and pounding of computer keys continued to no avail. The accountant and programmer were thrashed with further verbal abuse, fired, and ordered from the premises. He would have Melvin deal with them later. David Laughlin's fury continued but all to no avail. Eventually the reality of it set in and the futility of hammering the keyboard subsided.

THE CALL BETWEEN COLE AND KEVIN CONTINUED as he struggled through the buys and sells to make sure what he was seeing was real. They were interrupted by a beep from D2; it was the expected call from the computer in Bear Lake. Kevin rattled the laptop's keyboard to bring in the surveillance camera images. He flashed through the images on the monitor and described it to Cole.

"Okay, you know the plan. Stay with it." said Cole and hung up.

Cole's thoughts were of the compound as he peered out from the trees in the direction of Laughlin's mansion. Tonight would be no different than pursuit training, except it would be no game. Pursuit training was a variation of capture the flag with paintball guns, drones, and combative physical contact. Sometimes it was three-on-three; sometimes it was one-on-five; sometimes it was against an unknown force; sometimes it was with limited paint ball ammunition;

sometimes it was against overwhelming forces with drones, infrared optics, and unlimited ammunition. Strategy varied but for tonight he would assault, retreat and ambush, which would leave Laughlin with no defensive forces. Then he could readily move in to finish off Laughlin.

With the rifle well hidden in the trees, Cole returned to the car with a short stick in hand. He started the car and slowly crawled down the lane towards Laughlin's mansion. He stopped directly in front of the mansion and, as he'd done months earlier, pointed the handheld video camera at the front door. Cole studied the furthermost dormer with the light on. He thought he might have seen a figure inside and zoomed the camera's focus. Two figures were presumably having some kind of discussion. One of the figures waved their hands suggesting the conversation was animated. Cole quickly accelerated away to circle back around. The third pass would be the critical juncture, assuming the Artie was on its game. But that wasn't tonight's plan.

Cole stopped short of the mansion and verified the length of the stick he had brought with him; it would work. He drove straight to the mansion and turned up the narrow drive and then onto the lawn to bring the car's nose pointing directly at the front door. Flood lights came on and some kind of internal alarm sounded. Cole stopped fifty feet short of the front door and got out of the car. He shoved the stick hard against the gas pedal and wedged its other end in against the seat. The car's engine revved to 5000 RPM and he pulled the shift lever into drive. Tires swirled in the grass as the car took off. As its speed increased, the car veered off target to the left. It's speed further increased to propel it into and then part way onto the deck with a nose up jolt that struck one the house's main pillars and stopped the car's forward momentum. Fluids spewed forth and a column of steam rose. It was not exactly the path Cole had envisioned, but the message delivered was just the same.

Tires on a car at the rear of the mansion squealed as the front door opened. Cole took off in a dead run across the front lawn. He jumped the runoff ditch along the road just as the car reached the end of the driveway. They were no more than fifty feet away, which was too close. Again, not the plan he had envisioned. He needed them out of the car pursuing him into trees in the park where he could pick them off one-by-one with Melvin's rifle. But they had reacted faster than anticipated and now they had him. At this distance, he could easily catch a bullet from the spray of a fully automatic weapon. Cole's options were limited. Even with evasive running maneuvers, there was no way he would make the trees. Time to act, he concluded.

Cole re-directed his feet and began running at full stride directly toward the oncoming car. Cole saw the surprised expression on faces of the car occupants:

who would assault an oncoming car with no apparent weapon? An Uzi appeared out the passenger window and Cole shifted his path to the right side of the road, increasing the difficulty of getting a shot off across the windshield. Cole's body, as well as his mind raced: thirty feet and closing; less than three seconds. The driver jerked the wheel to his left to target Cole with the hood of the car. As the car jerked to its left, the Uzi fired a burst in an errant skyward direction. Cole darted to his left with only a second-and-a-half before impact and the driver reacted; jerking the wheel hard right to follow. Cole dived into the borrow ditch just as the car's front wheel passed directly over him, momentarily and lightly thumping him on the back of his leg; again not to plan. Ordinarily it would have been disastrous but the cars angle to the ditch left three of its wheels on high ground. His leg received a second thump as the car's rear wheel passed over.

Cole's boot knife was already in his hand as he emerged from the borrow ditch behind the stopping car. Cole knew the armament MO from the experience in the industrial park: driver – pistol, passenger – Uzi. A second car was now emerging from the back of the mansion as the passenger door of the first car began opening. Cole closed the distance catching the passenger as his foot hit the ground and he began to stand. With his back still turned, Cole sliced up and through the man's right armpit severing axilla blood and lymph vessels, subscapularis tendons, and nerves.

     Brian David Simmons

Cole swiftly and fluidly transitioned his knife to his left hand and repeated the motion to slice through the man's left armpit while reaching around under the man's now failing right arm to grasp the shoulder harnessed Uzi. Cole didn't aim; he didn't even see the driver; he just spayed the inside of the car with the Uzi.

With the second car now coming down the drive and two men emerging from the front door of the mansion, Cole jerked free the Uzi from its shoulder harnessed position as the man in his arms screamed and fell to his knees. He fired a quick burst in the direction of the two men running at him from the front door and then emptied the clip in the direction of the oncoming car. The two men, one with an Uzi and one with a long gun similar to Melvin's, dove to the ground. The car came to a sudden halt and then began slowly rolling down the driveway. Cole didn't wait to confirm his hits, or lack thereof, and took off in a dead run in the direction of the trees in the park.

A car squealed around a distant corner and Cole put all his energy into accelerating his pace. As the engine roar of the approaching car became audible, the tires of yet another squealed around the distant corner. That made at least four assailants plus however many he had left at the mansion. The roaring car came into view just as Cole reached the edge of the trees. The car proceeded on down the lane towards the man-sion. Cole pressed on into the trees but didn't hear the engine roar of the second car. It must have stopped short, Cole surmised. As he worked his way through the trees and neared the hidden rifle, he heard just barely audible voices and hit the ground. He lifted his head slightly and his eyes studied every detail ahead. The wet-cold crisp air had settled into the trees and Cole's ears went on high alert. He waited, looked and listened, and then inched forward. Again, he looked, listened, and inched onward, repeating the process until Melvin's rifle was within twenty-five feet. As he crept, Cole's mind captured and processed the sounds and sights; occupants from the second tire squealing car were in trees coordinating through their little headsets with those at the mansion. It was a trap, just like he'd seen months earlier. Only this time he would turn the hunters into the hunted.

No doubt, they were creeping through the trees searching with their night vision gear, perhaps thermal and heat imaging, which could be a problem. Thermal imaging would reveal him standing, sitting, or laying and there was no way to avoid it, even in a complete void of light. Others from the mansion had now joined the coordinated night vision search and they would all be whispering through their little headsets. Cole needed one. He crept onward towards Melvin's rifle. A crack of a branch under foot echoed in the forest as if it were the snap of a full size tree branch. Cole's mind processed the direction of the sound and slithered up to hide behind a large tree. It happened again; only this time the sound was much more subtle,

     Brian David Simmons

but closer. Cole adjusted his position behind the tree and estimated distance. He waited. The noise had night vision; he had none. And would the noise have its finger on the trigger? Would the invisible nine-millimeter Uzi be pointed in his direction? Or would it be sweeping left and right as the noise crept forward? Ordinarily, fifteen feet was his kill radius. Less than fifteen – attack. More than fifteen – flee. But that was for an adversary not poised to fire a weapon. A frontal assault was not an option. He waited. The forest was silent, crisp and cold. Night air should reveal every step and every concealed headset communication, but there was only silence .

Moments passed and turned into minutes. Then he heard it; not a foot step; not a voice; but odd, perhaps mechanical, indecipherable sounds coming through a headset earpiece. The man was right there, not more than three steps away, and Cole delicately adjusted his position around the tree to keep it between him and the man. Cole listened intently to the now perceptible steps and envisioned the position of the man. He was slowly working past the tree and momentarily his back would be to the tree - and Cole. Cole bounded from the cover of the tree and before the man could turn, he used his great strength to thrust his knife into the man's back, between the fourth and fifth ribs, to penetrate the heart. Cole cupped his left hand over the man's mouth. The man struggled and squirmed and Cole twisted and shoved the knife ever deeper. The man continued to struggle for what seemed like minutes; his feet were kicking, stomping and creating a horrific racket. Cole withdrew the knife and went for instant death; he sliced first one carotid artery and then spun the man to slice the other. The man let out a cry, but it was short lived – so was the man. Unconsciousness came to man within seconds and death would follow within minutes.

Cole removed the man's headset and night vision goggles. The goggles were thermal imaging and could see in total darkness. They were much better than the ones he'd brought with him and stashed with Melvin's rifle. Cole put on the man's headset and thermal imaging goggles. He studied the surrounding forest; no one was within sight, but the headset beckoned for a Johnny. After no reply, the request came again in a whispered tone, "Johnny."

Cole responded, "Here?"

Cole searched the now unconscious and still dying man, relieving him of his forty-five calipered 1911, nine-millimeter Uzi and all his ammunition.

"Did you hear the disturbance in your local?" came the voice.

"Checking," replied Cole as he concentrated on the heads-up display inside the goggles; it was longitude, latitude, and a compass. He swung left and right checking his perimeter, still no one visible. Cole moved forward towards Melvin's rifle and his stash. It was less than thirty feet away and he quickly and quietly arrived in moments.

     Brian David Simmons

Another voice, but this one was strangely mechanical, maybe computer like, came over the headset, "Fourteen, proceed thirty-two degrees northeast."

An odd second set of GPS coordinates began flashing on the display in the goggles. Cole studied it momentarily; it was a few fractional seconds different from the steadily displayed coordinates. "What the fuck?" thought Cole.

The mechanical voice returned to his headset, "Fourteen, proceed thirty-two degrees northeast."

Cole shouldered Melvin's rifle and picked up his Nighthawk night vision monocular. The dead man's night vision he was wearing were thermal imaging, but his infrared Nighthawks had better resolution and zoomable to 4X. Cole placed all his acquired ammunition in the backpack along with the zoomable goggles, shouldered the pack, and verified accessibility of the 1911 slipped into the back of his pants. Long gun, Uzi and backpack were about all he could carry but now it was his turn to become the hunter. He began a slow trek back towards the mansion when the mechanical voice commanded again.

"Fourteen, proceed thirty-two degrees northeast."

Cole studied every tree and shadow as he slowly crept towards the mansion. Both the steady and flashing coordinates on the goggle display changed as he advanced. He listened intently at every opening in the trees before then venturing forward. He could see the edge of the trees and was nearly within sight of

Laughlin's mansion when the mechanical voice inter-rupted his advance.

"Fourteen, proceed thirty-two degrees northeast."

He crept onward; moving from tree to tree, stop-ping and listening, and then advancing again. The car that had nearly run him over was still in the grassy area just beyond the borrow ditch. The passenger door was still open and a man sat motionless in the passenger seat. Cole's eyes strained. The driver was slumped over, having falling towards the the other man. The car on the driveway had rolled down the lane and its motionless driver was clearly visible. The passenger, however, had presumably joined the hunt. The car he had sent roaring towards the mansion now sat silent with subtle vapor rising in the cold air. Its nose and front tires had managed to bump up onto the front porch. The battlefield scene in front of the mansion was now dead still in the crisp chill of December and the question came to mind: where are the hunters?

The thermal imaging picked up movement to his left and Cole unshouldered Melvin's rifle. It was time see how well Melvin had sighted in the rifle. Cole reached up to remove the night vision when the mechanical voice came back on the head set again.

"Command check," the voice stated.

Then came a series of differing human replies: "Zuzu," "Delta," "Tango," "Echo," "Whiskey," "Bravo," "Charlie," "Kilo," "Papa," "Uniform," "November."

Cole froze wondering what was transpiring. Maybe Johnny back there was supposed to reply as well. Cole replayed the responses in his mind and then, with random choice, added, "Foxtrot." The head set went silent and he breathed a momentary sigh. Maybe he'd gotten lucky – probably not, he concluded. He'd chosen one of twenty-six, minus eleven, call signs. What were the chances? But at least now he had a number. There were eleven pursuers for him to deal with, which was double what he had expected. The night was not going to go well and certainly not to plan, he concluded. Then, it got worse.

The mechanical voice came back on the headset, "Strategic convergence on subject target. Coordinates: 33°44'56.239" N 84°23'24.712" W."

Cole glared at the heads-up display inside the goggles and spoke out loud, "You dumb ass." The steady and flashing coordinates were exactly the same and matched the commanded convergence coordinates. They had his exact location right down to the fractional second.

Chapter Twenty-Seven

ASSAULT

KEVIN SAT SHIVERING IN THE AIRPORT RESTROOM stall studying the video feed. Motion detectors had picked up several intruders patiently waiting in the trees within sight of the cabin. His hands shook as he alternately portrayed views from each of the cameras and checked status of the motion detectors. Waiting was terrible and the moments dragged by as minutes.

The screen on his laptop showed no movement from the trees. "Shit," Kevin mumbled to himself. "How am I going to do all this?" His part of the plan required multiple events to take place all at once and his hands shook even more violently than they had before. He studied the screen and strained to search out detail. He wished they would just hurry up and charge in, just as much as he feared it.

THE REALIZATION CAME TO COLE SLOWLY. THREE times the voice had directed "fourteen" to proceed northeast and "fourteen" had failed to comply, three times. Coordinated subversion of police calls, redirected traffic, and direction of the hunt was a massive orchestration. The mechanical voice could only come from one source; he was being hunted by the Artee.

The Artee was playing him like one of Kevin's analogical chess games. There was no way to win playing within the Artee's game constraints. The mansion, with its concealed Artee, was within sight through the trees. How long would it take to cross the open ground, contemplated Cole? Time to change the game, concluded Cole; the Artee was the real target and it had to die. He dropped Melvin's rifle; shed the backpack, headset, and goggles, keeping only the 1911 tucked into the back of his pants and the knife sheathed in his boot. Cole bolted from the trees at breakneck speed heading for the car half way up on Laughlin's porch. He was nearly to the lane and it's borrow ditch when he heard the now familiar ti-ti-ti of a silenced fully auto weapon. As he jumped the borrow ditch, Cole pulled the 1911 from his waist band, and without looking, fired a single, unsilenced forty-five caliber round in the general direction of the weapon. The gun boomed and echoed in the night air. It bought him a few more seconds of flat out charge at the mansion, but eventually the ti-ti-ti returned and this time coming from two directions to his rear. Cole zigzagged left, zigzagged right and then back to the left. A thick wet dew was forming on the grass and challenged each direction changing step. Again, he fired a single booming forty-five round rearward as he straightened his path and dug from his inner depths to muster every ounce of speed. He reached the car parked half way onto Laughlin's porch and rolled underneath just as the ti-ti-ti started again. Bullets splattered the rear of the car, some piercing all the way through and nearly striking their intended target. Cole smelt a whiff of gas, as one of the bullets had penetrated the car's tank.

"Fucking computer, let's see how you deal with this!" said Cole as he rolled rearward and stabbed his boot knife into the plastic gas tank, furthering the leakage of fuel. Without further hesitation, Cole rolled out from under the car and, while shielded by the rear tire, fired a single muzzle flash in the direction of the gas fumes. Combustion was instantaneous and engulfed the underside of the car. Gas spewing from the tank was in full ignition and feeding a now vigorously growing fire. The tank was only moments from intense heat softening its plastic and fully rupturing when Cole bolted from his shielded position to the stairs and onto the porch.

He crashed through the front window as all structure of the gas tank gave way, sending flames and billowing black smoke into the air. Intense heat and flames followed Cole through the window as he rolled to a shooting position against the far wall. It was a small formal living, or receiving, room with access only from the hall serving the front door: one way in, one way out. Cole burst out of the room into the hall way and open foyer, which seemed like a hub for halls leading elsewhere in the house and included an elegant stair case to the second floor. It was clear but he heard voices coming from the second floor.

Cole edged into a hallway just out of sight of the stairs. The voices became louder and frenzied elements of discussion became apparent. As they scurried down the foyer stairs, Cole caught pieces of what sounded like one-sided instructions: "out back," "car," "wait," "computer," "safe-room." It had to be Laughlin giving instructions. Flames and smoke now began appearing from the little receiving room. Pace of the voices increased as they neared the bottom of the stairs. Cole listened carefully; it was only two having a conversation.

Cole stepped out of hiding and aimed the 1911. It wasn't two. It was four. Two men in the lead coming down the stairs were more fully armed soldier goons. Behind them was an older man with a pot belly and another soldier. Cole adjusted his aim at the fat man and pulled the trigger. The fat man had seen the assault coming was already pulling the man next him over as cover. The shot missed both. Both soldiers reaching the bottom of the stairs, began elevating their Uzis. Cole adjusted his aim and fired, catching the man on the left's center of mass. The man on right's Uzi came level just as Cole fired. The Uzi spit nine-millimeter bullets in Cole's direction; Cole fired again with the realization this was his seventh and last round but at least the Uzi quit. As the 1911 slide locked open, having fired its last round, Cole's thumb slid over the release to discretely snap the slide back into place. His mind registered a tinge of pain, first in his abdomen, and then another from his shoulder. But the signs of pain paled in comparison to the knowing he'd fired his last shot.

The fat man and the other soldier were scrambling from the stair case. Cole aimed the now empty 1911 at the fat man; the soldier was swinging his Uzi into position. Cole saw his imminent death but the fat man responded as he had before, shoving the soldier goon in Cole's direction to shield himself; the Uzi erroneously fired. Cole burst forward to meet the man driving him back to the stairs and toppling onto the two now dying soldier goons. Out of the corner of Cole's eye he saw the fat man heading for a door down one of the hallways. Cole was on top of the man, who was grasping his Uzi with both hands trying to get it into a firing position. Cole grabbed the weapon with his left hand and kept it pointed way. He raised up and then quickly dropped to crash his right elbow into the man's nose. He raised again, this time fully extending his left arm, and then snapped a knuckled punch with his right into the man's throat. The man released the Uzi and both hands went to his throat.

Cole was instantly off, Uzi in hand, to the door he had seen Laughlin approaching; beyond it was a stair case and he flew down it. He emerged in a large open area with what appeared to be fifties vintage automobiles. A Cadillac, Two Fords and Chevrolet were in a line facing windowed garage doors, which led to a driveway level with the rear of the mansion. Cole charged towards the windowed garage doors, but as he checked left and

     Brian David Simmons

right, he heard a door close somewhere to his right and rear. Cole changed directions and ducked behind the Cadillac. It was a convertible and he bopped his head over the driver's door to get a glimpse in the direction of the sound. It wasn't an ordinary door; it was a metal door reminiscent of a safe. Cole slowly raised his head to get a better view. The room was clear. Cole glanced down at the interior of the Cadillac: immaculate – and with a key tethered to an authentic looking tab labeled 1959 Cadillac in the ignition.

Cole charged across the open room to the metallic door. He jerked on the door with no response and then studied the keypad. Laughlin was in there and this was not the way it was going to end. The soldier goons outside were probably marshaling for an assault. The Artee was probably giving them all instructions with its mechanical voice and a coordinated response to his assault was probably already underway. Fire suppression water sprinklers had come on in parts of the house. Hopefully, the fire department and police would still react to smoke and flames from the car; and also hopefully, it was another distraction for the Artee to manage.

The Uzi in Cole's hands was no match for the steel door, all it did was reminded him of the wounds it had inflicted. Both wounds were survivable he concluded. The bullet to his abdomen had sliced through scar tissue from his previous injury and was now extremely painful to the touch. The bullet to his shoulder had taken flesh and throbbed, but it too was survivable.

Chapter Twenty-Eight

ERASED

SEVERAL PEOPLE ENTERED THE AIRPORT BATHROOM and Kevin's whole body began shaking. He stared at the gap under the stall door fearing feet would appear and the door would burst open. Someone at a urinal said in an attempt at humor, "Long flight. Oh what a relief it is." Kevin went back to studying his laptop.

He saw movement from the trees in the video feed from the camera over the cabin front door. They had guns, just like the machine guns on TV. Kevin mustered his concentration to slow the quivering of his hands and focused his eyes on the keyboard. He sent a command to the 4056 to send all Laughlin's clients trading data to FINCEN. It was sent undisguised using his own 4056 IP address and name, making it clearly traceable back to him and the cabin. Kevin quickly went back to the video feed. He zoomed in on one of four men approaching the front of the cabin. He was wearing a funny little headset. He zoomed out; so were the others. There was little doubt in Kevin's mind that it was Laughlin's goons.

Kevin dialed from his cell phone while continuing to watch the screen. A transmitter laying on the table next to the cabin's 4056 beeped and then dialed 911.

INSTANTLY A MALE VOICE CAME ON THE LINE, "911. Is this an emergency?"

Kevin was already panting with nervousness and yelled, "Yes, God dammit. There's men out there with guns."

"Okay. Slow down. What's your name? Last name first and then first name."

"Kevin McKuel and I'm here with Cole Davis."

"Okay Kevin, now can you give me an address?"

"420 Pine Drive, Bear Lake. Hurry. Please hurry."

"Okay. I just confirmed your location. And - and - dispatched local authorities."

KEVIN SCANNED THROUGH THE FEED FROM THE video cameras. He thought the lead man was one that Cole had described. He was clean cut-looking with a small mustache, crew-cut hair, business suit, and odd little headset. In fact, they all had headsets, except one. It was Melvin. He was taking up the rear, letting his troops take the lead as they neared the cabin.

KEVIN MENTALLY PUT HIMSELF INSIDE THE cabin. "They're coming," he cried into the phone.

The 911 operator coolly responded, "Okay Kevin, let's just remain calm. Stay on the line with me. You say you're there with a Cole Davis. Are you both alright?"

"They're coming," Kevin cried again.

Help is on the way. Are your doors locked?"

"All of them, yes. Dead bolts too."

"Are your windows locked?"

"Yes. Please hurry. They have machine guns. They're going to kill us!"

They all had machine guns, except Melvin. Three men stepped out of view of the surveillance camera above the front door. Kevin switched cameras. A momentary notification appeared on his laptop from the 4056; all files had been sent to FINCEN. A perimeter violation was recorded at the back door and moments later a figure appeared inside the cabin. He was quickly followed by a second, advancing in SWAT team style. Kevin typed four letters into the laptop and prepared the BOOM command for sending.

"Oh my God! I think they're going to break in!" whimpered Kevin into the cell phone. "They just broke in the back door," he yelled into the phone.

"Quickly exit the house!" commanded the 911 operator.

On the monitor, the front door crashed in and a man leaped through, rolling left to take firing position on the floor. A second followed, staying high on the right. He swung his machine gun left and then right searching for a target.

"We can't. We're going to die!" cried Kevin into the phone.

The intruders, two from rear and three from the front, began a systematic search of the cabin. Bathroom, bedroom, kitchen, closets, were all methodically checked and they convened in the living room. Melvin stepped through the door. One of men motioned for Melvin to join them at the table in front of the computer. All six intruders stared at the humming computer in the middle of the living room. They studied it and the note taped to monitor. Kevin could see their faces from the monitor's camera and he recalled what Cole had written on the note:

> Melvin:
> Sorry I can't be there.
> Sorry I can't give you the promised disembowelment.
> This will just have to do.
> Say hello to the Devil for me, will you.

They looked at each other in wonderment. Melvin's glaring malevolent eyes pierced through the computer screen's camera as he studied the note. His lips moved as if to say something.

The 911 operator inquired, "Are you still there?

Kevin didn't respond.

Kevin felt the intense stare coming through the video feed as if Melvin knew it was him. Kevin's inner self trembled with fear and his body shook uncontrollably. He looked at the "enter" key on the laptop and whispered, "Fuck me." His hand was quivering over the keyboard as he stared the key. The black key glowed red in his mind. It was evil. It was wrong. How could he? He closed his eyes and his hand slowly descended to the keyboard. He separated himself from the actions of his hand and then his forefinger dropped to the "enter" key. The BOOM command arrived milliseconds later at the cabin's 4056, terminating video feed to the laptop and the relayed cell phone connection.

A hypergolic initiator filled the attic with flame, igniting the dry blend of sawdust, aluminum powder and ammonium nitrate fertilizer. Two milliseconds later, pyrotechnic igniters fired in all four corners of the cabin, igniting a dense packed blend. The attic over-pressured, driving a shattering ceiling to the floor and filling the cabin with 5,500 degree Fahrenheit gases, instantly killing its occupants. Sheetrock on the walls imploded, driving converging deflagrations to the cabin's center. Pressure waves reverberated to the walls, accelerating the burn rate of the explosive mixture, driving the pressure higher and turning the interior of the cabin into a combustion chamber with rocket engine temperatures. Pressure continued to increase driving the explosive mixture's burn rate even higher, which in turn generated more intense all-consuming heat. Chairs, tables, beds, computers, and bodies all became combustion fuel and converted to gaseous products and ash. At 5500 degrees Fahrenheit, body muscle, fat, fluid, bones and teeth were reduced to little more than calcium sulfate and salts of sodium and potassium, making DNA identification impossible.

Fifty-five-hundred degree flames shot from the doors and windows to relieve the ever-increasing pressure. As pressure reached critical, the roof was incinerated, releasing a jetting torch toward the heavens. Moments later, the walls were consumed, and the cabin was gone.

Kevin sat motionless staring at the blank laptop screen, questioning what he just done. Tears formed in his eyes and he pressed the power button.

Chapter Twenty-Nine

Terminal Terminal

Laughlin's hiding place was some kind of safe room but it had odd equipment that serviced it from outside. A large pressurized cylinder of some kind, what appeared to be a generator and some kind HVAC unit were further down the wall, away from the door. The cylinder was plumbed to a control of some kind and then had additional piping leading up the wall. The other item was certainly a generator, concluded Cole. It had its own plumbing taking exhaust outside and electrical conduit going up and through the wall. It also had a five gallon gas can sitting next to it. The HVAC unit had what Cole assumed to be inlet and outlet ducts penetrating through the wall. In front of him, he stared at the steel door and then back down the wall. The wall that housed the steel door was concrete and unpenetrable, making the door the only possible avenue in.

Cole turned to stare at the rear bumper of the 1959 Cadillac convertible. The massive chrome metal structure from days gone-by gleamed in the light coming through the garage door windows. Cole had his plan. The key with its tag were in the car's ignition switch and the car slowly started after its massive engine rolled over several times. Cole pulled forward and angled the car slightly, pulled the shifter to neutral, let it rev, and then put the lever into its reverse slot. The Cadillac squealed rearward accelerating until the corner of the bumper crashed into the metallic door. The Cadillac's bumper crumbled as the door deformed, fractured, opened slightly and pulled free of its hinges.

Cole was instantly over the seat and sliding down the trunk towards the now ajar door with Uzi in hand. The door was open just enough for a man to squeeze through and off it's hinges just enough to see inside the room towards the other end of the room. The room was well lit and contained a long series of racks, each full with electronic boxes displaying LEDs: some flashing, some green, some red, some blue. They were computer servers of some kind, assumed Cole. The row of racks had to be at least twenty feet long with at least twenty server boxes in each rack. The realization hit Cole like a sludge hammer; it was the fucking Artee: complete with its own HVAC system, inert gas fire suppression system, and backup power generator.

The soldier goons would no doubt be approaching soon; he was out of time. It was time to flee, but not until Laughlin and the Artie were dead, dead, dead. Through the partially open door, Cole could see the fire suppression system's large diameter galvanized piping and periodic nozzles running the full length of the room. He fired the Uzi through the door gap at the pipe, penetrating it at multiple locations allowing abundant release of its high pressure inert gas. He fired again providing even more avenues for the gas to escape into the room. If he had minutes, he could have waited until the inert gas displaced enough air to incapacitate Laughlin and then just held his breath, walked in and shot him. But time wasn't going to allow it to happen that way.

Leaving the Uzi on the trunk of the car, Cole bolted for the generator and its standby five-gallon gas can. It was full and Cole unscrewed its cap as he ran back towards the Cadillac and the partially open door. He peered through the partially open door and the gap at the hinge side; Laughlin was nowhere visible. He was presumably hiding behind the racks of computer equipment and probably pointing a stub-nose thirty-eight in the direction of the door. What kind of gun would the fat man carry? Maybe none considering his army of soldier goons? Questioned Cole. It didn't matter. Cole fired a quick burst with the Uzi into the interior of the room, took a deep breath, and slipped inside. He moved in only far enough to reach the central point of the computer sever racks to toss the gas can on top. Gas began flowing down through the cooling vent passages of the top server box and then into the next and the next. Cole retreated and slipped back out the door just as a single round boomed and stuck the door. There was enough oxygen in the room to sustain combustion surmised Cole. Or maybe Laughlin was just holding his breath. But it really didn't matter.

Gas was now reaching the floor and it's heavier than air, heavier than inert gas, fumes would begin spreading right at floor level. Cole fired three shots from the Uzi through the trunk of the Cadillac, piercing the trunk lid, trunk floor and gas tank. He waited momentarily. It dawned on him that all of the cars in the basement could be 1959. The Cadillac was for sure because of its classic tail fins and bullet taillights. He starred at the horizontal fins and eyebrow taillights of an El Camino; it was probably a 1959 as well.

Cole slipped the muzzle of the Uzi under the Cadillac and fired. Flames were instantaneous and Cole bolted for the El Camino. He hit the open button on the windowed door in front of the car and the garage door slowly started upward. He fired and emptied the magazine of Uzi in the direction of the high pressure inert gas container to accelerate the release of fire retarding gas before sliding into the El Camino. The car started instantly and Cole pulled the column mounted shift lever down only to the sound of a horrible grinding. He tried again, only to receive the same result. His heart raced as a soldier goon appeared at the opening door. Clutch pedal he realized; this was three-on-tree. He'd never driven one, but his time he depressed the clutch pedal, pulled the shift lever down, fully depressed the gas pedal, and then took his foot off the clutch. The car jumped forward and through the door, catching the bottom edge of the still rising garage door. The soldier goon was raising his weapon to get off an aimed shot, but the El Camino bumper caught him at knee level and he briefly bounced forward partially on to the hood before his feet began pulling him under and then he disappearing from the view across the hood as the car bumped up and over.

Behind him in the basement, the Cadillac became fully engulfed. Flaring fumes at ground level in the secure room were pulling in more and more combustible air. Intense heat from the Cadillac aided ignition of more and more gasoline inside the room. Eventually, it became fully engulfed in flame as plastics and circuitry from the server boxes became fuel as well. Laughlin and the Artie would be no more.

Cole accelerated and found second gear as he rounded the corner of the mansion. As he passed the front of the house, a group of soldier goons had convened and were staring in his direction. A momentary question of who was driving one of Laughlin's prized automobiles kept weapons pointed down. When one of the goons realized it wasn't Laughlin, he raised his Uzi to fire, but it was too late; Cole was already gone.

 Brian David Simmons

Chapter Thirty

Anti-climax

In reality, they had had enough of each other. The money didn't matter. They finished making arrangements for special packages and made personal calls. After a verbal tirade from Kevin about being a psychotic, insane, mentally diseased malefactor, Cole reluctantly sat next to Kevin to read through newspaper stories pulled up on Kevin's computer.

The papers were full of stories. In the Sunday edition, details of how Omicron had resurfaced and now had a new variant, Demonicron, which were spreading and competing for hosts. Hospitalizations in Florida with lax mask, restaurant, and vaccination regulations were strangely down while New York and California, with the strictest regulations, were setting new hospitalization records. Phizer and Maderna were both shipping new Demonicron vaccines nation wide in anticipation of FDA emergency approval.

In the business section, the big news was the volatility of the stock market. Friday was another record day of trading activity. The flurry of daylong wild swings in both the Dow, NASDAQ, and S&P 500 had set records for the widest single-day point swings in history. At the end of trading on Friday, both indexes ended in positive territory, leaving investors relieved but worried about the Christmas week that followed. The futures markets had made such frenzied and erratic swings that investors speculated new regulations would be forthcoming.

In local news, a page one story in the Atlanta Times was about David Laughlin and the apparent shootout at his mansion. Details were still forthcoming, but there were seven dead, illegal weapons, hundreds of rounds fired and nine men in custody. David Laughlin had disappeared and was being sought for questioning by both Federal and local authorities. Money laundering, racketeering, and income tax evasion topped the list of alleged crimes. The list of lesser crimes—credit card fraud, grand larceny, and extensive traffic violations - was still growing. Laughlin, who was not at the mansion crime scene, had apparently avoided authorities, and was suspected of fleeing the state.

A story on page three of the Atlanta Times was about Isaac Bartrum found hanging from the rafters of his garage. It looked like a suicide, but foul play was suspected. He was found by an employee delivering a Christmas present. Bartrum's wife and two daughters were staying with relatives in the Memphis area and were not home at the time of the suicide. His wife had no comment.

A buried story in the Salt Lake Tribune was about a cabin fire and death of potential occupants. The local investigation was continuing and it had been joined by federal officers from the FBI and FINCEN.

News didn't change the mood. Kevin was still sick with the thought that he had intentionally killed six men at the cabin. It wasn't in his nature and Cole had made him do it. Cole was fed up with Kevin's onslaught of taunts about being a psycho killer and worse. Kevin packed his computer equipment; Cole packed his duffel bag. Cole thought of his Grandmother as he packed his bag. She had raised him in his teen years. She wanted a religious environment: church, Sunday school, bedtime prayers, and dinnertime grace; Cole feigned compliance. The last few months had been so different. How can I spend Christmas with her? What would she think of me now? Kevin might be right. A psychologist wouldn't hesitate a second to have me committed. I don't feel anything for Christmas. The spirit just isn't there. Am I just a leftover from the Patriot Rebirth Society? What the fuck is the matter with my head? What am I going to do now? He continued to try and raise feelings from within, but they just weren't there. He was now an ugly human being that had fully reverted to the hostility of the compound. There was no excuse for what he had done. What's worse, there was no guilt. There should be guilt. But where was it? Can I ever return to some kind of normalcy?

The good-bye was short, with each promising to call, knowing full well they wouldn't. Kevin gave Cole a half-hearten wave as he got in his car and drove past the motel office. Cole turned right out of the driveway and disappeared from sight. It was over for them.

Chapter Thirty-One

AFTERMATH

IN CHICAGO, BUSINESSMAN AND REAL ESTATE tycoon Tiziano Vecelli analyzed his futures' losses with his accountants. In an adjacent room, a Sicilian cousin waited. When Vecelli didn't get the answers he wanted from his accountants, he excused himself and joined his cousin. The instructions were clear; the contract price was established; and David Laughlin and anyone else associated with him wasn't to live past year's end.

IN AN ELITE SUITE IN HARLEM, A HUGE BLACK MAN sat at the head of the table. A beautiful woman sat at his side stroking his arm in consolation. He pounded the table repeatedly and demanded, "What do you mean I owe thirty-seven million?" A small man at the far end of the table meekly explained again for the third time, "It was a margin deficiency. You failed to meet the margin call and the exchange sold off your contracts. Which means you have an unsecured loss on the contracts and owe them money." The large man again pounded the table and insisted, "It was that Laughlin. How can it be thirty-seven million? I'm not going to pay. But Laughlin and his associates are, with their lives!

I'm going track down anyone that could have been involved and hunt those son-of-a-bitches to the ends of the earth"

Jack Cross sat in his little-used apartment thinking about a Christmas eve by himself. A courier knocked and demanded he accept a special delivery package that had no return address. The courier was not to leave until Jack opened the package and agreed to make a very special flight. Jack opened the package to find fifty thousand dollars in cash and a printer-generated note. The unsigned note read:

> "Consider this a special bonus. And, by the way, I need your flying services today. Pick up Joe and Sylvia Atkins in Atlanta and fly them to Tobago. Have Christmas in the sun, on the beach, all on me."

Joe and Sylvia Atkinson were closing up the store early for Christmas Eve when a limousine pulled up out front, followed by a moving van. The limousine driver entered the store and inquired about a Joe Atkinson. Joe was presented with a package. He hesitated, then opened the package. Inside were photographs, passports, fifty thousand dollars in cash, an account statement, and a printed note. Joe handed the photos and cash to Sylvia as he studied the note. The unsigned note read:

"Congratulations on your recent success in the futures market. Your success entitles you and Sylvia to a life of leisure. A place on Robinson Crusoe's Island has been purchased in your name. Escrow will close on your new villa on Tobago Island next week. You need to be there to sign the paperwork, if you like it of course. The cash should tide you over until you get an account established on Tobago. Give your apartment keys to the moving van driver. Your personal belongings will be delivered. Go with the limousine driver. A private jet awaits you. Clothing, personal items, luggage and all that you should need has been arranged. Go now and enjoy. Thanks for everything."

Kevin's parents smiled knowingly. He wasn't going to join them for Christmas and they had been instructed to display an appropriate level of mourning to reports of his death. But, contrary to the instruction, they were doing some late Christmas shopping. Becoming instant multi-millionaires, they had arranged for a private showing of motor homes, the million-dollar variety.

THREE DAYS AFTER CHRISTMAS, TWO WOMEN silently stood at a memorial service for the late Hamilton Cole Davis. They had never met but both strangely knew they had something in common. Neither shed a single tear throughout the service for they had both received a special delivery package making them very wealthy women and giving them very special knowledge. After the service, Carol Meeks and Elizabeth Davis, Cole's grandmother, divulged and discussed the secret that they both knew: Jason would contact them soon.

Coming Soon

If you enjoyed reading Innate Hostility, watch for the following books coming soon.

Immanent Hostility – The Cole and Kevin partnership continues to thwart dire consequences for Israel and the United States.

Invited Hostility – The world of international spying draws Cole and Kevin back into action with a vengeance.

Leadership – Plain and Simple with stories from the workplace – Entertaining short stories every employee, manager, or CEO can relate to.

Bloody Mary Tours (by Connie Campbell) – Comical tales of life's adventures in search of the ultimate bloody mary.